For my mother, Dale J. McCorkle, who always believed that her 10-year-old son had talent.

For my wife, Fiona, who has put up with me all these years, and who saw me through the dark days of my cancer, and its continuing effects on my life going forward. You believed I would survive even when I thought I was toast.

You saved my life in more ways than one.

And to my Grandfather, Edgar W. Allen, Sr., who gave me my first typewriter in 1972.

PROLOGUE

Journal entry, Wednesday 25 January.

Damp, clammy darkness threatening drizzle greeted me when I reanimated tonight.

Nothing new there. I am always cold.

Throughout the daylight hours of the past 100 years, I succumb to the "Sleep of the Dead". When night falls and I come back to life - if one can call my existence living, I come back stiff as a corpse. Bone-on bone joints groan like rusty gate hinges. Atrophied muscles spasm as neurons fire electrical impulses across synapses and I recover from eternal nothingness.

Nothing new there, either. Just something that must be endured.

I do not dream anymore. I had never thought about it until recently, while reading a newspaper in a local all-night coffee house in Normal Heights. One of those beatnik bohemian places, funky and retro. My epiphany struck around four in the morning as I began to consider driving back to Kensington.

It does not disturb me, the fact that that I do not dream. Not since I was a young man. Not since when I still saw the world through human eyes. When I still felt the sun's warmth on my face.

Back when I basked in the sound of Danae's laughter. Reveled in the warmth of her body.

Before I became this thing that I became.

No point in self-pity, though. Bad things happen. Keep moving. Things are what they are; once things change, they cannot go back to the way they were. In real life, there are no "do-overs", so get it right the first time.

Quality counts.

Even if I could change the past, would I? Probably not. No incentive anymore. All that is long since gone. I do wonder sometimes about what life I might have had if Danee and I had escaped. If I had gotten out of the Life sooner. The Dark Path I now walk is a ripple effect, an unintended consequence of bad decisions made by a stupid, arrogant young man during a woefully misspent youth.

I do not blame society. I do not blame my parents. I do not blame peer pressure. I made my own decisions. I knew they were bad decisions. I knew they were wrong. And yet I made them anyway.

I brought this all on myself.

This is my blunt, brutal philosophy. Honesty in all things, both great and small. I "call it like I see it", even when it comes to me. It requires more strength than one might imagine.

I just "keep on keeping on", as a wary, laconic Texan I knew once advised me back in the summer of '47. Night after night.

Year after year. Ad infinitum.

And now, to the task at hand: I have a rather busy night ahead. I have not done what I am about to in a while. Quite a while, actually.

But I am confident I am up to the task. My skillset is unique to my Kind. And once lethal, deadly skills have been taught, learned, and perfected to the point their execution becomes a matter of muscle memory and instinct rather than conscious thought, they never truly leave.

Those skills stay with you, live within you the rest of your days. They lurk just below the surface, savage serpents underneath a thin veneer we call civility. Taut springs, waiting to be sprung. Waiting to be called upon once again.

Wanting, more than anything, to be called upon once again.

Concentrate on the work. Deadly work is afoot tonight.

Not for me. Oh, no. Most certainly not for me.

I do not concern myself with getting caught or killed. I cannot remember the last time I did. If I die tonight, then I die.

After all, I have already died once. It was not so bad. I remember I was bleeding out at the time. A quick pierce of my carotid, a flash of exquisite pain bordering upon pleasure. A momentary flash of white light, then swirling darkness and welcoming shadow. And then - serenity.

Like I said, not so bad. That unique experience delivered me into an existence devoid of fear. Who amongst you can make that claim?

Nowadays, men shudder in fear of ME.

Men fear that which they cannot contain, control, classify, or comprehend. They do not hear me treading behind them in the night. They do not see me coiled in the shadows, eyes wide and unblinking, ready to strike with the blackness of the night.

They never know what is happening until it is already too late, their lives draining away. Spilled like thick red water, splashing with a sickening wet sound across the floor.

I am that glimpse at the edge of the light. I am the thing that goes bump in the night. I am the demon nightmares are made of.

I have been called malevolent, corrupt, evil.

I have been called Monster-

Satan walking the earth. Death incarnate.

To which I respond, yes. I am all of that.

And more.

I live quietly. I work. I consume. I go out for a meal occasionally. I keep the human race at arm's length. I am indifferent to their affairs. I would ignore them entirely but for one compelling interest: they are my food.

I choose my targets carefully. The others, I leave in peace. But I declare here and now, may God have mercy upon anyone who tries to hurt me or mine. For I, most assuredly, will not.

Which brings me back full circle to tonight's work. I shall once again hide in the shadows, partner with the darkness, strike without warning, and slaughter without remorse. Once again I shall prove why mortal men are right to fear me.

To tremble at my name.

I.

Am.

VAMPIRE.

CHAPTER ONE

Rudy Valdez popped the collar up on his brown leather bomber jacket against the damp night. January in San Diego meant cool days and cold nights. Thick cloud cover usually burned off in late morning. Then as temperatures dropped, another heavy bank of clouds – the Marine Layer – would form over the water, creep up the coastline, engulf the bay, and slither inland a few miles. Drifting in from the Pacific Ocean, tonight's fog blanketed everything it touched.

Congested, Rudy sniffed, wondering if his stuffy head was a reaction to the temperature change, the ever-present pollution, or if he might be coming down with a cold. But what, at this point, difference does it make, he asked himself. Forget it for now. I have more immediate, more important things to worry about tonight.

Standing on a seldom-used dock in a run-down section of the city south of the high rise hotels and tourist attractions, but north of the Naval Base with its sleek, modern warships, with the still, dank night air beading moisture on his jacket, he heard a foghorn, forlorn and monotonous in the distance. It sounded far to the north and west, out on the water, past the channel, heading out to sea. Probably a heavy freighter, loaded with cargo, sailing on the high tide.

The foghorn certainly did not come from the *Sulu Sea*, the rusty, hulking 180 ft. freighter currently moored at the dock. The ghostly gray and black ship squatted next to the pier. She bobbed slightly on the tide, her neglected hull devoid of fresh paint, its topside lights off. No smoke unfurled lazily from the stack above the engine room. No boilers stoked in preparation for departure. Her engines were at cold iron.

In the darkness of the moonless night, and with the haze from the fog, Rudy could barely make out the gangway that stretched from the ship's quarterdeck down to the concrete pier.

Beyond the freighter, San Diego Bay remained obscured by mist. Silent waters swirled liquid black. The sky above tinted a dull gray from the lights of downtown reflecting against the cloud cover. Although the lights created a muted glow against the clouds, the hotels and skyscrapers of downtown San Diego hid, completely blanketed.

Compactly built, muscular and wiry, Rudy gripped the AK – 47 just a bit tighter. He'd been around firearms all his life. He cradled it easily in his hands, the weapon as much a part of him as his own beating heart.

Raised in Tennessee by a decent but emotionally aloof police officer father, he left home at 18, right after high school, and joined the Marines. He and his dad got along well enough, but did not talk much. Rudy's teen years seemed spent pretty much with him on auto-pilot. Both father and son seemed fine with that. He told his father about joining the Corps that evening after he had already signed the papers. His father, mildly surprised, grunted over his burger and fries, nodding his endorsement of his son's decision.

Nothing more was said.

Six years and three combat tours later, and spending his last year stationed at Camp Pendleton, Rudy left the Corps. He didn't have a problem with killing, and he had escaped the ravages of PTSD that had devastated so many of his fellow Marines. Rudy was grateful to whatever God lived in heaven that he had not been burdened with an overactive conscience.

His command tried repeatedly to convince him to reenlist and "Stay Marine!" as the posters barked. But Rudy was convinced he could land a good paying job in a matter of days or weeks. He considered going to work for the CIA, NSA, or some other alphabet organization. He figured the work would be similar to what he'd already trained for; he could make more money, and enjoy better living conditions. But during the early stages of applying, he saw the same Government bureaucracy shoved under his nose by the very pencil pushers with the power to hire him or tell him to take a hike. Inefficiency and redundancy had gotten good men killed when he was in the Marines. He wanted no more of it. He decided to explore other opportunities.

But the economy was the worst it had been in 80 years. Jobs never materialized, or went to others. Resumes never elicited responses. On the rare occasion when he did get a callback, promises from managers and HR personnel were nothing but blue sky. Eventually, with a growing sense of anxiety and indignation, Rudy realized he was officially in deep shit. His options were gone. Time to swallow his pride. He'd apply to return to the Marine Corps.

The meeting lasted less than ten minutes.

Rudy listened in shock as grizzled Gunnery Sergeant Grimes delivered the bad news. Combat grunts were coming back to the Corps in droves because of the crap economy and high unemployment. The Recruiting District had already met their quota for returning veterans for the Fiscal Year. The bottom line was, the Corps couldn't do anything for him. Rudy knew the Gunny was giving him the straight skinny. Too bad it didn't help.

Going home to Tennessee never entered his mind.

Six months back, in some dive bar in Imperial Beach, Rudy overheard a drunken jerk badmouthing Marines and worse, the Marine Corps.

"Hey! Anybody know what the Marine Corps calls a Marine who can put the right size nut on the right-sized bolt? Skilled labor!" the drunk, a mountain of a man with a Navy tattoo on his arm guffawed.

"What do you have against the Corps?" Rudy asked, turning full on him.

The drunk sized Rudy up and sneered at his diminutive size. "Why? You want to be a Marine when you grow up?"

Rudy simply stared at him, his face betraying nothing. The sailor stood over six foot two, weighed an easy two hundred and forty pounds. He possessed arms the size of Rudy's thighs, but his gut was bigger than Rudy's chest.

The silence grew taut. "What the fuck you staring at, pee-wee?"

"The biggest, dumbest, drunk piece of shit Squid I've ever seen."

The drunken sailor's eyes registered confusion. "Huh?"

"Were you born this Goddamned stupid, or did you have to fucking work at it?"

The big guy swung at Rudy.

Big mistake.

Rudy nimbly ducked the sailor's sloppily thrown haymaker, and knocked him out with one powerful punch square to the point of the chin, hard enough to sublux the jaw, dinging the nerve centers under the ear. The sailor's face registered shock and disbelief for an instant, then his eyes rolled up in his head. The lights went out, and he fell backwards to the ground, landing with a great thud on the floor.

Bottles rattled on the bar and nearby tables.

There was a brief moment of stunned silence in the bar. Everyone stared down at the unconscious behemoth, then up at Rudy, who stood all of five foot seven and weighed one sixty dripping wet. When the unconscious ass-hat's friends decided to jump him en masse, Rudy obliged by fully demonstrating what one well-trained, highly motivated Marine could really do in a combat situation.

Less than two minutes later, four other sailors lay scattered across the filthy floor, either unconscious or wishing they were. All were bleeding, two of them profusely. At least one would never sire an offspring.

And standing at the center of it, not even breathing hard, grim and determined to not be taken down, stood Rudy

"There a back way out of here?" he asked the bartender.

The bartender motioned his head towards the back of the bar. Rudy retreated, sliding out the back.

Outside in the parking lot, a man approached him. A big Hispanic man, expensive clothes. Lots of bling. Rudy recognized the two men with him as bodyguards, obviously professionals, and obviously men not to be trifled with.

So Rudy simply stood his ground.

"Guillermo Calderon," the Big Man introduced himself. Everyone calls me El Gecko."

"Rudy Valdez."

"You got skills. I want you to come work for me."

"Doing what?"

They all smiled. Rudy had no idea who this guy was.

El Gecko, in a rare moment of complete veracity, told Rudy: "I am an international drug smuggler. Marijuana and heroin, mostly; we bring it up from Latin America into the U.S. I like keeping violence and bloodshed to a minimum. It draws the attention of law enforcement. Prices go up, profits go down. Bad for business."

"Basic law of Economics," Rudy replied. "What does any of this have to do with me?"

"When violence occurs, I don't want undisciplined cowboys going wild, shooting everything and everyone in sight," El Gecko answered. "Innocent bystanders, children." He shook his head. "Bad karma. No, I only want professionals who know what they are doing."

"Admirable," Rudy said, "but again, why me?"

"You're a Marine. You're cool under pressure, and know how to take out the garbage."

"How much money?"

"About ten times what you made on active duty."

Rudy couldn't help but smile "Then it looks like I'm you're man."

Now here he stood, six months later, tired and in a foul mood, pulling what was essentially glorified guard duty on a foggy dock on a cold night, searching the shadows for anyone who was not supposed to be there. All he really wanted was a mug of strong coffee, followed by a good night's sleep in a warm bed. But here he was, and he was making almost ten times what he had made in the Corps.

He breathed in and out slowly calming his nerves. Nights like this limited his vision and narrowed his potential kill zone. Truth be told he'd simply watched way too many old horror movies as a kid when the Old Man was pulling double shifts at the precinct to make ends meet.

He moved forward, striding across the dock, his tightly laced steel-toed combat boots sounding dull thuds with each step. The cold dampness seeped through his blue jeans. He felt the skin on his thighs contract, the hair follicles rising. His boots kept his feet warm, at least. Next time he was out here, he told himself, he'd wear thermals.

He stopped near the middle of the dock, pulled out a small flashlight. He turned it on, waved it in a modulated, horizontal back-and-forth pattern towards the ship. Moments later, a tiny yellow beam pierced through the night, a prearranged response from the guard on board. Satisfied, Rudy turned the flashlight off and moved forward once again, continuing his patrol.

Stay sharp, he told himself. Stay alert.

His index finger slid off the side of the weapon to caress the trigger guard, a subconscious sign of his anxiety. Something isn't right tonight, he thought.

Trouble's coming. I can feel it.

At he top of the gangway, Stephen Thompson, better known to his friends as "T-Ball", stepped off the ship. Gaunt and haggard, he wore threadbare, tattered clothes, unlaced sneakers, and unkempt dreadlocks. He stood over six feet, but weighed less than two hundred pounds. He was wasting away beneath his ill-fitting clothes. He was smoking meth, "sucking the glass dick" again, and was not eating properly. Malnourishment combined with the chemically enhanced hyper-driven metabolism had him losing almost five pounds a week. He could see his ribs now when he looked in a mirror, and his muscles were atrophying, looking like corded ropes under his blemished skin.

T-Ball was feeling the effects of downing a half bottle of rotgut whiskey he'd purchased a scant hour and a half ago. His head buzzed, but not in a good way. His chest felt tight, like he couldn't expand his lungs to take a deep breath. His stomach roiled and heaved, threatening to spill upwards at any moment.

Detox was a bitch.

Cold to the bone, he clutched his soiled Army Surplus field jacket closer to his unshaven throat. He shuddered, then lurched down the gangway. Looking as if he might pitch face forward at any moment, he finally made it onto the pier. Wobbly legs stood upright like rickety splinters underneath him.

T-Ball shuffled towards the dull red metal shipping containers. Stiff knees refused to bend properly, so his gait resembled that of a robot in an old Buck Rogers show.

Stacked three high, nine containers crouched on the dock, waiting to be loaded onto the freighter.

He leaned against the door of one of the containers to help steady himself, lighting a cigarette with quivering hands. Rudy had told him several times not smoke while on watch. The glowing cherry of the cigarette, he'd said, could be seen a quarter mile away. It would give away their position to an enemy force.

But fuck Rudy and all that Joe Jock Military bullshit, man. If T-Ball wanted a cig, T-Ball was gonna have a fucking cig.

T-Ball took a drag, pulling the smoke into his lungs. The nicotine acted quickly, giving him a pleasant sensation of spreading warmth and harmony. He closed his eyes, held his breath, then blew out bluish gray smoke.

T-Ball opened his eyes. Smiling and satisfied, he put the cigarette back between his lips and stepped away.

At no time did T-Ball notice the unholy thing less than eight feet away, squatting low, knees spread, hands flat on the pavement, arms shooting down between his legs from muscled shoulders. Barely breathing, black narrow eyes unblinking, the preternatural creature hunkered down pressed against the cold metal of the rusting shipping container. The thing's muscles tensed, waiting for that moment of release through explosive motion. Using the darkness it knew so well as camouflage, it glared at T-Ball. The monster inhaled, its nostrils filled with T-Ball's putrid scent of disease, decay, and lack of hygiene. The creature's pale face wrinkled as it cringed in disgust.

Completely undetected.

The perfect predator.

Shivering from withdrawal as much as from the cold, T-Ball hoped walking around would make him feel better. Get the blood circulating, that's what he needed. Just get through this gig tonight, get paid, then take some time off.

Go get laid.

In the shadows, the creature touched a sharp, pointed fingernail against the concrete, then purposefully dragged it over the rough ground.

A soft sound stopped T-Ball in his tracks. He couldn't place it. He glanced around holding his AK – 47 awkwardly, close to his chest. Sweat popped out across his forehead. He had been formidable once. As a kid, he'd been a Golden Gloves champion. He had even thought about Olympic tryouts, going pro. Make some real money. But a series of screw-ups took him away from all that. The drugs sealed his fate, withering him down to a pathetic shadow of his former self.

T-Ball was no longer a mercenary. He was just another junkie. Just another fucked up loser, and knew it. Get it together, motherfucker, he told himself. Maybe you should think about going to rehab or something.

In the dark, the creature grinned sadistically. A malevolent, ugly smile revealed two fangs refined by evolution, by God or Satan, for piercing through pliant flesh.

A night bird called, its screech piercing the quiet. Gasping in terror, T-Ball spun around, his weapon held high in front of him. Eyes wide, panting like a dog, he scanned the nearby rooftops and the dull gray sky, looking for the source.

Nothing.

From the nearby shadows, the creature tried hard to keep from laughing. This was just too easy. If this lame excuse for a human being was the best his enemies had to offer, he was going to be done here and back home in time to watch the early morning cable news shows.

Finally, disgusted with himself, knowing he had lost his edge, T-Ball relaxed a bit. He lowered his weapon to a more casual-ready position, something Rudy had taught him. T-Ball knew El

Gecko would kill him if he ever found out how bad things had gotten.

El Gecko had made his position crystal clear when he hired T-Ball. Relaxation away from the job made for a better worker. A few drinks, a snorted line or two, a joint here and there was fine. He had no problem with his men blowing off steam. But addiction, El Gecko would not tolerate.

He called it El Gecko's Rule *Numero Uno*. Addiction among customers was a good thing. It kept them coming back. Supply and demand, Economics 101. But addiction among drug suppliers? Bad for business. El Gecko told him he respected men who handled their business, took responsibility for their actions and their lives. Those who were addicts, and who could not or would not clean themselves would be "retired".

Damn. Rehab it is.

On the other side of the dock towards the south end, Rudy continued his patrol. He glanced to his left towards the abandoned buildings at the edge of the property. Two by four studs pounded into a concrete foundation, cheap plywood walls and roof covered in dull, colorless metal. Two rows of black windows, staring out at the night like soulless eyes. Long forgotten offices, he surmised. Years empty, abandoned, occupants long since retired, moved away, or deceased. The buildings' only occupants now would be rats, spiders, and the occasional homeless person looking for a place to squat out of the cold.

Rudy's eyes darted with practiced precision from one strategic point to the next. He calculated angles and vectors, gauging trajectories in his head. The buildings sat less than 50 yards away. It offered an unobstructed view of the dock, the ship at its mooring, and the road leading onto the property.

A good place for a patient, savvy sniper to set up and wait for an opportunity.

Rudy reached down under his jacket to the web belt, a holdover from his military days, which held up his jeans. He unclipped a small black walkie-talkie. Out of habit, he glanced down at the channel indicator. El Gecko's crew always used the same channel, and Rudy knew the settings had not been changed. But familiar, methodical habits gave him a sense of security and comfort. You could never be too careful in a business where the slightest slipup, the smallest inattention to detail, could end up costing you your life.

Standing in the open, in the middle of the sniper's Kill Box, Rudy looked around. No cover nearby. Those buildings, squatting like trolls, gawking at him made his skin crawl. He had not been shot yet. Perhaps an indicator that no sniper lay hidden. Then again, maybe they weren't set up yet. Maybe they were waiting for the bigger fish to arrive.

Rudy glanced again at his watch. The bigger fish would be arriving soon. Rudy squatted, took a knee, reducing his silhouette. Caution is beautiful thing, he smiled grimly to himself.

He held the device near his face and keyed the mic. "T-Ball. Rudy. Come in," he said in a hoarse whisper. No response. He keyed the mic again. "T-Ball. Rudy. Come in."

T-Ball, standing on the other side of the dock near the freighter, slung his rifle over his shoulder. He frantically fumbled through the pockets of his clothing until he found the walkie-talkie. He fished it out of the deep cargo pocket on the bottom of his field coat.

"Yeah, Rudy," he brayed, too loudly, his thumb stabbing the key button. "What up?"

Rudy rolled his eyes. He had tried repeatedly to get T-Ball and the rest of the security crew to adhere to a more professional demeanor when speaking on the radio. It had been to no avail. Fucking cowboys, he thought. Goddamn amateurs.

"Did you sweep and clear these office buildings earlier today?" Rudy asked.

T-Ball thought Rudy had just spoken to him in a foreign language. "Did I do what?" He pushed a limp dreadlock out of his face.

"Did you perform a sweep and clear?" Rudy repeated, impatient now with his so-called colleague.

"I heard what you said," T-Ball bit back. "Do you really think I 'performed' one of those?"

Rudy bit his lip to keep his temper. "Of course, T-Ball. I'm sorry. I don't know why I asked. Keep a sharp eye. I'm going to check the buildings."

"Yeah, yeah," came T-Ball's response. "Perform some of that 'sweep and clear' bullshit."

Rudy gritted his teeth as he clipped his walkie-talkie back onto his belt. He repositioned his rifle into a relaxed ready position. He stood up and moved silently through the fog towards the buildings.

T- Ball had always been wilder than Rudy, louder, quicker to throw down, and less disciplined when he did. Rudy always thought things through, considered consequences, contemplated contingencies. T-Ball jumped in with both feet, no matter what. He gave no thought to what might happen next. Initially that go-for-broke enthusiasm had been part of T-Ball's charm. Now, he had become reckless, and that meant dangerous. Unpredictable.

Untrustworthy.

Rudy knew T-Ball had fallen off the wagon. He was to sucking the glass dick again. If El Gecko found out, he would peel T-Ball's skin off his body, layer by layer, with a knife dipped in human shit.

Just to make a point. To send a message.

Rudy considered dropping a dime on T-Ball, outing him to El Gecko. Nah, he decided. Never been a squealer. No reason to start now. Most people wind up getting what they deserve in this world, he reasoned. And as raggedy-ass as T-Ball was flying these days, it would be only a matter of time before he fucked up and El Gecko would punch T-Ball's ticket himself. Rudy would just sit back and watch.

God knows, he had seen worse.

T-Ball tried to stay alert like Rudy had taught him. He tried all the little tricks and mind games, but it was a losing battle. He hated to admit it, but he admired Rudy's discipline. He wished he had that kind of discipline. Maybe he should have joined the Marines back in the day.

Too late for that now. He was thirty-six years old, an alcoholic, a drug addict, a heavy smoker, a carrier of Hepatitis B, and a convicted felon. Not exactly a Marine Corps recruiter's prime candidate.

He drew deeply on his cigarette. A shadowy movement caught his eye. He peered through the mist. A shadow moved on the main deck of the freighter. He concentrated, looking harder, stepping forward across the dock.

There it was again. The shadow was of someone large and hulking, moving near the cargo hold main doors.

T-Ball's dug into the recesses of another pocket. He pulled out a small metal-bodied flashlight. He pointed it towards the ship's main deck, and signaled three short bursts of light through the fog.

A few seconds later, the shadow on the deck solidified. A huge Oriental man stepped out of the blackness near the gangplank. He responded to the signal by sending a three-flash burst of his own, then moved back, fading into the darkness once more.

Donnie Chen, T-Ball reminded himself. A kung fu expert. Crack shot with a gun, and deadly accurate with a knife, a sword, all manner of blades. A consummate killer, he did not kill indiscriminately, but could kill with great efficiency and zero hesitation.

Not someone to have pissed at you.

The creature in the darkness watched the two humans signal each other. He shook his head in amazement. Like something out of a bad movie, he thought. What next? Morse code? Carrier pigeons?

T-Ball was still nearby, still clueless, still sloppy. The man was completely oblivious to how close to death he was.

The creature wrinkled his sensitive nose again at the man's pungent odor. He would be shed of this assault on his senses soon. The creature glanced up at the ship, observing the Chinese man. He knew instinctively by the efficient manner in which he moved this man was, in human terms at least, a dangerous individual.

Wait 'til they get a load of me.

He flicked his tongue across his fangs, anticipation rising at the thought of the horror that would flood their faces at the sight of him. He glanced at his wristwatch. Even in the utter darkness, his vampire eyes read the dial easily.

Time to get things started.

CHAPTER TWO

T-Ball took another drag from his cigarette. As he savored the familiar sting of the smoke roiling within his lungs, he noticed a newfound steadiness in his hands. Then he heard a low sound.

A breath, gently sucked in on the night air, whispering his name.

"T-Ball."

Practically jumping out of his sagging skin, T-Ball whipped around, his weapon at the ready. Eyes, bloodshot and bulging scanned behind him.

Nothing.

He scanned the area again, gun barrel moving left to right, back to left, up to down. He detected no follow up sounds or movement.

T-Ball finally heaved a great sigh, his body crumpling into its usual bad posture. The weapon in his gnarled hands dropped to the ready position. He tossed his cigarette onto the pavement, crushed the glowing orange end with the heel of his scarred Dingo boot.

Must be my imagination, he thought. Fuck these drugs, man! They're turning me into a little pussy.

On the weather deck of the Sulu Sea, Donnie Chen looked down at T-Ball shuffling around in the mist, huddling next to the crates like a bitch. He rubbed his own pockmarked face in thought.

T-Ball was definitely someone Chen would call TFL – Total Fuckin' Loser. Personally, Donnie would have liked nothing better than to beat T-Ball's skinny little tweaker's ass within an inch of his miserable life, then toss him out of the cartel, penniless and broken. Or perhaps kill him outright if that pleased El Gecko more.

But Donnie liked Rudy, which was noteworthy in itself, because Donnie Chen rarely liked anybody. But Rudy was honest, reliable, trustworthy. He could handle himself in a fight, and was not given to killing civilians. And he covered for T-Ball, demonstrating loyalty to others. Donnie respected that, too.

So, Donnie said nothing, and kept his reservations concerning T-Ball to himself. But Donnie knew the truth. He saw all the signs. Bad skin, dull hair, receding gums and hairline, weight loss, lack of basic hygiene, and some alarming neurological symptoms. T-Ball walked with a shuffling gait, suffered from bouts of dizziness and vertigo, and had developed a facial tic under his right eye in the past two weeks.

T-Ball was back on crystal meth.

Donnie didn't like drugs very much; he never had. He never took drugs himself, and had no respect for those who did. He did not drink or smoke. Ever since he was six years old living in Orange County under the tutelage of his first kung fu instructor, Donnie had always walked the narrow path of a warrior. Never fight for no reason, but always be ready to fight. Be polite and courteous to everyone you meet, but always have a plan to kill them if need be.

Always plan an escape route.

Donnie turned his head seaward, and gazed across the glassy black waters of the bay. He could barely make out distant lights, obscured by fog. More clouds billowed in from the bay. The Maine Layer was particularly thick tonight, thicker than he had seen it in months. Donnie still carried his traditional upbringing, so he took this as an omen, a malevolent harbinger of bad things to come.

He looked back down across the docks. It reminded him of those old spooky movies he had watched on TV as a kid. T-Ball was standing at the edge of Donnie's sight, a ghostly figure hovering close to the ground.

Right then, at that moment, Donnie realized didn't much like the drug trade, either. It profited off the weakness of others, traded in human misery, destroyed human lives. It started people down a sure and certain path to self-destruction. Others had told him druggies were going to get their drugs one way or the other. Why not from them? And druggies chose their own path, right? Free will and all that shit.

But Donnie had never really bought into that. People chose their own path, yes. That much was true. But it seemed to Donnie that addiction actually stole that very freedom away from the addicted. And that was what made drugs so bad. Not that someone got high or got a buzz going but that they could not deal with reality when the ride came to a stop.

And every ride, no matter how hard, how long, or how high, must come to an end.

Donnie was about to look away, but something caught at the corner of his eye. A black shadow, deeper and darker than normal, seemed to have materialized, taken on shape and weight, right behind the oblivious T-Ball. It seemed to pause and then spread near the top, as if it had arms, ready to engulf its prey.

But that couldn't be really what was happening, right?

On the dock, T-Ball was unaware that one of the ancient predators that had haunted men's souls for eons had uncoiled and slithered silently up behind him.

Repulsed by this piece of human garbage, sickened by the smell of tainted blood and old urine, the undead creature relished the thought of killing him, wasting him, slaughtering him. A complete waste of a human being, T-Ball had squandered whatever opportunities life had offered him, and the vampire was disgusted by that fact.

He wanted to torture T-Ball, beat him, slice him, kill him slowly, drain him within an inch of his life, then start IV's on him, replenish T-Ball's fluids, bring him back from the brink. Then torture him again.

And again.

And again.

That would be a fun time.

Practical concerns precluded that. More humans on their way, and he needed to stay focused on the big picture.

Moving so swiftly he was nothing more than a dark blur, the vampire closed the gap of the last few feet, wrapped one arm like a constricting coil over T-Ball's gun hand, his other hand slapping across T-Ball's face, covering nose and mouth so fast T-Ball never even had a chance to scream. T- Ball was held so securely, he may as well have been attacked by an anaconda.

The unholy thing leaned his toothy mouth towards his victim's ear.

"T-Ball."

He then wrenched backwards, dissolving back into the same shadows from whence he came. T-Ball was lifted off his feet like a rag doll, completely overcome by forces he could not have understood even if he had known what they were.

The creature grabbed the AK 47, ripped it from T-Ball's hands as easily as a parent takes away a toy from a naughty child. He spun T-Ball around, who looked up, eyes wide and uncomprehending, into the mist and shadows. At first he was not sure what he was looking at.

A pale face, devoid of any true color or pigmentation. Skin so waxy it appeared yellowish in the smudgy light, almost translucent. A hint of bluish veins running like delicate latticework underneath down the cheeks to the chin. Across the forehead. Black hair on the skull above, long and limp, hanging like seaweed, falling past the top of the ears. Black eyes, pupils dilated full open to bring in every scrap of available light. No whites at all, giving the creature the look of a Great White Shark. The sallow skin around them seemed dead. The mouth opened into a cavernous gash below the pointed nose, exposing two canines, elongated into sharp fangs, one on each side of his incisors.

T-Ball's bladder emptied right there.

The last thing T-Ball saw on this Earth was that fearsome mouth rushing forward and down. The fangs punctured the flesh over his carotid artery. The lower jaw clamped down over his windpipe, cutting off his air and his ability to scream.

Oxygen-rich arterial blood pumped from of the left ventricle of T-Ball's fading heart, pulsed upwards and through the open gash, past the vampire's lips and teeth, over his tongue, down his throat, and into his stomach. The junkie's blood tasted terrible, bitter and brackish, foul and impure, but the vampire needed to feed. He needed strength for what would come next.

But his stomach could only hold so much. When the vampire had his fill, he wrenched T-Ball's neck until he heard a familiar, sickening crunch. He lithely tossed T-Ball's limp body aside. It landed hard, a tangle of arms and legs, head twisted at an angle incompatible with life.

T-Ball was dead now. Dead as a doornail; deader than fried chicken. His eyes glazed over in that unmistakable blank expression of a corpse.

Once a person has seen the eyes of the dead, the truly dead, he or she will remember it all the days of their life. One never forgets the cool smooth skin, limp body, dead weight. Eyes open because all the muscles, even the ones around the eyelids have relaxed.

T-Ball's eyes stared outward, looking into forever, and seeing nothing.

Although T-Ball's heart had already stopped beating, blood continued to pool from the deep wound on his neck. It spread slowly along the concrete, obeying the laws of gravity and the physics of warm liquids.

The vampire stepped back, not wanting to get blood on his clothes. He did not want to track blood around, leaving footprints the police could trace. He also did not want DNA of the victims on his person, or any of his possessions. Also, having been a snappy dresser for over a century, the vampire *really* liked his clothes. He pulled a dark blue handkerchief out of his pocket and wiped the blood from his mouth and chin.

Above the dock, on board the *Sulu Sea*, Donnie walked slowly around the main deck, looking for trouble, sensing it but finding none. That pleased him. Now that he had decided to get out of this life, he didn't want some bad shit to go down where he got killed on his last day of work. He pulled out a cigarette, quickly lit it, then continued walking. The cigarette smoldered lazily, dangling from the corner of his mouth.

As he strolled down the port side, going aft, he glanced out across the bay, barely able to make out the lights of Coronado Island to the southwest. Looking northeast, the dark docks and old Port of San Diego buildings eventually gave way to Downtown San Diego and it's famous Gaslamp District. He could barely make out the Convention Center. Petco Park was dark – the Padres were in their off-season – but he knew it was out there, lurking in the gloom, waiting for the next event to ignite its lights.

Donnie rounded the edge of the aft cargo hold, strode port to starboard, and gazed past the gunwales to the dull dock below. All appeared quiet. He eased slowly forward, alert for any changes. He knew from listening to the earlier radio traffic that Rudy was checking out the old office buildings. He could not see him from his position, but he knew Rudy was there, doing his job, a true professional.

He calmed his mind as he walked, eyes alert. Something cold on the wind tonight. The omen had been right. Evil was close by. He stopped at the gangplank and looked down at the edge of the shipping containers.

No one was there.

Donnie frowned. T-Ball was supposed to be there. It was all part of the bigger security coverage for tonight's business. It was all part of Rudy's plan for interconnecting field of fire in case they had to "go hot".

Donnie keyed up his walkie-talkie. "T-Ball. Come in." He waited.

No response.

He double-checked the radio frequency, then keyed the mic again. "T-Ball. This is Donnie. Come in."

In the shadows of the shipping containers, the vampire squatted near T-Ball's corpse. He listened to the radio transmission coming from the device stuffed into one of T-Ball's jacket pocket.

"T-Ball, this is Donnie. Come in." A burst of static, then nothing. A pause. *"T-Ball, where the hell are you?"* Another burst of static, then silence. He noticed Donnie's voice was beginning to show strains of both impatience, and concern.

Things were moving along nicely.

On the South side of the compound, a rusted metal door swung open with a grating protest. Rudy stepped outside, going from the darkness of the buildings to the gloom and mist of the night. The buildings were clear, and he felt much better for it. He had fought off the temptation to cut corners, but had instead gritted his teeth and taken the time to do the job right.

One of his old Drill Instructors had once told him that integrity was the ability to do the right thing, even when no one else was looking. Rudy had never forgotten that.

He grabbed his walkie-talkie off his belt. "Donnie. It's Rudy. Report."

"T-Ball's not at his post and not responsive to radio," came Donnie's response.

Rudy frowned. "Where did you see him last?"

"The shipping containers."

Rudy glanced in that direction, roughly north of his position. The containers, hulking black rectangular metal cubes, sleeping monsters stacked three high and six wide, waited to be loaded tomorrow. All was quiet. Quiet as the grave, Rudy mused.

But now something felt different. Heavy. Threatening. Like the air itself had somehow gained weight. His muscles contracted, his breathing deepened. His pupils dilated. Pulse and blood pressure elevated. The hairs on his forearms and neck stood up.

Something was out there, all right. Something he could not see; something he did not want to see.

Whatever it was, it was Evil, and Rudy Valdez was afraid of it.

CHAPTER THREE

In the shadows by the shipping containers, the vampire squatted low, motionless. He knew the young Latino - Rudy, he believed his name was - could not see him there from where he was standing. The vampire saw him with perfect clarity; but to Rudy, the vampire blended into the black, simply part of the fabric of the night. Indistinct. Nonexistent.

Human eyes were simply not like vampire eyes. The vampire's retinas contained rods and cones just like when he had been human. But now, as a creature of the night, he possessed more rods than cones. Like a cat, he saw clearly in what for humans appeared as near total darkness.

The vampire considered his options. He instinctively knew from the Latino's scent and aura that Rudy was no degenerate like T-Ball had been. Rudy obviously had military experience, evidenced by the disciplined manner in which he carried himself, the efficient, no- nonsense manner in which he moved. He handled the weapon in his hands like it was a part of him. Like he had been born with it in his hands. He also exhibited an admirable work ethic in executing his duties.

The vampire respected that.

It was rare to see that kind of dedication these days when so many seemed content to remain undisciplined, unskilled, lazy. Living mundane lives and settling for second best. Their existences punctuated by mediocrity, they mistakenly believed that "good enough" was indeed actually, good enough. Never mind trying to achieve perfection; most never bothered to achieve excellence or even at a bare minimum, a level of proficiency.

More was the pity.

The vampire believed discretion the better part of valor, so he stayed where he was. He was curious to see what this Rudy would do faced with a sudden adversity.

Still alert, with a heightened sense of his environment, Rudy continued staring to the darkness in the distance, expecting to see movement, something that would give away the position of an enemy, or law enforcement. Without taking his eyes of the dark, he held the walkie-talkie close to his mouth.

"T-Ball. Come in." He spoke in a low tone.

Silence.

"T-Ball. This is Rudy. Come in, Goddammit."

Silence.

Rudy rolled his eyes in exasperation. "Donnie."

"Go ahead."

"Something's not right."

"He's probably taking a dump or something."

Rudy did not think so. "I hope you're right."

"We should talk about this later."

"Copy that."

Rudy detected movement to his far left. He turned his head to see a faint yellow glow coming from the other side of the hill near the dockside entrance. The glow grew, became more intense.

Headlights approaching.

Rudy immediately jogged towards the tiny guard shack by the entrance. It was a good one hundred fifty feet away.

"They're here," he barked into the mic. "You and I will have to handle this without T-Ball."

"No problem," Donnie replied. "I'm just sick of having to carry the guy, you know?"

Rudy was almost there. "He'd better have a damn fine explanation when this is over. That's all I'm saying."

Rudy slowed to a walk. The guard shack was really three metal walls and a roof, slanted to one side for water runoff. The fourth wall was missing, acting as both window and door.

Headlights pierced the darkness, yellow beams bouncing upwards into the fog, stabbing at the clouds, dissipating quickly. The front of the car appeared over the ridge, cresting over the top of the road. The high beams plummeted downward, illuminating the fog close to the ground as the car continued towards Rudy's position.

Rudy grabbed the gate. It had been reinforced cyclone fencing once. He pulled hard. The gate slid back, protesting with squeaks and rust vibrating off the metal. He yanked again, and the gate slid back wide enough for the oncoming car to drive through the checkpoint without slowing down.

Another twin group of headlights pierced the darkness and bounded over the top of the hill. A second car was coming, coming a bit too fast, trying to close the distance between itself and the first car.

Rudy stepped across the gate entrance and stood, gun at the ready, at a vantage point where he could unload on the driver without a second's hesitation if he sensed something wrong.

The first car, a dark full–size American four-door sedan, slowed as it neared. The driver's window opened. Rudy heard the faint whine of the motor inside the door pulling the window glass down.

Mongo, the driver, leaned his head out and nodded to Rudy. Rudy recognized him instantly, nodded back. Mongo was black, bald, close to seven feet tall and weighed three hundred pounds. His face was pockmarked from acne as a kid, and a delicate latticework tattoo traced its way around his left cheek, eye socket, and ear. An ex football player with a weakness for the ladies – the younger the better, age was no boundary! - he had been El Gecko's driver and bodyguard for close to three years.

Mongo drove by. The window rolled back up. Rudy turned his attention to the next car, which was pulling forward.

The second car, a black Mercedes, stopped. The window rolled down. Rudy recognized the driver. A thin, rather effeminate-looking Latino named Aldo. And if Aldo was driving, that meant *Juanito Lobo* was in the back with his bodyguard.

Rudy nodded to Aldo, motioned for them to pass. Aldo rolled up the window. Bulletproof glass, Rudy noted. He assumed all glass panels n the vehicle were the same. The car moved on towards the dock while Rudy grabbed the gate and manhandled it shut on its rusty wheels and corroded ground guide with all his might.

Juanito Lobo was a poser, a clownish buffoon, as far as Rudy was concerned. First off, his real name was John Wolf, which became "Johnnie Wolf", or sometimes "Johnnie the Wolf" because Johnnie was definitely an alpha male type. Loud and proud, he made it a point of perverted honor to do his own killing. He was new to the drug business, and "Juanito" was about as Latino as an apple pie. He had blonde hair, blue eyes, and had never been south of San Ysidro.

But he had money. Lots of it. Rudy had no idea where the money had come from initially. Ultimately, it did not matter. He always paid in full. He always paid on time. He never cheated on a deal. That was why El Gecko dealt with him. He knew Johnnie's word was good as gold.

And that was precisely why Rudy did not trust him. It was nothing about Johnnie's rather peculiar sexual tastes, Rudy shrugged that kind of shit off all the time. In this business, one had to forget what one saw very quickly. No, it was something else.

He could not put his finger on it, but there was something simply.... *off* about Johnnie Wolf. He was, in a word, *too honest!* In this lousy business, there was no such thing as honor among thieves. No fraternal obligations, no true loyalty. Everyone tried to fuck over, double cross, or kill everyone else at one time or another. It was just the nature of the business, and Johnnie Wolf simply did not fit the mold.

Rudy looked behind him, scanning the crest of the road for movement. Seeing none, he trotted towards the dock, still scanning backwards, providing rear security as the cars pulled up next to the ship. Red lights flashed bright as the cars stopped.

Rudy jogged towards Johnnie's car, slowing to a walk as he came up on the driver's side. Aldo was watching him through the driver's side window, his gun hand inside his jacket. Rudy, his weapon pointed downward, halted. He swung outward, away from the car, raised his weapon to the ready position.

Inside the car, Aldo relaxed. He opened the door and stepped out, instantly feeling the cold and dampness seep in past his clothes, icy fingers wrapping around his legs, tickling their way up.

Aldo gasped softly in surprise. He closed his door and stepped to the rear door as Rudy studiously kept watch, covering their position.

By this time, Mongo was also out of the first car, senses adjusting to the night. He looked around. Something was off.

"Hey, Rudy," he called.

"Yeah?"

"Where's T-Ball?"

Mongo noticed Rudy hesitate for just a fraction of a second. "Oh, he's around."

"Why isn't he here, covering our right flank?"

"I'm here. Donnie's coving from above."

Mongo huffed out a sigh. Shaking his head, he reached for the back door handle. Likewise, Aldo reached for his. Both doors opened at the same time; a ritual that had been performed a hundred times before.

El Gecko stepped out, all dark skin and hair, slicked back and perfect, his fashionable, expensive clothes custom fitted over his thin, muscular swimmer's physique.

Johnnie Wolf emerged his Mercedes. Pasty *gringo* skin, oily with a bad complexion. Blackheads like peppercorns around his nose, pimples on his cheeks and chin. He had tried to grow a beard, but had been only partially successful. His long hair, the color of used dishwater, hung in disheveled, nappy dreadlocks. His ill fitting, mismatched attire did nothing to minimize his massive belly, which bulged against the inside of his wrinkled shirt, and jiggled like jelly when he moved.

After Johnnie stepped away from the Mercedes, Arthur, Johnnie's bodyguard and his lover, stepped out. Arthur scanned the area with intense beady eyes that never stopped moving. Arthur was about Rudy's size, red hair and pale skin. A quiet man, Rudy did not know much about him because the man hardly ever spoke. He had done time in the military, and had maintained his discipline after he mustered out. The fact he was gay made no difference to Rudy one way or the other.

Finally, Jorge, El Gecko's bodyguard exited the car, and instantly began scanning the area, alert for danger. Young, black, handsome, his caramel skin tone indicated a multiracial ancestry. So did his piercing green eyes and high cheekbones. Naturally baby faced, he had grown a beard in recent weeks. Now he looked closer to his actual age. He leaned in close to El Gecko, and whispered in his ear, "Right flank exposed."

El Gecko glanced to the right, nodded, then whispered back, "Right flank, Jorge."

Jorge pulled his .45 ACP pistol, flicked the safety off. He always kept a round in the chamber. He immediately took position on the right flank.

Johnnie grinned from behind a pair of dark sunglasses. Ridiculous really, considering the time of day and inclement weather. "Hey. Gecko. What's the problem, bud? Something wrong?"

El Gecko forced a smile. "Nothing's wrong. Just taking care of business."

"That's good, *amigo*. "I'm all about taking care of business."

El Gecko motioned with his hand. "Oh course. Right this way."

The drug smugglers and their bodyguards moved away from the parked cars and walked towards the gangplank. Rudy moved in behind them.

The drivers, as was customary, stayed with their respective cars. Mongo and Aldo looked at each other, and sighed.

"Another night standing out in the cold," Aldo said.

Mongo shrugged. "Yeah, but if we didn't do this for our money, we'd have to go out and get *jobs!"*

They both laughed.

The small cluster moved towards the gangplank of the *Sulu Sea*. Johnnie and El Gecko walked side by side in the center, flanked by Arthur to the left, and Jorge to the right. Rudy provided rear security.

From the main deck over twenty feet above the dock, Donnie watched as the group edged closer. They stopped at the edge of the gangplank. He stepped out of the shadows and stood at the top of the gangplank. He waved a hand lazily over his head, signaling all was clear.

"Let's do some business, shall we? After you," El Gecko smiled.

Johnnie grinned that greasy grin that secretly repulsed El Gecko. "That's what I like about you," Johnnie said. "You're so polite. He's polite," he added towards Arthur, who nodded in silent agreement.

Johnnie stepped onto the gangplank first, followed by Arthur, Jorge, and El Gecko. Rudy made a move forward, but El Gecko looked back at him, put up his hand to immediately halt him. El Gecko spoke briefly, under his breath, words tinged with anger.

"Find T-Ball."

CHAPTER FOUR

The vampire flowed languidly among the shadows, no real exertion, effortlessly blending in. He disappeared like a wraith, enveloping night itself. He rubbed a white, almost translucent hand through his hair, flicking the moisture condensing on his skin off and away from his expensive clothing. Perhaps he should not have worn silk tonight.

From his vantage point he saw the group moving up the gangplank in sharp, garish color. His gaze passed over each of them, stopping and on a young black man carefully providing right flank security.

Repulsed by the evil emanating off the rest of the two-legged vermin, he focused exclusively on the young man they called Jorge.

This was the young man the vampire had come to find.

First things first. Kill the drivers. Disable the cars. Then slaughter the rest at his leisure, in any manner that provided him amusement.

Rudy was coming his way. The vampire moved, faster than the human eye can follow, a black blur against the sackcloth of night.

Rudy, rifle at the ready, moved towards the unfriendly containers. He assumed T-Ball was dead.

Somehow, they were under attack. It wasn't cops. Cops would have pounced once all the players arrived, all lights and sirens and megaphones announcing their arrival. It wasn't a rival gang, either. If it had been, the ensuing firefight would have already happened, and everyone would be dead. But someone was out there, all right. Someone good enough to take out T-Ball without making a sound and evade both Rudy and Donnie.

Whoever, whatever was out there stalking them, it was worse than cops or rival gangs.

Much worse.

Just then, something passed by, whooshing with great speed, barely sensed, not fully heard nor seen. A cold gust shimmied over him, freezing him in his tracks. He knew it was not simply the night weather.

Rudy had just been touched by the wings of Evil.

And was that a faint hint of laughter, already fading away?

Trembling with an all - consuming fear and dread the likes of which he had not felt since early on in his first tour in Iraq, Rudy briefly considered turning tail and running. But the thought left him as quickly as it had come. His pride and discipline would not allow him to do something so cowardly. He also knew if he ran, El Gecko would pursue him as long as they were both alive.

Rudy gulped, gripped his weapon tighter, and took a step forward. He was not at all certain he would survive the night. He was not at all certain that any of them would.

Aboard the dilapidated *Sulu Sea*, Donnie stepped back from the quarterdeck as Johnnie and El Gecko arrived atop the gangplank. He hoped the deck had not rusted through.

"Good morning, sir, " Donnie said.

"*Buenos dias,* " his boss said back. "Everything ready?"

"Yes sir."

"What's up, Donnie?" Johnnie interjected.

Donnie nodded. "Mr. Wolf. Lovely to see you again."

Johnnie grinned yellowed teeth and pointed towards Donnie with both stubby index fingers. "You too, dude."

Donnie nodded silently to Arthur, who nodded back. "This way, gentlemen." Donnie led them aft to an open hatch in the deck, with a metal ladder heading down below.

It was pitch black down there.

Donnie slung his weapon over his shoulder and took the lead, walking down the ladder first, his hands gripped loosely around the rails on each side, ready to grab if his boot slipped on the steel step. When he got to the bottom of the ladder he stepped back and looked upwards expectantly.

One by one, the rest of the men each descended the ladder into the bowels of the ship. Jorge was the last one to descend. Almost as watchful for danger as Rudy, Jorge kept his gun trained upwards as he walked down the ladder to the steel plate at the bottom.

Once they were all standing there, waiting, Donnie simply turned around and began walking. They followed silently, single file. At the far bulkhead of each watertight compartment, they had to step through an open hatch to continue their journey. Doing so required picking up their feet and striding forward while simultaneously ducking their heads to keep from scraping their knees or knocking themselves out on the metal flanges.

After several episodes squeezing through hatches, as they moved aft, the group stepped into a compartment much larger and better lit than the rest. Several tables scattered around, with attached seating, bolted to the deck in rows. Light glared downward from several battery-powered spotlights erected at strategic locations around the room. Though the room was better lit than the passageway compartments, it was not, by any means, lit well. The harsh lights, with no scrims or diffusion, created areas awash in bright whiteness surrounded by black pools of shadow and darkness. A dark, abandoned food service area could barely be detected in the distance going aft.

"What is this place?" Arthur asked.

"The old mess decks," Donnie answered.

Rudy inspected the shipping containers where T-Ball should have been. Halted by the blackness, Rudy again pulled his small flashlight out, hit the button on the end, and felt comfort when the small white LED light burst forth.

Holding the flashlight in his fist with the light coming out near the bottom of his hand, he played the intense white LED light across the containers. Painted a dull blue that had faded over time and was peeling from years of sun, salt water air, repeated cycles of heat and cold, the containers in front of him all displayed heavy beads of moisture, condensation from the dank night air and low temperature. The light danced across the metal. Further down the side of the ground- level container, something dark red wet had been sprayed across the side.

Curious, Rudy moved closer until he caught the unmistakable coppery smell he knew all too intimately. The light refracted off the rusty spray, and he recognized the splatter for what it was – a splash of thick blood, still fresh, not yet coagulating in the moist night air. He paused in his tracks, his jaw clenched tight as his thumb flicked the safety off his weapon. His index finger snaked up to caress the trigger. He moved the flashlight slowly down towards the ground.

The white beam finally illuminated the twisted mound of old clothing and dark flesh that was T-Ball's corpse. Rudy frowned at the tangled wreck. He was no stranger to death in all its grotesque, vicious presentations. Yet he could hardly believe this mangled pile of flesh and bone had ever been a living being.

At the cars, Aldo and Mongo relaxed, chatting to ward off boredom. These meetings could last minutes, or hours. One never knew. Aldo smoked his expensive Turkish cigarettes. Mongo stoked a fifty-two ring, seven-inch cigar, an "*El Presidente*".

"How long to smoke one of those things?" Aldo asked.

Mongo took the cigar out of his mouth, glanced at it, appraising. "About an hour, hour and a half," he replied. "That's assuming I smoke it all in one sitting."

"Oh?"

"I can always cut off the lit end, stick the remainder in my pocket, and light up again some other time."

Aldo held up his thin, brown cigarette. "I'm done in five minutes. Efficient, yes?"

Mongo shrugged, unconcerned, then shoved his beloved cigar back into the left corner of his mouth. He inhaled, the smoldering end of his dark cigar glowing a luminous orange, then dying back down as he blew smoke out between his teeth.

Glancing up at Aldo from his cigar, Mongo half-saw, half felt a blur with an accompanying gust of wind sweep past, moving left to right between them.

He gasped, caught off guard, as he heard the faintest hint of a sadistic laugh. He looked at Aldo, confused. "What was that?"

Aldo did not answer. He stared back blankly, eyes wide and unbelieving, mouth agape, expensive brown Turkish cigarette falling from his lower lip. His mouth moved, but no sound came out.

He glanced down at himself to see four distinct red stains spread across the shirt covering his abdomen, blend together, become one. Blood spilled downward and over his belt, then cascaded in rivulets down his legs. Then his abdomen gaped open, its contents heaving out of him, spilling heavy and red onto the concrete, splattering everywhere, wet steam immediately rising in the cool air.

Mongo stepped back, eyes big as saucers. His cigar, forgotten, fell from his mouth. Aldo's dead body collapsed in a wet heap just a few feet in front of him. Mongo stopped when he bumped into the car behind him.

The jolt brought him around. He drew his handgun, looked around wildly. Adrenaline injected into his bloodstream, rushed throughout his body, surged by a rapidly rising pulse and accompanying blood pressure. Fight or flight, baby. Mongo already had a round in the chamber; he cocked the hammer back.

Deathly and unexpectedly afraid, Mongo promptly forgot the protocol Rudy had so carefully set up and painstakingly practiced with him and the rest of the security team. Mongo was supposed to key the radio and sound the alarm. Let Rudy know his location, and that Aldo was down. Have Donnie and Jorge get El Gecko the hell off the boat. Then they fight their way out and to safety.

None of that entered Mongo's mind. His only priority was his own survival. Gasping for breath, gun held out in front of him, his eyes scanned the blackness.

The night had returned to quiet peace. No sound out of place. No revving cars. No helicopters overhead. No attacking gunmen. Only the sound of his own breathing. In his near panic, the ensuing silence frightened him even more.

He glanced back over at Aldo. He needed to confirm the reality that Aldo was indeed dead, and that he had indeed seen what he secretly knew he had seen. Aldo's remains lay in a tangled heap on the ground between the cars. Most of the steam had finished rising as the blood and intestines cooled against the cold pavement.

At least Mongo wasn't taking leave of his senses.

A quiet rustle to his left. The barest hint of movement. Close.

Mongo turned in one swift, precise motion. He did not see anything, only felt a great impact at the wrist of his gun hand. Astonished, he looked at his gun, which had magically dropped and clattered on the ground. What was that dark brown thing attached and wrapped around the handgrip of the gun?

Oh yes. Of course.

It was his hand, severed neatly with surgical precision, a single incision slicing through flesh, bone and sinew. Mongo's index finger still gripped around the trigger.

Mongo's gaze drifted upwards from the ground to his right arm, which now somehow ended at the end of his forearm, and squirted hot red blood into the air.

None of this made any sense to him. His hand had been there just a second ago, right?

His brain began to register pain. Mongo instinctively grabbed his arm with his remaining hand, clamped down on it in a viselike grip, trying to stop the unfettered flow of blood out of his body.

He heard a mewling sound, like a soft growl of a cat, off to one side, approaching swiftly. He turned to his left. His eyes grew wide once again.

Then Mongo's brain simply checked out.

The last thing Mongo ever saw in this world was an expensive suit, dark and immaculate, an open mouth filled with razor sharp teeth, long nose, alabaster skin, and black, evil, deep-set, hate-filled eyes. After that, he felt a brief and terrible rending of flesh at his throat, and then he was floating downward, downward, ever downward.

CHAPTER FIVE

Mongo was dead by the time his massive body thudded to the ground. Blood pooled out from his jagged neck, engulfing his head.

The vampire stood over his two latest kills, scanning his handiwork, grinning with smug satisfaction. He had managed to take them both out without either one of them raising the alarm. Of course, with the big man, the vampire had sliced through his throat, rending vocal chords asunder, his sharp nails going through flesh like a warm knife through butter. He dabbed the blood from his fingers with his linen handkerchief.

"Mongo, Rudy. Come in." The harried voice on the radio sounded tinny, far away.

"Mongo, come in." A pause. "Mongo. Come in." The voice sounded urgent. Pleading.

The vampire stepped away from the carnage. His eyes flickered up to the hulking, decrepit freighter tied to the dock. Drugs, he thought with disgust.

Repulsive.

He was a demon of bloody vengeance this night, and they were all going to get what they deserved.

Rudy tried Mongo one more time as he squatted beside T-Balls ragged remains. When he got no response, he switched his radio to the reserve frequency, the one they had all agreed would only be used in case of catastrophic emergencies.

"Mongo. Mongo. Come in. Abort. Abort."

No answer. He stood up, his mind slipping into combat mode, ready to engage the enemy.

"Donnie, Rudy. Come in"

Static.

"Donnie, Rudy. Come in!"

More static.

Radio communication from outside to inside the ship was useless. Assuming Mongo and Aldo were dead, Rudy moved towards the gangway. He would have to go get them himself. Expecting to die at any moment, Rudy broke into a dead run, crossing the concrete towards the gangway as fast as he could. Surprisingly, no gunfire erupted, no bullets whizzing past his head, chewing the concrete around his feet...

Something big slammed into him from the side, unseen, tripping up his feet. Rudy's momentum sent him sprawling, skidding across the pavement. His head bounced off the concrete a couple of times, skinning his forehead, rendering him unconscious.

Spare the brave, the vampire thought as he shot up the gangway, nothing but a black blur.

Inside the belly of the freighter, no one knew anything was amiss outside. Standing on one side of a dining table, across from Jorge and El Gecko, Johnnie nodded to Arthur at his side. Arthur lifted the black briefcase he had been carrying, placed it on the metal table. He flicked the spring-loaded tabs open, then opened the lid. He then turned the open case around, careful not to make any sudden movements. He pushed the open case towards El Gecko until the contents appeared directly under the light.

Leaning forward, El Gecko smiled. Inside the case sat a small flash drive, held in place by foam buffers filling the inside of the briefcase. A shallow cutout held the drive. He glanced up at Johnnie, who smiled from ear to ear like an idiot, and to Arthur, whose face wore no discernable expression.

He took a step back, glanced to his right, and nodded to Jorge.

Jorge stepped forward, leaned down and reached underneath the dining table. He searched for a moment, then stood up and produced a sleek laptop computer from somewhere under the table. He opened the top, booted up the computer.

Jorge looked at Johnnie. "May I?"

"Please. Be my guest."

Jorge reached out, a measured movement to not agitate any itchy trigger fingers in the room. He plucked the flash drive out of the briefcase, and plugged it into a USB port on the side of his computer. The drive engaged automatically, lighting up iridescent green at its tip. Jorge immediately began typing. El Gecko and Donnie kept a close watch on Johnnie and Arthur. They stood perfectly still.

Seconds passed. "Are we happy?" Johnnie asked, an overgrown child.

Jorge continued to study his computer screen.

El Gecko glanced at Jorge. Behind him, Donnie's grip on his AK – 47 tightened slightly, almost imperceptibly. Tension rose in the room.

"Well?" El Gecko asked. "Are we happy?"

Jorge finally looked up from his screen. "Oh yeah. We're happy."

The tension dissipated immediately. Even Donnie smiled faintly. Johnnie held his hands out wide beside himself. "Told you, man. You can always trust me to honor my word."

El Gecko extended his hand. "In this business, one must to be careful."

Johnnie pumped his hand. "Well, you can always count me as a friend."

El Gecko shrugged, unapologetic. "Friends are friends, but business is business."

"And speaking of business, friend, I just paid you four million dollars." He pushed his ridiculous sunglasses up on his greasy nose. "Where's my merchandise?"

El Gecko snapped his fingers in the air. Donnie walked over to a work light and moved the toggle switch. The light snapped on, illuminating a series of crates, each covered with nondescript blankets and covers. Donnie pulled the covers back on one. He opened the hinged top, reached inside, and pulled out a large, black weapon. Vaguely resembling an M-16, but much larger and heavier, it looked like something from a science fiction movie.

"What the hell is that?" Jorge asked.

"That," Johnnie replied, "is the AA-12. The world's most advanced automatic shotgun, and the world's most dangerous and deadly troop - carried weapon." Donnie pitched one over to Johnnie, who caught it with an ease that surprised Jorge.

"What the hell you gonna do? Start a war?"

Johnnie's dopey grin faded. "Something like that."

Donnie tossed him a large circular canister, about eighteen inches in diameter by four inches thick, with what looked like a notch cut out at the top. Johnnie caught the preloaded twenty round ammo canister with one hand. With practiced ease, he slapped it into place on the bottom of the weapon, and expertly chambered a round.

El Gecko stepped in. "Two hundred units, just like you asked," he said. "Plus both the twenty – round and the thirty – two round drum loaders as requested." Behind him, Donnie proceeded to uncover the other crates. "Plus the more conventional small arms, ammo, grenades."

Jorje felt a tickle of fear shoot up his spine.

Up on deck, the vampire moved smoothly through the darkness, his sensitive ears picking up the tiny, muffled voices from below. He moved aft. The voices got a bit stronger. He moved aft again, following the gathering sounds, until he found himself standing at the top of the ladder on the aft cargo hold.

And as he drifted downward into the hold, ephemeral as a wisp of smoke, his nose picked up their blood. Now, following his nose as well as his ears, the vampire strode confidently through the passageway. He lifted his legs and ducked his head, passing through the hatches without hesitation. Glancing at his watch, he noticed time was becoming a factor.

He strode faster.

Jorge looked around and did not like what he saw. This was supposed to have been a routine purchase of heroin for Johnnie's contacts up north, not an arms deal.

Neither Donnie not El Gecko seemed at all concerned that Johnnie Wolf, a known wild card and unpredictable man, suddenly was armed with a very dangerous weapon and twenty live rounds. Johnnie laughed like a kid on Christmas morning, dancing around in sheer, unbridled glee.

Jorge's hand discreetly moved to the small of his back, where he kept his gun.

"Know what this bitch can do, Jorge?" Johnnie asked. When Jorge shook his head, El Gecko grinned, then glanced at Johnnie. "It can fire a standard double ought buck shotgun shell, or an armor piercing round, or custom, high explosive anti- personnel rounds. This thing, when it's on full auto, can fire up to three hundred rounds per minute."

Johnnie laughed. El Gecko joined in. Arthur too. Even Donnie grinned in the shadows. Sweat started beading across Jorge's upper lip.

Johnnie took a step forward. "I could start a war with anybody. Another drug cartel member?" El Gecko shook his head no in an exaggerated fashion. "With a small Central American republic?" He shrugged. El Gecko shrugged in return.

Then Johnnie lowered the weapon until it pointed straight at Jorge. Jorge pulled his gun, aimed at Johnnie.

"What the fuck you doing, you junkie-assed motherfucker?"

Johnnie kept the AA-12 pointed at Jorge, but reached up with one hand, took off his sunglasses. He tossed them aside onto the metal table.

"I'm starting a war," Johnnie whispered intensely. His eyes went cold. His mouth was a thin, cruel line across the lower part of his face. "Against law enforcement. And you'll be the first casualty..... *COP!*"

Jorge's heart threatened to explode. "Do I look like a fuckin' cop to you? I ain't no fuckin' cop!"

"Our contact within the police department says otherwise," El Gecko stated.

"Then your contact's fucked up. I ain't no fuckin' cop."

"Have it your way."

"This should be fun," Johnnie said. "You wanna go get something to eat after this? I know a great all-night diner up on El Cajon Boulevard."

El Gecko grinned, and it was ugly. It reminded Jorge of pictures he'd seen on TV of jungle predators right before they rip into their prey.

Then, incredibly, Johnnie's abdomen ripped open, from right to left, intestines spilling out. Jorge dived for the floor as Johnnie's finger squeezed the trigger, firing off a wild round.

Pandemonium ensued.

El Gecko lunged for the door. He got about three steps before some impossible blur, an unseen force, neatly decapitated his head from his body. Bright red blood spewed ten feet from his spurting neck, peppering the overhead. His body dropped like a load of bricks to the deck.

Donnie opened fire in the direction of El Gecko, hoping to kill whoever had just killed his boss. While lying on the deck, Jorge shot Arthur, who had gone for his own gun. Arthur took a slug to the leg and fell to the deck, putting him down to Jorge's level. Then he got two slugs to the chest. His head dropped to the floor, dead weight.

Jorge scrambled for cover behind a metal storage cabinet. He pointed his gun in front of him, trying to find the next target.

Donnie stopped firing. Silence enveloped the compartment. He waited, listening. He heard nothing. He ducked behind a crate for cover.

"Jorge," he called. "Is it true? Are you a cop?"

"Fuuuuck no, it ain't true, mortherfucker," he replied. "You ever seen a cop do the shit I've done on this job?"

Donnie thought about that. It made sense. "Stay where you are. There's someone else here. I'll kill them first. Then we'll talk."

Jorge gulped. He knew what it meant when Donnie wanted to "talk". He was not out of the woods yet.

Donnie slowly rose until he could barely see over the crates. Eyes scanning the pools of bright light and juxtaposed depths of darkness, he couldn't really see anything. But he knew someone – something! – was in here with them. And it would never let Donnie walk out of this compartment alive. He decided it prudent to double back, attempt to outflank whoever was doing this.

He slowly crouched down, head out of sight. He spun on one foot one hundred eighty degrees..... and his heart stopped.

White skin, blazing black eyes, unearthly evil, and a razorblade mouth filled his eyesight. The vampire grabbed the muzzle of the rifle, pushed it out of the way. He moved in for the kill, wrenching Donnie's head to the side so quickly he did not have a chance to scream. Long fangs sank into the carotid, his powerful lower jaw crushing Donnie's windpipe.

Donnie, kung fu expert, expert marksman, consummate warrior, died in a matter of seconds.

From his hidden position, Jorge could see nothing. He had thought he had heard something, but it stopped quickly, and he had not heard anything else after that. With the exception of his own breathing, there was no sound at all on the mess decks.

He looked back to where Donnie had last been. No movement. But he noticed a black stain on the floor. As he looked at it more closely, he realized it was not black, but a deep crimson red, liquid, and it was spreading across the deck.

Something massive was heaved upwards out of the darkness. Jorge fired twice, both bullets hitting the mass. It fell with a thud onto the tiled deck. He peered from his position and realized that what had been tossed out like last week's garbage was Donnie Yen's corpse.

"Jorge." A whisper. "That is what you call yourself?"

The voice came from nowhere, and yet came from everywhere.

"Who the fuck are you?"

" Someone who knows you are not like these others.

"What the fuck are you talking about?"

"They are trash. Human garbage. Pathetic dregs from the shallow end of the gene pool. Their lives mean nothing. Their deaths mean less. You, on the other hand, are different. I mean you no harm."

"Then step out where I can see you."

From behind an iron column, something that resembled a human body, still clinging to the shadows, as if made out of thin air. Whoever it was stood there, hands by their sides, not moving.

Jorge kept his gun trained on the person's center of mass. "Step out where I can see you." The person started to slowly walk forward. "Hands up where I can see them!" The person walking towards him complied.

Then he stopped right at the edge of the light. Jorge could see his shoes. Italian. Expensive. The pants leg. Dark blue. Pinstripe, maybe. Nicely tailored. Clean lines. Proper length, ending precisely at the top of the instep of the foot, the fall of the fabric immaculate.

The rest of him remained hidden in shadow.

"Step out where I can see your face."

"No."

"Motherfucker, I'm about two seconds away from putting two rounds in your chest."

"Please do not."

"Why not?

"My shirt."

"What about it?

"It is quite expensive."

"Then step out where I can see you."

"No."

"Why's that?"

"So you will not be forced to lie later when they ask you what I look like."

"Who?"

"Your colleagues in law enforcement."

"Man, I told you, I ain't no fuckin' cop!"

"There is no need to continue your charade, Reginald." The vampire noticed the look of shock on Jorge's face. "I came here this night for you."

"To kill me?"

"To protect you."

This made no sense. "Have we met?"

"Not the way you mean."

"Even if I was this Reginald cat, why would you want to help me?"

The vampire glanced at his watch again. "Time has become a factor for me. I really must be going." He stepped back, deeper into the shadows. "Tell the truth. They will believe you."

"Wait!"

The vampire stopped.

"Who... No, *what* are you?"

"Something... not quite human."

"Hold on!"

"Yes?" The terse response carried an impatient edge.

"Did you kill everyone outside?"

"All but one brave Latino."

"Rudy."

"Rudy. I rather like that name." The vampire turned to walk away.

"How did you do all this?" Jorge yelled.

"Magic, my boy. Magic"

Wait!"

"Do not despair. We shall meet again under less traumatic circumstances. I promise. Ta-ta for now."

And then he was simply… gone.

CHAPTER SIX

The new day dawned, cloudy, overcast, and gray. Angry, low-hanging clouds threatened a drenching downpour. Fog continued to envelope the docks and the shoreline, a undulating white blanket. The sun, a pale white orb mostly obscured, hung close to the gloomy Eastern horizon. The air, still cold and damp, remained stagnant. Heavy. Condensation beaded on every exposed surface.

A typical January morning in San Diego.

The docks, quiet the night before, now buzzed with police activity. Vans, police cruisers, and ambulances parked haphazardly, scattered about, roof lights silently flashing. Coroners and technicians huddled together, examining the carnage littered across the pavement. Even the most hardened cops stood aghast.

A police videographer walked around, stone-faced and grim, eyes concentrating on his two-inch viewfinder as he documented the scene. He slowly tilted and panned his camera, sweeping in smooth steady movements. Every so often, he would stop and move in for a close-up of something significant. Nearby, Detectives stood, coffee cups in one hand. Pointing around with their free hands, they spouted theories of what had happened here. They claimed certainty on how each victim had been killed.

None of them even came close.

Detective Sergeant Reginald Downing, San Diego Police Department, on loan to a Federal Joint Task Force, who until recently had been known as Jorge, sat, feeling removed from it all. Eyes distant and unfocused, bloodshot from exhaustion and shellshock, he perched himself atop a massive Marine cleat on the wharf beside the gangway to the *Sulu Sea*. Resting his elbows on his knees, his spent firearm dangled loosely between the intertwined fingers of both hands.

He mentally replayed the events of the last few hours over and over in his mind. Stark images assaulted him, a sadistic videotape on continuous loop in his head. Questions flooded his mind. How had the others found out was undercover? Contacts within the force, huh? They had planned to kill him, so why would they lie? But who? And how many? Did the cartel's reach go as far as Reggie feared it might?

It made sense, though. Reggie knew when El Gecko was bluffing, and last night he was not. Wealthy, powerful men like El Gecko and Johnnie had informants everywhere. They had to. It was often a matter of survival.

It could be a beat cop on the street, or an administrator in an office. You find someone who's underwater on their mortgage, has alimony or child support problems, a sick parent in the hospital or a nursing home. Grease their palm every once in a while with enough money to keep them afloat, and you've got your stoolie. If they step out of line, get greedy, or grow a conscience, you threaten their family. Keeps 'em in line every time. Trapped by their own dishonesty, they feed you intel until they retire, get caught, or commit suicide.

Of course, you can get lucky and find a cop who's just greasy enough to be greedy. They take the money to supplement their lifestyle, or to fund a more comfortable retirement than an honest cop's pension provides. Or maybe they simply get off doing something dirty under the table.

And if they get out of line, no sweat. You just kill 'em. Make the body disappear. Make sure you leave no forensics. Find another stoolie (never hard to do!), and you're home free.

But someone in his own Police Department had dropped a dime on Reggie. He had to find them, and plug the leak. Good thing he had no idea who that might be. If he knew now, he'd simply take them out.

No arrests, no warrants, no trial by jury. No due process; just pure revenge.

Summary execution.

Reggie's eyes darted furtively around the dock. He watched the forensic videographer swoop silently in for a close up of Aldo's intestines. Real Academy Award winning stuff this guy was going for. Beyond him, Reggie saw two white coverall-clad technicians attempting to put T-Ball's remains into a body bag. The pieces fell apart under their own weight.

To his right, ambulance attendants and uniformed cops hauled body bags, heavy and cumbersome, down the gangway from the main deck of the freighter. About fifty feet away, two senior homicide detectives, both of whom he had met in the past and neither of whose names he could remember, huddled together talking. To him, they looked deep in conversation. Something serious. Discussing clues, blood spray patterns maybe?

Then they both grinned and, heads back, laughed uproariously. They continued to sip their coffee and eat the Danishes they held in their hands.

Disgusted, Reggie glanced further to his right. In the distance, he could make out Rudy, bloodied and solemn, sitting quietly and ramrod straight in the back of a police cruiser, hands cuffed behind him. Rudy stared straight ahead, eyes unfocused – the thousand-yard stare - like the good soldier he was, and never looked Reggie's way. He'd go to prison, take the full weight. He'd never say a word, never cop a plea. It would be a matter of honor to him.

Reggie absently rubbed the side of his face with his forearm, then looked down at the concrete. One person killed seven armed people in a matter of minutes, got away without a trace, and left him alive.

But why? Reggie did not recognize the voice he'd heard. And the mystery man admitted they had never met in person. What did this guy care if some nameless undercover mid-career cop got killed in the line of duty?

And this drug thing wasn't over, either. Not by a long shot.

A late model police car, unmarked but unmistakable to the trained eye, crested the small hill in the distance near the guard shack. It slowed as it moved down the dirt incline and onto the dock.

Reggie noticed the car, a dark brown Crown Vic, as it stopped and the engine cut out. Reggie wondered, did this kind of "unmarked car" really fool anyone?

He knew what they wanted. A part of him tensed, dreading the confrontation. But another part off him was just too tired, too scared, too confused, and too pissed to give a damn. After last night, the last thing Reggie cared about was getting his ass chewed by an overweight, over-the-hill, too-long-in-the-tooth admin pogue. He just hated having to deal with the Departmental bullshit.

The car doors clicked opened, swung wide, like the spreading wings of an ugly steel insect. Detective Sergeant Nick Castle got out the driver's side. Tall, thin and wiry, he had runner's legs and a fighter's body. A Hispanic man with a Caucasian name, he had boxed as a kid to keep from getting picked on, and currently trained three nights a week in mixed martial arts. He seemed to be scowling behind his unnecessary sunglasses. Not because he was angry, but because he was always under stress, didn't handle it particularly well, and wore a perpetual frown. An honest cop, he wore an older, inexpensive suit, cheap store-bought tie, and ten - year old scuffed shoes.

On the passenger side, a large foot, adorned inside a shiny black oxford shoe, stomp to the ground below the open door. Reggie's eyes moved up as Captain Morris Horn pushed his massive body out of the seat. The car lifted visibly as Horn's weight shifted onto his tree trunk legs.

Horn, a very dark black man, adjusted his eyeglasses atop his nose. Dark eyes, bloodshot, having not slept well. Built like a grizzly bear with a legendary temper to match, he smoothed his deep blue tie against the pale blue shirt covering his barrel chest. At six foot four, over two hundred and eighty pounds, a touch of gray over a deeply lined face with pockmarks from acne when he was a kid, Morris Horn looked more like a retired pro football player than a veteran cop with twenty years on the force, seven major felony convictions that put perps in jail for life (or more!), ten Departmental Commendations, and two Medals of Valor.

Horn's hard glare focused on Reggie across the busy dock and zeroed in on him with laser-like intensity. The corners of his mouth turned downward. The lines across his forehead deepened. He grabbed his trouser belt at the sides with both hands, giving it a slight, mindless tug upwards across solid belly. Horn was not obese; he was *thick*, a refrigerator on legs. He stalked forward, an unblinking predator closing the distance on his prey.

Reggie knew what was coming. He realized suddenly he was still holding his firearm in his right hand. The barrel seemed like an extra finger jutting downwards. He shoved his handgun into the waistband at the back of his pants.

As they got closer, Reggie stood up and put his hands behind his back. He willed himself to relax, concentrating on his breathing, feeling his heart rate drop. He watched serenely as Capt. Horn jabbed an accusatory finger in his direction.

"Downing!" he barked from fifteen feet away. "What the holy motherfuck happened here?"

"Good morning to you, too, Captain." A calm voice will turneth away anger, right? He nodded to Castle, who looked apologetic. "Nick."

Castle nodded back. "Reg. You all right?"

"I'm good."

"Don't give me any of your super-cop smartass bullshit," Horn growled. "You got a lot of explaining to do, Mr. Kid Fuckin' Genius!"

"Don't worry, Captain," Reggie said, wishing the old bastard would just fucking retire. "I'm fine."

"'You're fine'? 'You're fine'? I don't give a flying fisted fuck if you're fine. I wouldn't give a flying fisted fuck if you were laying in that meat wagon over there with a Goddamn tag on your toe." He pointed to the ambulance. "Looks to me like there was a goddamned bloodbath out here last night, and somehow, miraculously," he gestured towards the sky, his condescension dripping with scorn, "you're the only one left standing."

Reggie nodded, already bored, already knowing what was coming next. "You're right. That's exactly what happened." He paused.

"So who did this?"

Downing raised his hands in a timeless gesture of innocence. "Not me, Cap'n."

Horn, caught off guard, was silent for a moment. "I know it wasn't you. Who was it?" He glanced around at the carnage. "A rival gang?"

Reggie shook his head.

"How many of them were there?" Castle asked gently.

"Just one. He was enough."

"Don't be bullshittin' me this early in the morning, Whiz Kid," Horn warned. "I haven't had enough coffee for this shit."

Reggie remained unmoved, imagining a life without Horn in it.

"I told you, Cap. Just one."

Now both Horn and Castle were speechless. They were accustomed to being lied to, by everyone, all the time. They knew the truth when they heard it. Reggie was telling the truth.

"One man took out seven people, all armed, most military trained, at multiple points on the dock and aboard that ship, but left you alive?"

"Yes."

Mentally digesting this, Horn and Castle both looked around the docks at the body bags, the blood, the mess. This sheer magnitude of slaughter, all at the hands of one man?

Incredible.

"Who could have done this and gotten away clean?" Castle asked. "Mercenary? A Special Forces commando, something like that?"

Reggie shrugged. "Maybe. He seemed to know how to use the night."

" 'Use the night'?" Horn echoed.

Reggie nodded. "He made sure I never saw his face. He moved fast. No sound. He used darkness and shadow as camouflage. Like a ninja or something."

"You saying a ninja did all this?"

"Of course not," Reggie replied. "But this guy was definitely a trained killer. And he wiped out a mid-level cartel in a matter of minutes, stopped a major arms deal, and saved my ass," Reggie confirmed.

"Let's talk about that," Horn said. "Why didn't he kill you?"

"He didn't say. But if he'd wanted to kill me, I couldn't have stopped him."

"You're a veteran cop and trained martial artist," Castle said.

"And he was out of my league. Out of everyone's league. If he had wanted me dead, believe me, I'd be dead."

Horn eyed Reggie with suspicion. "What aren't you telling us?"

"Gentlemen, I think that's enough." The voice came from behind. Surprised, Horn and Castle turned around. A middle-aged man, full head of hair gone gray, with a moustache and small goatee beard greeted them. Wearing jeans, sneakers, a threadbare gray sweatshirt and a military style leather jacket, the only thing that identified him as a cop was the DEA badge dangling from a lanyard around his neck.

"Well. Special Agent Coulter. So nice of you to drop by." Horn's words seared with hostility.

Walt Coulter smiled, letting the insult pass him by. He stepped forward, ignoring Horn and Castle, and stopped in front of Reggie. "You okay, cowboy?"

"Fine, sir."

He put an avuncular arm around Reggie's shoulder. "Come on, kid. I'll buy you a breakfast burrito and a coffee. Then we'll talk." He started to lead Reggie away.

"Now hold on a goddamned minute, Coulter," Horn exploded. Coulter stopped. "That's my officer there. He hasn't been debriefed."

Coulter smiled over his shoulder. "Your officer was assigned to me for the Federal joint task force. Signed over to me personally by you, as a matter of fact. That makes him *my* officer until such time as I say otherwise, understand?"

Coulter jabbed an index finger in Horn's direction. "You want to talk to *my* officer? You have questions for *my* officer? Submit a written request. Maybe I'll grant it. Maybe I won't. Either way, he's off limits to you. Got it?" He and Reggie resumed walking away.

"We're not done here, Coulter!"

Coulter turned around. This time, he was not smiling. "Yes, we are. *My* agent barely escaped with his life. He's hungry and tired. I'm taking him to breakfast. I'll copy you his report later this week after he's submitted it – if you're lucky." Coulter pointed a finger again. "And it's 'Special Agent Coulter' to you. You will call me by my proper rank. Understand -- *Captain*?" He walked away without waiting for a response.

Horn stood there, eyes wide, mouth agape. He simply could not believe he had just gotten into a pissing contest – with a fucking *Fed*, no less! – and lost. He turned and looked at Castle, who had wisely turned his attention elsewhere, watching the forensics team collecting evidence and blood samples for processing.

"Come on, Castle," Horn said, deflated. "Let's get the fuck out of here."

Back in their unmarked police car, Horn turned to Castle.

"Did any of that seem strange to you?"

Castle looked at him. The whole thing seemed strange to him.

"Like something from the Twilight Zone, right?" Horn pressed.

"Something."

Horn stared out the windshield for a moment. "Why leave Downing alive? He killed everyone else – "

"He didn't just kill them, Cap. He slaughtered them. The entire scene was like a meat packing plant from Hell. Oh, and by the way, he left someone alive," Castle corrected. "Rudy Valdez is alive."

Horn nodded. "Why those two? A low-level foot soldier and an undercover cop. What kind of message does that send?" He began counting things off on his fingers, one by one. "To law enforcement? To rival gangs? To the cartels?" His hand opened, palm up, an unanswered question. "It just doesn't make any sense."

Castle thought for a moment. No hypothesis came to mind. He mentally connected the dots, but no discernable pattern emerged.

"A guy like this," Horn said, softly, like he was thinking out loud, "his kills are fast. Clean. They're messy, they're bloody, but they're not reckless or random, you know?"

Castle nodded. "I'm with you so far."

Horn thought a moment longer. "If this was a regular murder scene, and you saw this kind of carnage in the method of execution, what would you think?"

"Crime of passion. Like the killer knew the victims and hated them. A lot."

"Yeah." The moment hung. "or something cold and calculated, deliberately brutal to send a message."

"What are you thinking, Cap?"

"Not sure."

The moment passed. Horn got back on track.

"Point is, Downing's right. This guy's been trained. He doesn't do random. He doesn't make mistakes." Horn paused a moment, formulating his words. "There's a reason for every decision he makes."

"Professional killers tend to be perfectionists," Castle said. "Acute attention to detail. They live in an unforgiving profession that allows no margin for error."

"Those two were left alive for a very specific reason." He turned and looked at Castle. "I'd like to know why."

Castle grinned. "Well, things being what they are... if we can't talk to Reggie..."

"We can talk to Rudy Valdez," Horn finished for him.

A dull white Toyota Celica, a relic from the late eighties, pulled into the parking lot beside an outdated greasy spoon called Mama's Diner. The car wheezed its way into a parking stall. The engine sputtered, backfired in a belch of sparks from the rusted tailpipe, then died. White smoke wafted upwards, smelling of burned oil and cheap gasoline, like the car had farted.

Doors creaked open, stiff hinges groaning their protests. Coulter, who had been driving, got out on the left. Reggie practically fell out the other side.

"Why is it I'm more scared riding in this car than what I was doing last night?" Reggie asked.

Coulter grinned, swatting at the smoke wafting his direction from the tailpipe. "Show some backbone, kid. This car's a classic!"

"A classic clunker," Reggie persisted as they walked towards the restaurant. "Why don't you turn her in to the state? They'll pay you a thousand dollars for it."

"Wait 'til I get this baby restored. She'll look like she belongs in a museum."

"She belongs a salvage yard."

Coulter patted Reggie on the shoulder, all in good fun. "You gotta have faith things will work out."

Once seated inside, they ordered. Reggie opted for scrambled eggs, sausage, and toast. Coulter ordered coffee and toast. Coulter watched as Reggie stared out the window for a while. Reggie wasn't ready to talk yet. Coulter knew that from experience. Give him time. He'll come 'round on his own.

Coulter sipped coffee that tasted like battery acid while Reggie devoured breakfast. He raised his empty cup towards the waitress. She noticed, came over with the pot, and topped off his mug. She disappeared while Coulter stirred his sugar and cream into his coffee.

"Feels good, doesn't it?" he asked.

Reggie wiped his mouth with his napkin. "What?"

"Being alive."

Reggie grinned, pointed at Coulter with his fork, then went back to eating.

Coulter stared out the window a moment. "Why are you still alive?"

Reggie put his fork down. His plate was mostly empty now. He grabbed his coffee mug, took a sip, swallowed.

"Honestly, I got no fucking idea," he said. Elbows on the table, he held his mug with both hands near his mouth. "This one guy. He..." he shook his head. "I should have been in a body bag this morning." He inhaled as if to continue speaking, then exhaled quickly, completely, more like a sigh than anything else.

Coulter noticed the change. "What?"

"It's nothing."

"Everything's always nothing until it becomes something," Coulter said.

Reggie hesitated. Coulter sat in silence. "He wasn't there to kill me."

Intrigued, Coulter leaned forward. "What do you mean?"

"It was almost like..."

"What?"

"Well... like he was protecting me. Like he was there to take care of me."

"What makes you think that?" Coulter asked in a carefully modulated tone.

"He knew I wasn't a criminal." Reggie leaned forward and whispered, "He knew my real name, Walt. He knew I was a cop."

"How?"

"Don't know. But we've got another problem. Johnnie Wolf and El Gecko knew I was a cop, too. Johnnie was going to turn my pancreas into mincemeat with one of those AA-12's. They claimed they have someone inside the Police Department."

Coulter sat back in his seat once again.

The waitress buzzed back in, silently topped off Reggie's cheap stoneware coffee mug. She threw him a smile, then flitted away. Reggie doctored his coffee, took a test sip before speaking again. When he did, his voice was low.

"Walt, I believe them."

"I do too."

"You know something I don't?"

"It's the only thing that makes sense."

Reggie sipped his coffee, put it down. He interlocked his fingers together, elbows on the table. He furrowed his brow, thinking.

"What?" Walt asked.

"My mystery savior knew I was a cop, but there's more." He looked Walt directly in the eye. "He knew me, Walt. Everything about me. My life story."

Walt glanced around, casing the place. Looking for danger.

Reggie leaned over the table towards Coulter. "Johnnie and El Gecko were garden-variety traffickers. Take them out, and what changes? Someone else just fills that void. But their bosses are gonna want to know what happened. So if the cops know I survived..."

"The cartel will be gunning for you."

A door leading out of the kitchen banged open. Reggie spun, grabbing for his gun, but relaxed when he saw it was just a bus boy, about sixteen or seventeen years old. Probably working to save for college, or maybe sending money home South of the border.

Coulter thought for a moment. "You need to go to ground, son. At least for a little while."

Reggie stood up. "I figured something like this would happen sooner or later."

"You have a plan?"

"I've got a 'go bag'. Cash. Gun. Ammo. New I.D."

"Can I drop you off somewhere?"

"I'm safer on my own."

Reggie walked towards the back of the restaurant. Glancing around, he slipped through the metal swinging doors into the kitchen. He silently moved past the mildly surprised grill cooks, and pushed the back door open. Sunshine spilled in, blotting out his body as he stepped outside. Then the door swung shut, clipping off the invading sunlight.

It was as if Reginald Downing had never been there at all.

CHAPTER SEVEN

Horn and Castle parked directly outside precinct Headquarters. Horn had been quiet during the drive back, which was unusual. Castle had expected to endure yet another barrage of profanity–laden conspiracy theories about God knows what, with a few baseless accusations that Reggie Downing was a dirty cop. Instead, Horn had sat still and slightly hunched, staring out the window. Castle had glanced at him a few times, and his position never changed. Horn simply sat there, his right elbow propped on the door near the window glass, his thumb and forefinger cupping his chin.

Castle killed the engine. He looked over at Horn, who did not budge. "Ummm, Captain?"

Horn came out of his mental meanderings. He opened his door, got out. He closed the door, but did not move. He turned to look at Castle.

"Let's assume for a minute that Downing wasn't yanking our chain," he started. "Now, there's no way just one guy could take out all those people without the others seeing him and sounding the alarm, right?"

"But Downing said there was only one."

"Exactly," Horn replied, "and that's what doesn't fit."

"But you said we're assuming he didn't lie to us, sir."

"I don't think he did."

"I don't follow."

"All Downing really said was that he saw only one guy in the cargo hold, right?"

"Right."

Horn threw up his hands in a *voila!* movement. "But that doesn't mean there weren't others outside. Downing just didn't see them."

"Our mystery man on the boat claimed he did it all himself."

"He lied," Horn said simply. "And in his highly emotional state, Downing believed him."

"That makes sense."

Horn turned and headed towards the sidewalk. Castle followed. "We got a lot of work to do."

"What?"

"Listen and learn, kid," Horn said, stopping. "If I'm right, a new crew's in town. Someone's going into business for themselves."

Castle moved when Horn turned and lurched towards the Police Building front entrance. "You mean someone's going to war with the cartels?" he asked.

Horn nodded and said, "Assume they got better intel than us. Assume they know who survived last night."

"And that Reggie is a cop."

Horn pointed a finger at Castle. "Smart boy. No wonder you're a Sergeant in only eight years."

"They'll come after him."

"They know what happens when they kill cops," Horn answered. "It's bad for business. But if they do make a move, well, Downing's no pushover. He can handle himself."

They pushed through the front doors and entered the building. Telephones rang, insistent, unanswered, while the soft rumble of a dozen conversations combined and filled the background with white noise.

To Horn's left, a uniformed cop handcuffed a sullen young teenager to a bench. Based on his extreme youth and paint-stained fingertips, Horn pegged him as a tagger. When the cop told the boy to sit still and wait, the kid flipped him off and said, "Fuck you, Cop". To his credit, the cop ignored the little shit and went about the business of calling the punk's parents.

To Horn's right, a Detective sat at his desk, interviewing an exhausted woman slumping in her chair he had seen before. He could not remember her name, but knew every line on her sagging face. Her rap sheet came to mind. A career prostitute, she sold her badly aging body to support her drug habit. She'd lost a real career, a husband and two kids somewhere along the way. Now she gave twenty-dollar blowjobs in the stairwells of dingy alleyways.

Just another day at the office.

The Greyhound bus terminal experienced a lull in activity. The last of the morning busses, bound for places like Los Angeles, Reno, and Phoenix, had pulled out minutes ago. The next wave of arriving busses weren't due to arrive for another half hour, around noon. Porters stood near the loading docks, talking, or listening to music on their phones.

Inside the terminal, a few passengers sat in uncomfortable chairs. One old woman dozed. A young couple in their teens made out in the corner. A Marine in uniform ordered a sandwich and coffee at the short order grill. The middle-aged woman who worked the newsstand had no customers. Bored, she read a tabloid magazine she had taken out of its rack. When she was done, she would put it back.

No one noticed the sloppy, hunched over figure that careened past the front doors and staggered towards the bus station lockers. Tall and thin, the man wore an oversized dark blue hoodie up over his head, his face in shadow. Black sunglasses hid his eyes. A small, half empty bottle of cheap whiskey protruded from his back pocket.. Smelling of alcohol, he stumbled towards the lockers mumbling to himself.

He careened closer, detecting the surveillance camera on the ceiling pointed at the lockers. He tucked his left shoulder, dipped his head a bit, and cast his gaze down. He babbled incoherent conspiracy theories about invisible laser beams from surveillance cameras entering his brain and stealing his thoughts.

When he stopped in front of the bank of lockers, all the surveillance camera recorded was the image of what appeared to be a street person, maybe a burned out druggie limping in.

He fumbled around, looking for something. He patted the pockets on his shirt, his hoodie, his pants searching. His search grew more urgent.

"Oh Jesus Christ," he muttered as he continued to pat himself down. Finally, frantic fingers found a familiar piece of thin brass. Smooth on one side, carefully serrated on the other, with a plastic ball on top.

A wave of relief washed over his body. He pulled his hand out of his pocket, held his fist up a few inches from his face. He willed himself to open his eyes and his fisted hand to open. What he saw resting in his palm allowed the weight of the world to fall from his shoulders.

A bus station locker key.

He memorized the number etched into the plastic top, then found the corresponding locker number. After a couple of bungled attempts, he managed to insert the key and turn the lock. Inside, a nondescript dark blue duffle bag waited. He hauled the bag out and slung it over his shoulder.

He took an unsteady step backwards. The spring-loaded locker door slammed shut the moment he let go. He flinched at the loud bang as the door slammed shut. Keeping his back to the camera, he lumbered away. The bum staggered deeper into the passenger waiting area. The passengers studiously ignored him. He stopped to rest near a door that lead out to a loading platform. The sign above the door stated PASSENGERS WITH TICKETS ONLY BEYOND THIS POINT.

His eyes moved upwards at the sign, then around. Passengers still ignored him. The old lady still slept in her chair. The Marine stood at a high bar table, consuming his sandwich and coffee. He knew the Marine noticed him. But Marines are trained to be aware of their surroundings, so this did not alarm him. He concentrated on the two uniformed Greyhound employees on the other side of the room, talking.

Something didn't feel right. One of them threw a glance his way, then went right back to her conversation. Neither employee looked his way again.

Ah, being homeless. The surest way to become invisible. No one saw you. No one *wanted* to see you. Hide in plain sight. Where no one will notice.

He turned his body in one movement and discretely pushed past the platform door and slipped out. He eased the door back closed so it latched with a soft click.

A few blocks away from the bus station, the hunched, limping homeless man staggered down a squalid alleyway. Litter, rotting food, dirty pavement, overflowing dumpsters. The alley ran directly behind a high-rise hotel, one of San Diego's best and most exclusive. He felt positive this view was not in any of the San Diego tourism brochures.

He looked around, over his shoulder, making sure he was alone. He also scanned the tops of the buildings, looking for security cameras covering the alley. There were none. To his right stood a large trash bin. From the smell emanating from it, the garbage truck was long overdue. One more series of glances, and the man disappeared behind one corner of the dumpster.

He unslung the bag, dropped it to the pavement. Standing up straight, he took off his silly sunglasses, revealing piercing green eyes. He pushed the hood backwards, off his head, revealing his face.

Reginald Downing glanced around once more. No such thing "too careful" when you're an undercover cop on the run. Satisfied for the moment no one was shadowing him, he knelt down and unzipped the bag. A quick, cursory inspection told him everything he needed to know. He noted a change of clothes, a forty-caliber handgun with a loaded clip in the mag, three more loaded clips in the bag, three boxes of ammo, and thirty thousand dollars in cash.

He stood up, unzipped his hoodie all the way down to his waist, peeled it off. He unceremoniously shucked T-shirt underneath, and placed the 9mm he had been carrying atop the bag. You know, just in case he needed to reach for it quickly. He stood up, unbuckled his belt, and dropped his trousers onto the pavement. He stepped out of them, a fabric puddle around his ankles. Now naked except for his briefs, he quickly donned the new clothes – a pair of tan khaki pants, military–style web belt, white T shirt, thin Navy blue pullover sweater, brown leather loafers, a black ball cap.

Reggie gathered his old clothes in his arms. He wasted no time shoving them into the dumpster beside him. He stuffed them down, making them more difficult to notice. He pulled a bag of garbage back down over them, further obliterating them in this contained ocean of refuse.

He put his shades back on, stuffed his 9mm in his waistband at the small of his back, then slung the duffle filled with cash and firepower over his shoulder. He walked easily down the alley until it opened onto a city street.

Reggie turned right and walked away, melting into the crowd.

The main dining room at *la Trattoria* bustled with activity. The noontime rush was in full swing, with most tables and booths occupied. Situated in the heart of San Diego's famed Gaslamp District, the pricey Italian eatery attracted the well-heeled of the downtown business crowd. Investment bankers compared notes in a booth. The market was up today, but was it going to stay up? Four well-dressed women sat at a table, drinking white wine spritzers while they waited on their meals. The elaborate array of department store bags sat under the table at their feet.

Waiters and bussers swarmed, busy bees carrying out a delicately staged and meticulously choreographed dance. The dance whisked customers to their table or booth, courtesy of the vivacious young hostess. Complimentary water got delivered by the busser, who then took their drink order. He was followed by the server about three minutes later, who made sure their drink order was correct, and then took their food order.

Deeper in the restaurant, at the bar, the bartender, a tall, lean young man with blonde hair, a long, angular face, and darting blue eyes, mixed the drinks and poured the cocktails. He placed them on serving platters for the servers, occasionally throwing a wink of an eye or a flash of a crooked grin to the women he found attractive.

Off to the left of the main dining room hid a smaller room, arranged with a discreet single row of booths situated lengthwise along the far wall. The area was strictly reservations only, only for the most special of guests and VIP's.

A maître d', decades older than most of the other workers on duty, stood guard beside the single arched entryway. Thick iron gray hair, which set off his dark eyes and deeply lined face. Between his nose and his lips grew a pencil – thin moustache, which he had cultivated and groomed to perfection for over thirty years. The maître d' fastidiously brushed a tiny piece of lint off the sleeve of his impossibly white and impeccably crisp shirt. He ran his hands down the front of his jet-black vest, smoothing nonexistent wrinkles. He tugged gently at his throat, adjusting his matching bow tie, so black it did not appear to be a color, but seemed somehow to simply suck all the light from around it. A black hole bow tie.

From his vantage point, the maître d' surveyed the entire restaurant. The bar to his left along with the narrow hallway to the bathrooms, the main dining room in front of him, and the entrance to the restaurant on his right where people came in from the sidewalk. He could also see part of the patio where still more patrons dined al fresco.

So of course he noticed the rough man who passed by the hostess with not so much as a look or a break in his stride. Wearing jeans, cowboy boots, a black T-shirt under a brown leather jacket, he did not fit the usual lunchtime clientele. Muscular, thick through the neck and shoulders, he possessed a crooked nose that had been broken too many times. His steely gaze and set jaw accentuated his mouth, which was not much more than a thin cruel line above a square chin.

Someone you definitely did not want to mess with.

He walked up to the maître d. "Hey, Giuseppe," he said, extending his hand.

Giuseppe, the maître d' shook his hand. "Mr. Oakley," he greeted. "Lovely to see you, sir. It's been a while."

"Too long." Rick Oakley tried to smile, but failed. Small talk and banter had never been his strong suit. "Is he in?"

"Always for you, sir," Giuseppe nodded.

Rick stepped past Giuseppe and into the almost deserted VIP room. Farther from the street, the light was dimmer. Rick waited a moment while his eyes adjusted. Then he moved forward towards the back booth where he knew his boss would be reading the newspaper and eating lunch. Nervous, he wiped his palms on his pants.

As he continued walking down the aisle, his boss came into view.

Antonio Vargas.

A large man, black, with very dark skin, he wore his hair shorn close to his skull. Clean-shaven, he wore a slate grey herringbone suit and an olive green mock turtleneck. He was finishing a plate of penne pasta alfredo with a charbroiled chicken breast. He looked up from his meal and motioned to Rick.

"Richard," he said. "Don't be shy. Have a seat."

Rick slid into the seat across from Vargas.

"Have you eaten yet?"

"I'm fine, sir," Rick responded. He fidgeted in his seat.

"You look nervous."

"I hate relating bad news to you, sir."

Vargas wiped his mouth on his linen napkin. "We knew bad news was coming. How bad is it?"

"Seven dead, including El Gecko and Johnnie Wolf."

"Damn," Vargas huffed. "What about Mongo?"

"Mongo, too."

"Awww, that's too bad," Vargas said. "I liked Mongo. Do you know how hard it is to find a good driver in this town?"

"It gets worse, sir," Rick warned.

"It always does," Vargas said. "How much merchandise did we lose?"

"None of our own."

"Say what?"

"The Gecko and the Wolf were doing something off the books."

Vargas frowned. "A side deal?"

"Arms shipment. Crates of AA-12's.

"What the hell is an AA-12?"

"It's a fully automatic combat shotgun."

Vargas turned this over in his mind. Gun running was not this thing. Arms dealers gave him the creeps. "So none of our business got exposed?"

"No sir."

Vargas nodded, satisfied for the moment. "Too bad about El Gecko. We'll have to find someone else to handle the weight."

Rick cleared his throat. "I'm not done yet, sir."

Vargas got quiet and serious.

"Rudy Valdez survived," Rick said. "He got nicked by the cops."

Vargas felt a migraine coming on. "What else?"

"Remember Jorge, El Gecko's bodyguard? Well, turns out his name's not Jorge."

"No?"

"He's really Detective Reginald Downing, San Diego Police Department, on loan to a Federal Anti-Drug Task Force."

The expensive food in Vargas's stomach turned rancid, curdled, threatening to come back up. With Herculean effort, Vargas fought back that tide. He swallowed hard, willing himself to stay outwardly calm.

"Please tell me he's one of the seven."

"He survived, sir."

Vargas thought hard and fast. "Get Rudy bailed out. Bring him to me."

"He's still being processed. He hasn't been arraigned yet."

"Let the lawyer deal with that shit," Vargas said. "Just get him out."

Rick nodded. "Done."

"Secondly," Vargas said, "Damage control. Have all the El Gecko records destroyed. Hard drives, laptops, support packages, phones, text messages, emails, standard drill. No electronic trail. I want it completely sanitized. You know what to do."

Rick nodded again. "I understand, sir." He stood up from the booth and turned to leave.

"And Richard?"

Rick stopped. "Yes sir?"

"Kill Downing."

"He's a cop, sir."

"I know."

"He's off the grid."

"I don't care if he's been kidnapped by a UFO and flown off the Goddamned planet. He's been embedded for almost a year. He knows our business model, our administrative structure. He knows me. He knows you."

Vargas paused. Rick stood there. He knew the boss had more to say.

Vargas continued. "We have no idea what he's turned over to prosecutors, or how damaging it is. But evidence doesn't convict without corroborating testimony."

Vargas paused again, took a sip of wine to clear the unpleasant taste in his mouth. "I don't care where he is. I don't care how long it takes. Track him. Find him. Kill him. Nothing fancy. Don't go all Scarface on him. Just make him dead."

"Yes sir."

Rick turned and walked out.

Vargas sat in the booth, looking tough, until Rick disappeared from sight. Then his entire body slumped. He wiped away the sweat that had popped out across his upper lip.

He looked down and saw his almost empty plate. The mere thought of food nauseated him.

He pushed his plate away.

CHAPTER EIGHT

The century–old red brick and mortar building stood on K Street, between Tenth and Eleventh Avenues, on the border between the Gaslamp District and San Diego's newest neighborhood, the East Village. This southernmost part of downtown had sat fallow twenty-five years ago, its residential motels populated with pensioners, druggies, and the destitute one step away from homelessness.

People at the bottom of society with nowhere else to go.

A recent influx of money, urban redevelopment, and newly affluent hipsters flooding San Diego seeking biomedical and tech jobs had changed all that. The poor got evicted. The homeless got rousted out; the criminals and hustlers arrested. Real estate values skyrocketed. Long neglected buildings got retrofitted and brought up to code. They converted to condos, live/work lofts, or otherwise repurposed. In addition to the *nouveau riche* tenants, trendy bistros, organic grocery stores and freshly paved parking lots sprang up with breathtaking rapidity.

The building on K Street, its facade still aged and faded, had escaped gentrification. Heavy iron front doors hung so they could swing out from the center, stood mute testament to when in the late 1890's it had been a fire station. Six men and four horses pulled a water truck. San Diego's Fire Department mechanized in 1917, and shined as one the most modern, professional departments in the country. The horses went to the city yards and hauled garbage to the dump.

In the 1930's, the station was shuttered. The Company moved to new facilities several blocks away. San Diego hurt for cash during the Depression to provide essential services. The city debated renting the property, or selling it. Renting meant steady income, but selling meant a cash windfall initially, and property taxes in perpetuity.

Edmundo Boroquez bought the building. A man of honor, Boroquez enjoyed strong business contacts across the Southwest on both sides of the Border. He needed a warehouse to store goods until he could truck them out.

His business prospered. He stored and shipped coffee, engine parts, tractor tires, firewood, flour, cattle feed, sugar, and beans. When they were old enough, Edmundo's sons started working at the warehouse, learning the business from the ground up. He sent the oldest, Ernesto, to college in 1948. Raymundo enrolled in 1952. Both graduated, and took over the business as partners. Boroquez and Sons continued to prosper throughout the fifties and sixties.

Edmundo happily handed over day-to-day operations to his sons. His health had been slipping, and he was diagnosed with high blood pressure and a heart condition. Retired and content, he spent the rest of his days with his wife. He grew bell peppers and tomatoes in his back yard. He passed away peacefully in 1969.

The bottom fell out of the economy in the early 1970's. Boroquez and Sons began a downward spiral. Increased operating costs and weak wholesale prices cannibalized profits. The county reappraised the building. Property taxes went up over nine hundred dollars. In 1971, California closed several loopholes in the State Tax Code, and killed several deductions, which effectively raised business tax rates significantly.

Through no fault or malfeasance of their own, the brothers went from prosperous businessmen with country club memberships to barely scraping by, paying their workers and having little left over to continue operations.

In 1973, OPEC quit selling oil to the United States in response to the U.S.'s rearming of Israel during the Yom Kippur War. Supplies of gasoline and diesel dwindled, prices skyrocketed, and gas rationing ensued. The embargo would last for over a year. When the Boroquez brothers lost out on what would have been a lucrative Navy contract, their fate was sealed. They limped along, but they knew it was all over but the slaughter.

In 1977, Boroquez and Sons closed for good. They laid off their six remaining workers, gave them severance pay out of the brothers' own pockets, sold the inventory at cost, sold their trucks and barely broke even.

It was ugly, but it got done.

Ernesto sold his interests in the building to Raymundo. Having been in the business to please his father, he was relieved to divest himself. He moved to a small beach house in Ensenada where he pursued a passion for painting. His acrylics and watercolors would hang in some of the most prestigious galleries in Latin America by 1984.

Raymundo felt a deep need to hang on to the building. The warehouse represented the life's work of two generations. Rather than sell, he decided to rent. He hired a management company to handle the details. Because of the blight in the area, property values had plummeted, along with their taxes. Raymundo, like his brother, was in a position to retire.

Raymundo, married, with one child in college – pursuing a *liberal arts* education, of all things! – relaxed, visited his brother in Mexico, and every once in a while, imported a few hundred boxes of top quality cigars from a certain Caribbean nation to sell to a small, elite clientele he personally cultivated and maintained.

In 1984, a hotshot young Investment banker named Josh Hamm got a couple of college pals to help him finance a boiler room investment firm. They rented the old building because it was cheap. They illegally tied into the power lines outside and stuffed the main floor with rows of computer stations manned by bright, young brokers who were pressured to close the deal, close the deal, close the deal. Commissions, commissions, commissions.

Money flowed like the wine. Deregulated markets opened up new possibilities, and the young wolves on K Street were only too eager to exploit them. After all, it was legal, right? Morality never entered into it. The Friday evening parties became the stuff of legend. Food, booze, hookers hired for the night. Nothing off-limits.

They started staying open twenty-four hours a day to piggyback off the foreign markets – Hong Kong, London, Tokyo. The partners lived in the building.

Over time, their clients expanded from doctors, lawyers, restaurateurs, and dentists. They handled pension funds for outside companies, investments from other brokerage houses, and local branches for international banks.

Josh Hamm himself was flown first class to Barbados. He was greeted at the airport by some very polite Latin gentlemen. He was given the finest accommodations, the finest foods, and the most enthusiastic women for his amusement. Life was good.

The very next day, these same gentlemen escorted Josh to a private meeting at a single -story villa nestled discretely amongst banana trees and old sugar cane in the central highlands of the island.

Josh Hamm met five wealthy men who had substantial funds to invest, reinvest, and then reacquire. And while their current cash happened to be in various currencies, they would prefer to reacquire their money in American dollars, either delivered personally in the form of a bank draft, or delivered electronically via international wire transfer. Naturally, Mr. Hamm and his company would be compensated for their efforts. They suggested a two percent commission of the gross amount moved, taken at each step of the process.

Mr. Hamm responded his commission was usually quite higher. They all smiled mildly, glanced at each other, and told him they felt they deserved a "volume discount" and that two percent at each step, which would add up to six or eight percent total, would be more than satisfactory over time.

Hamm took a drink of his mojito, mulled things over a moment. Glancing around the room, he wanted to figure out a polite way to thank them for their hospitality and then decline their offer.

Then he noticed the three men in the back of the room. They were much younger than his prospective clients. Wearing sunglasses inside, they had muscular chests, trim waists, tough faces. It was only then he noticed the faintest glint of metal inside the coat of one of them, and only then did he notice the bulges in their jackets below one armpit.

Josh Ham took the deal.

Hamm and Associates invested the money, moved it around between different investments, then cashed out, taking two percent at each step. By the time the money was wired back his clients in the South, the money was in clean, untraceable, American dollars. Everyone was happy. So happy in fact, his clients decided since Hamm and Associates had proven themselves competent and honest with a measly sixty five million, the *real* money could start flowing.

And as it turned out, his Caribbean clients had been right. The two percent at each step had worked out well for Hamm and Associates. Josh Hamm felt he was untouchable. He could close deals with gun smugglers, drug dealers, launder their money under the FBI's own nose, send it back to them, and no one was ever the wiser. God, he could do anything he wanted.

And that was precisely the moment he started to push the envelope further. He got sloppy, became reckless. He didn't even bother to cover his tracks any more. And that was precisely the moment when he sealed his own fate.

Nothing is more dangerous than when people tell you you're the greatest and you start believing them. And Mr. Hamm started to believe his own press.

The FBI raided them in 1987. The brokerage was funneling over two hundred million dollars a month. Everyone, including Josh Hamm, went to Federal prison. The property was seized.

The property stayed in Government hands. That is why this old, long-abandoned, nondescript red brick firehouse, warehouse, and boiler room investment house was the perfect choice. The tech nerds spruced the place up with modern wiring, cable jacks, phone lines, state of the art computer systems with military-grade encryption and high speed Wi-Fi.

It became headquarters for a covert DEA-administered Joint Task Force targeting international drug smuggling coming through the San Ysidro and Otay Mesa border crossings, and the Port of San Diego.

Late afternoon clouds pushed *en masse* from the southwest, across the ocean and the bay. They obscured the sun, darkened the horizon. The temperature dropped. The wind kicked up, funneling through the narrow streets and alleys, picking up speed, gusting cold and relentless.

A poorly maintained car engine wheezed, strained, coughed, almost stalled. The old Toyota Celica careened around the corner and lurched onto K Street. The engine caught, jumped again, the front end almost coming off the ground. A gear shifted. The transmission protested, then third gear locked into place.

The car rattled along, white and bluish smoke belching from the same rusty tailpipe. Finally, the car pulled hard to the left, shifting its weight to the right, almost going up on two wheels. It came to a rude stop next to the warehouse.

Walt Coulter churned the keys towards him, turning the ignition off. The engine kept sputtering, coughing, the timing way off. Coulter inserted the keys again, turned them to the "on" position.

The engine caught again and idled. He waited, then turned the keys "off" again. The engine died with a mournful wheeze.

Walt unbuckled his seat belt. He would never admit to anyone else that sometimes even he wondered about the car's safety. He also wondered if it was going to explode some day in a fireball of flame and rusted bolts.

He reached for the tiny door handle. He pulled, and nothing happened. No click from inside the door frame, nothing. He nudged gently against the door. It did not budge.

Well. This is new.

He pulled again, making sure it was pulled as open as possible without snapping off in his hand. He shouldered the door harder, to no avail. Frustrated, he shouldered the door harder still.

The door flew open with such force Walt halfway fell out of the car. Quick reflexes saved him. He flung his outstretched hand to steady him on the pavement. His other hand darted up to stop the car door on its arc back towards his face.

Maybe everyone's right, he conceded. He'd owned this beater for years, and he'd done no restoration work. Maybe he had bitten off more than his high school auto mechanics class knowledge could chew, and take it to a professional to get done correctly.

Walt climbed out of the car, adjusted his gun in his shoulder holster. He glanced around the deserted street. He noticed the cold, glanced upwards at the roiling sky. He reached in the back seat and grabbed his old college letter jacket and threw it on.

He pushed the open car door closed, but did not latch it. He was going to get in later, and he wanted the door to actually open. Even he would admit that at fifty-four he was just too damned old to shimmy in and out of the driver's side window.

Coulter walked towards the old building. He could see the faded remnants of the "Boroquez and Sons" sign that had been painted in huge blue letters. Now all that was left was "Boro..." and everything else had peeled off.

Eyes dating around, the veteran cop constantly scanned the area. The concept of situational awareness had been drilled into his head. He reached the steel reinforced door secured by electromagnetic lock. He punched a six-digit code onto the keypad at the doorframe. An awkward *BUZZ!* sounded and Coulter heard a metallic *CLUNK!* as the internal mechanism released.

Coulter grabbed the handle and pulled hard. The door resisted until he put his shoulder and back into it. The heavy, supposedly impenetrable door swung slowly on reinforced titanium hinges. A crack opened between the door and its frame, blackness beyond it. The crack crept wider, wide enough for him to slip through. Coulter turned his shoulders and moved past.

Coulter's eyes adjusted quickly to the interior lighting. It was not truly dark inside; the light was simply more subdued than the ambient light outside. He turned to his right, punched in another six-digit code into a touch pad on the wall. The door stopped automatically, then reversed direction, closing. It always unsettled Coulter just a bit. The door closing hermetically sealed everything and everyone inside.

Coulter walked across the expanse of the main room, where horses and firemen had once lived and worked. Now the room sported several large desks, facing each other in pairs, so partners could look and speak to each other. Coulter wanted transparency in his unit. So all the rank and file worked together. Even their computers monitors were set at an angle to the side of the desks, so his crew could have an unobstructed view of their partners' faces.

Coulter's office, the same office Old Man Boroquez had worked out of, sat off to the side. When the place had been refitted for Agency use, Coulter had insisted on having clear, albeit bulletproof glass installed floor to ceiling, including the door. He wanted his people to always be able to see that he was working just as hard as they were.

Most of the desks were empty. It was late Friday afternoon. Most of his officers were either in the field, or had knocked off for the weekend. The only person left was Miriam Arroyo. A twelve–year veteran, she had worked the streets for five years, then six with the Sheriff Department's Tactical Narcotics Team before being hand-selected by Coulter for his Task Force. She now sat at her computer, near the back of the room, frowning at the computer screen.

"Miriam. It's late. Go home."

Startled, she looked up. "Sorry. I thought I had the place to myself."

"Go home. Get some rest."

Miriam pushed her dark hair back behind her ear, and Coulter was reminded how beautiful she was. "I'm trying to confirm a new piece of intel concerning the bloodbath at the docks. I'm waiting to hear back."

"They contacting you via email?"

"Yes."

"Then go home. Have a glass of wine. Watch a movie. The email might not even come through until Monday."

She sat back in her chair and sighed. "You're probably right." She raised her arms, ran her hands through her hair, clasped her fingers behind her head while looking up at the ceiling. Coulter was reminded that not only was she smart, tough, and beautiful, she had a great rack, too.

Determined to outwardly maintain his professional demeanor, Coulter turned away and pushed the door to his office open. He rounded the desk and hit the power button on his computer. He heard the tiny fan inside kick on as he sat down.

Movement to his right caught his attention. He turned his head and saw Miriam, purse over her shoulder, walking towards the main door. She smiled and waved, a friendly wave. Coulter smiled and nodded upwards in her direction.

Relieved, Coulter turned his attention to his computer. He quickly typed in his user name and password. The screen changed immediately, welcoming Walt Coulter into the Joint Task Force and Drug Enforcement Agency system and database. His fingers flew across the keys, lightly depressing as he went. He hit the ENTER button.

A mug shot of El Gecko immediately appeared on the screen in the upper left corner. The details of his many arrest reports filled in down the right side of the screen. Coulter knew most of it by heart. He scrolled down to the color photos of his bloody corpse, sans head. He noticed the dark stains under the arms, and the dark stain between his legs and the puddle underneath. El Gecko's bladder had emptied when he died. Over to the right of the screen was a very clear photo of El Gecko's severed head. His facial expression, frozen in time, was one of absolute astonishment.

The next photo was also El Gecko's head, laid on its side. The photo was taken from the neck up, clearly detailing the trachea, cervical spine, and carotid arteries and jugular veins had been severed in one clean, powerful slice, by something incredibly sharp. The skin showed almost no tearing or jaggedness of any kind.

Eyes darting across the photos and back again, Coulter took it all in. El Gecko had been in the drug business almost seventeen years. He had survived assassination attempts by rival gangs, disgruntled underlings, hell, he'd even ferreted out traitors within his own organization. The last one had been skinned alive, slowly, starting at the feet and working upwards, using a machete dipped in shit.

And yet here he was decapitated, a violent man who met a violent end.

Coulter wondered what would happen if he ever caught the guy who'd done this. Would he arrest him, or give him a medal?

"Couldn't have happened to a nicer guy."

Coulter, startled, pushed himself away from the desk at the sound of the disembodied voice in the darkness. He went for his weapon, pulled it out in front of himself, a snarl of fierce determination on his face. He flicked the safety off, knowing he already had a round in the chamber.

"Whoever you are, step forward slowly, with your hands up. Show yourself."

The shadows near the door languished, then started to coalesce, taking on a faintly human form as whoever it was slowly stepped forward. He had his hands up, fingers splayed out.

"That's it," Coulter said. The person stepped closer, coming into clearer view. Dark, slightly reddish hair, cropped close to the skull. Baby-smooth face, freshly shaven. Tan cargo pants, Navy blue pullover. And the most intensely green eyes.

Reginald Downing!

Journal entry 28 January

Why do I keep a journal?

They say that talking to oneself is a sign of mental illness. Writing my thoughts down allows me to talk to myself in a socially acceptable manner. Not that I consider myself part of society though. Even in life, I never felt that deep connection most people feel for those around them. I loved my mother of course, and I was singularly passionate about Danae, but that is about it. I believe that may explain my brief yet disastrous life of crime.

Journaling allows me to work things out and meditate on them as I continue to seek the truth.

But as Pontius Pilate famously said, What is truth?

Where do we come from? Why are we here? Where do we go from here?

I possess no insight into any of that. I had hoped that once I became the thing I am, that answers that eluded mortal man would reveal themselves to the Dead and all would become clear.

Truth is, I am still just as confused now in death as I ever was in life.

And so, like this journal, I simply... continue.

Tonight, I ponder my limitations. Sunlight and my vampire integument don't mix. A cruel twist of nature and evolution precludes daylight hours.

Ever see an albino who has been in the sun for an hour? Imagine that same albino in the sun after twelve hours. That is what would happen to me in less than two minutes. I do not burst into flames like on those ridiculous movies and cable TV shows (I said before, I love them for their comic appeal!). But I do redden, blister, boil, and char. My skin cracks, bleeds. My body temperature skyrockets.

Instant heatstroke. It is agony, let me tell you. It takes me a long time to heal.

And blood. Lots of blood.

Sunlight is one of the few things on this planet that will actually kill me. Decapitation, too. Vampires are not immune to the laws of physics. Bullets anger me. They hurt like Hell. Wooden stakes will not slay me (thanks again, Hollywood!), but such a barbaric act puts me in a demeanor most foul.

Back to my wake-sleep cycle. I reanimate at dusk. I work. I read, and I feed. I visit libraries, museums. I enjoy classic horror movies, so Midnight Madness screenings are my favorites. I love taking off my sunglasses and watching these films around humans costumed and made up into images of... me, really. I often pass unnoticed among them. The few who do notice me think my "makeup" is "rad", and ask me how did I get my eyes to do that? And of course, my personal favorite: Where can I get fangs like yours? They look so... so... REAL!

Oh, sweetie. If you only knew.

CHAPTER NINE

A featureless interrogation room. White tile, drop ceiling. Soundproof walls, painted gray. A barely functional door, painted the same color as the walls. When closed, it blended into the background, disappeared. All the better to disorient an interrogation subject. One long mirror, obviously two-way glass to anyone with an IQ over 50.

Rudy Valdez sat in the bare steel Government-issue chair made somewhere in Middle America by the lowest bidder. Staring ahead at the mirror, he ignored the discomfort, his eyes focusing on nothing. He modulated his breathing. His heart pumped around fifty-four beats per minute. He inhaled through his nose, exhaled out his mouth. In his head, he repeated his multiplication tables, memorized back in grade school, from one times one up to twelve times twelve. He started at the beginning, went all the way up, then started over at the bottom again.

Cuffed at the wrists, his hands in front of him, handcuffs chained to a bolt in the table. The gray jumpsuit did not fit properly. The legs were way too long. During intake, he had told them an inseam of thirty-six inches was too long for someone five foot seven. He guard simply grinned and had shoved the jumpsuit into his hands.

The room was hot and stuffy. Rudy correctly surmised the air had been deliberately turned off. They wanted him sweltering, uncomfortable, sweaty, distracted. Tougher to keep the lies straight when you're sweating like a pig.

Shifting in his chair, he realized the chair legs were uneven. The adjustable caster on the right rear leg had been removed. The slightest shift of weight caused the chair to tilt unexpectedly.

Rudy recognized these subtleties as pre-interrogation techniques designed to produce a specific psychological effect. Later, during the interview, in response to his request to turn on the air conditioning, an interrogator might offer to do just that, in exchange for some piece of damning evidence Rudy might have.

Fat chance of that.

So Rudy sat there, skin greasy, sweat staining his underarms and collar, trickling down his back downward to his gluteal cleft. Placing his feet flat on the floor, he balanced himself, taking the uneven chair out of the equation.

The door separated from the surrounding wall, swung open. A large black man who looked like a refrigerator in a suit lumbered in, followed by a taller Hispanic man Rudy had seen earlier that morning. Come to think of it, he'd seen the back of the refrigerator's head, too.

"I'm Captain Horn," the big man said. "This is Detective Sergeant Castle." They both sat down across from him, each opening the folders they had brought in with them.

Rudy zeroed in on Castle. "Castle, huh? Shouldn't it be Castillo?"

Nick blinked his eyes, determined to not let this guy get to him. "My mother is Mexican."

"We have some questions for you," Horn interjected.

"My name is Rudy Valdez."

"We know who you are, "Horn replied. "Your military service, family history. Must have been tough growing up a cop's house."

Rudy shrugged.

"We talked to your dad just now before we came in here," Horn continued. Rudy's eyes met his. "You know what he said?"

Rudy waited.

"He hopes you rot in jail."

"Score one for the old man."

Castle leaned forward. "You don't seem too broken up over his remarks."

"We were never actually what you'd call close."

"So what the hell happened to you, Rudy?" Horn asked. "You had a good start in life. Decent home, strong father figure. Good grades in school. You served with honor in the Corps."

Rudy waited.

"So... how do you go from an All-American childhood and proud Marine to being a hired gun to a drug runner?"

The corner of Rudy's mouth slowly lifted into a crooked, Clint Eastwood type grin. "My name is Rudy Valdez."

Horn exhaled, leaned his head forward onto his hands. He was clearly frustrated. Valdez simply sat there, silently, staring at the top of Horn's head. No compassion. No remorse.

"Let's talk about the bloodbath on the docks this morning," Castle said.

"My name is Rudy Valdez."

"Who lets himself get taken out, his boss get decapitated, and all his buddies slaughtered like that?"

Rudy's eyes narrowed in anger. "My name is Rudy Valdez."

Horn spoke softly. "Tell me, Rudy Valdez, why didn't he kill you?"

Rudy's eyes drifted away, low and to the right. The anger left his face as his brain remembered and replayed the events in his mind.

"Why didn't he kill you, Rudy?"

"I don't know." Rudy whispered. All pretense and attitude fled. He slumped back in his chair. "I never even saw him. Never heard him. He... used the night."

"He what?" Horn asked.

"He used the night. He blended into the shadows. You ever watch a lion stalking its prey, blending in to the environment so the prey can't see him? He was like that."

"You're scared?"

"Damn right I'm scared."

"Of what? The cartel?"

"The worst they can do is kill me. I'm lucky if they don't have a hit out on me already."

Horn and Castle waited for the other shoe to drop.

"So who are you afraid of? Him?"

Rudy looked unblinkingly at Horn. "This guy operates on a whole different level of deadly. He's like some ninja assassin; like something out of a Goddamned monster movie."

Rudy relaxed his hands, slumped back in the seat. Both Horn and Castle recognized the body language. Rudy Valdez had given them everything he was going to give. No amount of questioning, leveraging, interrogating, or threatening would make him say another word.

The door opened again, unexpectedly. The sudden movement disturbed the still air, causing a whoosh to move across the room. It faintly fluttered Rudy's hair.

Everyone turned his attention towards the door. In strode a middle-aged man, morbidly obese, bland features, although he tried to cultivate an air of importance. He wore an expensive suit, power tie, carried a Gucci briefcase, and wore stern face. "Don't say another word," he barked at Rudy. "This conversation is over."

"And who the fuck are you?" Horn asked, standing up, looking intimidating.

"Michael C. Law," the attorney announced. "I'm Mr. Valdez's attorney."

Rudy folded his hands in his lap and smiled. He looked completely serene now.

Castle flipped his folder closed and stood up. "I know you," he said. "Well. I know of you. You're a mob lawyer."

"Captain, put a leash on your dog here."

"Fuck you, you Goddamned shyster," Horn spat. "You're a fucking mob layer, and everyone here knows it."

"Well then, you'd better watch your mouth," Law returned. "Talk like that can ruin my reputation. That's called slander, and it's a crime, *Detective*. Maybe they didn't teach you about that in the Academy? Or maybe they did, and you just don't care?"

Horn picked up his folder from the table. "It's only slander if what I say is known by me to be untrue at the time I say it. Didn't they teach you that in Mobster Law School? Or maybe they did, and with you being a fucking mob lawyer and shit, you just don't care about that?" He grabbed a grinning Castle by the shoulder of his rumpled suit coat and walked him out the door.

Once they were gone, Mike Law put his briefcase on the table. He walked over and closed the door, then walked over to the two-way glass and adjusted a small dial to zero, effectively muting the sound in the room so anyone in the observation area could not hear what was being said.

He turned around to Rudy. "What did you tell them?"

Rudy eyed this new addition with open suspicion. "I don't know you."

"I have been hired by Rick Oakley, at the request of Antonio Vargas, to represent you in this matter."

Rudy's eyes narrowed. "Can you get me out of here?"

"It's too late in the day," the lawyer replied, shaking his head. Rudy noticed the extra flesh under his chin waddled a bit. "It'll be tomorrow before we can get you arraigned and get bail set."

"What do I do until then?"

"Don't say a word to anyone. Not the cops, not the guards, not the other inmates. Code of silence. You got that?"

Rudy nodded his head.

"I'll try to get your arraignment scheduled for as early in the day as I can. I know a judge who may be sympathetic to our plight."

Rudy relaxed visibly.

Law put his hand on his briefcase. "By the way," he said, "I heard about the incident at the docks. It doesn't make sense to me."

Rudy just stared at him.

"Between you and me, what really went on down there?"

"Privileged?"

Law smiled, waved his hand.

"I don't have the first fucking clue," Rudy raised his right hand. "Hand to God, all I know is, my friends starting got ripped apart, limb from fucking limb, and I got knocked the fuck out. By the time I came to, the cops already had me in cuffs."

Michael C. Law, attorney for the defense, stood there, motionless, looking at Rudy. He knew Rudy was telling the truth.

"Stay strong. I'll have you out tomorrow." He grabbed up his briefcase.

"One other thing."

Law stopped at the door, hand on the knob. "Yes?"

"It's past seven o'clock. I haven't had anything to eat."

"What would you like?"

"Carne Asada burrito."

Law nodded. "I'll see to it."

Another thought occurred to Rudy. "Hey. Counselor. It's Friday night. How are you gonna get me out tomorrow?"

Law smiled. "I know a judge sympathetic to our plight." Precisely what he had said before. Then he pushed himself out the door, and was gone.

Rudy knew he was supposed to feel better, but he did not. He was not out of danger. Word was already out he had been a tough sumbitch with the cops. They might reward him, get him out. Or they could have an inmate shank him, or pay a guard to make sure he "accidentally" hung himself with his bed sheet.

He still had to survive the night in lockup.

Darkness spilled across San Diego. In a frantic dash down the western sky, the sun slid behind heavy cloud cover and faded to a dull white orb, hiding from the night's onslaught. The sun plunged below the horizon, conceding defeat to the night.

The vampire's corpse lay in bed, mostly covered with blankets and a quilt. Heavy fabric curtains, held together with Velcro tabs, covered the solitary south–facing window in the room. The bedroom, like the rest of the house, was completely dark.

In bed, the vampire was nothing more than a dried, desiccated carcass. Muscles and sinew atrophied, his lips pulled back away from his teeth in a kind of permanent rictus. Eyes closed, mouth slackly open. Yellowish waxy skin, stretched like parchment across forehead, cheeks, and chin. No heart pumped within him. No air entered or exited his lungs. No blood circulated. No autonomic life activities or brain waves functioned.

He was simply dead.

As then, it had every night for the last century, the vampire's body shuddered a bit, as the heart began to unnaturally beat, and beat, and beat. It beat against all the laws of God and nature. And it continued to beat as blood, thick as sludge, surged through collapsed blood vessels.

Fingers, thin and bony, brought into a curl on both hands, unfurled now as circulation returned. Arms and legs moved.

Glassy black eyes popped open and his consciousness came bursting forth all at once from the nothingness of his True Death. In that same instant, he took a deep, painful, beautiful breath. Chest on fire, lungs burning as bronchi expanded, and alveoli inflated once again.

He sat up and coughed, his ribs aching with each exhalation. He rubbed his sternum, smacked his lips. He was still dehydrated. After sitting there a few moments more to let the room quit spinning, the vampire swung his legs outward and placed his feet gingerly on the floor. He pushed off the bed with his hands, and stood up.

He staggered down the short hallway and into his kitchen. He opened his refrigerator door and peered inside. He had unscrewed the light bulb inside, so the fridge upon opening, resembled a dark gaping maw, with white wire shelving for teeth.

He found what he was looking for, pulled it out. He looked at the blood bank bag, filled with packed red blood cells – donor blood he had bought illegally from a local blood bank technician with an uncanny ability to always bet on the wrong sports team.

The vampire tossed the bag into the microwave. He programmed a few seconds, just enough to take the chill off, then punched START. When the bell on the microwave sounded off with a perky *DING!* he pulled the warm bag out. He twisted open the plastic stopper on the top of the bag, opened his mouth wide, and upended the bag over his head. The blood dripped like red syrup, in stringy dollops into his mouth. The first glop hitting his tongue caused him to exhale with a satisfied shudder.

Like an addict getting their fix.

A few more mouthfuls, and the vampire felt better. He put the stopper back in the bag, tossed the bag back inside the refrigerator. He stepped over to the faucet, filled a glass with water, and drank it down. While blood was his main source of sustenance, he could drink water in moderate amounts, especially when he was washing down packed red cells.

The vampire walked out of the kitchen, knees steadier, legs stronger with each stride. In his bedroom, he pulled the curtain back and stared outside. He still had not turned any lights on. Darkness allowed the ciliary muscles in his eyes to relax and his pupils to dilate. Less eye fatigue that way. The vampire often wore sunglasses at night, especially inside nightclubs and bars.

Easier hunting prey when they don't know a predator is among them.

Peering outside, he saw everything clearly. Living less than a block north of Adams Avenue, he saw the main thoroughfare and it's trendy eateries, coffee houses, and wine lounges.

The vampire liked where he lived. He felt content, safe here. Nice neighborhood, mature, sedate, dignified. He lived in Kensington, one of San Diego's oldest and more exclusive neighborhoods. Real estate here maintained its value well, even in the face of the recent economic downturn. Other San Diego markets, as with most of the rest of the country's housing markets, had not fared so well, having gone into harsh tailspins.

Living in a 1940's adobe Spanish-style two-bedroom rental, the vampire was taking a break from decades of home ownership. Technology had made it too difficult in recent years for him to simply will the property to himself, pretend to die, and then show up a day or two later as a long lost heir, just in time to inherit his own fortune.

His current landlord liked him and left him alone. The vampire had explained to him that he was a day sleeper, his job required him to work odd hours, mostly at night. He could not go outside during the day because of a rare, but severe medical condition – a severe allergy to sunlight. Even the briefest of exposures to sunlight would cause him severe skin burns and excruciating pain.

The landlord had assured the vampire it would be no problem. When he inquired what the vampire did for a living, the vampire had stated matter-of-factly that he handled financial investments in the Asian markets, hence the odd hours.

Again, the landlord accepted the vampire's logical explanation. He then happily accepted the vampire's bank draft for first and last month's rent, plus a discrete thousand dollar cash "bonus" tucked into a dark envelope so the landlord rented to him and not someone else.

Since that time four years ago, the vampire had always gone out of his way to be a good tenant. He was unfailingly faithful to his word, making sure he dutifully fulfilled all of his obligations to the letter under his rental contract. He always paid his rent in full, on time. It was a matter of pride to him.

He enjoyed his music, classic rock, mostly. He still enjoyed the older talents like Louie Armstrong, Duke Ellington, the crooners like Frank Sinatra, Dean Martin, Sammy Davis, but once rock bands like the Stones and the Beatles came along, the vampire was, as they say, hooked. He still listened – on vinyl, of course! - almost every night. He just made sure to play it low enough to not disturb his neighbors.

Mainly, the vampire kept to himself, lived quietly and alone. He never hunted where he lived. He was pleasant enough to the few neighbors he encountered. He ran into them infrequently, never engaged in long conversations, and always politely declined any invite – no, really, I have to get back to work - to their apartments or houses for a drink.

The vampire dropped the curtain. It fell back into place, settling down with a ruffle and a slight furl. Realizing he was naked, he reminded himself to put some clothes on before going out tonight. It was a Friday evening, and he had not fed completely for several nights now.

He was hungry. Tonight, he needed to prowl.

He would hunt in the Gaslamp tonight, he decided. The sidewalks would be an ocean of people, surging from restaurants, then flowing to clubs, bars, or movie theaters. The vampire would be just another face in the crowd, hardly seen, mostly unnoticed, easily forgotten. He would move among them unfettered, sliding easily between warm bodies, thrilled by the sounds of their heartbeats, intoxicated with the unmistakable scent life gives off.

Ordinarily, the vampire hunted the overflow of trendy bars for the sake of expedience. But tonight, he craved something more... *esoteric*. So instead of his usual Italian suit perfectly tailored to a trim fit, the vampire chose cowboy boots, leather pants, a silk T-shirt, and black leather jacket he'd stolen off the corpse of a biker he had slaughtered back in the seventies.

Friday nights downtown attracted all kinds: students, workers blowing a week's pay in one night, hipsters trying to not look so proud about being so fucking cool, business executives wining and dining clients, men and women looking for a hookup, and so on. But the Gaslamp also brought out certain predators: drug dealers, pimps, pickpockets, muggers, rapists, carjackers, and worse, all in these same clubs and bars.

They slithered about, preying on the young, the naive, the weak, the addicted. Anyone they could exploit for money or sexual gratification. Selling drugs to some investment banker, the money and merchandise handed off under a table; or getting a girl drunk and then whisking her into a car or van conveniently parked with the engine running in a side alley when she stumbles to the bathroom. They could "disappear her" in a matter of seconds, most likely never to be seen again.

But these predators, these would-be "bad people", were too stupid, egotistical, shortsighted to contemplate there might be something else out there lurking in the blackness, stalking them even as they stalked their own prey, poised to strike in the blink of a human eye.

They could never comprehend that something more evil, more malevolent, more demonic was hunting them, stalking them, then taking one of them down, ripping them apart limb from bloody limb so fast they would still be able to see what was eating them alive before they died.

The vampire pulled the leather pants up over his naked skin. Then he thought better of it, and peeled them back off. He had made the mistake of wearing leather pants while not wearing underwear – "going commando" as he had once heard it called – and had regretted it. Living or dead, the laws of physics and friction still applied. The chaffing had been nightmarish to the say the least.

Now, he grabbed something out of his nightstand drawer, then unfurled it in front of him, between his hands. Bending over and stepping in, the vampire pulled a stretch spandex pair of leggings on. The synthetic material caught at his ankles as he pulled them up, creating a new layer of protection, a "second skin", as he tugged the top of the waistband. He adjusted himself up front, then snapped the grommets to hold them up. He picked up his shirt and jacket and walked, holding them off the floor.

Stepping into the bathroom, he turned on the light. The bulbs blared, and he averted his eyes for a moment. His pupils adjusted, and it no longer like he was being stabbed in the skull. While he did not need light to see himself in the mirror, he wanted to see how he would appear to others.

The vampire's skin was ashen white, a hint of yellow, waxen. His dark hair hung limp, falling from his head exactly the same length as the night he had died, with no body, no fullness at all. His nose was long and narrow, slightly pointed at the end. His cheekbones sat high, but his long angular face made for sunken cheeks, winding their way down to a thin-lipped mouth and pointed chin. He had died clean-shaven; now he never had to worry about five o'clock shadow.

The vampire picked up a bottle of liquid makeup foundation, opened the cap. He dripped a small amount onto his fingers, then massaged it onto his skin. Foundation could only do so much to make him appear living. But hunting in places where the lighting would be low made it easy to "pass" for human. He applied the makeup to his entire face and forehead, then ran it down his neck so his T-shirt would cover the rest. He took care to smooth out any unevenness.

His eyes drifted downward at his reflection. His pallid torso was fit, trim, no body fat. His was a wiry physique, broad shoulders and narrow hips.

He had been blessed with the lean body of a runner, or a swimmer. He was grateful that in his time, people had eaten less food and had taken in fewer calories. Since everything eaten then was freshly grown – "organic", they now called it – food had contained less sugar, less fat, no chemicals.

People had been leaner, healthier. And since he had been a man then, physical labor had been a familiar friend. No gym memberships required; you just worked a job. Thank God, he thought. I'd hate to have to go on through the nights of eternity fat, never able to lose weight.

Then his eyes came to rest on three rather peculiar circular scars on his chest. Old memories, best left in forgotten, came raging up to the front again. Two scars, each about three eighths inch in diameter, grouped close together over his sternum and left chest. The third sat lower on his anterior torso, to the right over the lower rib cage.

Over his liver.

That's what you get when you take up a life of crime, you stupid ass. You get killed, and the people who love you wind up betrayed, hurt, and alone.

Self-loathing was a wasted emotion, so the vampire pushed it out of his mind, back into the cobwebs of the past. He stretched his T-shirt on over his head. He shrugged into the jacket, adjusted a bit as the heavy garment came to rest across his neck and shoulders.

The vampire took one last look at himself in the mirror. He pushed his lank hair away from his face, but it cascaded back across his skull and coming to rest in precisely the same place and orientation as before. He had performed this act many times over the years, always with the same result. He didn't really expect any change – he was a walking corpse, after all – but it had become a ritual for him.

He walked out, turning off the light as he went. He grabbed his car keys on the counter on his way out.

He also remembered his sunglasses.

At barely past nine o'clock, the vampire pulled his Lexus into the pay lot at the corner of Tenth and E. As he killed the engine and got out, he knew he was still early. But as a child of the night, he loved reveling in it on occasion. With no attendant present, he dutifully stuffed a ten-dollar bill into a pay machine that resembled a miniature ATM. He sniffed, bemused that even a minimal effort, minimum wage job like Parking Lot Attendant could be phased out and replaced by a piece of technology.

The machine hummed and clunked, and somewhere inside, plastic gears ground together. A ticket spat out into a compartment near the bottom, protected behind a small clear plastic shield. The vampire flipped the shield up and extracted the ticket, which was adorned with the large letters, THIS TICKET LIMITS OUR LIABILITY! A litany of legal jargon printed in a font so small even the vampire could not make it all out followed. The tiny tirade printed thereon claimed the lot owner was not responsible for any damages, and could not be held liable if your car was broken into, stolen, vandalized, or firebombed while parked in their lot. You assumed all risk parking there.

Walking back to his car, the vampire wondered if such a generalized disclaimer would stand up to judicial scrutiny if a lawsuit ever made it to court. Probably not, he decided, but the company probably already knew that too. They'd settle out of court, complete with a bilateral non-disclosure agreement and a disclaimer stating that while agreeing a settlement, the company was admitting no wrongdoing or liability, whatsoever, now or in the future.

He shook his head in disgust. No one stood behind their work, their product, their service anymore. Everyone – corporate or individual – was just looking for a way out in case something – anything! - went wrong.

No one had the balls to accept responsibility for anything anymore.

Back at his car, the vampire opened the door and leaned inside, placing the ticket on the dashboard in plain view. He did not want his car towed for nonpayment if he needed to make a hasty getaway later. As he pulled himself out of the car, he accidentally bumped his head on the doorframe, knocking his sunglasses off his face. He blinked in surprise as they clattered on the asphalt.

Just at that moment, two young women, dressed provocatively even by today's standards, emerged from their own car nearby. One, a pretty, plump redhead with curly hair and large breasts stuffed into tight clothing, looked his way, and did a double take. She gasped at his eyes.

The vampire had already detected their heartbeats, and clearly heard her gasp from thirty feet away. He instinctively looked directly at her for an instant, always the predator, mouth thin and cruel. Then he averted his eyes and looked down.

"Jesus, Leslie," she said to her friend. "Did you see that?"

"What?"

"Look at that guy's eyes!"

Leslie, taller, slimmer, small breasts and darker hair, looked around. "What guy, Amy?"

The vampire had already squatted down and was retrieving his sunglasses. He tucked his chin to hide his face and placed them on the edge of his nose while still squatting. Then he rose, using an upward push of his index finger to thrust them higher up on his nose and across his eyes as he stood up.

"Those are sunglasses, silly," Leslie chided her friend.

Amy looked perplexed. She inhaled and opened her mouth, then said nothing. The vampire simply looked at them, then touched his finger to the side of his temple, a sort of half-salute. Then he smiled, careful to not show any teeth.

Walking away, he picked up the rest of their conversation. No, there really was something wrong with his eyes, but Leslie had not seen it. Why wear sunglasses at night, Amy wondered. Leslie: Maybe so he'd look cool, or maybe so the cops wouldn't stop him if he's high. Amy doubted that.

Stopped at the corner by traffic, the vampire waited for the light to turn. Then he crossed, walking west on E Street, deeper into the Gaslamp. Most of the buildings here were over one hundred years old. Having been used for various industrial purposes, most had been rezoned and converted into pricey condos with ten-foot high ceilings and live/work lofts. They sold for mid to high six figures.

The vampire had considered buying near here two years back, ultimately choosing to continue renting. Money was not the issue. At over eight feet tall, the windows, some of which faced west towards a setting sun, were simply too big. And since the vampire refused to sleep in a coffin, it was too big a risk.

As he walked, he glanced upwards across the street. He saw a man, youngish, red hair and freckles, sitting in a fabric Director's chair on the balcony of his condo. An open bottle of wine breathed on the tiny table beside him. The man brushed some breadcrumbs off his white shirt, gently, with the back of his first two fingers. He sniffed – which the vampire heard with clarity - and glanced downward from his perch.

Their gazes met. The moment hung.

The man smiled and waved. He raised a glass of wine and nodded in the vampire's direction.

The vampire grinned and waved back, casually, never breaking stride. He nodded upwards, returning the silent greeting. Nothing wrong with being polite, he thought.

In fact, he often went out of his way to be polite, and always felt better doing it. One of the problems in the world today, the vampire felt, was a rather complete lack of old-fashioned manners. Oh sure, parents still taught their children the most rudimentary of perfunctories; "may I", "please", "sorry", and of course, "thank you". But these pleasantries nowadays served only as a function of what the children could get out of it themselves, not because it was the right thing to do.

He crossed Ninth Street with the light. The old Public Library took up the entire block. Now closed, dark, and dusty, it still held reminiscence of its former art deco glory. Built in the early 1950's, it had served the community well. The vampire himself had spent time there, reading newspapers from all over the country. Of course, that was in the days before the Internet. Technology made things more efficient, more sterile. But the satisfaction of pouring over real books, real newspapers had been left in the dust, just like the old library.

The vampire felt a pang for something lost.

A new library had been built at great expense. It had just opened, several blocks to the south near Petco Park, the baseball stadium where the San Diego Padres played and sometimes tried to win. At a total construction cost of one hundred eighty five million dollars, the library stood nine stories high, complete with a three-story entrance and lobby. A high school taught on floors six and seven. The high-domed structure was unique enough to change the skyline of downtown.

The old Library had become a congregating place for the homeless. Some huddled together believing in the safety of numbers. Some preferred to move off by themselves. Sometimes solitude can bring its own sense of security. And either out of plain paranoia or out of bitter experience, they kept their shopping carts and wire baskets loaded up with all their worldly possessions close by. Anyone coming too close to their stuff alerted them, made their jaws set and their eyes go cold.

"Hey Mister," came a tiny voice. "Spare a dollar?"

The vampire stopped and looked down. On the concrete, next to the section of rented portable chain link fencing that had been strung around the library to keep the homeless out, sat a young girl. Dirty, hungry, dark hair that had not been washed in weeks, from what he smelled. Desperation emanated from her. He also smelled blood, old and dried, but could not quite locate her wound. Senses tingling, he knew she was here through no fault of her own, that she had wound up here so fast she had no idea how it happened, or what to do about it.

He dug a bill out of his pocket, kept it concealed inside his palm. He squatted down, getting closer to her. That's when he placed the origin of her blood smell. She had been raped recently, and the dried blood still clung to her crotch and inner thighs.

"You do not belong here," he said.

Tears formed at the corners of her eyes. "I got nowhere else to go."

He cocked his head slowly, looking down at her. Behind his glasses, he felt an unaccustomed emotion – compassion.

"Yes, you do." He took her hand, stood up, bringing her up with him. The connection was intimate and immediate. " There is a hostel three blocks from here."

"I got no money."

"I do. Come on."

She grabbed what few ragged garments she had off the ground. Her eyes sparkled with gratitude. He nodded, keeping his own feelings in check. They started walking west, the way he had been moving in the first place.

"So. Gonna get some of Rosie's pussy tonight?"

The taunt came from somewhere behind them and to the vampire's left. The vampire spun around, instantly angry, zeroing in on a disgustingly dirty man with a balding head, grey, disheveled beard. Open sores dotted his cheeks and forehead. A bottle of cheap whiskey stayed clutched firmly in one hand. He wore a withering sneer across his lips. And what was that smell coming off of him?

Something the vampire had smelled before.

The vampire was on him in two strides. He grabbed the old man's shirt and heavy jacket with one hand, and pushed HARD, lifting the bum off his feet. The vampire slammed him into the temporary fence with such force the entire block of fencing shuddered in response.

"Hey." The old guy put his hand up in front of him, a sign of surrender. "Chill out. You'll like her. Trust me."

The familiar smell was Rosie's blood. The vampire realized it emanated from his crotch. But the smell was tainted, a mixture of semen, urine, and filth.

Seething with rage, he made sure Rosie was behind him. Then he snatched off his sunglasses and pushed his face within inches of the old geezer.

He bared his fangs and hissed softly, like a serpent.

The old man's eyes bulged in an all-consuming fear. His bowels evacuated on the spot, brown grease sliding down the insides of his thighs. His entire world was filled with nothing but the face in front of him, a vision from hell itself – black eyes, animal teeth, and no mercy.

The vampire, satisfied for the moment with the old man's reaction, put his sunglasses back on and released his viselike grip. The geezer's feet hit the ground with jarring force, sending pain shooting sharply up his shins.

"See you later," the vampire whispered.

The vampire turned around and walked away, leaving the old geezer to drink from his bottle and realize he had no clean change of clothes. The vampire gently took Rosie by the arm and guided her along the sidewalk.

The vampire had no idea what the city had planned for the old Library property. They'd probably raze the current structure, and build more condominium high rises. Such is the price of progress, he thought.

They slowed as they approached the hostel's entrance. Originally a brothel back in the late eighteen hundreds when prostitution was legal, the hostel boasted a small check-in area in front, with bathrooms and showers farther back, all on the first floor. A staircase near the back led upstairs to the second and third floors, where dorm style rooms slept four with wooden bunk beds.

He opened the door and allowed Rosie to enter first. He closed the door behind him.

A tall, rail thin young man stood behind the desk, situated to their left. His nametag announced him as Brian.

"Good evening," Brian opened. "May I help you?"

"This is Rosie," the vampire stated. "She's new to San Diego, and will be leaving tomorrow."

Brian eyed her up and down, very skeptical. "Really?"

"Yes," the vampire said. "I would very much like to pay for a room for her."

"Well, we don't usually just "rent" rooms to people off the streets," Brian said.

The vampire's smile faded a bit. "Is that right?"

"We need to see either a Government – issued I.D., or a foreign passport, and documentation of future travel."

The vampire turned his head towards Rosie, who silently pulled a faded, crumpled Nevada driver's license out of her coat pocket. She handed it over to Brian. He looked at it, still unsure if this was all on the up and up.

"And documentation of future travel?"

The vampire's grin returned. He stepped closer, leaned on the desk. "That is where we could use some help, Brian," he said. "She needs to get home to...."

Brian glanced at the driver's license. "Reno?"

"Reno!" the vampire echoed. "Of course. Now, this place looks pretty modern. I bet you've got computers and Wi-Fi here, yes?"

Brian nodded.

"Outstanding," the vampire clapped his hands together and smiled. Brian thought he saw a hint of long, sharp teeth. Suddenly, he just wanted to get this over with, and get this guy out of here.

"I need you to help her buy either a bus or a train ticket back to Reno. You print out a copy of her itinerary, and *poof!* You have documentation of future travel."

"Sir, this is highly irregular."

"I am certain it is," the vampire replied. "I shall make it worth your while." He reached into his pocket, and produced a thick wad of neatly folded money. They appeared to be all one hundred dollar bills.

Brian's eyes grew wide. His jaw dropped just a little.

The vampire slid two bills across the desktop. "This should cover her stay tonight, some food for her, and her ticket price for tomorrow, yes?"

Stunned, Brian stuttered. "P..pr..probably, yes."

The vampire pushed another hundred-dollar bill across the desktop. "Let us make certain, shall we?

Brian nodded emphatically.

"Good. Now, whatever is left over from this," he pointed at the money, "you give her every penny of it. Understand?"

"Sure."

"Good." The vampire peeled off two more bills. He reached out across the countertop and stuffed the bills into Brian's shirt pocket.

"All of this stays between us, yes?"

Brian nodded.

Brian was telling the truth, and the vampire knew it. Lies had a smell to them, just like sin and death. Evil exuded a scent, a scent he could pick up, identify, and locate. And if he could touch the particular person, similar to how he touched Brian when he put the money in his shirt pocket, he could see into their very souls. No lies, nothing hidden.

The vampire still did not know if this ability of his was a blessing or a curse. He had seen a lot of sinful things that, once seen, could never be unseen. And he carried those memories around with him in his head, like a perverted video loop.

He turned to Rosie. "Look, Rosie. You are going to be fine now."

She reached out and touched the cool skin of his arm. Instantly, his mind flooded with an image of her home in Reno. Nice place. Middle class, near a park and a school, nothing fancy. A mother and father sick with worry, sick with grief, sick with regret of angry words harshly said. Incredulity and remorse that they had actually pushed her that hard, that she'd actually leave. That they'd wake up one morning, and their baby was simply.... gone.

"Don't leave me," she said, her plaintive words bringing him back to the present.

He patted her hand. "This is where you and I part ways." He noticed the disappointed look on her face. "Brian is going to make sure you're provided for." He spoke up. "Right, Brian?"

"Right, sir!"

She leaned in and whispered, "Well, I thought maybe we could.. you know."

He understood immediately shat she meant. She intended to pay him back for his kindness. He chose his words carefully. "I have.... well, I have a condition for which there is no cure."

Rosie's look of shock and sadness nearly warmed the walking corpse's long dead heart. "Is it.... contagious?"

The vampire chuckled. "No." There was really nothing more he cared to say.

Rosie had to let that sink in a moment. Then she nodded her understanding of the situation. "Thank you. For helping me, I mean."

"You are quite welcome."

"Why are you doing this? Why help me, of all people?"

"Because one time, a long time ago, I was like you. In a bad place. Bad decisions. And because of it, I became... what I am now." He paused, a rare moment of real emotion rising within him. "I wanted to give you something I never got – a second chance. But it is up to you to do something with it. "

Rosie threw her arms around him and hugged him tight. He hugged her back.

"Thank you." Tears spilled down her cheeks.

He smiled, under control again, and took a step back. "You want to thank me? Go home. Your parents love you. They miss you. They are worried sick about you."

She looked frightened. "How do you know for sure?"

"Trust me," he replied. "Go home. Enroll in school. Build a life for yourself. No one is going give it to you. It is okay to ask for help once in a while when you need it. And everyone needs help now and then. But no one hands you anything in this world. The world does not owe you anything. You have to do the grunt work on your own."

She nodded. She had heard this speech before, but this time, where she was, in front of his mysterious man who wanted only to help her and expected nothing in return, the lesson finally sank in.

Satisfied, the vampire gave one last look over Brian's way. Brian said nothing. "Keep your word to me. Make sure she is out of this city tomorrow." He paused for effect. "If not, I will come back. It will not be pleasant."

Brian shuddered involuntarily at the thought of this person coming back. The vampire grinned slightly.

And then, the vampire was out the door. Melting into the distance, swallowed up by the crowds on the sidewalk, he disappeared into the night.

Like he had never been there at all.

But it would be several more minutes before Brian's pulse dropped back down to a normal rate and rhythm.

CHAPTER TEN

Back out on the street, the vampire sailed seamlessly through the crowd, cutting an unerring course through the ocean of people. A gentle breeze brushed his lank hair off his forehead. Various scents, smells, and odors wafted, swirling around him, overloading his senses: perfume, cologne, sweat, lavender soaps, semen, laundry detergent, menstrual blood. Occasionally, he intentionally brushed a shoulder here and there. He needed the brief physical contact as he hunted.

He did not detect those he chose to hunt, the worst of the worst – pimps, drug dealers, wife beaters, rapists, pedophiles. A young mother out for the first time in months, the vampire would give a pass. Likewise the father working two or three jobs to make ends meet and feed his kids. But if someone who fit his special criteria blundered across his path...

The vampire could be a messy eater.

He rounded a corner on Fourth and F, the heart of the Gaslamp, and stopped. Across the street, in the middle of the block, a large powder blue neon sign spelled out the word, FETISH in jagged, fractured letters.

He could smell prey even from this distance. The faintest hint of a smile curled his lip. This would serve as his hunting ground for tonight. He had never hunted here before. He would never hunt here again. Security measures.

He noticed a line already forming at the entrance, replete with Fetish's rather distinctive clientele: leather, Bondage, dominatrix, submissives, wannabes and posers who just dressed the part. Not his scene, that was for sure. Not when he was a man, and certainly not now. As a walking corpse who drank blood, he had no sexual function, no sex drive. He did not miss it, the distraction of it. And in any case, without Danae, well then, what would be the point? But people did what they did, and he was in no position to judge them for it.

The vampire crossed the street with the light. Part of staying safe in this modern world was keeping his secret about what he really was. All he needed would be for a truck to plow into him doing forty, and him get up from the pavement with nothing more than a pissed off disposition.

He walked up to the end of the line and stood there. "Is the line moving?" he asked the young couple in front of him.

"We've been here about ten minutes," the girl replied over her shoulder. "We haven't moved at all."

Her male companion nodded his pierced, bare, and tattooed skull. "Yeah. Man. Sucks, doesn't it?"

Several minutes ticked by. The large muscular bouncer at the door stood impassively at the front of the line. The club entrance, a metal door adorned with several peeling layers of old paint, sexually explicit graffiti, and punk–inspired stickers, stood embedded in the white brick wall immediately to his right. The couple in front shifted their weight, the girl now clutching her arms across her chest. The tattooed young man pulled her closer, trying to warm her.

The vampire leaned forward, so they only could hear him. "Come on. Follow me." Then he was moving to the aside of the line, towards the doorway and the enormous guard. The couple obediently moved in behind him.

The bouncer, whose nametag on his upper left pectoral proclaimed his name as Antoine, focused as they approached. His arms dropped to his sides.

Walking up, the vampire and offered his hand. "Good evening, sir."

"Yeah. Good evening." Antoine's reply was merely perfunctory. He took the vampire's cool hand, shook it, and his fingers curled around the three hundred dollar bills folded up in the vampire's palm.

A quick glance into his own hand, and the bouncer looked at the three in front of him. "Can't let you in," Antoine said.

The vampire pulled out two more bills, slapped them into the bouncer's waiting hand, approximately the size of a catcher's mitt.

Antoine deposited the money into his pocket, then folded his arms across his chest once more. "Can't let you in."

The vampire understood completely.

"Well," he finally sighed, holding out his hand once more, "You can't blame a guy for trying. No hard feelings?"

Antoine, certain he had won the confrontation, thrust forward his Thanksgiving turkey - sized hand, and shook the vampire's.

The smile on the vampire's face disappeared. His mouth flattened into a cruel, thin line across the lower half of his face. His visage changed from disarming to sadistic in the blink of an eye.

Suddenly, the bouncer's face froze. Confusion, surprise, and fear and pain washed over Antoine's face as the tiny man in front of him crushed his hand in an impossibly viselike grip. He tried to reach out, break the grip with his other hand. The vampire in front of him simply batted it away as if it were nothing more than a minor nuisance.

Sweat appeared across Antoine's upper lip and forehead. He tried reaching for his hand again, but the vampire batted the other arm away with a swing so strong it felt like being hit with an iron rod.

"What is the matter, sir?" the vampire asked calmly from behind his sunglasses. "Changing your mind, perhaps?" He tilted his head, inquisitive. Then the vampire compressed again, and this time rolled his right hand inward, towards his thumb.

Antoine, realizing he was in way over his head, let out a sharp cry as his arm twisted outward and a bone inside his wrist snapped. He grabbed his shoulder with his other hand, an instinctive ploy to prevent the shoulder socket from dislocating forward with a loud pop.

Antoine dropped to one knee. He grunted in agony. A tear formed at the corner of one eye, spilled downward across his cheek.

"Think you can let us in now?"

Antoine, the humiliated bouncer, desperate to escape, tried to form words, but no coherent speech came out. So he simply nodded yes.

"Get the door for us." It was an order, given with a dismissive air. Antoine knew this creature in front of him saw him as nothing.

The vampire, never releasing his grip, helped the big man stand up. The injured bouncer reached for the door with his good hand, opened it, then moved aside. The vampire motioned for the couple to go in first. Scared by what they'd seen, they scurried inside.

The vampire turned his attention back to Antoine. He moved in close, so no one else could see. He took off his sunglasses.

The big man inhaled in panic as he dropped to one knee again.

"Do not scream," the vampire ordered, a low, whispered warning.

Antoine the former bouncer obeyed. The vampire allowed his fangs to show for the first time.

"Never overestimate yourself. Never underestimate your opponent." He made certain Antoine's saucer eyes were on his fangs. "I am the last person on this entire planet you want to anger." The vampire put his sunglasses back on. "We have an understanding then, yes?"

The vampire released his grip on the hapless human's now useless hand. Antoine winced. His whole body seemed to sag. By the time he looked up, the vampire was already gone, inside.

Antoine looked up, hit by a tsunami of embarrassment. The partygoers and revelers he took so much pleasure in teasing, extorting, and otherwise fucking with, were all still there waiting to get in. Some looked worried. Some looked scared. Some grinned, exhilarated that he finally had gotten what he deserved.

He staggered to his feet with Herculean effort. He stood up, wobbly on unsteady legs. He still cradled his ruined appendage. He tried to put on a brave face. Epic fail. Everyone stood there, waiting.

Antoine the Defeated unlatched the velvet rope and let it drop to the ground. He stepped aside. "Go on in. I don't care."

He stepped further back as one girl stepped forward and opened the door for herself. She paused, looked over at him with compassion.

"Sorry about your hand." Then she was inside.

The next person in line stepped up, followed by a couple. Then the rest began filling through the door so rapidly, the door had no chance to close between them.

Antoine watched the last one enter, the door slamming shut behind her. Suddenly alone on the sidewalk, he looked around. It was uncharacteristically quiet. He heaved a great sigh.

"Fuck it," he muttered under his breath.

And then he turned and weaved erratically down the block, still tenderly cradling his wounded wrist in his other hand.

"You know, feeding you is starting to become a fulltime job," Walt grinned over a Styrofoam container of mostly eaten cheese enchiladas, decimated refried beans, and untouched rice.

Reggie smiled as he wiped his mouth on a cheap napkin. "It's much appreciated, Boss."

"Maybe I can claim you as a dependent on next year's taxes."

Coulter and Downing sat at Coulter's desk inside the fortified Boroquez building. It was pitch dark outside. Two lights on Coulter's desk cast unfiltered, garish light at odd angles, partly obscured by deep blackness.

"Next time, you buy the grub."

"Deal."

"So what's next for you?"

"This place is the best kept secret in the city," Downing stated. "I'm staying in the duty room tonight."

"Hell. Stay the weekend. There's pizza in the fridge."

"Can't. Gotta keep moving. I will need to swing by my place."

"That's the first place they'll look," Coulter said.

"Not my cover flat. My real place."

"They know who you are," Coulter continued. "They probably know everything."

"I have to risk it."

"You need to lie low. Go watch TV or something."

Downing yawned. "Good idea." He stood and gathered up the remnants of his meal container. "See you later." He threw his garbage in a trashcan at the door.

Walt Coulter watched through the glass as Downing padded deeper into the building. He disappeared into the shadows as he climbed the back stairs to the second floor. From his office, Coulter could hear the aged wood creak under Downing's weight. When Downing made it to the duty room, Coulter knew. The boards stopped creaking, silence followed.

Coulter turned back around in his desk. He pushed his meal trash aside with a swipe of his left arm. He grabbed his keyboard and pulled it close to him.

He began typing furiously.

CHAPTER ELEVEN

FETISH undulated with wall-to-wall people. Drinks as colorful and as varied as the customers floated in their hands. Some people leaned in close to speak; others to hear over the din of thrash metal music and thousands of conversations.

Everywhere one looked, leather corsets pushed breasts upwards, creating or accentuating cleavage. Leather pants and skinny jeans announced the young males' endowments. A latex–clad, redheaded dominatrix with large breasts, flat stomach, and curvy hips lead her "slave", an overweight middle-aged man wearing sneakers and an adult diaper, through the crowd. A black leather dog leash attached to the front of the silver spiked collar latched snugly around his thick neck. They headed single file towards the main bar.

Behavior would get you arrested elsewhere was "self-expression" here.

The entire place throbbed with house music, interspersed with the occasional surging cacophony of death metal. Blue, green, and red lights flashed in beat to the music. People danced anywhere and everywhere, even in line at the bar or the bathrooms.

Rick Oakley, wearing his trademark black T shirt and brown military bomber's jacket, jeans and motorcycle boots, shoved his way through the crowd, trying to ignore as much of this hedonistic debauchery as he could.

He had work to do, so he continued through the pulsating people. He bumped into people, and sometimes people bumped into him. In some cases, people even groped him. The occasional hand, coming from any direction or no direction at all, and could be male or female, might grab his ass or cup his cock. Anywhere else, Rick would simply leave the offender lying in a puddle of their own blood.

But here, the rules were different. Acceptable interaction here was whatever went on between consenting adults. Close body contact was inevitable here, permitted, encouraged. If the place were to break out into a mass orgy of fornicating bodies, the owners would simply lock the main entrance and join in the fun.

No one Rick knew would be caught dead here. It was one of the reasons he's chosen this place for a meeting.

In a corner booth to his left, he saw a young brunette woman thin and pale, crane her neck back, eyes closed in pleasure, as two men on either side of her kissed her mouth and neck, caressed her body. They already had her shirt open. One man caressed her pearly, smallish breast and teased his thumb over her nipple. The other one kissed her neck and had already snaked a hand up her leather mini skirt.

Oakley could not see fingers, but he saw the muscles in the young man's forearms fluttering under the skin, so he knew those fingers were busy. Whatever he was doing under there, the girl liked it. She gasped, arched her back, started grinding her hips against his hand. A few more minutes, and she would be having intercourse with both men simultaneously, right there in the booth.

Self–expression, indeed!

As Oakley moved onward, movement to his right caught his eye. A young man had crawled under a cocktail table. The other man sitting in the chair leaned back, eyes closed, a serene smile on his face.

More self–expression.

Oakley's eyes locked back on the booth in front of him. It was empty, which surprised him considering how crowded the place was. He snagged it before anyone else could. He sat down, eased himself back, made himself comfortable. Well, as comfortable as he could be in this type of place.

Regardless about cutting edge these people wanted to think all this was, the truth was, this was nothing new. Rick knew it. This entire scene, while definitely not his cup of tea, had existed for a long time, thousands of years in fact, back to the Romans, the Egyptians, the Mesopotamians. And would continue well into the future, just underneath that thin veneer called Civilized Society.

From his seat, Oakley could see most of the club in front of him. The main bar did a bustling business, crackling along about forty feet to his right. Beyond that, the stairs jutted upwards, leading to the ground level main entrance. The DJ booth lurked near the back wall in front of him, with the dance floor in front of that.

To the left, people occupied more booths, partying, drinking, scoping out potential sex partners.

Kid stuff.

People at some of the other tables definitely walked a darker path. Drugs snorted, leashes pulled short, brutal kisses that left lips red with blood instead of lipstick.

Impatient, Rick Oakley glanced at his watch. His contact was running late. All Oakley wanted to do was get the hell out of here, go home, wash the stink of this place off him, and go to bed. He adjusted the large caliber handgun stuffed into the back waistband of his pants.

A buxom waitress sashayed over to him. Dressed in a black French Maid's uniform, her hair dyed a raven black with streaks of fire engine red and a darker purple, her eyes cast off an impossible green color. Oakley assumed she wore contact lenses. She balanced herself deftly atop four-inch stiletto heels. Her smile was pretty, genuine.

He was old enough to be her father.

"What'll ya' have hon?" she yelled over the music.

Oakley leaned in to speak. "Diet Coke." She nodded. "I'm expecting someone. Can I also have an ice water?"

"You bet." She spun around on those impossible heels. Oakley was astounded she didn't fall over. And then she moved away, swishing her ample ass at him until swallowed up by the crowd.

Oakley sat back, his old counterintelligence training kicking in. His eyes constantly scanned, moving up, down, from one side to another, doubling back, checking the angles, trying to catch something – anything! – out of place.

That's when he saw The Predator.

Oakley would never forget that first sighting. The Predator revealed himself dimly, subtly, in the distance, across the room, partially obscured by partiers oblivious to the fact there were now TWO truly dangerous people in their midst. The Predator seemed detached, otherworldly. Like he had no real connection to the humanity around him. He moved fluidly as a wraith, ethereal as a wisp of smoke. He moved among them, aloof, not one of them.

Dressed in leather pants, a plain, unimportant shirt, and motorcycle jacket that seemed a part of him like a second skin, this Predator simply curled past everyone else. Slow, meticulous, prowling. Scanning the heard.

On the hunt.

Oakley knew blood would spill tonight; life would drain away, crimson rivulets swirling down a back alley drain. Whoever this guy was looking, Oakley pitied them.

A portly, balding middle-aged man appeared. Looking pathetic, gasping like a fish out of water, he saw Oakley and headed directly toward him. The man's face was red, blotchy, and sweaty. He obviously was not a regular here.

"Counselor. So nice of you to come."

Michael C. Law, obese attorney to drug dealers, wiped his pudgy face with a white linen handkerchief. "What kind of place is this?"

"Somewhere we can talk without being disturbed." Oakley motioned to the cushion beside him. "Take a load off."

Law plopped down. He tugged at his drenched collar, loosened his damp tie. His skin lost some of its redness. He looked around, his head on a swivel.

"Relax, Counselor. No one is going to rape you here."

The waitress returned, glasses balanced on a small serving tray. She placed the drinks in front of the two men. She gave a curious glance was Law, then looked at Oakley.

"That'll be fifteen dollars, hon."

Oakley put a twenty on her tray. "Keep the change."

"Thanks, hon. Anything else?"

"Just a bit of privacy."

She looked incredulous. "In here? Good luck with that."

Oakley grinned. "Point taken."

"I'll be back later to check on you," she said. She gave one more glance to the guy in the suit. He looked like he was going to throw up. "It's okay, hon. Don't take this shit seriously. No one else does." Then, like the good waitress she was, she walked away.

Law continued looking around, aghast. He gulped the ice water in front of him. Oakley enjoyed seeing the normally smug, self-centered fat fuck in such acute discomfort.

"Let's get this over with," Law said.

Oakley's grin vanished. Like a veil descending, he put his game face back on. "Very well, Counselor. Mr. Vargas wants to know what kind of shape Rudy Valdez is in."

"He's a Marine," Law replied. "He's at summer camp, compared to some of the places he's been."

"Is he scared? Did he talk? Did he name names? Do you think he'll talk later?"

"You know what he was doing when I came in? Toying with them. Infuriating them. He was running counter-interrogation techniques, trying to get them to lose control."

Oakley's respect for Valdez ticked up a notch.

Law glanced over at the next table. A young woman straddled her male partner, eased herself down, and began having deep intercourse with him. Law swallowed hard as his heart rate increased. He felt an unaccustomed stirring between his legs.

Shaken, he looked back at Oakley. "The only truthful thing he said was that he was knocked out early on, and it was all over before he came to."

Oakley stared at Law a moment. He knew the lawyer was too afraid of him to lie. And with good reason. Oakley would have no problem with showing up at the lawyer's house some night. He could kill him and his entire kill his family: the wife, the live–in maid, both kids, even the goddamned dog! And then he could burn their house to the ground, cover his tracks, and sleep like a baby the next day.

"So," Oakley sighed, "you're saying we have nothing to worry about from Rudy Valdez."

Law nodded, finished his water.

"What about arraignment?"

"I called a judge friend of mine," Law stated. "He pressured the D.A. to send someone to lockup tomorrow morning. It'll take about an hour."

Oakley nodded. His eyes glided over the crowds, moved left, froze for an instant, then darted back to the right. He zeroed in.

In the distance, at the far edge of the dance floor, stood The Predator. He stood casually, eyeing Oakley while leaning against a support beam that kept the building from toppling down upon everyone in the club. Arms crossed, each hand cupping the opposite elbow, legs crossed at the ankle. Not a threatening stance, just one that said everything that needed saying: they were hunters in a world of the hunted. They knew of each others' presence and proximity.

Finally, The Predator smiled a crooked little smile, one corner turning upwards. He nodded. Subtle. Practically imperceptible. Without really thinking about it, Oakley gave him an uptick of the head, a nod in return.

Professional courtesy.

Law reached out and put his hand on Oakley's arm, startling him. "What?" He blinked at the attorney.

"I said, are you all right?" Law repeated.

"Yeah, sure," he responded. He looked back to where the other nameless predator had been standing. Naturally, he had disappeared by now.

Law nodded his acknowledgement. He stood up, grabbed the cowhide leather briefcase he'd been clutching since he came in. He did not even say goodbye to Oakley. He simply walked away as briskly an out of shape lawyer who hadn't seen the inside of a gym since high school could.

Oakley sat back against the cushions, cleared his throat, and casually sipped his drink. He intently scanned the room once more, looking for the fellow he had seen twice now. There was no mistake. Two killers in the same club, on the same night. What significance did this have?

After scanning the room three times, Oakley was convinced he had not seen him again. The pathway to the stairs to his right had cleared a bit. The stairway itself was sparsely populated with people. One Goth girl squatted in front of her male partner, who leaned against the wall, gazing upwards, his eyes opening and closing, breathing hard. The back and forth bobbing movement of her head left Oakley with no doubt as to what she was doing down there.

Oakley glanced at the room and to his left one more time. Though he was not afraid of any man, he felt it prudent to avoid a confrontation in a public place like FETISH.

Confident he was safe, Oakley got up from the booth. He looked around again quickly, one hand casually behind his back, near his handgun. He turned to his right and strode forward.

Glancing to his left and to his right, mindful of a rear attack, he made his way towards the stairs. He saw the handrail rising at an angle towards street level. A last glance backwards assured him he was not being followed. He reached out for the handrail at the bottom of the stairs. He rounded the corner and began his steady, controlled ascent upwards towards the streets, and way from FETISH.

If he never came back here, it would be just fine with Rick Oakley.

From the shadows where he could not be seen, the vampire watched the Dangerous Man leave. He sat on a bare wooden chair in the slightly damp concrete-walled corner. Arms and legs crossed, jacket collar turned up to minimize his silhouette, the vampire peeked out over the top of his jacket, exposing only his forehead and eyes.

He had known instantly, even from a distance, upon seeing the bald human that he was a Dangerous Man. Not just someone who thought he was badass, mind you. This human was the real deal, and the vampire knew it. It emanated off of him like perverted heat waves. It was plain as day for anyone to see, if they only paid attention.

And pay attention the vampire did.

That is why he allowed the Dangerous Man to see him twice. He wanted the DM to know that he was not the only creature on the prowl this night. But the DM was not his designated target here, oh no. Not that the vampire was not intrigued. This was precisely the type of prey that invigorated the vampire the most.

But there was so much easier prey in abundance here, all equally as deserving of the vampire's hatred. Perhaps more so. And most of them all too eager to be led into an ambush as only he could set.

Behind his sunglasses, his eyes shifted, scanning the crowd. He had seen a couple of people that had sparked his interest, but they were passing fancies, nothing more. But time was beginning to become a factor. The club would be forced to close in a couple of hours.

A new emanation caught his attention. He did not move his head, but his eyes darted to the right. On the other side of the small dance floor, two men, a "Mutt and Jeff" combo that made the vampire smile to himself, both dressed like wannabe TV vampires – all leather, studs, long hair, white makeup, dark circles around the eyes – stood side by side, looking in his general direction. The tall one was more muscular, heavier. Outwardly, he appeared to be a typical alpha male. But it was Slight One, standing beside him that caught the vampire's eye.

Blonde hair an impossible yellow, gelled and spiked to ridiculous extremes, soft pale skin, thin lips, the Slight One stood a good six inches shorter than Alpha Boy. A black cape draped across the back of his narrow shoulders. Evil wafted off him like black heat. The Slight One's gaze finally fell on the vampire, and came to rest there.

Alpha Boy was looking off in another direction. He moved away, as if to walk towards the bar, but Slight One stopped him without a word. He simply reached out from underneath the draping cape, touched the back of Alpha Boy's wrist, and shook his head. Alpha Boy was immediately brought back into tow, and this subtle exchange told the vampire everything he needed to know.

Game on.

The vampire uncoiled himself. With neither worry nor hurry, he planted his feet flat on the deck and stood up from his chair. Outwardly, he made no movement to indicate he was aware of the pair, much less that he had targeted them both for death. He moved at an angle, not only so he could keep them in his line of sight, but so they would not lose him in the crowd.

He planned to do some reading before sunrise, so the vampire devised a plan for a quick kill. The bathrooms were situated behind where the pair stood. Beyond that, a narrow hallway lead to an emergency exit required by the city's Fire Code. The exit opened into a small concrete rectangle, oblong, boasting a set of concrete steps and old iron handrail going upward to ground level and emptying into the filthy alley.

The vampire grinned. This should be fun.

He ambled leisurely in their direction, moving his head, slipping past people. As he approached them, he glanced directly at them. The Slight One puffed out his thin, Whippet-like chest, curled his lip downward, and nodded with an uptick of his head. The vampire walked by like they were nothing.

The hallway leading to the rear was so narrow two people would have difficulty getting past each other. Inadequate track lighting provided sketchy illumination. Tape lighting, the plastic and LED pin lights type often used in modern movie theaters to line the floors and stairs for safety, snaked along the floor back past the bathrooms to the rear exit.

Slight One and Alpha Boy watched the stranger careen down the hallway, occasionally putting a hand to a wall for support. Slight One grinned to himself. On wobbly legs like that, the guy's obviously had too much to drink. He looked up at Alpha Boy, who bent down so he could whisper something into his ear.

Down the hall, the vampire spun ninety degrees to his right. Before him stood a dark recess in the wall. Within the recess, which was only about four feet deep by maybe six or seven feet wide, resided the two bathroom entrances. Men to the left, women to the right. Of course, in FETISH, these bourgeois gender delineations were only for the benefit of the County Health inspectors. Such trivialities were only partially and then only marginally, adhered to. The vampire launched himself forward, into the recess. He leaned left, aimed at the Men's room door.

As soon as the stranger disappeared from their view, Alpha Boy moved forward, flexing his muscles. Full sleeve tattoos rippled as if alive. A girl, thin and sickly, all red leather with black trim, staggered down one side of the hallway. She turned her shoulders to nudge past him against the wall. He allowed her to pass without so much as a second glance. He never had much use for girls, anyway.

He dug his fingers into the shallow pocket on the front of his pants. He found what he was looking for, two small sharp objects he enjoyed using in these situations. He pulled him out, glanced down at the fake vampire fangs cradled in his palm. He expertly popped them into his mouth, pushing them into place over each of his own canine teeth. He ran his tongue over them, making sure they were in place.

They were.

He burst through the Men's room door forcefully, whacking the door against the wall with a loud *THWACK!* He stepped through the doorway, all menace and concentration. His eyes darted around the enclave, searching.

A lavatory hovered in the left corner, unused. An ancient, moderately rusted metal towel dispenser sprung out from the left wall. To the right, along the far wall hung the trough urinal. Porcelain poured over and iron core, the urinal was approximately six feet long by eighteen inches wide and another eighteen inches deep. Standing shoulder to shoulder, men pissed into it without any privacy It floated approximately two and half feet off the filthy floor, held up by metal grommets and the attached plumbing, which piped into the plaster wall behind.

Alpha Boy did not see his quarry. He stepped deeper into the crowded bathroom. Farther to his right, the three narrow toilet stalls squatted. One of them had lost its hinged swinging door at some point in history. Inside, A young man sat on the toilet, and a young woman, short and plump, sat, straddling his pelvis and facing him. Their arms wrapped around each other, they kissed deeply, passionately. They were oblivious to anything else around them.

The other two stalls still possessed doors. Both were closed. Unsure what to do, he hesitated, considered checking the Women's bathroom next door. Self doubt and fear of failure crept up his spine as the moments ticked by. He wavered, took a step back.

The last stall door opened and the stranger came striding out. He ignored the men at the urinal as he passed them. Alpha Boy almost shuddered with relief. The stranger, thin and intense, approached him as he stood near the doorway. His massive body effectively blocking the exit, Alpha Boy did not move.

The stranger stopped in front of him. "Get out of my way."

Startled at the intensity of the snarling command, Alpha Boy moved without thinking it through. The stranger shouldered past him without another word. Alpha Boy frowned, anger taking hold in his dull brain. He turned and followed the stranger out.

Outside the bathroom in the hallway and glanced towards the main club. His companion was there, glaring in his direction. Alpha Boy's head snapped around in the opposite direction. The snapping motion sent his dark hair flying out from his head. He saw the stranger moving towards the emergency exit.

Emergency exit, huh? I'll give him an emergency.

He lumbered down the hallway after his quarry. He saw the stranger hit the heavy metal door and fling it open. He was surprised with the ease with which such a small guy could throw his weight around. The stranger looked back over his shoulder at Alpha Boy, grinned, then disappeared outside, the door slamming behind him.

Alpha Boy hit the door seconds later. He pushed against the metal bar, and heaved the door open, spilling outside. The cold damp fog of the night kissed his face and neck. It was colder now than when he had first arrived. He glanced around, and stopped as the door closed behind him.

The stranger stood waiting for him, several feet away. His shoulders squared, hands at his sides, feet wide apart. Back straight, head up, eyes forward. Completely unafraid.

Ready for battle.

The vampire knew this was the best place to take care of business and not be seen. The steps behind him led to the alley. His fallback position, should he need it. Anything could happen in the heat of battle.

The metal door banged open again. The Slight One strode through. Behind him, the vampire could hear the music, smell the sex, sense the desperation and despair inside. The door clanged closed, cutting those distractions off.

"You know, my friend and I have been coming to this club for over a year," the Slight One said. He nodded towards Alpha Boy and walked a slow diagonal line, angled so he could see the vampire unobstructed. "We've never seen you here. Have we?"

Alpha Boy pursed his lips, shook his head.

"Why is that?" the Slight One asked.

The vampire said nothing.

"Now you see, that's just rude," Slight One said, "ignoring me like that. My friend doesn't like it."

Alpha Boy flexed his muscles, pushed his chest out, shoulders back.

"Is this slab of beef supposed to scare me?"

Slight One smiled. "There you go again being impolite. Chester – " Alpha Boy looked his way – "Why don't you introduce yourself?"

Chester, formerly known as Alpha Boy, puffed his chest out and drew himself up to his full height. He opened his mouth and threw his head back, exposing his fake fangs, plastic implants over his real canines. He hissed and spit like all those bullshit vampires in all those bullshit movies.

Unimpressed, the vampire stifled a laugh. "Cute."

Chester lunged forward, fully committed to a ferocious attack. The vampire lithely stepped aside and twisted around, punching his attacker hard in the side of the head. The impact sent the off-balance Chester to the dirty concrete like a sack of bricks.

Chester bounced his head on the pavement as the vampire took a step back.

"That all you got, Chester?" The vampire sounded disappointed.

Chester, shocked, pushed himself up from the pavement, brushed off the front of his shirt. He glanced at Slight One, who seemed genuinely shocked by what had just happened. He punched at the Stranger, who ducked, bobbed, and sidestepped once, twice, three times. He did it easily, all grace and style.

"Chester, Chester, Chester," the vampire shook his head. "I had hoped for more from you. Give me *something* to work with here, will you? Make this interesting for me."

Frustrated, Chester grimaced and screamed. He hauled back and threw a punch that would have broken bone if it had landed on a fellow human. But that is not what happened. He threw the punch, his hand thrusting outward from his body, at the end of his arm, traveling straight and true, a flesh–covered sledgehammer.

It suddenly, incredibly, came to an immediate stop.

Then a nuclear burst of pain, bright and white and beyond understanding, blinded him.

The vampire had caught the last punch in mid swing with one hand. He gripped Chester's lower forearm with is other hand and applied massive pressure and a downward, wrenching movement, efficiently snapping three bones in Chester's wrist.

Chester's eyes bulged in terror and agony. His mouth fell open, his useless fangs mere novelty store trickery.

The vampire kicked Chester hard in the back of leg, sending the big monkey down to one knee. Further twisting the wrist with one hand, the vampire quickly moved behind Chester's now helpless mass of muscles. He reached around with his free hand and grabbed Chester's esophagus at the front of his throat underneath the jaw. His thumbnail pressed inward on one side, the other four fingers pressing down on the other. Sharp fingernails, almost to the point of qualifying as claws, indenting the skin, threatened to draw blood at any second.

The vampire looked up at Slight One, who stood still, shock and fear covering his face. Slight One, trembling, looked helplessly at Chester, tried to choke out some words. He failed.

The vampire roughly gripped down on Chester's esophagus, until his fingertips touched behind the windpipe, deep in the neck. The claws punctured the skin, knives through tender flesh. Blood spilled down Chester's neck and onto his chest.

Blood vessels ruptured in Chester's pleading eyes as his oxygen–deprived face quickly deepened from red to purple. The vampire twisted with a savage grunt and rent outward, ripping the esophagus out completely, rupturing both carotid arteries, and pulling out supporting musculature in the process. It sounded like wet sackcloth being torn.

Arterial blood spewed six feet.

Slight One's eyes popped large, his mouth dropped open in an attempt to scream. All that came out of his mouth was a small, high-pitched wail, like a puppy suddenly afraid of the dark. He watched in disbelief as the blood continued to gush and gurgle out of the grapefruit – sized hole in Chester's neck. He saw the stranger, still behind Chester, holding the mass of red, wet tissue high and out to the right, carefully avoiding the spraying crimson from Chester's rapidly dying body. The vampire then tossed the dripping neck tissue aside and roughly pushed Chester forward, away from him. Chester was dead by the time his nose and front teeth broke against the pavement.

The vampire bent down and wiped his hand off on Chester's clothing. He stood back up, calmly, pushed his glasses up on his nose. Slight One stood there, paralyzed. On any other night, the vampire might have felt sorry for him.

But not this night.

He stepped forward, closing the distance between himself and the Slight One. Slight One stepped back, but had nowhere to run. Slight One panicked and reached for the door. There was no outside knob or latch, just his frantic palm slipping over smooth metal.

Slight One's hand snaked behind himself. Towards a weapon in his back pocket, the vampire assumed.

The vampire opened his mouth, bared his fangs.

Adrenaline kicked in for Slight One. In true fight or flight mode, he pulled a large lock blade knife out of his back pocket. He brought it up and out, opening the blade with his thumb. The blade, already in an arc, locked into place with an audible *click!*

Grunting with effort, Slight One caught the advancing vampire by surprise and actually managed to plunge the knife directly into his left chest. The blade buried a full four inches up to its hilt. The vampire coughed and growled, staggering backwards.

Slight One smiled, triumphant. "Take that, bitch. Fucking die!" He waited, expecting his enemy to fall to the pavement, as dead as Chester. "Fucking die!"

The vampire grimaced in pain, steadied himself on his feet. Slight One watched with a spreading satisfaction, confident this Stranger was dying, his chest cavity filling up with blood. His face fell when the vampire shook it his head, clearing it, as if shaking off a bad dream.

"Now look what you did," the vampire chided. He gripped the knife embedded in his chest, and with one quick, sharp motion, pulled it out. No blood whatsoever. "You ruined my jacket."

Slight One tried to not piss his pants.

"I got this jacket for over forty years ago. Do you know how hard it is to find one of these now?"

The vampire lifted the jacket away from his chest, and checked the wound inside. Through the jacket, ruined the shirt, between the ribs, and through the heart. Punctured the lung, too, dammit.

Painful as hell.

He would be fine by tomorrow night, of course, but that was not really the point, now was it? This bottle-blonde twinkle-dee arrogant little bastard had fucking *stabbed* him!

He tossed the knife over his shoulder. It clinked onto the ground somewhere behind him. Angry, vindictive, he focused on Slight One and surged forward.

"You know why this night has gone so bad for you?" he asked.

Slight One trembled, unable to speak, unable to comprehend what he was seeing.

The vampire, slinging off his sunglasses, grabbed Slight One and hauled him up off his feet. " Because *my* fangs are real."

Slight One dangled several inches above the ground and stared downward at the unholy creature beneath him. Black eyes, bottomless.

Remorseless.

Evil.

The type of evil Slight One thought was hip, and edgy, and oh so cool; the type of evil he aspired to. But now he saw what Evil was, now understood for the first time what it took to carry something like that within oneself, and he realized this was out of his league.

His bowels moved involuntarily. The foul stench lifted upwards, and he began crying, blubbering for his life. All he wanted to do was go home.

The vampire, disgusted with Slight One's cowardice even more than his smell, held him outwards so he did not get any of the loose stool dripping out the bottom of the pants legs on him. He set the hapless human on the ground, then grabbed him by the throat. With a forceful downward pressure, he forced his victim to his knees. He wrenched Slight One's head back, so he had no choice but to look at him.

Slight One's eyes bulged in deep, primitive, primordial fear. The last thing he saw in this world was the vampire's gaping maw, lined with sharp teeth and fangs, descending savagely upon his throat. The vampire clamped down, cutting off respiration.

All that came out of Slight One was a small gasp and a gurgle.

His vision narrowed, the periphery fading to black. For a moment, it appeared as if he was peering down a long tunnel or section of pipe. There was something down there at the end. He could not make it out.

Then, even that fell behind a veil, thickening to black nothingness.

CHAPTER TWELVE

Anxious and waiting for a phone call, sleep had eluded Antonio Vargas. Insomnia frequently visited him, an occupational hazard due to the stressful nature of his work, so this came as no surprise tonight.

He stood on the balcony of his twenty-fourth floor condo, with views of the bay to the west, the airport to the northwest. In the distance lay Point Loma, Ballast Point, and the great Pacific Ocean beyond. Of course, at three in the morning, the airport was dormant, and he could not see beyond the lights of the bay. The Ocean, deep black molasses, remained enwrapped in mystery.

Standing there in slippers, silk pajama pants and a matching robe left untied exposing his thickening middle, the cool night air clung to the hairs on the backs of his hands. Vargas could discern the tiny droplets clinging to his skin.

He could not move forward with his next order of business until he got the call, and he chaffed at waiting. As someone who ran a drug empire that generated three million dollars a day, he had not succeeded by being patient. But El Gecko's death had come at an inopportune moment. Antonio was overextended because of a legitimate real estate deal he had invested in that was taking longer than planned to generate returns. And with Downing still alive, Vargas found himself completely jammed up. His buyers were impatient for more product. If they did not buy from him, then they would buy from someone else. He had urged patience, and they were giving him the benefit of the doubt. For now.

Sighing, he pushed himself off the safety rail and padded inside, leaving the sliding glass door open. Earlier in his life, he would never be so careless. What if an assassin with a high-powered rifle was in position in a nearby building? Nowadays, Vargas conceded that a sniper's bullet might be the quickest solution to his problems.

He walked across the living room's thick carpeting and into the open-concept kitchen. He threw melting ice into a glass, poured Diet Soda from a two-liter bottle. Tan bubbles popped and fizzed on top as the darker liquid flooded over the ice cubes until they floated and clinked together.

The irony did not escape him.

He himself did not drink, smoke, or take drugs of any kind. He had tried all these things when he was younger, of course. He kept cigars in his humidor for friends and party guests, but that was it. He took medications prescribed by his doctor. He was no druggie. He just got rich by selling to people who were.

He sipped, felt the slightly acrid taste wash over his tongue and cascade down his throat. He gulped down half the glass right then.

Pure Nirvana.

Vargas retraced his path across the living room carpet, glass cradled in his hand at waist level. He stepped back out onto the frigid balcony. The lights of the Gaslamp glowed beneath him with pulsating energy, though the streets were mostly quiet now.

To the north, the area known as Banker's Hill, where commercial and residential real estate merged and commingled, the lights were sparse. Looking right, his gaze drifted eastward, to a huge black hole in the night. Very few lights at all. Balboa Park, sleeping the night away. On the other side of the park rested the San Diego Zoo.

He sipped again, unsettled. He realized he was frequently unsettled these days. Insomnia. Tension headaches. Increased irritability. Stomach problems, too. Dyspepsia was a bitch. Getting worse.

Merely maintaining his status quo, just keeping what he had, had become a full time job. Doing what he enjoyed, the actual deals, had almost become incidental to that. The deals were easy. He only dealt with people he knew and had dealt with successfully before. He brought money; they brought drugs. He bought the drugs, and sold to his buyers down line. Hell, he was more like an Amway distributor than a drug dealer.

He again thought of getting out of the Life. He had toyed with the concept a lot lately. Let someone younger and hungrier fight for the scraps. Sure, there could be a vacuum left if he split the scene, but nature abhors a vacuum. The others would be happy to fight over it. He could anoint his own successor, and retire to a non-extradition country. Easy peasey.

Antonio already had his "out" whenever he decided to use it.

He had deposited fourteen million dollars, discreetly of course, over time in a bank in Costa Rica. He had bought that two bedroom, two bath bungalow on the beach just a few miles outside Puerto Limon, on the Atlantic side of the country.

A leather duffle hidden in his closet contained over forty thousand dollars in various world currencies, some toiletries, a handgun, and a change of clothes. He could grab the bag; leave everything in the apartment.

Be gone before anyone knew.

Instead of heading to the San Diego airport, which is what everyone on both sides of law enforcement would expect him to do, he would slip across the border at Otay Mesa or Calexico – NOT at San Ysidro - take a taxi a few miles to the airport, and pay cash for a flight to Costa Rica. He could be beyond American jurisdiction in a matter of minutes, and safe in his bungalow in less than eight hours.

As long as Vargas greased a few palms with the local officials, he could live there the rest of his life. American Law Enforcement would never touch him.

The wind kicked up, chilling him. He balanced his glass on the safety rail and pulled his robe around him. He tied the silk belt – it was actually more sash than belt – around his waist. It did not help.

The cell phone in his robe pocket lit up and vibrated in its staccato *bzzt* – pause pattern pleading for Vargas to answer. His hand snaked into the pocket, grabbed the phone and retrieved it. He grasped his glass off the railing as his thumb punched the button on the phone he now pressed to his ear.

"Vargas."

At the other end of the line, Rick Oakley spoke. "Here's what we know, sir." Vargas listened, knowing Oakley would likely answer all his questions without him having to ask them.

"Is there anything else?" Vargas asked when Oakley completed his report.

"No sir."

"When he's done, send him to me."

"Understood, sir."

Vargas pressed the END CALL button without even looking. He sat down in one of the lounge chairs on the balcony. He sipped his drink, staring blankly out across the city nightscape.

He felt better now. Rudy had taken his pinch like a man and not told the cops anything. Vargas had figured that's what would happen, but Rudy had never been arrested before. And you simply don't know if a tough guy is truly tough until everything turns to shit, the world slides sideways. In times of adversity, people show the world precisely who they are. Rudy Valdez had proven himself worthy as far as Antonio Vargas was concerned.

Yet sleep still eluded him.

As a younger man, this had never been a problem for him. The more successful he became, the more plotting and strategy he had been forced to employ. Now, his entire life seemed like nothing more than one long chess game. He couldn't go to the bathroom, or get laid without running a mental checklist of how it might affect the rest of his day, the rest of his week.

Hell. No wonder he couldn't sleep.

His bed, a gigantic California King, squatted comfortably in the middle of his bedroom. Two women slept there. One white, and one Latina, both of them spent. Vargas could not remember their names, but he had appreciated both their enthusiasm, and their willingness to work together. But even after that delightful interlude, true peace still escaped him. They had fallen asleep on either side of him, and he knew the girls would welcome him back, all warm bodies, caressing hands and legs, soft kisses.

And yet he continued sitting in his chair on his balcony, staring out across the city at three in the morning. He considered yet again the matter of Reginald Downing. This sneaky bastard had infiltrated his organization. What a con he had perpetrated. Everyone had been fooled, Vargas included.

And that's really what hurt most of all. Vargas had considered Downing – in the guise of Jorge – as more than simply an employee. He had considered him a confidant, and even a friend. Downing had deceived them all, plotting their downfall. What's worse, Downing had all the intel to build a Federal case that would put them all in prison for life, perhaps send some to Death Row.

So Downing had to die, die, die. There was no going back. Even if he wanted to, he could not. His rivals, who already knew he was vulnerable, would see it as weakness, and weakness around drug traffickers is like blood in shark-infested waters – it turns into a feeding frenzy.

Vargas did not like killing cops. It guaranteed law enforcement on your neck with relentless intensity. Cops considered an attack on one as an attack against all.

He considered alternatives, explored contingencies. He made a few more momentous decisions. Once done, he had a viable plan that tied up all loose ends.

For the first time in a long time, he felt rather good about things. Now all he had to do was work his plan. He held his cold glass up to his mouth and tilted backwards, draining the rest of his glass.

The showerhead exploded projectile water droplets downward into the vintage claw foot tub. The water warmed almost instantly, and was steaming up the bathroom mirror in less than a minute.

Stripped naked, the vampire stepped into the tub and closed the shower curtain around him, enshrouding himself in a plastic cocoon. Blood and makeup ran down his face and body, turned to rivulets coursing their way down his legs, off his feet. The cloudy water circled the drain once, maybe twice, before gurgling its way downwards through the pipes.

It had been after four in the morning when he finally pulled his Lexus to a stop in the parking area reserved for residents near his apartment. Still covered in sticky blood from earlier when he threw the two corpses into that nearby dumpster, he considered his options.

Checking quickly to make sure no one was out, he dashed at vampire speed from his car and up the stairs to his dark apartment door. There was no bulb in the light fixture above. He had taken it out long ago. He silently turned his key, opened the door a split, and dodged inside, a wisp of smoke, not really seen, only half-sensed.

Locking the door behind him, the vampire peeled off his bloody clothes as he walked. The punctured muscle in his chest twinged tenderly as it stretched and moved when he shucked off his jacket, and then his shirt.

Holding the garments in his hand, the vampire strode into the bathroom. Two laundry hampers waited by the door, side by side. The one nearer was for his regular laundry. The far one, lined with a plastic bag, was for clothes he needed to burn or otherwise dispose of. He tossed his clothes in this last one, then hooked the edge of the front of one foot on the heel of the other boot, and heaved upward.

His stocking foot came out easily. Standing on one leg, he raised the other foot upwards and inwards, making his legs look like he was creating the number 4. He grabbed the toe and heel of the remaining boot and pulled.

He inspected the boots closely. Some blood splatters remained, but nothing major. He placed them by the door, then peeled off his leather pants. Somehow no splatters had contaminated them.

Naked, the vampire moved to the toilet. He had not peed since waking up, and he had fed recently, so the need was great. He aimed towards the water and let go. What came out was not urine in the human sense. His body had ingested and filtered the plasma in the blood, so what came out was actually a more intense lemon yellowish fluid, thicker than water, almost syrupy. There was no pain in urination for him, as one might expect if a human eliminated such a viscous fluid. Rather, the vampire only felt a relief similar to what he had experienced in life. He wiped the last globules, which tenaciously hung to the underside of his penis, with a square of tissue paper.

As he finished up and his thoughts turned to taking a shower, a faint but familiar pressure in his lower abdomen made itself known. The vampire smiled. Of course, he thought. I've fed, and my last meal, already digested, must be eliminated.

He turned around and sat down on the toilet. He relaxed, clearing his mind. He realized this was an apt metaphor for his entire vampire existence. A lot of it was similar or the same, except for those parts that were different. And oh, those parts that were different...

The vampire realized he had finished defecating. Like billions of humans before him, he wiped, tossed the paper in the toilet. He stood up and reached out for the handle to flush.

His eye drifted down to the water. In it, submerged, was his scat. Intensely black, semisolid, and thick. Like roof pitch or road tar, with red tendrils drifting out, digested blood infusing into the surrounding water in the bowl. It looked just the same as it had been for over a hundred years.

No change at all.

The first time he had seen his own stool after he had been reborn to the night, he had been shocked and frightened. He was sure something was terribly wrong. He was certain some strange malady afflicted his body. Well, of course a strange malady afflicted his body. And of course, something was indeed terribly wrong. He was a vampire.

He had immediately gone to a library. Large cities like Hoboken, right across the river from New York, had libraries open very late indeed. Some of the finer ones even had separate reading and smoking rooms. One could even order a scotch or a whiskey, if one was so inclined. One could spend several hours in the evening in one, large, quiet, baroque room of the library, sip whisky (or scotch!), smoke a cigar, and read newspapers, magazines, or books. One would be left alone in peace. One could wile away half the night there, if one was so inclined.

The vampire had calmed himself during the walk to the venerable old building. He had wondered briefly why it was that library buildings, no matter what their true age, always looked old, stodgy, and ready to crumble at any moment? Walking in out of the night, he had asked the librarian on duty for the Medical Reference section.

She had glanced up blandly from her bookkeeping work, then her mouth fell open in shock. His fedora brim pulled down low, he had tilted his pointed chin downward to cover his eyes from her. If she had seen his eyes, she would have screamed. Then he would have had no choice but to kill her.

He had told her he realized he looked a bit pale, and that was the purpose for his inquiry. Fearing he might have something contagious, she had directed him to the appropriate section of the library, which just happened to be located in the basement of the grand, old, crumbling building. He had found some general medical books, and had begun pouring over them furiously. When he found his answer, he had almost cried with relief.

The new vampire discovered it was a known medical fact that when a person swallowed blood, or had an upper gastrointestinal bleed, like from a perforated ulcer or similar condition, the blood would move along the digestive tract just like anything else. And the small intestine would try to digest and extract nutrients out of it just like with anything else. Sodium, potassium, hemoglobin, everything.

Once this mixture - called "*chime*", as he discovered - passed into the large intestine, the large intestine, the body's water recycling plant, would do its job. It would extract all or most of the leftover water, firming up the consistency of the stool. After that, peristaltic action, a series of smooth muscle contractions exerted on the intestines, pushed the stool along its track until it passed through the rectum and exited the body.

As it turned out, this was true of both humans and vampires. Who would have thought?

And there, standing naked in his bathroom in the early twenty-first century, the vampire smiled at his former ignorance and naiveté. Live and learn, he thought. Well, in his case, true learning leading to wisdom did not occur for him until after he died.

And now, as he rinsed the shampoo out of his hair, he thought back to earlier in the evening when he had killed the Slight One. Part of his Dark Abilities was being able to sense the evil in people. The other side was, if he touched them, made physical contact, his brain was bombarded with visions and memories of the perversions these people enjoyed. Usually it was shocking, even to him. But sometimes, just sometimes, it was actually painful, like an intense blade, forged of intense bright white light, stabbing him directly in the front of the skull.

Tonight had not been like that, thank God. When the Slight One's blood had flooded the vampire's mouth and spilled down his swiftly swallowing throat, he had been blasted with visions of whips and chains, gay sex with Chester and twisted servitude. Chester had been the subservient one. Slight One had been the "top". Chester had gone out with Slight One whenever the Blonde Dom had wanted, bringing home sometimes willing partners for a time of true debauchery.

The vampire turned the water off. The showerhead trickled off rapidly. A few extra drops fell into the bathtub, then nothing. He pushed the curtain back, metal curtain rings grinding along the rod. He grabbed a towel hanging on a nearby rack, stepped out. He towel dried his hair first, then systematically worked his way from top to bottom.

He padded silently to the lavatory. He gazed at his reflection in the mirror. His eyes seemed clearer now. The blood meal earlier had given him much needed sustenance. His skin no longer had such a waxy pallor. Indeed, except for his eyes and fangs, neither of which ever changed, he could almost pass for human.

The knife wound on his chest had already closed. By tomorrow night, there would be nothing but a scar.

He pulled out his toothbrush and toothpaste. Indeed, another example of how similar his vampire existence was to the human one he had foolishly tossed aside. He still had to brush his teeth and floss, otherwise his breath would smell like Death itself.

When he finished, he walked through the dark apartment and into his bedroom. He threw some comfortable lounging clothes on, then headed into the other bedroom. He had set it up as a combination office and study. He had placed a modern, tubular aluminum computer desk near the window. Even though heavy curtains adorned this window, as indeed on all windows in the apartment, he always made sure left the curtains slightly parted. That way, when he was working, trading stocks and commodities for his Asian clients, he could keep an eye on the coming daylight.

He enjoyed his job, felt a sense of accomplishment when his advice or actions helped his clients save money in a bad market, or make money in a good one. The ebb and flow of the financial markets, much like the rise and fall of the ocean's tides, fascinated him. Sometimes he became so intensely concentrated, he would lose all sense of time.

When the first yellow fingers stabbed their way across the windowsill, he knew it was time to shut down work and get some rest. Depending on the time of year, the Asian markets would already be closed by then. But in late spring and summer, when the sky began to lighten well before five thirty, it could become a problem.

The vampire sat down at his computer desk and opened his laptop. He depressed the ON button, then powered up the printer. Although Friday and Saturday were his weekend days because of the time difference between the U.S. and the Asian stock markets, like any broker, he had to stay atop international business developments as they occurred over the weekend. These developments often had a direct influence on markets.

A CEO stepping down, a quarterly profit report that fell short of expectations, a management shakeup and shuffling of personnel, could all spell trouble for a company's stock price, and could set off a cascade of events that could affect other companies, other sectors, even the market system itself. Even natural disasters like tsunamis, hurricanes, or in the case of commodities like corn, soybeans, or wheat, a summer drought could kill a company. The closest markets usually bore the brunt in the first instance, but often other markets would become affected, like waves rippling out across the electronic pond.

The vampire's main screen lit up, a real-time evaluation of the Hong Kong and Tokyo markets. Hong Kong was down twenty-nine points from their opening numbers. Tokyo was down forty-two. Along the bottom of the screen, a stock price ticker scrolled from right to left, showing companies by ticker symbol and closing price. The vampire's eyes danced across the numbers, as he formulated preliminary plans on what he might do with his own money, and what he might advise his clients Sunday night.

He punched a few buttons on his computer, and his screen changed instantly. The graphics for the New York Stock Exchange and NASDAQ appeared. The corresponding ticker ran from right to left across the lower band of the screen. He studied it for a few moments, making sure he double-checked his numbers.

Satisfied his investments were doing well, he sat back in his chair and stretched. The ancient bones in his back crackled and popped audibly. His gaze drifted around the room and fell to the windowsill. A pale blue glow infiltrated from outside, through the glass pane, and across the white paint. The dawn was coming, but actual sunrise was still at least a half hour away.

Still a bit peckish, the vampire shut down his computer. He rose from his chair and crept silently into the kitchen. With no lights glaring, the kitchen waited for him in what humans would perceive as pitch darkness. But his vampire eyes saw the room in swirling gloom, shadows like black puddles, colors desaturated almost to the point seeing in black and white.

He grabbed the refrigerator door handle, pulled the door open. He reached in quickly, grabbed a bag of the expired Blood Bank blood. He let the door swing shut while he rinsed out the same glass he had used earlier. Holding the bag upside down over the glass, he applied steady pressure, squeezing thick goopy blood into the glass until it was about half full.

The vampire paused, considering whether or not that would be enough. Eventually, he decided gluttony was unseemly, so he tossed the bag on the counter. He picked up the glass, placed it inside the microwave. Closing the door, he set the timer for thirty seconds. That would warm it to somewhere close to human body temperature, but not so warm he would not be able to drink it.

He had made that mistake once before. In his ignorance, he had microwaved a blood meal for too long a time. It had, of course, overheated, and had begun to cook. The vampire found out that if blood got too warm, the red blood cells would explode - a phenomenon familiar to laboratory workers called *hemolysis* - releasing all potassium and hemoglobin from inside the cells into the circulating blood itself. Furthermore, the protein within the base of the cells denatured much like an egg white when fried. The sloppy result turned a perfectly enticing glass of warm red blood into a disgusting brownish mess with the look and consistency of melted chocolate.

Naturally, such a debacle was undrinkable. It stunk to high heaven, too. It had taken him several nights to get the smell out of his house.

Now, the vampire waited patiently. The microwave completed its cycle. The rotating plate inside provided for even heating. The dim light inside the chamber went off, and the microwave bell went off with an optimistic *ding!* The vampire had always thought that bell was an electronic equivalent to someone jumping up and proudly yelling, *"ta data!"*.

He opened the door with the push of a button. He gingerly wrapped his fingers around the glass and pulled it out. He smiled almost instantly. His fingers warmed, not burned. The red liquid swirled and ran down the inside of the glass. The vampire lifted the glass, not unlike a connoisseur judging wine. He brought the glass to his lips and sipped, savoring the taste.

He drank again, more deeply this time. He drank one last time, emptying the glass. He sighed and smacked his lips. He rinsed the glass out at the sink and placed it upside down on a towel on the counter to dry.

Pleasantly full, the vampire glided through the hallway. He glanced into his office room. He noticed the pale blue glow that had been spilled across the windowsill was now wider, brighter, and had morphed almost to pale yellow.

Sunrise was just moments away.

The vampire headed into the master bedroom. As was his custom, he closed the door to the hallway, locked it with a deadbolt from the inside. He crossed the room; double-checked the Velcro fasteners on the window curtains. Assured they were secure and windows locked from the inside, he felt better.

Nobody believed in vampires anymore. There were so many fakes around, so much silly merchandise, movies, CD's, DVD's, and all that. Vampires had now been thrust into the modern pop culture. But now, the old monsters who used to be seen as unholy villains were now revered, seen as tragic heroes, romantic Lotharios, or worse, pop icons.

This whimsical view of something ancient and evil the humans thought of as nothing more than wisps and shadows, worked for the vampire. Anonymity had become his greatest weapon, the strongest tool in his arsenal to ensure his continued survival.

The greatest trick the Devil ever pulled was convincing the World he did not exist, right?

The vampire, deep in thought now at the end of his night, pursed his lips. Naked, he sat down on his bed. Fatigue washed over him.

But the Devil *WAS* real, he knew. The vampire had seen enough Evil in the world over the years. It ebbed and flowed, surged and waned, always getting defeated, but always circling back around in some other form.

The slave trade.

Nazi Germany.

The rise of the Soviet Union.

Public lynching in the South carried out by racists with an agenda.

Communism in Cuba, Korea, China.

Dictators that live like Gods while their own people starve outside the palace gates.

Sheiks, strangling the world's economic neck like a proverbial chicken because they wielded control over production and export of a black gooey substance that existed mostly under their sands.

Religious fanatics that guided their flocks to mass death and destruction in places like Guyana.

But God existed, too. There was goodness in the world, too. There was compassion, mercy.

People dedicated their lives to servitude and poverty to help their fellow human beings. High-priced American doctors, who every year, spent part of their time in third world countries providing free medical care to the world's neediest patients. Even the random young person who helped an old lady up the stairs with her groceries qualified.

These two forces were continually at odds. Diametrically opposed, they constantly battled one another to a stalemate of sorts, forever, throughout time.

Yes, God definitely existed; the vampire was certain of it. But the vampire did not understand Him.

Shrugging off melancholy thoughts, the vampire laid down in bed. He pulled the heavy quilt up, way up, past his chin. He was not cold, but if anything happened to the curtains, the quilt was thick enough to protect him from sunlight shining across the bed.

He quieted himself, as he had learned so many years ago. He stared at the ceiling, but did not focus his eyes. He looked through the ceiling, past the ceiling, and into nothing at all.

Then, the dawn broke outside. The sun peered over the horizon, bathing the treetops and the streets with golden light. Inside his apartment, snug in his bed, the vampire... died.

It happened in the same manner it always did, every morning, every dawn. A small sigh of air escaped his lungs. His black eyes changed, went pale and milky. His skin dehydrated, sank around the bones, stretched across the hollows of his body, sticking to the tendons. His lips pulled thin across his lower face, then slowly retracted back in rictus, exposing his teeth, his fangs, which yellowed and turned dull. Skin cells, dead and desiccated, curled upward and flaked, forming a light dust across his grayish blue forehead.

Barring any kind of unforeseen circumstances, the vampire's lifeless corpse would lie in the bed, unmoving, quilt pulled up past its chin, dead to the world. And it would lie there until nightfall, at which time, the vampire, through twisted forces of nature he still did not comprehend even after all this time, would come back to life, reanimate, and continue on with his long, slow nocturnal existence.

Journal entry, Monday, February 1st.

In 1897, a drunken Irishman, well known and laboriously tolerated for his notoriously highbrow aspirations and his equally notorious lowbrow abilities published what would become his most enduring literary achievement. It was not the only contrived and vulgar ghost story he would impose upon the world, but it would be associated with him throughout his life, after his death, and on to this day. In his novel, he called vampires "children of the night".

And for one brief, shining moment, he was absolutely correct.

Bram Stoker, a modern man of his day, had not believed in his own product. He had approached his story from the position that his main character and his strange brides, the infamous "children of the night", were nothing more than myth. A fable to tell around the campfire and frighten children.

Stoker could not have been more mistaken.

Stoker's vampire was a fictional composite, based on a real-life Romanian warlord of particular brutality who had fought the Turks during the Middle Ages. The vampire brides were pure fiction, plot devices to up the sex factor as they seduced their victim, Jonathan Harker.

I think Stoker was afraid of women, afraid of the sexual powers they lorded over men. He published during the so-called "gay 90's", something of a sexual revolution for that generation. Of course, syphilis and gonorrhea became more prevalent, so the old "promiscuity equals death" thing was an underlying theme in his novel, along with seductive women being only out for a man's body fluids.

Stoker paid real vampires a disservice, due to his ignorance and lack of belief. He was constrained by his own fears and sexual hang-ups, so I forgive him. He drew all the vampires in his fable as one-dimensional characters, pure evil, only after blood and domination, motivated only by lust. And to be fair, I have met a few vampires like that in my time.

But I have also met vampires who with an affinity for humans. Even after death they identify with mortals, have a problem drinking blood from a living host. I personally don't get that, but, whatever. Maybe they stay connected with their past.

I find the practice impractical and imprudent. I only felt close so few people when I was alive, and felt a disconnect from others. So I keep humanity at arms' length, especially since I have been dead for almost a century.

Stoker makes me giggle.

We do not turn into wisps of smoke. We do not turn into wolves, bats, or anything else. We cannot command the beasts of the field, nor the winds, nor the seas. Nor do we hypnotize our prey or put women into a swooning trance of orgasmic delight. The only place where that happens is the Late Late Show.

We simply... are what we are.

Vampires are not social creatures. Apex predators, we are solitary by nature. Continually in motion, we spend our time searching for prey.

Some of my kind prefer their food to come to them. Ambush predators, I call them. Hanging out in alleys, stalking Skid Row, pretending to be drunkards, meth heads, whatever. If that is how they wish to do it that is their business. I find it inefficient.

As a rule, we have no need to set ourselves up for "vampire groupies". Quite frankly, I have never understood the attraction. To see someone become so enthralled that they willingly submit to periodic draining.

That whole "moth to the flame" thing, I guess.

They eventually get drained one too many times and they die. Then the vampire responsible must make a choice. Either welcome a newborn vampire into this world of shadow and mist, or destroy the body immediately.

We pass for human as long as no one looks too closely. On the occasion that we cross paths on the hunt, we give each other a wide berth.

Too many hunters panic the herd.

But, of course, Stoker had not known any of this; that the legend of the vampire is much more than legend, more than an allegory to explain the humans' fear of death. It was more than a Victorian "smoke and mirrors" cover up for sexual intercourse and its accompanying transmittable diseases.

If Stoker had known the truth of our existence, and had understood what we really are, I can't help but wonder and ponder one simple question.

What kind of book would he have written about us then?

CHAPTER THIRTEEN

The same sunrise that sent the vampire under his covers cast piercing light through the slightly parted curtains of Captain Morris Horn's tiny bedroom. Horn lay sprawled across the bed on his stomach, legs straight, arms flung out from his thick body. The yellow shafts drifted across the quilt, fingers inching ever closer towards his pug face. He frowned in his sleep and turned his head away.

At precisely seven o'clock, the alarm clock on the bedside nightstand erupted into infuriating, relentless beeping and chirping. Horn budged, but did not jump. He finally reached out a blind arm. His hand slapped at the nightstand, looking for the snooze button. Not finding it, his bleary eyes opened.

"Shut the fuck up!" he growled. He brought his clenched fist down on the snooze button hard enough to snap it off and send it flying onto the floor.

Regretting having to face yet another day, Horn rolled over and swung his legs over the edge. He suddenly found himself in a sitting up. Damn. Fog enshrouded his mind. His head throbbed. He closed his eyes and rubbed his temples to no avail.

Horn had not slept well the night before.

He had come home to an empty, dark apartment, long after nightfall. Typical. He had swung by the grocery store and had bought one of those pre-cooked chickens in a bag, the kind kept warm in the store by heat lamps near the deli case. The store helpfully placed accompanying items like pre-made mashed potatoes in gray containers, pints of pre-made macaroni and cheese, flavored cornbread stuffing.

Upon entering, he had turned on the light, then dropped the chicken on the counter. He strode over to his musty living area and dropped the case files of "the *Sulu Sea* debacle" on his stained, rickety, grimy coffee table. He knew he needed to clean the place top to bottom. But Horn just didn't give a shit. He had more important things on his mind.

He stepped into his small, single bedroom, kicking off his uncomfortable black oxfords. They needed polishing. Badly. But that never crossed Horn's mind. After standing, sitting, and walking all day, his feet hurt, and that's all he cared about.

He yanked his tie away from his pinched throat, fumbled with the top button, then made his way down his chest and belly, opening the shirt wide. His dark skin appeared oily black against the pale fabric in the semidarkness. Shrugging his shoulder holster off, he laid it atop the nightstand, then tossed the shirt onto the floor. He pulled his belt out of his waistband, peeled his pants off.

Standing there in the quiet apartment, alone in his underwear, Horn looked around, wondering how his life had come to... this.

He'd gained and lost a wife and two children somewhere along the way. Her name was Mandy, short for Amanda. They had two children, Adam, and Abigail. He had been a cop when they'd met, he told himself. She knew that. And he made sure she knew what that meant, that she understood what impact that being a cop – and being married to a cop! - could have on a marriage.

He had been honest with her from the start. Being a cop – or being a good cop, at least - was not a job, but a lifestyle. And that lifestyle would always have to come first. The stakes of what he did were too high for anything less. Mandy had assured him that she could handle it.

Mandy had been wrong.

They had been married about eleven years when things finally came to a grinding halt. Long enough for the marriage to be considered a "long – term marriage" under California divorce law. He knew he would not get away cheap. Even if Mandy was civil and decent, he was going to take a bath in a divorce, and he knew it.

Things had been going poorly for a long time, but he had never seen fit to take the time and effort to fix it. There was always some scumbag who needed to be caught, convicted, jailed, taken out of societal circulation. There was always a report that needed to be filed. Evidence to be inventoried. Night School to be passed. A Bachelor's Degree to be obtained. A career to build. Promotions to be made.

And when it was said and done, Horn had succeeded. He had moved up through the ranks, from Patrolman to Sergeant, then to Detective, Detective Sergeant, Lieutenant, and now Captain. Not bad for a black kid from the wrong side of the tracks in Texas who had landed in San Diego by luck of the draw when he had joined the

Marine Corps. But he had been an absentee father, cool and aloof, and had been a neglectful, even uncaring, husband.

The marriage ended with a whimper, not a roar. No high drama, no screaming, no yelling, no recriminations. No thrown frying pans; no broken dishes. Just one Saturday evening, he was home sitting on the sofa, watching TV, a glass of iced tea in his hand. Mandy had walked into the room, and calmly stated that she wanted a divorce.

Horn, shocked, turned off the TV. He took a sip of his sweet tea as she stood there, awaiting his response as he turned this over in his head. Mandy stood several feet away, holding her hands nervously in front of her. He realized how much courage she had mustered up to come in here and tell him that.

Rather than react violently (as she had feared he would), he nodded his head with a long, exhausted sigh. He told her he understood, and that he understood why. When she tried to continue, he cut her off with a wave of his hand. She didn't need to justify herself. He got it. He promised to do right by her.

Mandy got the kids, the house. She got child support, and she made sure Horn had liberal visitation. She turned down spousal support. She made more money. In the end, he moved out of the nice neighborhood with the great schools and CCR's, into the dingy apartment east of downtown he now occupied.

Had it already been six years?

Now the kids were both teens, heavily involved in school activities. They rarely had time for him nowadays. Adam was a junior, already thinking about college. With excellent grades and a keen intellect, scholarships from prestigious schools were in the lad's future. A whiz in science and math, he wanted to study Chemical Engineering.

Abigail, a sophomore, played violin in the orchestra. Not as academically inclined as her brother, she had middling grades – strictly B's and C's with A's in music. Abigail also played guitar, drums, and keyboards. Hell, she was damned musical prodigy as far as Horn was concerned.

She must have gotten it from her mother. Horn knew damn well it didn't come from his side of the family. She jammed with some neighborhood kids in a garage band, and she had many friends.

Adam, more introverted, was content to stay home most weekends and read books.

Mandy had recently made partner in her law firm. Good for her. Corner office, nice view, big pay raise, and now, profit sharing. He suspected she was seeing one of the men there. He knew her well enough to know that little spring in her step when she was sexually satisfied. She had it in the early days of their marriage. But he had not seen that gleam in her eye for a long time. Now it was back. He never pried, and she never volunteered anything.

He knew the mature, sophisticated thing would be to be happy for her. The best he could manage was to accept it as none of his business.

Horn opened a top drawer on his scarred, Salvation Army dresser. He pulled out a faded red Hensley shirt and a pair of blue jeans. He grunted a bit as he pulled his new ensemble on, then slipped his dry, cracked feet into a well worn and sublimely comfortable leather loafers.

Shuffling into his living area, he used the remote to turn on the TV, a nineteen-inch flat screen. He tuned in to the local news. He grabbed a beer from the fridge, then heaved himself onto his sofa, which groaned under his weight. He screwed off the top and took a deep swig.

The *Sulu Sea* incident was the top story, but nothing in the report he did not already know. When a commercial break came just twelve minutes in, Horn got up and grabbed the bag of chicken, a roll of paper towels, and sat back down. He sat back down more gingerly this time. He smiled when the couch did not again creak in protest.

Leaning forward, he pushed the file folders to the side and placed the bag on the table. He opened the bag and wrenched a leg portion – both thigh and drumstick – off of the roasted bird's body at the hip. He held it over the bag, letting the juices drip out of the way. Then he bit deeply, rending succulent flesh and savory meat clean off the bone.

As he ate, he found out the weather was going to be lovely tomorrow in America's Finest City. After a few days of warmth, the temperatures would drop once more. Typical weather for San Diego this time of year. He zoned out the rest of the newscast, not paying particular attention. It was always the same – after the weather came a station break, sports, and then the fluffy, feel-good human-interest stories.

Horn consumed the other leg and thigh, the tail, and had started pulling flesh and muscle from the back and breast by the time the newscast ended. In that time, he had finished his first beer, and his second.

When the newscast ran end credits, Horn turned the TV off, then licked his fingers and wiped his hands one last time. He threw the sticky paper towels in the garbage can at the end of the kitchen counter top. He put the leftover chicken on the top shelf inside his almost empty refrigerator.

He would be handling documents, photos and reports that likely would be submitted into evidence. He washed his hands at the sink, dried them on a threadbare hand towel he kept stuffed into the door handle of the barely working freezer on his refrigerator. Horn bought the fridge himself when the one that came with the apartment gave out and the manager dragged his feet with a replacement, Horn found it at a Goodwill for sixty bucks. He was certain the damn thing dated back to the 1970's.

Rubbing the bridge of his nose between his thumb and forefinger, he staggered back towards his measly living area. He flicked on another lamp, a tall one that stood like a metal stalk behind the sofa and illuminated from overhead. The bulb inside was of smaller wattage, so a softer ambient light glowed.

Satisfied he could see without too much eyestrain, Horn sat back down on the sofa. He moved his nearly empty beer bottle away to the far left. He pulled out his new glasses and placed them low on his nose. He tilted his head slightly upwards, and cast his eyes downward, looking down past his nose, mouth partly open.

Damn, he thought. I've lived long enough to become an old man.

He placed photos from the scene in a certain geographical order for where on the dock and ship events had transpired. The photos documented the carnage inflicted. And while Horn did not feel bad for them – they had chosen their path in life, after all – he felt a bit horrified at the absolute brutality. What type of monster could do this to other human beings?

Moving to the preliminary medical reports, he read again and again about the violent causes of death. Disembowelments.

Decapitation. Necks snapped. Multiple massive exsanguinations. One guy, Johnny Wolf, had even had his fucking *heart* cut out – no, not merely cut out, but *ripped* out of his chest, for Christ's sake! - by some weapon or apparatus, origin unknown.

None of it made sense to Horn. And that made him feel insecure, like he was sailing into uncharted waters on this one.

Deep down, he knew Downing was a good cop. He was honest, not on the take. Horn respected that. But Downing as a grandstander, and Horn had disdain for that. Downing had been dubbed a Golden Boy by the Department, even before he graduated the Academy. Young, smooth – skinned and handsome, he had been designated by the Powers That Be to be the new Face of the Department. But the kid had bought into the hype just a little too much for Horn's comfort.

Horn believed Downing had been promoted too quickly, part of a PR agenda that marginalized the efforts and accomplishments of older, more experienced, less photogenic officers. Downing possessed good instincts and had a solid arrest record and a high conviction ratio. But his youth and lack of experience could be a severe liability in the field. Hell, the kid had managed to blow his cover, alert the bad guys, and nearly get himself killed. He was alive because unknown players had decided to show mercy.

That's not inspired investigative police work. That's just dumb luck.

The pieces were there, right in front of him. Horn knew it. He just could not make them fit together into sensible answers. Without answers, he could not build a case for prosecution.

Back to Square One and one hell of a headache. Horn closed the files and shoved them across the table. He tossed his glasses onto the sofa beside him, leaned his head back. He closed his eyes and rubbed his temples against the stress. His breathing slowed, but his headache did not dissipate.

He sat there, feeling like an idiot, knowing he was not going to have any breakthrough tonight. So he hoisted himself up off the sagging sofa, and stumbled to the bathroom.

Like everything else in his apartment, the bathroom was nothing to write home about. It was utilitarian, not luxurious. Fittings consisted of a chipped porcelain pedestal sink, medicine cabinet with dull mirror, a toilet, and a claw foot tub Horn only used for showers. A pale yellow shower curtain, devoid of any design or decoration, hung from a curved aluminum rail that snaked its way around the ceiling, following the outline of the tub.

Horn flipped the light on. Glaring light pierced his eyes and skyrocketed his pain. He pulled open the medicine cabinet door, grabbed a bottle of pills he'd been prescribed for these pesky predicaments. He looked at the label just to make sure he was getting the right thing, but he knew he was. The double check was automatic, like muscle memory.

He pushed down on the top and cracked open the childproof cap, shook two tablets out into his waiting palm. Holding them in place with three fingers, he screwed the cap tight and placed the bottle back on its narrow beveled shelf. He turned the water on, popped the pills into his mouth. He filled a plastic cup with water, took a swallow, then knocked his head back hard as he swallowed again.

The two pills scraped down the inside of his throat, tasting bitter. Try as he might no to, his entire frame shuddered involuntarily. He gulped again, this time tasting bile. It was ironic. Here he was, a big, tough guy, a Marine and career cop. But a simple thing like taking a pill by mouth always gave him the heebie jeebies.

Some things you never outgrow.

He looked at his reflection. How long since he'd cleaned this bathroom, anyway? It didn't matter. Nothing much mattered. His fate was sealed, he knew it – hell, he *accepted* it! - and all that mattered was what good he could do in the world. How many bad people he could catch before he retired, or died?

He turned away from his sad, hanging features: down-turned mouth, red-rimmed eyes. He hit the light off with a down stroke of his hand as he lumbered past the switch. Careening past the useless living room, Horn staggered into his bedroom and threw himself across the bed. He fell flat across the sheets and quilt on his stomach, arms stretched outward, legs straight, feet hanging off the edge.

Horn's massive frame sagged as his muscles finally uncoiled and relaxed. A faint smile danced briefly across his face just before his eyes closed. He was asleep in less than three minutes.

And now, here he was, on a Saturday morning, hitting the snooze button, trying to steal an extra nine minutes of blessed sleep.

Saturday was just another workday for Captain Morris Horn.

Detective Sergeant Nick Castle rode his meticulously maintained vintage motorcycle up to the Police substation. Moving with fluid grace, he braked to a gentle halt. He rode a cruiser. A heavy bike that hugged the pavement for better traction, a big forest green tank up front, big front light for visibility, and with single leather seat slung low over the massive back tire.

He killed the engine with a flick of his right thumb on the handlebar control. With an almost involuntary movement of his left foot, he pushed out the kickstand until it snapped into its position of function. He gingerly leaned the big machine to the left until the kickstand pushed downward into place, holding the entire weight of the motorcycle in a delicate balance, keeping it from tipping over and crashing onto the concrete.

Castle threw his right leg high and wide, rotating on the heel of his left foot. The leg cleared the seat and swung downward, coming to rest flat on the concrete next to his left. He reached up under his chin with gloved hands, loosening the full-face helmet's nylon strap. He yanked, pulling the straps through the eyelet and out. He grabbed the helmet below the face shield and lifted up and back, freeing his head.

His longish dark hair fell back into place. He blinked a bit behind his riding glasses. He bent down with his helmet and secured it by its eyelet into a small locking mechanism located on the side of the bike underneath the left side of the seat.

Castle stepped back a pace and unzipped his leather jacket. It was still cold, but the early morning sun promised to warm things up. He peeled his gloves off, rolled them tightly in his hands, and shoved them into his side jacket pocket.

A dented, slate gray unmarked police car rounded the corner. As it approached, Castle heard the engine, and looked over. He saw Horn's unmistakable face at the wheel. He waited by his custom bike as Horn maneuvered the car towards the slanted parking spaces and pulled into one next to him.

"Morning, Captain," Castle greeted as Horn hauled his girth out of the car.

"Morning," Horn returned tersely. He grabbed the files he had failed to crack the night before, then locked the car door. "How is it you look so refreshed this early on a Saturday?"

Castle shrugged. "Clean living, vitamins and exercise," he said.

Horn thought about his own health and eating habits. "You might have something there."

Castle reached into the custom saddlebags on his bike. He pulled out his copy of the same files Horn possessed. He also pulled out a small, oil-stained bag, filled with an onion bagel and a packet of cream cheese for himself, and two raspberry cheese Danishes for Horn. He held the bag up between them, saying nothing. He swung it gently, side to side.

Horn's face cracked into an uncharacteristic grin. "Now that's what I'm talking about."

Castle knew his best way to his boss's good side was through his stomach. They walked towards the front doors.

"You make much headway last night?" Horn asked.

"Not much," Castle replied.

"Me neither. I tried, but I fell asleep."

Castle looked at his boss, concerned. Horn did not look well. When was the last time this guy had gotten a checkup? When was the last time he'd gone on vacation? Hell, when was the last time he'd gotten laid, for Christ's sake?

"You probably needed the rest."

"Probably."

Horn and Castle walked up the sidewalk and alighted a short flight of steps that deposited them at the front entrance to the Station. Castle grabbed the handle, depressed the latch and swung the door wide. He held it open as Horn passed through, then allowed himself to enter.

The main waiting area was quiet. During the week, a certain level of noise, confusion, and conflict was considered normal as detectives and uniformed police dropped off suspects, processed paperwork, and interviewed witnesses. Compared to that, the place was practically deserted.

The Desk Sergeant, an older cop with a crew cut, a thick handlebar moustache and a thicker torso, looked up from his computer logs. He gave them a perfunctory salute, then went back to his duties. Horn nodded back. He remembered the old cop's name was Jenson, and was waiting for his retirement papers to be approved. Jenson's shift was almost over, his weekend about to begin. He wanted to get done and gone, with everything wrapped up neat and tidy, by Change of Shift.

Horn could not blame him for that.

Castle's dark, all seeing eyes darted around the room. He saw the large biker, all tattoos, long hair, and beard, handcuffed to a bench that was bolted to the floor. Wearing his club's colors with pride, he sat still and glared straight ahead, unblinking, unseeing, silently daring anyone – *ANYONE!* – to try and fuck with him.

Castle noticed the hooker, all attitude and indignation, and all of sixteen years old. She argued with an arresting vice cop who had busted her for solicitation.

She was not a hardcore hooker. She was too clean, too well nourished, and too talkative. She was no street urchin. Street urchins don't have French tipped nails and Brazilian blowouts. More likely she would prove to be some spoiled rich girl who decided to get back at Daddy and the trust fund. So she went slumming with Daddy's Beemer and Visa card, crashed face to face into what the rest of the world liked to call "reality", and found herself in over her head.

She saw him looking over. She snapped her head around, trying to be tough, auburn hair and baby fat in the cheeks and chin.

"What the fuck you looking at?"

Castle grinned as the girl turned back to her Arresting Officer, who had just told her to shut her fucking mouth and wait for Daddy. Castle smiled more broadly as he walked on. Sometimes, you just had to laugh at the stupid shit in life, or it really started seeping into your core, your soul, fundamentally changing you as a person. Castle had seen it happen with a lot of cops. He'd seen it happen with Horn over the years. No way he was going to let it happen to him.

That was why he wore his hair longer, way past the tops of his ears. That was why many of his friends away from the job were not cops. They had nothing to do with law enforcement, and he rarely talked about his job away from the precinct. And it was why he rode his motorcycle whenever he could. These were things he had enjoyed prior to becoming a cop, and these were the things he would enjoy long after he retired.

Castle and Horn pushed open the double doors that opened onto a smaller hallway leading to back offices and interrogation rooms. They quickly turned left at Horn's office door. Horn shoved his key in the lock, turned it as he simultaneously turned the knob. The door pushed back and in, then they were inside.

Castle immediately headed for the coffee maker, which stood, waiting to perk, on a small table off to the side along the far wall. As he passed Horn's desk, he tossed the bag of pastries onto its surface.

Horn rounded the desk and sat down in the worn, comfortable leather high-backed chair. He tossed the file folder on the blotter in front of him. He watched in silence as Castle got the coffee maker filled with water.

"You know," Castle opened as he put a paper filter into the basket, "you should consider buying a ten-dollar coffee grinder and keeping a decent quality whole bean coffee up in here."

Horn thought about this as Castle closed the lid on the coffee maker and hit the ON button.

"You're serious?" Horn asked.

"Why not?" Castle replied, dusting his hands off in front of himself. "Rank has its privileges, Captain. You deserve to drink a decent cup of coffee, not this cheap-assed, Government–issue, mass market swill."

Horn jutted his lower lip out in thought as Castle sat down on the other side of the desk. Horn nodded. "Maybe you're right."

Castle grinned. "Of course I'm right." He pulled his onion bagel and cream cheese packet out of the bag. "That's why I'm a Detective Sergeant in eight years, on the fast track to Lieutenant." He shoved the bag towards Horn. *"Bon appetit!"*

"Ahhhh," Horn sounded. "You have high hopes for yourself."

"Nothing wrong with upward mobility," Castle said.

Horn opened the bag and peered inside just long enough to glimpse two large pastries with tell tale red jelly and yellow custard fillings juxtaposed in the middles.

"You know me all too well," Horn said.

Castle shrugged. He spread cream cheese across the inner surface of his bagel with a small plastic knife. "I'm a cop. I'm supposed to notice the little things, subtle things. Pay attention to the details."

Horn nodded absently, pulling a Danish out of the crumpled white bag in front of him. He bit into the pastry, chewing thoughtfully.

"And what details of our case are you paying attention to?"

Castle smelled the coffee brewing. "All of them," he stated with surety.

"Your conclusions, Sergeant?"

"Only one, sir."

"And that is?"

"That Reggie's account of events is one hundred percent true and accurate. There was only one wild card on the pier. And whoever he was, he killed them all by himself, by hand, as it were, without conventional weaponry as we understand it. And, he spared Reggie's life."

Horn stared at Castle a moment. He knew Castle was completely serious. Castle never showed much humor on the job. He also knew Castle's intuition was seldom off target.

"But why would anyone do that?" Horn asked, thinking out loud. "Why would anyone in the drug trade knowingly save a cop's life?"

"You're assuming whoever did this was in fact in the drug trade,"

This brought Horn's train of thought to an abrupt halt.

"Fact is, Cap, we don't know that. Since we don't know who he is, we have no idea what he is"

"What are you thinking?"

Castle thought a moment longer, then gestured with his hand as he theorized off the top of his head, speaking as quickly as the thoughts formed. "It really kind of feels like something personal, doesn't it? The killer's efficient, effective, practiced at his craft. But these are not 'traditional' professional hits. The killer didn't just kill them, he *slaughtered* them. Like sheep or something. Bloody. Brutal. Grotesque. Like he was sending a message."

Horn got up and poured two mugs of coffee, handed one to Castle. "And he not just let Reggie go, he made a point of letting Reggie go."

Castle pointed at Horn, his thumb and index finger in the classic gunpoint pose. "Exactly."

Horn turned this over in his mind. It actually made sense, even though there were still gaps to be filled. That was why he could not make any progress on his own the night before. He had gotten too hung up on filling in the gaps instead of looking at what conclusion the evidence supported.

He sat back down behind his desk, scolding himself. He knew better than that. He took a sip of his coffee to calm himself back down.

"So this Mystery Man," Horn started. "He moves in unnoticed, kills everybody dockside. Spares Rudy Valdez for some reason. By the way, any idea why he would spare Rudy Valdez?"

Castle shook his head as he ate.

"Okay. He gets aboard the ship, kills the rest of 'em in the hold, saves Reggie, and then disappears. Thin air and shit. Makes good his escape under cover of darkness."

Castle nodded. "The timeline, the physical evidence and the forensics support the theory."

"Does the timeline, physical evidence or the forensics support any other theory? Like, say, multiple killers, a kill squad, attacking from multiple vantage points?"

"Nope."

A migraine began behind Horn's left eye. "I didn't think so."

Horn and Castle finished their breakfast in silence. Castle wiped his mouth and lips with a white napkin as Horn bit into his second raspberry cheese Danish. Horn truly enjoyed his raspberry cheese Danishes. It was one of the few pleasures he had ever seen Horn indulge himself in, and it made Castle smile.

Sometimes, people treasure the simplest things.

"So let's assume you're right," Horn said at last. This time, he was speaking softly, not in his usual booming baritone. "Let's assume this was personal. That means this Mystery Man knew Reggie."

"Makes sense to me."

"And yet, Reggie says he doesn't know who he is. He never saw the guy's face, just his shoes and part of a pants leg. He didn't recognize the voice, and the guy stayed in the dark. Used the shadows to conceal himself. How do we reconcile that?"

Castle thought for a moment before responding. "The guy obviously knew Reggie, knew who he was, what he did for a living"

Castle supposed. "That does not necessarily mean that Reggie knows him."

"He's a stalker?"

"More like a Guardian Angel."

Horn thought for a moment. "No. An Avenging Angel."

The old school black rotary phone on Horn's desk erupted with a loud classic bell ring. He had the volume turned up so loud, the phone actually vibrated as it rang. The ring was ear splitting in the silence of the Saturday morning.

Horn glanced at his watch. Not even nine yet. He reached out and grabbed the receiver, pressed it to his ear.

"Horn," he spat. He listened a moment, his forehead wrinkling as he did. "You're sure about this?" He paused. "How the hell are they getting away with that?" He listened a bit more, rubbed his hand down his face, suddenly feeling very old and even more fatigued. "I'm on my way. Thanks for the heads up. I owe you."

Castle watched Horn slam the receiver down, all tension and anger once more. "What's up, boss?"

"We've got a problem over at Central Jail."

Rudy Valdez woke up in his cell at six o'clock, just like everyone else. He cleaned up quickly, combed his hair. He made his bed while his cellmate, a tattooed gang banger named Demetrius, brushed his teeth.

At six twenty, the ringer buzzed, the electronically controlled doors on all the cells clanked open. Rudy and Demetrius stepped onto the line with everyone else on their block.

Time for breakfast – such as it was. Rudy turned right when told to, fell into a slow ambling gait behind Demetrius, as the line of human baggage snaked its way to the dining facility. Rudy smirked at such a pretentious name for such a utilitarian place. His military mind thought of it as the mess decks.

Rudy opted for scrambled eggs, potatoes, an unusually large and ripe orange, black coffee, and ice water. He had seen what they offered up in the jail, so he always stayed away from breakfast meats. Bacon and sausage, rarely ham. They were almost all high in fat, and the prison system bought its food supplies from the lowest bidder. When it came to meats, that meant even less real meat, and more added fat as filler. He had no desire to see his cholesterol go through the roof.

He sat at a table off to the side, so he had a good view of the entire area. He ate his meal quietly. He kept to himself, minded his own business. His eyes continued to move around, though, looking for any danger headed his way. Currently, there was none. Demetrius was sitting with some of his gangland homies on the other side of the room, eating, talking laughing.

Like jail was some kind of a vacation or something.

Fuck that noise.

Professional criminals did not get caught. They did not do time. That's why they were professionals. They approached what they did with the same care and attention to detail as a Wall Street executive, a policeman, a doctor. Rudy considered himself a professional. As far as he was concerned, spending time in jail was a sign of failure on his part. He needed to learn from his mistake, and make certain it did not happen again.

Rudy finished up. The powdered scrambled eggs and institutional potatoes that somehow appeared gray had been cooked up without seasoning of any kind. This was typical with institutional food preparation. Rudy had seen the same kind of thing in chow lines back when he was active duty. He assumed it was so no one eating the food had an allergic reaction to some spice. The only seasonings available were salt, pepper, and hot sauce. So salt and pepper it was.

The highlight of breakfast was the orange. The coffee was bad, stale. The ice water was simply for hydration. The ice made the unfiltered San Diego water, full of sedimentation and minerals, more palatable. On the outside, Rudy drank bottled water when on the go. He had a filter on his kitchen spigot at home.

Once his glass was drained, and his tray consisted of orange peels and a few grease smears from the eggs and potatoes, Rudy stood. He placed his plastic utensils across the middle of the tray, picked everything up and turned around.

Rudy stopped short, momentarily startled as he nearly walked right into two guards walking up on him. One guard was older, heavy, but obviously someone who knew how to handle himself. A veteran corrections officer, his face seemed lined into a perpetual scowl.

Hell, Rudy thought, if I did this for a living, I'd fucking scowl, too.

The other guard was younger, tall but slim. With a smooth face and no evidence of razor burn, he did not look like he had a lot of time on the job, or a lot of meat on his bones. To Rudy, the kid looked like a cheetah cub that was just now losing his spots.

They stood silently, looking at each other, a span of about three feet between them. Rudy's eyes darted back and forth between the two. He knew the older bull, obviously in charge, would speak first.

"Clean up your shit, inmate," the older guard spat. "You've got an appointment this morning."

Rudy was instantly on guard. It was only around seven on a Saturday morning. "What kind of appointment?"

"How the hell should I know?" the guard growled. "Just toss your trash and come with us."

Rudy glanced back and forth at the two. Something was not right. As the moments ticked past, he noticed the old guard's fingers drifted to his can of mace. Rudy nodded without speaking, and moved deliberately towards the trashcans near the end of the "dining facility". The two guards followed closely behind.

Rudy threw away his trash, placed the reusable polyurethane food tray into the small window in the wall, where an inmate on the other side slid it away and pre-rinsed it with water heated to a scalding one hundred eighty degrees.

Rudy turned slowly, looked at the guards again. He could tell the Youngster was a simple kid, just following orders, trying to do his job, and most importantly, trying to not screw up and avoid embarrassment. He was no threat to Rudy. The older bull was plainly the force of the operation, and had been around the job long enough for his disillusionment to sink into anger, loathing, a bit of self-hatred, and an overall sense of bitterness.

"So. Where we going?" Rudy repeated.

"Turn around, " the guard grumbled. Rudy turned around. "Hands behind your back." Rudy grimaced as handcuffs were applied, a bit too roughly. The guard grabbed Rudy's wrists in order to control his direction and movement. "Let's go."

Rudy found himself propelled from the dining facility the same way he had come in. Instead of turning to walk up the stairwell towards his cell, he was pushed past it, moving along on the same level, heading towards the interrogation rooms and administrative spaces.

Rudy began to relax a little. At least they weren't taking him anywhere near the kitchen, the laundry, or the showers. In any of those places, he was sure he would be killed. Punishment from Vargas or Oakley for the sin of getting caught, and a preventative measure to make sure he did not cut a deal and talk.

They walked silently down the corridor, made a turn away from the admin offices and towards the interrogation rooms. The guards pulled Rudy up short in front of Interrogation Two. The youngster pushed opened the heavy grey metal door, and Rudy was manhandled inside and pushed down into a seat. The Old Bull removed the handcuffs, bringing a wave of instant relief, along with a tingly rush of blood back into Rudy's fingers. As he sighed and relaxed his shoulders, the old guard cuffed his hands to a short chain that was bolted to the table in front of him.

Rudy pulled against the cuffs, gently, not trying to really break free. He was just testing the strength of the chain. He realized the chain was much stronger than he. No reason to be an idiot about it. Then he watched as both guards simply turned around and left the room, closing the door behind them.

The room became very quiet. Rudy could hear nothing, save for the soft sound of his own breathing. He sat back in the uncomfortable chair, obviously made by the lowest bidder and with little concern for quality. The room was rectangular, approximately ten feet by twelve. The walls were plain gray, and covered with a sound-absorbing material. Even at that, Rudy was certain there were microphones and video cameras hidden at various vantage points around the room, both in the walls and in the ceiling. And the oblong mirror on the far wall was nothing more than one-way glass, with an observation room on the other side.

He wondered if anyone had come in on the other side yet. Probably not yet. It was still early. But they would, and he knew it. Rudy could see it now – two or three cops, maybe an assistant District Attorney, drinking their cheap-assed, overcooked, ineptly prepared, burned coffee while stuffing their mouths with day–old doughnuts, glazed sugar flaking off, dropping like snow, dusting white across their chins and their shirt chests.

Disgusting.

The attorney, of course, would not engage with the blue-collar shenanigans of the cops. Too much school, too much education, too much "refinement" for that. No, sir. He or she would look at them with a certain mixture of forced camaraderie and secret disdain, knowing working with cops was a necessary evil, but not wanting to get too dirty while doing it. And the lawyer would be drinking a no-fat latte, and be more concerned about wrapping whatever this was up, and getting out on the links by one o-clock.

For an instant, Rudy considered whether or not that fucking narc cop would be in there. What was his real name? Oh, yeah. Reggie.... something. Then he decided probably not. If Reggie had any smarts at all, and Rudy had to begrudgingly concede that he probably did, then Reggie had gone to ground until the other cops could figure out a security plan for him, and rounded up more guys like Rudy.

Moments turned into minutes. Rudy tested his chair. The legs were level. Sometimes the cops would adjust one leg to make it shorter than the others. Then the suspect was off balance. They spent most of their time while being interrogated mentally distracted because their chair was wobbly. And all humans have an instinctual fear of falling.

Sort of a poor man's Jedi mind trick.

But that was not going on here this morning. The temperature and humidity in the room had not been cranked up. In fact, it felt quite pleasant. So this was not going to be a high-intensity interrogation. Rudy's mind rocketed to the inevitable question, what exactly was going on here?

The door in the wall opened inward. Rudy watched as a thin, balding, middle-aged man shuffled through the door, hunched over. The man, who looked like a bird or something, dressed in corduroy pants, shirt and tie and pullover sweater, carried a relatively light, but unwieldy load. Essentially, he brought something in that looked like a miniature typewriter supported atop a thin, pedestal stand and would be stabilized by a broad base plate. Rudy recognized the contraption as a portable stenographer's machine. In the stenographer's other effeminate, untanned hand, he carried a cheap collapsible stool. The stenographer, whose brown hair never made it past his forehead and whose bushy moustache could have used a trim, nodded towards Rudy, but did not speak.

Rudy nodded back, almost without thinking.

The stenographer put the stenograph and stool down, then uncoiled the electric cord attached to the base. He glanced around at the lower area of the nearby walls, looking for an electrical outlet. He saw one, moved towards it. The cord went taut, the base rocked a bit. Embarrassed, the stenographer grabbed the stenograph by the thin pedestal stand underneath the machine, and moved the whole thing closer to the outlet. He plugged the machine in, and unfolded his stool.

"Hey. Buddy," Rudy called.

The stenographer looked at him as he put his weight on the stool. "Yes?"

"What's going on?"

The stenographer looked surprised. "They didn't tell you?"

Rudy shook his head.

The stenographer glanced at the one-way glass, then leaned towards Rudy, as if about to reveal a deep dark secret. "I really shouldn't be the one telling you this, but you're getting arraigned this morning."

Rudy frowned. "On a weekend?"

"You must have some pretty important friends."

Rudy sat back in his chair. Michael C. Law, Esq., had come through. A pleasant warmth spread over him. Once bail was set, he'd be out of this motherfucking place.

A contented smile spread across Rudy's lips.

The stenographer's fingers probed on the underside of the machine, clicking the ON button. He then gazed down at the machine and began typing, peering intently at the resulting code being created.

Testing the equipment, Rudy assumed.

The door opened again. This time, Rudy Michael C. Law, attorney at law, squeezed his girth through the narrow doorway. Dressed casually in a pullover sweater that barely covered his massive belly and a pair of jeans that looked like they had been constructed from a circus tent, Law hoisted his briefcase onto the table next to Rudy. He began to immediately shuffle papers.

"Counselor," Rudy said, perfunctorily.

"Morning," the attorney responded, not looking away from what he was doing.

"Would you like a seat?"

"Nah," Law said, finding what he was looking for. He grabbed a document out of his briefcase. "We won't be here long."

Rudy turned this over in his mind. "Should I be worried?"

Law looked down at him, and smiled. The smile was intended to infuse Rudy with confidence. But Rudy had been in too many situations too many times in too many places on the planet to feel any new confidence infused.

The door opened yet again, and a short, harried young woman, wavy red hair severely pulled back in an exaggerated bun and poorly dressed in a crumpled suit that looked like it had been slept in, spilled inside. She teetered on heels too early in the morning. She yanked on a small aluminum handle gripped in one hand behind her, pulling a small professional document carrier. Her bleary eyes scanned the tiny room with growing alarm.

"Where the hell am I supposed to set up?" she asked to no one in particular.

Rudy indicated one side of his desk that was unoccupied. "Open space here, Counselor." If he remembered correctly, her last name was Russell.

Russell hesitated, looking at Rudy like he had leprosy. The moment lasted, Rudy and Russell staring at each other. Finally, Rudy simply shrugged his shoulders and turned his head away from her, disinterested.

Realizing she had no other choice in this outrageous situation, she sighed with exasperation. She opened her document carrier and began slapping case files onto the other end of the desk.

"I don't know what strings you pulled or whose palm you greased to pull this off, Michael" she growled.

"Counselor, I am injured," Law replied, feigning hurt feelings.

"Oh spare me, Mike," She spat. "An arraignment on Saturday? Unheard of!"

"It's highly irregular, Stacy," Law grinned. "Highly irregular."

"Exactly."

"But not illegal," he said, shutting her down. Stacy knew he was technically correct. As long as the legal requirements were met as far as procedural matters and parties present and represented, an arraignment could be done whenever a judge felt like it.

"It's all in the interest of justice," Law grinned. His trademark sleazy smile.

Stacy cringed. Remnants of breakfast clung to his teeth.

The far door opened yet again. An older man, gray hair and matching moustache, heavy set beneath black robes, entered. He carried a laptop computer scooped up under his left arm.

"Judge Mauser," Law said. "Nice to see you."

Mauser threw him a poisonous glare. He harrumphed under his breath, threw an eye dagger glance at Rudy, and set his computer down on the table in front of the defendant. He opened the lid and hit the on button.

"Let's get this shit over with."

"Your Honor, please," Law protested, his flabby arms spread wide. "I hope your early morning mood won't adversely your judgment when it comes to my client."

Anger flashed in Mauser's eyes. "I know my job, Counselor. You just do yours."

Law put his hands up in acquiescence. "My humblest apologies, your honor."

In the Observation Room, a door opened from the hallway outside. Horn stormed in, followed quickly by Castle, who closed the door behind them.

Horn stared through the glass, recognizing all the players. "What the hell are they doing?" He flipped the intercom switch, and the voices from the Interrogation Room filtered in.

"Your Honor, we request remand..." Stacy announced.

"Your Honor, my client has never..." Law countered.

"I still want to know how the hell got an arraignment on Saturday morning," Castle said.

Horn shook his head, feeling defeated. "Money. Power. Blowjobs. Grease the right skids the right way, you can get anything done."

"Bail is set at five hundred thousand dollars, cash or bond," Mauser decided. "Court is adjourned. Let's get the hell out of here."

Through the glass, they watched as Mauser unzipped his robe and headed towards the door. Stacy threw document folders back into her pull-along mobile office case. Law closed his briefcase while Rudy sat where he was.

"I can't believe this," Horn muttered.

"The universe just served us a shit sandwich, boss," Castle said. "We have to take a bite."

Horn lunged to his left and opened the door leading into the interrogation room. He did it so fast, Castle had no time to react or hold him back. He was striding into the next room before Castle could even realize a big man could move that fast.

The door swung open and banged against the wall. Horn found himself staring into the pale, troubled eyes of Judge Mauser. He could tell by the look on the judge's face that the judge was in no mood to be trifled with. Well, fuck that, because neither was Horn.

Horn stood his ground, filling the doorframe. "Judge Mauser."

The judge squared his shoulders and nodded. "Captain."

They stood there for a moment, silent, staring at each other.

The judge gestured at Horn and beyond through the doorway. "May I?"

"What the fuck, judge?" Horn blurted.

Mauser stiffened.

"I mean it. What the fuck just happened here?"

Mauser, fighting his own conflicting emotions, calmed himself. "We had an arraignment," Mauser responded.

Rudy sat still, watching intently.

Horn cocked his head. "You know," Horn continued after a pause, "I'm thinking someone high up pulled a lot of strings to arrange an arraignment for a low level foot soldier of a dead mid-level drug dealer on a Saturday morning."

Mauser pursed his lips, as if in thought. It did not wash with Horn, though. He knew the judge was simply buying time, trying to diffuse this situation, and beat a hasty exit. Well too fucking bad.

" I think it best we don't speculate on hypothetical matters," the judge responded.

"But it makes me curious who has that kind of influence over a garden variety case like this. And it makes me wonder who has that kind of influence over you?"

The tiny room immediately went dead quiet. The air became heavy. Neither attorney spoke, moved, or even breathed as Horn and Mauser stared each other down.

Mauser, his face awash with rage, stepped forward one pace, entering Horn's personal space.

Horn made it a point to remain precisely where he was. He did not budge an inch.

"Shut the fuck up, Horn," he growled under his breath. "Or you're gonna find yourself in deep shit with me."

"Are you attempting to threaten and intimidate a sworn peace officer – *Your Honor*?"

"Get the motherfuck out of my way." Mauser shouldered past Horn and stormed out.

Both attorneys seemed shell-shocked by what had just transpired.

"Well. That was entertaining," Rudy chimed in, loud and brash and breaking the silence with the subtlety of a turd in a punchbowl.

Everyone turned and stared at Rudy, drop-jawed. It was as if he had just spoken Swahili.

He shrugged his shoulders. "What?"

Michael Law gently placed what he hoped would be interpreted as a comforting hand on his client's shoulder. "We'll post bail immediately," he said.

Staci felt completely defeated. How had she so completely botched what should have been a slam-dunk arraignment with this creep getting remanded right back to his cell? She left wondering how she was going to explain this to her bosses Monday morning. Her next thought was whether or not they would still be her bosses come Monday morning.

May be time to shake the dust off the old resume, she thought to herself.

"Guard!" Law yelled out. "I'd like my client unlocked immediately, please!"

Horn and Castle watched in impotent muteness as a young Corrections Officer appeared in the doorway and entered the room.

This was a different young recruit from earlier, Rudy observed. His ID badge identified him as Treese.

Treese, probably barely out of Corrections Officer Academy, just a few years out of high school, tried to assume an air of control. He was slender and smooth shaven, boasted youthful features, but built with strong, broad shoulders. With skin a caramel brown and naturally curly hair cropped close to his scalp, Treese wore his uniform with pride: a cleaned, pressed shirt, crisp straight creases down both the front and back of the legs of his trousers, shoes buffed and polished to a high gloss.

Treese pulled a set of keys out of his pocket. They jangled as he looked for the right one.

Rudy sized him up rapidly. Muscular underneath his uniform. Moving with grace and an understated agility. Calluses on the guard's knuckles and along the outside border of his hands. Rudy concluded the guard was into martial arts. Classical karate training for sure, mostly likely as a child. Maybe he dabbled in MMA these days. A lot of athletic young guys did. Smart for Treese, considering his line of work, seeing as Corrections Officers did not carry guns.

Treese found the key he was looking for and slipped the key into the lock. "Hold still a moment, and I'll have you out of these things."

"Okay," Rudy responded pleasantly enough.

"What the hell are you doing?" Horn yelled as Treese turned the key in the lock and the handcuffs cracked open.

Treese looked in Horn's direction. "You talking to me?"

"You damn skippy I'm talking to you. What the hell you gotta treat him so good?"

"What, you mean by acting like a professional?" he asked. On the other side of the table, Rudy stood on stiff legs and rubbed his sore wrists.

"He's a criminal," Horn said.

"He's still a human being."

"He's a scumbag."

Law touched Rudy on the shoulder, and Treese motioned for Rudy to follow him. Treese stepped out the door on the opposite wall, followed by Rudy. Law smiled triumphantly in Horn's direction, then closed his briefcase.

"This isn't over, Counselor," Horn growled.

Law looked up over his glasses at Horn. "No, it is not," he conceded. "But that's fine. I'm just going to trounce all over you at trial, just like I did in here today."

Blind rage flashed in Horn's eyes. He lurched forward. Castle, alert and nimble, moved in a blur and grabbed Horn from behind, restraining him.

Castle whispered into Horn's ear. "Don't be stupid."

Law picked up his briefcase and moved towards the door. "You should listen to your friend," Law advised. "He seems to know more about the law than you do." Then he was out the door.

Horn pulled away from Castle. Castle did not try to hold on. Horn turned to Castle, furious at the situation. Looking at Castle, standing there so calm, so Zen like, his own anger began to dissipate.

"Thanks," he said.

"My pleasure."

"Come on then," Horn said. "Nothing we can do here now."

Treese walked down the corridor, Rudy in front of him. The only sound was the slap of their feet echoing off the tile flooring and bouncing off the cinderblock walls.

Up ahead was the turnoff to go back to the cellblock. They got closer, and just as Rudy moved to go left down that way, Treese nudged him to the right.

"Your dress-out cell is this way."

Rudy complied, with some internal consternation. This was not the way releasing a prisoner on bail usually went. Usually, they went back to their cell, gathered up their personal belongings in a pillowcase, then waited for a guard to take them to another cell or holding area where they could change into street clothes, then wait for authorization for final release. Rudy assumed now he was being set up for assassination.

It probably wouldn't happen here in the hallway. It would probably happen in the dress-out cell. Closed space. Nowhere to run. No other choice. Make a stand. Fight to the death.

Live.

Die.

No middle road.

Meet the Grim Reaper like a man.

He wondered from which direction it would come. Probably not from the guard following him. Treese was a real guard. Young and idealistic. He was bright enough to get through training, and stupid enough to follow orders without question. A rookie, he did not yet know just how much he *didn't* know about the job.

Treese was no hardened criminal with a badge, Rudy decided. And he sure as hell was no assassin. This was an All-American kid. Probably had a girlfriend, some former high school sweetheart, a cheerleader, prom queen, whatever. He was planning to marry and have a gaggle of kids. Buy a home. Get a dog. Mow the yard. Invite friends over for dinner. Eat terrible backyard barbeque on the weekends, go to church on Sundays and pray for his sins.

All that wholesome shit.

Good thing for him, Rudy thought. Best thing for him.

Sure, in normal circumstances, Treese could probably handle himself pretty well, but he's no match for someone like me. He hasn't had the kind of training I've had. I'd be able to tell. From his walk. His general demeanor. By the way he carried himself, that certain and unmistakable aura given off by professionals, for whom killing is simply a function they perform. Part of the job. Part of the Life.

One on one, I'd kill this kid in less than sixty seconds.

They continued walking down the unfamiliar corridor in silence. Rudy noticed a wall made of prison bars at the far end, embedded in both the flooring and the ceiling, with a heavy, locked gate placed in the middle. Rudy looked past the bars, and saw a guard desk lay beyond the wall on the left, which looked over a small antechamber. Rudy assumed this was a waiting area. He could make out a few chairs from his restricted point of view. No one waited. On the other side of the room stood a thick glass door leading to the outside.

Freedom.

The World.

Rudy smiled to himself.

They walked closer to the bars. Rudy noticed an opening on his side of the bars, a doorway without a door, on each side of the corridor. Obviously, these led to small rooms, and one of these were his destination. But no doors meant no privacy, and he glanced upwards, taking notice of the small gray cameras that moved slowly but surely, following him and Treese as they made their way down the corridor.

As a prisoner soon to be released, all this might have made one feel better and more secure about getting out without being shanked.

But Rudy knew better.

He had to keep his guard up because he knew, all too well, how easy it is for a guard or another inmate to turn a blind eye and a deaf ear to the agonizing pleas of a dying man as he bleeds out. Cameras cannot see around blind corners. And tapes or hard drives can be deleted, corrupted, lost, destroyed, or altered.

"You're on the left," Treese announced when they were about ten feet away.

Rudy grunted and nodded. If an attack happened, it would be inside the room. No cameras. And a blind spot along the inside of the front wall until he was already past the doorway. So he paused at the doorway, sucked in his breath a bit, going into combat mode. The room was small, square. He saw the clothing he had been arrested in, neatly folded and waiting, on a low bench that ran the length of the back wall. He glanced inside, looking for the blind spot.

He glanced to his left inside the front cinderblock wall. No one there. Silently breathing a sigh of relief, he relaxed.

"There a problem?" Treese asked.

"No problem."

"What are you waiting for, then?" he asked. "Your bail's been paid. Don't you want out of here?"

Rudy stepped inside the small room, the Marine in him staying in combat mode, staying alert of what was around him, behind him, above him. Treese did not follow him inside. He took up a position outside near the door, waiting.

Rudy kicked off his prison-issued shower shoes and socks, unzipped the front of his prison jumpsuit from neck to pubis. He shrugged out of the sleeves. The garment's own weight caused it drop off him and land with a muffled flop on the floor, forming a fabric puddle around his ankles. He stepped out of them, kicked them away. They slid across the cell and against the far wall.

No one had darkened the doorway yet. Maybe he was going to get out of this alive after all.

He peeled the prison-issue white T-shirt off, his muscles defined and rippling underneath. Now clad in only his jockey shorts, he quickly pulled on his blue jeans and buckled them. Next his long-sleeved black T-shirt. Then he sat down to pull on his socks and his tan brown, soft and supple desert combat boots. Only his weathered, worn, dark brown bomber jacket still lay on the bench.

As he laced up his boots, from the top of his peripheral vision, he noticed a shadow fall across the floor. Here it comes, he thought. He froze where he was, glanced up, and saw Treese standing in the doorway. His face was unreadable. He simply stood there, motionless.

"You almost ready?"

"Just lacing up my boots."

"Someone's here to pick you up."

Rudy began to dare to believe he might actually walk out of this Godforsaken place alive. Perhaps, Rudy thought, Mr. Vargas trusted him enough to know he would never, ever, give the cops anything, even if it meant he himself went to prison for a very long time.

He tied the lace on the other boot, tucked the excess lacing inside the top of the boot, and pulled his pants leg down. He stood up, grabbed his jacket, then paused for a bit, the tactical side of him still unsure about his safety.

He looked at the open doorway, saw the barred gate and wall to the left at an angle, and the waiting area beyond. He did not see anyone in the waiting area. Hadn't Treese just said someone was waiting for him? And exactly where was Treese, anyway?

Uh oh.

Suck it up, Rudy. Be a warrior.

Go out like a man.

Rudy squared his shoulders, exhaled deeply. He tilted his head to one side, cracking his neck. He bunched and rolled his shoulders, loosening up. Ready for what might come, he moved forward. Towards the door, towards Heaven or Hell, striding through the doorway and —

Out into the hallway once more. Treese, a few feet away, facing him.

"Ah. There you are."

Rudy looked at him, a bit confused. The attack he had been convinced was coming, was nowhere to be found.

He glanced around to his left, through the bars. He saw the desk in the corner, manned by an aging Corrections Officer. Gray hair, receding hairline, reading glasses. The guy had to be late fifties, early sixties. Near retirement, that's for sure. The bulging gut underneath his straining shirt showed testament to Rudy the old guy had definitely seen better days.

Standing beside the desk was Michael C. Law, attorney to the low life scumbags of the Underworld. He waved amiably towards Rudy. Nearly swooning with relief, Rudy managed a nod in his direction.

Treese stepped towards the gate, rattling his enormous key chain. "Okay. Let's get you out of here, shall we?"

Rudy watched him as the young Corrections Officer sifted through the keys on his brass ring. Big ones, small ones. Gold colored ones, silver colored ones. Even a couple that glinted a pale redness, illuminated by the sunlight from the waiting area.

Treese finally found the key he was searching for. He grinned as he shook the ring in his hand, the other keys jangling loudly as they fell out of the way. He pushed the key into the locking mechanism located at waist height on the barred gate. His hand cranked to the left, and the tumblers inside fell with a satisfying series of clicks and clanks. He pulled on the gate, and door swung open.

Rudy glanced at Treese, glanced behind him. No one else was in the hallway.

No one sneaking up behind him at the last moment.

He looked past his attorney and at the ancient Desk Sergeant, who seemed completely disinterested with the proceedings. His nose was buried in some cheap magazine he had brought with him.

Threat assessment: little to none.

Rudy stepped through the gate, and suddenly found himself in the waiting area. Law stepped forward, put out his hand. Rudy shook it, allowing a genuine smile to flit across his lips for the first time. Behind him, Treese closed the gate and secured the lock. Then he turned and walked back down the corridor, back the way he came, without so much as another look at Rudy. Mission accomplished, that's all. Now on to the next thing. Shift change was coming up.

"So how does it feel to be a free man once again?" Law asked.

"Feels good."

"Come on." Law motioned with his head towards the outer door. "Let's get you out of here."

Law pushed the door open and stood aside, allowing his client to step into free air first. Then he followed, still lugging his briefcase. The door behind them closed on its own.

Rudy noticed the birds singing. The fresh sweetness of the air. The crispness to the coolish temperature. It had been a long time since he had seen a sky so purely blue.

They strolled towards the parking area. "So. Where would you like me to take you?"

Rudy thought for a moment. "Home I guess. But could we stop off for a bite? Jailhouse food is shit."

Law never passed on an opportunity to eat. "Of course," he responded.

The pair walked across the parking lot to Law's waiting Cadillac. Rudy walked around to the passenger side.

"Just one more thing, Rudy," Law said as he paused at the driver's door. "Mr. Vargas would like to see you at his place of business at ten tonight."

Rudy knew "his place of business" meant the warehouse Vargas owned down on the docks. All kinds of things, both good and bad, had transpired there. Parties, drugs, hookers and semen exchanged, but also torture, murder, vital fluids spilled out. Everything washed away.

Like nothing had ever happened.

"What does he want to see me there for?"

Law shrugged. "He didn't say," he answered honestly. "I don't think it's anything bad."

"Probably not," Rudy said, not convinced.

Law unlocked the doors remotely. An audible *thunk!* rolled out as all the locks on all the car doors unlocked in unison. He threw his door open wide so he could swing his girth in, but paused as he looked over at Rudy.

"Rudy."

Rudy was still looking around.

"Rudy!" Rudy spun back around to concentrate on Law.

"You okay?"

Rudy nodded.

"What are you looking for?"

"Sniper fire."

"If Mr. Vargas wanted you dead, you never would have made it to arraignment," Law grinned broadly. "Come on. Get in."

Both men got into the car, closed their doors. The driver's side sank down slightly lower than the passenger side. From a distance, it looked like the car's shocks were blown on one side. Law turned the key in the ignition. The engine swirled to life, idling like a purring tiger. Gentle now, but lots of muscle just waiting to be released.

Law put the car in gear and hit the gas. The engine roared with excitement, and car accelerated out of the parking lot and onto the street beyond.

Journal entry, February 3rd

Another quiet evening. Like most evenings.

I spent about four hours after I reanimated working on some stock recommendations. My clients are high-value, high net worth individuals, or "HNI's", as we call them in my learned profession. They are understandably jittery with their investments in this volatile market. Some require more personal attention than others.

I spend quite a bit of time in front of my laptop, a small headset wrapped over my ears, a condenser microphone on the tip of a thin stalk-like extension in front of my mouth, calming them, pacifying them, coddling them, reassuring them.

What can else can I do? I have to make a living like anyone else, and the financial services industry pays well.

However, this "economic recovery", as the pundits and politicians are wont to call it, the one that supposedly has the United States, along with the rest of the world "recovering from the Great Recession", is a sham.

The U.S. is doing better, but there is a reason for that. The U.S. Federal Reserve Bank – the "Fed" - keeps artificially deflating the interest rates on the Prime Interest Rate – which rate at which banks charge to loan money to each other, which keeps consumer home loans and cars loans – and every other kind of consumer loan except for credit card debt – at "historically low rates", which in turn artificially props up the value of the U.S. dollar. And even though that rate has been raised by a quarter of one per cent, we are still deflating the rates to shore up the U.S. dollar on the currency exchanges. But that cannot go on forever.

Other countries have no such entity shielding them from economic reality.

And the reality is, the very same conditions that enabled the stock market crashes of 2000 and 2007 still exist today. There was no real

Banking Industry or Wall Street reform as was promised by the new President, so young, so dashing and handsome, so resolute of visage as he ascended into Office. He talked a good show, but in the end, he has done nothing to correct the real underpinnings of the problem.

Subprime loans are on their way back into vogue, and people who have no business owning a home are being told it is okay to buy a house they cannot possibly afford with no money down and an adjustable rate mortgage. The problem with adjustable rates is, they always go up.

The same thing is happening with car loans. A young janitor making less than ten dollars an hour is being told he can afford a thirty thousand dollar sports car with no money down, six years to pay, at a rate of fifteen percent.

When he quickly, unthinkingly signs on the dotted line, he is locking the cage of his own financial prison, and putting himself on the road to financial ruin, car repossession, an anemic FICO score, and possibly, a bankruptcy. But with his head swimming with visions of the respect he will soon get from his friends and the pretty girls who will somehow miraculously now want to go out with him, the modest janitor signs his name.

It is the economic equivalent of feeding a diabetic a candy cane.

CHAPTER FOURTEEN

Horn's office door clashed open swinging inward, clattering against the wall. Horn stalked in, still fuming about what had just happened at the jail. He had not spoken on the ride back, and Castle had known to not try to start a conversation. Now Horn lumbered across the few feet to his desk, and plopped down into his high backed leather chair. An older chair with a wooden skeleton and base, creaked under his weight.

Castle glided in behind him, padding to the chair in front of the desk where he had eaten his breakfast barely an hour ago. He sat down again, grabbed his coffee mug as he watched Horn rub his eyes like a man who had not slept in days. The coffee had gone cold, and Castle's nose crinkled.

He got up, poured a fresh mug from the pot, which was still hot. He added sugar and cream, stirred with a pen he kept in his pocket. When he turned around, Horn had placed both meaty hands, palms open, across his entire face.

Castle sat down, sipped his coffee. Across from him, Horn heaved a great sigh, the kind of sigh that said, I Hate This Fucking Job. He rubbed his hands across his face and moved them outward, until he held his face in his hands at either cheek, fingers extending close to his eyes, and base of the palms cupping his chin. Then his eyes snapped open, and he saw Castle, calmly sitting there, legs crossed comfortably, sipping his coffee.

Castle saw Horn looking at him. He motioned with his mug like he toasting him, then continued to sip his coffee.

"You don't seem to be very broken up over our hopeless situation," Horn observed.

"We're not in a hopeless situation."

Horn put his hands on his desk, leaned forward, resting his weight on his forearms. "And why's that?"

"The question is," Castle responded, "why do you think we've lost anything?"

Horn looked back down at his desk. He focused on the half-eaten raspberry cheese Danish, which lay in pastry puff tatters on a grease-stained napkin, growing stiff and stale.

Sort of like my career, he thought. Past its prime.

And even though he was looking at food, he had no appetite whatsoever. For the first time, wondered if it might be time to seriously consider putting in his retirement papers. Walk away from all this shit. What he did have left to prove to anyone?

But first....

"We needed to question that witness," Horn said. "He's the only one who might have seen something, and now he's gone."

"We can still get him in an interrogation room."

"Not without that mob attorney present."

Castle shrugged. "Yeah, but so what? We were going to have to deal with Michael Law anyway," he said. "It's not worth getting knocked off our stride."

"His lawyer's gonna stonewall us. He won't let Valdez give more than name, rank, and social security number."

"That's all we'd get from him anyway, Cap. That man is hard core."

"Great. So no matter what, we're back to Square One."

"Not exactly."

There was something in the way Castle had said those last words, a sense of surety that Horn picked up on.

"What are you thinking?"

"Rudy Valdez is not the only person who survived that night," Castle answered. "He's not the only person we can interrogate."

"You mean?" Horn ventured.

"Reggie Downing," Castle answered.

"He's disappeared."

"Everybody goes somewhere, Cap."

"Nobody knows where he is."

"Somebody always knows."

Banker's Hill was a largely residential area located just north of downtown San Diego and the Gaslamp District, and just blocks north of several large, world-class banks and investment banking institutions. Most small businesses in the neighborhood were law partnerships, medical offices housing both group and private practices, and architect and graphic design offices. The buildings were early twentieth century structures that had been upgraded over the years to meet changing building codes. Some had been converted into apartments or condos.

Traffic in Banker's Hill flowed through on a series of one-way streets. The north south streets were numbered, one through five, and were all one way. Sixth Street, closest to the Western border of Balboa Park, was two-way traffic. The cross streets, named for vegetation like Grape, Laurel, Juniper, also boasted two-way traffic.

Saturday morning traffic was sparse, almost nonexistent. By this time of day during the week, all four lanes would be filled, with an ebb and flow created by the Stop signs and traffic lights set up every few blocks.

But not today.

After being dropped off by his attorney at a corner market, Rudy Valdez changed direction and walked briskly back down the block. Most convenience stores and delis in this area supported the investment bankers during the week. They were closed on Saturdays and Sundays.

Rudy stopped into one of the few convenience stores open on the weekends. Though the outside possessed a updated sign and facade, the inside had not been updated in decades. More than merely a convenience store, this was a tiny, but functioning market and deli. The store had three aisles, stocked with everything from a small freezer section to canned goods, paper products, soft drinks and beer, and even a microscopic section for fresh produce. The only things out in the produce section were a couple bags of potatoes, some bananas, and a few apples.

Rudy glanced around as he browsed. The old guy behind the counter, Gary Kirchik, had owned the place since he inherited it from his uncle. His scalp was bare these days, his face deeply lined. Dressed in threadbare pants and a faded plaid button up shirt he'd owned and worn for twelve years, Kirchik chomped a cigar tightly at the left corner of his mouth. He read a newspaper by the register, holding the Sports Section in his gnarled hands.

He looked up from his paper. "Hey, Rudy."

Rudy looked at him.

"You want anything out of the deli case?" he asked, the cigar still clenched between his teeth. "I got some fresh garlic bologna I'll sell you at a discount."

Rudy considered the vision of Kirchik, cigar still in his mouth, leaning over the meat, slicing it with practiced precision, the ash of his cigar hovering precariously over the bologna.

"No thanks, " Rudy replied. "I'm good."

Kirchik shrugged, went back reading his paper. Rudy noticed there was no one else in the building. And even though Kirchik had surveillance cameras set up in the ceiling, Rudy knew they did not work. They were simply installed to deter amateur thieves from robbing him.

Rudy walked over to the glass- enclosed freezer section. He saw a turkey and dressing TV dinner, one of the few TV dinner varieties that he actually liked. He opened the door, grabbed it, and headed towards the front of the store. He placed the dinner in front of Kirchik.

"Anything else?"

Rudy picked a newspaper from the stack beside the register. Kirchik rang it up, gave him his change.

Outside, Rudy headed up the street again, his TV dinner and folded newspaper tucked underneath his arm. He suddenly bolted across the street at mid-block, moving gracefully like a fighter bobbing and weaving to escape his opponent's punches.

Rudy hopped onto the opposite sidewalk, turned again, and strolled leisurely in the opposite direction. As he strolled, he glanced around, to his left and his right, catching reflections of the sidewalk and street behind him. He did not notice anyone following him. Still, the constant zigzag approach, changing streets, changing directions, was a solid counter surveillance tactics. He did not think he was being followed, but still...

Twenty minutes later, Rudy strolled east on Grape Street. He passed by the large HMO building, a state of the art healthcare facility, complete with a weekend Urgent Care, owned and operated by one of the top Healthcare systems in California, possibly the country. Being a Saturday, the parking lot was mostly empty.

Rudy glanced at his watch. Just after noon now. The morning cloud cover was breaking up, replaced by lighter, whiter clouds floating across the blue sky. The sun peeked through, warming his face. His mood lightened, and he relished the thought of devouring his TV dinner, then catching a nap.

His studio apartment was located on the western-facing corner of a hundred and ten year old, pink stucco apartment building, sitting on the north side of Grape, bordering Third Street. From the top floor apartment, Rudy had a great view of the city tumbling down the hills towards the bay. At night, he could see all the twinkling lights of the ships and smaller watercraft, and he could watch the jets landing at Lindberg Field. On a clear night, he might be able to make out the light patterns of the aircraft carriers berthed across the bay at North Island.

He pulled his key ring out of his pocket, ready to enter the building through the locked, gated entryway. Rudy had been told once you could tell how complicated a man's life was by the number of keys he carried. The logic went, the more keys, the heavier was the man's burden of responsibility, ergo, the more complicated a man's life was. He inserted the key into the heavy deadbolt lock on the steel screened door.

He glanced over his shoulder one last time, making sure no one was coming up behind him. Some would call him paranoid. But Rudy Valdez was a survivor. He had survived his cop-based upbringing, had survived his tour in the Corps, along with his tour of combat, and he had survived working as a soldier for hire in the drug trade. Paranoid? No. He was careful. He was meticulous. He was disciplined.

He was a professional.

He turned the key, felt the weight of the bolt as the mechanism turned over, and the bolt slid back. He pushed the gate inward gently with his shoulder, and stepped inside. The door swung closed behind him, set on a pneumatic cylinder installed at the top of the door. He twisted the finger handle, sliding the lock back into place.

He climbed the stairs and walked down the hallway, passing closed apartment doors on each side. He did not know many of the other tenants in the building. They led quiet lives, and he kept strange hours, so Rudy pretty much simply kept to himself. Plus, civilian relationships complicated matters.

Rudy climbed another set of one hundred year old stairs to the third floor. The boards creaked under his weight. One board near the top actually sagged perceptibly. He made a mental note to call

the property management company so they could send someone out
to fix it.

He stepped onto the landing and paused, his senses on high
alert. He heard no shifting of body weight, no sounds of sucked in
breath that comes right before a blitz attack. He saw no shifting
shadows, no gun barrels, no flash suppressors or silencers.

He swung to his left, and walked down the hallway. The
sunlight from outside filtered in through the window at the end of the
hallway. The last door on the right stood resolute, solid, closed,
secured. Rudy's key ring found its way into his hand once more.

As he stopped in front of his door, another door down the
hallway clicked and swung open. Rudy's eyes darted to his right. He
relaxed as he saw a rather frail, gray haired lady, stooped with age,
joints swollen with arthritis, teeter out with the help of a cane. She
looked his way, Her face, lined with deep wrinkles not at all hidden
by the heavy makeup and garish red lipstick, moved upwards into a
smile. Tobacco yellow teeth gleamed in her mouth.

"Why Mr. Valdez!" she exclaimed. "Just now getting
home?"

"Good morning, Mrs. Loobner," Rudy said politely.

"Why it's actually a bit past noon by now," she announced.
"So who was the lucky woman? Anyone I know?"

"My odd hours are work-related," he parried. He could smell
the cat she kept in her apartment. The smell emanated from her
clothes.

"That's your problem," she stated with authority. "You work
too much. Young man your age should be spending time with a hot
girlfriend."

Rudy smiled. "Well, I'll have to work on that."

"You should," she said as she locked her door. She stepped
closer to Rudy, then glanced around to make sure no one was
listening.

"I had a Latin lover once, you know," she confided.

"Really?"

"Of course," she confirmed. "Nineteen sixty seven. I wasn't
always the seventy-four year old woman you see today, you know."

"I should hope not!"

Mrs. Loobner's face became wistful. Her eyes softened as
she accessed distant memories. "His name was Raul," she said, her

voice lilting. "He was thirty-one at the time, tall, thick hair, moustache." She looked at Rudy. "Hung like a horse."

Rudy nodded, trying to seem impressed.

"Best sex this skinny little white girl ever had, I kid you not," she finished.

Rudy grinned appreciatively, tried to keep from laughing. "So what happened?"

"Oh." Her face fell. Once again, she was seventy-four year old Mrs. Loobner, who lived alone in a stale apartment with a stinky cat and a malodorous litter box.

"He went back to Mexico," she said. "Work up here dried up, so he went back to his wife and kids."

"Awwwww. How sad."

"Yes. Well." She began to turn, leaning on her cane. "Nothing good lasts forever," she stated, with a sad resignation of someone who knew what she was talking about. She began to hobble off down the hallway.

Thinking the conversation over, Rudy turned his attention back to his door. The key was still in the lock. His fingers engulfed the key chain.

"You really should find yourself a nice girl, you know," came Mrs. Loobner's voice from farther down the hall.

"Why's that, Mrs. Loobner?"

"You work too much," she reiterated. "You're always working, keeping such strange hours, coming and going all hours of the day and night, being gone for days on end."

Rudy shrugged. "It's the nature of the work," he said simply.

Mrs. Loobner shook her head, not accepting that as an excuse. "You need more balance in your life. You need to find love. Share your passion." Rudy saw her eyes reddening as if she were beginning to tear up. "Now you listen to me, sweetie. I'm an old woman, but I am no fool." She paused, then said, "No one gets to the end of their life, lying on their deathbed, and wishes they had spent more time at the office."

Rudy realized the truth of what she was saying. He watched the sad old woman turn from him and totter away towards the staircase.

Rudy turned back to his door. As he turned the key in the lock, he understood what dear Mrs. Loobner was trying to say. She was trying to help him, warning him to not make the same mistakes she had made. She was a sweet, sad, caring lady, and her words had impact on him.

He opened his door and stepped inside. He closed the door behind him, threw the deadbolt into place. He smelled the stale smoke of a cigarette. Problem was, Rudy never smoked in his apartment. He spun around and froze, his heart hammering within his chest.

The other man in the room made no attempt to conceal himself. He sat in a worn easy chair Rudy had bought at a Goodwill store a few years back. The studio apartment was an open space, with TV area and easy chair on one side, A futon that doubled as Rudy's bed near the huge front window that opened out onto the city, the view Rudy loved, and a kitchenette area along the wall on the other side, complete with an apartment sized refrigerator, apartment sized stove and oven, a single sink and small food prep area, and a microwave, another Goodwill purchase, sitting atop the refrigerator, waiting to heat its next meal.

Rudy's lips went tight with tension. His eyes narrowed.

The man across from him sat easily in the chair, arms laid out on the arms of the chair, legs crossed casually. He sat back in the cushions, his smile seemed friendly enough, but one could never tell in this business. Often, it was your friend that came to kill you. However, this man had no weapon in his hand. His pistol was situated comfortably in its leather holster beneath his left armpit.

"How did you get in?"

"I have my methods," Rick Oakley replied.

"You're here to kill me?"

"No. God, no. Why would you think that?"

"I just got popped. I might have panicked, talked to the cops. Maybe cut myself a deal. Took a plea bargain to testify."

Oakley shook his head. "Someone else, maybe. Not you."

Rudy moved carefully to beside his decrepit dinette table. He put his newspaper and TV dinner down, emptying his hands in case this went south.

Rick stood up slowly, trying to convey he was no threat to Rudy. "You're a man of honor, Rudy. You still have that whole 'Marine' thing going on. And I think you always will."

"And what does that mean?"

"It means you'd let them cut out your tongue before you'd ever talk to the fucking cops."

Rudy thought for moment, nodded. "You're probably right about that."

"I'm ex-military, too. I know hardcore when I see it. And you're as hardcore as they come."

Allowing himself to relax a bit, Rudy tore open the box, tore off the corner of the clear film wrapping sealed over the food, then tossed it into his microwave. He set the timer for five minutes.

"You still haven't told me why you're here," he countered, turning full on to face Oakley.

"No, I guess I haven't."

Rudy waited. He said nothing, but was acutely aware of the sound of the microwave cooking, the faint smell of the dinner that would become stronger over the next few minutes, the curling window curtains at the front window, the cool breeze wafting in, and Rick Oakley's face, smiling smugly. Rudy was losing patience.

Oakley must have sensed it, because he stepped back and broke eye contact. "Sorry," he said. "Bad joke."

"So why are you here?"

Oakley took a breath, blew it out. "I need to ask you a serious question."

Rudy, confused, said nothing.

"I need to now precisely where your loyalties lie."

"My loyalties begin and end with the organization that has taken me in, given me a job, given me friendship, and camaraderie, and loyalty to me," he stated forcefully. His voice became harder edged as he spoke, his anger rising.

Oakley put his hands up, palms out. "Okay, okay. Take it easy."

"Fuck 'easy'", Rudy spat back. "Who the fuck do you think you are questioning my loyalty?" Rudy took a step forward.

Oakley took a half step back, planted his feet. He dropped his hands to his sides, ready for an attack. "I said, take it easy, kid. This is not what I came here for." There was no fear or stress registering from Oakley, only a warning tone in his voice.

Rudy carefully considered his options. Oakley stood stock still, not wanting to provoke a fight, giving Rudy time to think.

Before Rudy could make a decision, the microwave bell went off with a small *DING!*

Rudy stood here, staring at Oakley. Oakley's eyes flickered to the microwave. "Your lunch is ready," he said. Then he took a step back.

The tension in the room dissipated. Rudy's shoulders slumped as he relaxed from combat mode. He heaved a great sigh, grabbed a small towel. He opened the microwave door and, using the towel like a potholder, gingerly lifted the TV dinner out of the microwave and placed it on a nearby kitchen counter.

"Look. I've never questioned your loyalty to the organization. What I want to know about is your loyalty to Vargas."

Rudy opened a drawer and pulled out a fork. He grabbed his TV dinner, moved to the small dinette table to eat. He placed the dinner on the table in front of a chair, sat down. He applied some salt and pepper to the dinner from small plastic shakers sitting in the middle of the table.

He did not offer Oakley a seat.

"Mr. Vargas gave me this job," he said, as he cut into the tender meat.

"Actually, *El Gecko* hired you," Oakley countered. "But Vargas is – or was – his boss, so...."

Rudy ate the meat off his fork. "What are you getting at?"

Oakley shrugged, like it was nothing big. "Oh, you know how it is."

"No. I really don't. I'm kind of stupid like that. Explain it to me. In words of one syllable."

"Organizations can run almost on their own for a long time, right?" Oakley asked.

"I suppose."

"Procter and Gamble, US Steel, the movie studios, all big companies with complex organizations and all running like a well-oiled machine, yes?"

Rudy shrugged, ate a roasted potato. "I suppose so."

"My point is," Oakley said slowly, "is that within these companies, the heads of these companies come and go."

Rudy looked at him, guarded.

"But you know the really extraordinary thing?"

Rudy put another piece of meat product in his mouth, waiting for Oakley to continue.

"These companies continue on long after the founders or CEO's have moved on."

Rudy dipped a piece of meat into the brown gravy sauce, then popped it into his mouth. "What does any of this have to do with us?" He glared directly into Oakley's eyes.

Oakley noticed how Rudy sat, legs under him, ready to explode upwards at any moment. He also noticed Rudy held his fork in his fist, prongs up. Not as an eating utensil.

As a weapon.

Oakley smiled. "Direct. I admire that." He paused, and Rudy knew to wait. "There may come a time when Mr. Vargas decides to move on to greener pastures, Rudy."

Rudy did not like where this was going.

"If Mr. Vargas decides to retire, go somewhere, sit on his money and make babies the rest of his life, would you be loyal to him, or to the organization? Would you be loyal to the incoming CEO?"

"You're asking me to back you, while you plan on 'retiring' Mr. Vargas?" That combat mode stare was back in his eye in an instant.

"Good God, no," Oakley reassured him. "Not at all. I've known Vargas since we were kids in middle school. No, I'm asking precisely what I say I'm asking."

"Even if Mr. Vargas was gone," Rudy answered, "I would be loyal to the organization. I need to keep working. I'm not ready to retire just yet."

Oakley nodded, taking this new information in. Rudy was smarter, more forward thinking than Oakley had realized. His respect for Rudy went up another tick. "And if I was the head of the organization? Could I count on your loyalty?"

"My loyalty will always be to the organization, no matter who runs it."

Oakley appeared relieved. He moved to the door. "Don't be late tonight." Then he was out the door and gone.

Like he had never been there at all.

By three thirty in the afternoon, the sunlight was already fading. Sinking towards the western horizon behind the Point Loma's hilly terrain, the sun's intensity had lessened to the point where it was simply a yellow orb hanging distant in the sky. The daily Marine Layer was rolling in, thick gray cotton clouds off the Pacific. Condensation clung to cars, railings, and other exposed metal objects.

By four thirty, San Diego dimmed with an overcast twilight. Street lamps blinked on. Vehicles used their headlights.

At the vampire's apartment in Kensington, the covers on the bed stirred. The vampire resuscitated with pain and agony. Just like every night. He woke up gasping, hacking, coughing, grabbing his stomach. He sat up on the side of the bed, his thin pale legs dangling, feet not quite touching the floor. He was finally able to inhale deeply, completely filling his lungs, then blowing it out. His head started to clear. His senses sharpened.

Saturday night. Financial markets closed. What to do? Stay in and read? Watch TV? He felt no great need to prowl; he had fed well recently.

As he sat there contemplating, a new awareness encroached upon his consciousness. A vague danger. Not to him, but to the young cop he had saved. The feeling grew stronger, more specific, more imminent.

He could not let it happen. Not to this cop. This human. After all, Reggie was... well, Reggie was special, wasn't he?

Placing his hands palm down on the bed beside him, he pushed his body forward, towards the edge of the bed. His feet landed on the solid wood bead board flooring just as his butt slid off the edge of the mattress. He stood there, dehydrated and wobbly. He held onto the bed for support for a moment, his head swimming, his body listing a bit to the left. He blinked his eyes, pushed the lank, lifeless hair upwards and to the right, off his forehead. He shuffled forward on spindly legs and unbending knees, careening through the dark rooms towards the bathroom.

He stumbled into the bath, and headed straight to the toilet. He did not bother turning the lights on, since he could see just fine. He lifted the seat and peed, reddish urine, thick and syrupy, dribbling into the bowl. Once done, he put himself back into his underwear, and flushed. He lurched back out.

He headed into the kitchen, his mind clearing even more. By the time he warmed up some of his refrigerated blood in a coffee mug in his microwave, the vampire figured out what he needed to do.

It was a huge risk.

It meant exposing himself, more than he had done in almost a century. He remembered the last time he had revealed the truth of what he was to a human being.

He grunted at the memory. More of a snort really, without merriment. Things had not gone so well then, had they?

The vampire sipped the warm blood from the coffee mug. Realizing he was hungrier than he had previously thought, he quickly put the mug back to his lips and tilted back, slamming the remainder of the mug's contents down his throat. He swallowed with an audible gulp. He turned on the water at the kitchen faucet, rinsed the cup out, filled it with water. He wiped the blood from the corner of his mouth, then drank the water down nearly as fast as he had the blood.

Feeling satisfied, at least for the moment, the vampire sighed, like a connoisseur who has just imbibed from a very rare vintage wine. He put the mug down on the counter and walked out of the kitchen.

His senses projected outward. His body operating more efficiently now, he stood in his dark bedroom, considering what to wear. Outside, he heard cars more than a block away as they negotiated Adams Avenue. He heard the footsteps and the heartbeats of the young couple down below, as they walked along the sidewalk, blissfully unaware of the monster nearby.

He considered applying makeup, decided against it. Subterfuge would be inappropriate. He would rely on the young cop's innate goodness to not try to kill him. Still, one never knew how people would react in a stressful situation. Where their first, worst nightmares were confirmed, when the things parents always told children were imaginary, were suddenly real and in your face, and people had to face the terrible reality that monsters really do exist.

The vampire glided over to his closet, pulled the door back. He selected his wardrobe for the evening, black khaki pants, a navy blue cashmere mock turtle, a black London Fog trench coat that hung to his knees, and black loafer shoes.

He changed into the clothes quickly. He needed to find Reggie, tonight. That would take time. The vampire knew instinctively that time was something Reggie did not have in abundance.

Once dressed, the vampire walked into his living room. He took a deep breath, slowly and quietly blew it back out. He closed his eyes, calmed himself, and then concentrated, thinking about Reggie. His mind, usually awash with the sights, sounds, and smells of his surroundings and the people in them, began to calm itself. Another deep breath, in and out, and the calm filled with a gentle darkness the vampire always found both compelling, and comforting.

A few seconds later, it came to him. Not in a blinding flash of light like some kind of dramatic epiphany, but just a steady dawning of awareness. Reggie was alive, and in San Diego. He was in a dark place, no lights, but he was not afraid. He was at peace with his surroundings.

The vampire realized Reggie was asleep. Gentle, slow breaths, all even, in and out.

The vampire came out of his trance. There were forces afoot tonight, forces on both sides of the law that wanted Reggie Downing dead. The vampire's face darkened. In his mind, there was nothing worse than a dirty cop. A traitor to fellow officers, and a betrayer and exploiter of the public trust.

The vampire remembered his run-ins with law enforcement in his younger days. And he had certainly had his own experiences with dirty cops back in the day, had he not?

The vampire picked up his thin wraparound sunglasses, put them on as he moved forward. He snatched up his car keys, opened the door just wide enough for him to slither out. And then he was outside.

The deadbolt slid softly into place with a muted *thunk*, and then all was dark and quiet.

Outside on the landing, the vampire turned the collar on his trench coat up, and brought his fingers around towards his chin, making sure the collar popped completely, and stayed in its desired position. It had nothing to do with the dampness or the cold. Out of a heightened sense of self-preservation, honed for over a century, he simply wanted to hide his face as much as possible. And keep what could not be hidden in shadows.

He moved like a jungle predator, down the Spanish-tiled steps to the ground floor. His Lexus waited in a reserved parking spot in the alley out back. He made his way around the side of the building, enjoying the night. Enjoying the quiet.

Enjoying the darkness.

The vampire moved silently as the fog that enshrouded him, impervious to the moisture in the air, the condensation clinging to windshields, metal gates, fences. He paused at the back corner of the building, lifted the latch on the gate, and pushed through. He closed the gate behind him, dropped the latch back in place, and found himself in the alley.

He heard and felt raindrops right then, at the same time. Great, he thought. Now I'm going to get drenched, and my clothes will be ruined. Oh wait. I'm wearing London Fog. I'll be all right.

As he ambled towards his car, he picked up two racing heartbeats, somewhere out in front of him. They were lying in wait, thinking they were concealed. The vampire saw all buildings, cars, shrubs, and garbage dumpsters with his customary clarity. He sensed an evil intent from one. In the other he sensed fear.

The vampire did not have time for this. Not tonight. And certainly not in the damned rain.

He continued towards his car, seemingly oblivious. The two people appeared, rising up out of the mists from near a dumpster.

"Hey, fucker," one of them called out.

The vampire stopped on a dime, without turning around. "That's not nice, you know. To talk like that. He turned slowly. "To speak to another person like that."

Two of them, both Hispanic. Wearing gang colors. The vampire sighed. He had noticed the painted gang tags that had been cropping up on street signs around the area lately. It had never been an issue in the past. During the last year or two, however...

One was a bit older, maybe eighteen, twenty. No more. He was slightly built, with smooth features, but a cruel face. The other was still a child. Maybe thirteen, fourteen tops. His eyes as big as saucers, a mixture of fear and disbelief that he was actually doing something like this.

Probably his first time committing a crime.

Welcome to the deep end of the pool, kid.

They walked up to him, stopped about five feet away. "That your car?"

"Yes."

The kid pulled out a knife, clicked it open. The blade locked into place. "Give me the keys."

The vampire pretended to think it over. "No."

The kid brandished the knife threateningly. "Motherfucker, I said give me the keys. And while you're at it, give me all your money, too."

"No."

"Motherfucker, I'll cut your ass."

The vampire sighed, as if he was infinitely bored. He took off his sunglasses, deposited them into his inside coat pocket. He looked directly at them, no longer smiling, revealing his eyes.

Then his lips parted.

Were those really fangs they were seeing?

The younger one's jaw dropped. He took a step back. The older one, clearly scared, would not back down.

"You sure you want to do this?" the vampire asked, his voice slithering like snakes.

"What the fuck is wrong with you, man?"

The vampire took a step forward, wondered how to answer that question truthfully. "Where do I begin?"

The teen had expected an easy robbery, followed by an adrenaline high and dropping the car off to a chop shop for an easy two grand. But now, things were going sideways.

The vampire sincerely hoped they would turn and run. He disliked killing amateurs, people who were not committed to a life of crime. Or those young enough to still have a chance at rehabilitating themselves. If they ran, he could simply let them go. No one would believe the crazy story they would tell. Hell, everyone knew that vampires didn't exist, right?

But if this older *pendejo* decided to stand his ground and fight, it would seal the younger one's fate as well. If the vampire killed one, then he would be compelled to kill them both. Another essential part of Vampire Survival Strategy: never, under any circumstances, suffer a witness to live who has seen what a vampire can really do.

"Man. I'll cut you, man."

"No. You won't."

"I'll fucking stab you in the heart. I'll fucking kill you."

The vampire took another step forward. "No," he said gently, shaking his head. "You really won't. Trust me."

The vampire simply stood there, waiting. Seconds ticked by. The rain came down a bit harder. He was soaked, his hair plastered to his forehead.

He sighed. "Face it. You ain't gonna do anything, and I don't have time for this." He turned his back on the kid with the knife, began to walk away.

"What? Where you going?"

"Go home, kid," the vampire threw over his shoulder. "And take the little one with you."

Confused by his supposed victim's lack of fear, the older boy looked like he might start crying. "You can't do that!" His voice was hoarse. "You can't just walk away like that!"

The vampire unlocked his car, opened the door. Raindrops began pelting the fabric of the seat, newly exposed to the elements. "I'm doing it." He paused, waiting to see if his words would be taken as a taunt, propelling the knife-wielding youth into a stupid course of action.

"Go home, kid. Take Junior with you."

The vampire slid into the driver's seat, closed the door, flicked the door lock with one finger. He started up the car, turned on the headlights. Rivulets of water obscured and distorted objects outside as he peered through the windshield. He turned his wipers on. They moved smoothly, almost silently, wiping the rain off the glass, clearing his view.

The two youths still stood there, not moving. The vampire sighed again at their ignorance. He revved his engine. They jumped as if they'd been shot, and they moved off to the side. Inside the Lexus, he shifted the car into gear and tapped the accelerator. The car lurched forward, past the bewildered boys, and down the alley towards the street.

The older kid, secretly relieved, stared at the car and its receding red taillights. He felt his younger cousin tug on his sleeve.

"What?"

"Can we go now?"

He stared at his cousin in silence, unable to form words.

"I want to go home, Efren."

Efren nodded, trying to act tough in front of his cousin. *"Momentito, Hector. Momentito."*

Efren watched as the taillights glared bright and the collision light lit up, like a firework in the black wet night. The white Lexus stopped at the alley entrance. The yellow blinker went on, indicating a left turn. The car inched forward and turned left, and disappeared from his sight.

"I wanted to be sure that motherfucker wasn't coming back." He folded his knife and put it back into his pocket.

"He scared me."

"He was lucky." Hector looked up at his cousin questioningly. It was in that time that Efren knew Hector was not cut out for the "gangsta" lifestyle. Maybe Efren really wasn't, either.

"Come on. I'll get you a sandwich on the way home," Efren said. He patted Hector on the shoulder, and they walked up the alleyway as the rain continued to fall.

"I'd like a burger better," Hector said.

"Okay," Efren replied. "And on Monday, you're going to school."

Hector looked up at his cousin. "What?"

"You do it," Efren ordered, in a voice that Hector knew meant he had no choice in the matter.

"You should do it, too," Hector mumbled.

Efren pretended he was thinking about it for the first time. "Well, maybe I will."

Hector's face lit up with a broad smile. "Really?"

Efren nodded. "I could sign up for one of those adult courses. Auto mechanics, or something."

Hector smiled. Efren grinned back at him.

Finally.

Something that would make his mother proud of him again.

CHAPTER FIFTEEN

Rain peppered across the windshield as the Lexus approached the ramp for the southbound Interstate 15. Wipers wicked water away in a rhythmic beat, an automotive metronome. More rain pattered across the glass.

The vampire glanced into his rear view mirror. Rivulets of water cascaded down the back window. Driven by air movement from the car moving at thirty miles per hour, rainwater ran off the roof across the back, and down to the pavement.

He tapped his brakes at the red light, put on his left blinker. The vampire was a very good driver. He always obeyed the rules of the road, never drove over the speed limit, never rolled through a stop sign.

But it was more than simply decades of experience and fastidious attention to detail. As with so many other things in his life, he drove so as to not draw attention to himself.

The light turned green. He accelerated gently and cranked his wheel. The car moved forward in a leftward arc, turning onto the onramp from Adams Avenue to the Interstate. Once in the merging lane, he accelerated more aggressively. He signaled, merged left into rather sparse weekend traffic. Soon he traveled at over seventy miles per hour.

As he drove, his mind slowed. His body controlled the car, from muscle memory more than anything else. His mind became calm water on a moonlit lake. Shimmering liquid. Tranquil translucence.

Quiet as the Grave.

Black as Death.

Then he pushed. Concentrated. Discarded psychic distractions.

Zeroed in.

He felt Reggie's life force again. Heartbeat and respirations thumped faster before, but the vampire sensed no trauma, no undue stress.

Reggie was awake now. The longer the vampire maintained his psychic connection, the easier to pinpoint Reggie. Like a bat seeking out both prey and dangers via echolocation.

The vampire looked in his rear view mirror again, checking traffic behind him. He signaled, merged onto another curved onramp. He merged onto westbound State Highway 94, known as the Martin Luther King highway, or simply the MLK.

The rain had abated. He turned the wipers off. Ahead, glistening like multicolored jewels, the lights of downtown San Diego sparkled. What locals proudly called "America's Finest City".

Somewhere within that city, a brave, honest cop had been betrayed by one of his own, a fellow policeman sworn to uphold the law. And seriously bad, evil men had marked that honest cop for death. Men with no morals, no respect for the law, no respect for human life, no remorse for the evil they did. No guilt about the lives they destroyed, or the families they devastated.

Men who showed no mercy.

Well, the vampire decided, no mercy is what they deserve in return. And no mercy shall they receive from me.

Officer Reginald Downing staggered from the cheap bed. His back torqued in pain. The ancient, seen-better-days, overslept and under stuffed mattress lay atop an exposed box spring that looked like something from the Great Depression. The claustrophobic room boasted a thin line of black mold near the top of the wall along the seam where it met the ceiling.

The bed, the linens, the walls, the entire room smelled musty.

Reggie had tried resting at the Boroquez Building. Having grown up watching old horror movies on TV and listening to his Grandma's and Great Grandma's ghost and voodoo stories when he was small, isolation and silence always gave him the creeps. The pitch-blackness, the cold sounds, chilly echoes. So he had opted for a cheapie roach motel instead. He did not check out with Coulter or anyone else.

He just did it.

Reggie now shuffled to a small wood worn table. He fumbled in the shadows, and finally managed to turn a tiny table lamp on. Yellow light speared through the room, illuminating only part of it, casting shadows, bringing the farther recesses out of blackness and into muddy gloom. He stood back up gingerly, then tentatively arched, stretching his abdominal muscles. It did not hurt as much as he feared.

Clad only in his underwear, he looked down at himself. He was getting older, sure, but he still had powerful legs, a tight chest, and washboard abs. His shoulders remained broad, heavily muscled, his triceps still well defined. When he made a muscle, his biceps curled up to roughly the size of small cannonballs.

The tiniest trace of "love handles" were forming at either side of his lower back. It did not show from the front, and his pants size had not increased since he was a teen. All in all, he thought he was doing well for a career cop in his thirties.

Reggie had bounced from one flop house to another the past two days. Standing still gave your enemy time to catch up. He did not spend the night in the same place twice.

Tonight would be no different.

He would grab a shower, put on some clothes, then venture out. His planned to utilize counter surveillance techniques, moving through the city to downtown, and into East Village. Once there he planned to do the last thing anyone would expect him to do.

Reggie ambled with a stiff gait into the bathroom he had paid extra for. It was worth it. He had also paid extra for the night clerk to not tell anyone he was here. Whether or not that was money well spent, only time would tell. Things were looking good so far.

He turned on the light by pulling a white string that dangled down from above. The bare bulb swung overhead imbedded in a plain brass socket. Subpar black wiring held the assembly, dropping two feet below the peeling plaster ceiling. He gazed at himself in the mirror.

The wall behind him was cinderblock, reinforced with rebar. Painted several times over the years – white, yellow, and the current faded, pale green that was so pale as too almost be colorless.

He grabbed a cup, filled it halfway. Drank it down. He grimaced. The pipes were old, rusty, not up to code.

But it was more than that. San Diego had a problem with its water table. The water was chock full of minerals and particulates, which effected the taste.

He brushed his teeth, cupped one hand under the faucet. Water filled his palm, and sucked it into his mouth. When he had packed his go-bag prior to locking it in the buses terminal, he had forgotten to pack mouthwash or floss. So he made do with what he had.

Reggie placed his toothbrush on the side of the porcelain lavatory, so old and worn it exhibited rings of rusty brown from the iron core underneath. He peeled off his underwear, stepped out of them. He turned on the shower, wondering how long he would wait for anything akin to warm water. True hot water was beyond his hopes in a dilapidated beachside dump.

Suddenly frowning, Reggie strode out of the bathroom. He walked into the main area, glanced around. He padded to the bed, and reached under the pillow, still indented from the weight of his head. His fingers stretched, searching, until they touched something hard.

Reggie's hand encircled the grip of his handgun. He pulled it out from beneath the pillow. He smiled a bit, nodded, then turned and walked back into the bathroom. As he turned to enter the bathroom doorway, he glanced over at the main door that led outside. Door securely closed, knob lock locked, a security chain in position, deadbolt still in the locked position.

About as secure as possible in a dump like this.

He stepped inside the bathroom, looking for a good place to pre-stage his weapon, in case he needed to grab it fast. The cartel had eyes and ears everywhere.

He settled on the trashcan. He dumped what little trash was in there onto the floor in the corner behind the toilet. Then he turned the can upside down and placed it beside the shower at the back. He placed his handgun atop the inverted can, muzzle pointing towards the door. Reggie quickly closed and locked the bathroom door, then stood at the shower once more, beside the trashcan, familiarizing himself with this eye line in case the worst actually happened.

Warmth and humidity quickly changed the enclosed room with the inadequate ventilation. Steam smudged the mirror. He smiled. He was actually going to get a hot shower.

He stepped into the tub and pulled the shower curtain, the tiny metal rings singing their song along the aluminum rod above his head. The thin sheet of decorative plastic unfurled along the way. Satisfied he would not splash water onto his handgun waiting on the other side of the curtain, Reggie turned his attention to the shower itself.

Water dumped, an upside down steam geyser from the water spigot. He reached out and grabbed a tiny metal toggle switch just above the spigot. The toggle was pointed down. He pushed it to the up position. The downward geyser immediately ceased, follow by an audible and visible vibration from the exposed pipes that lead upwards to the antique shower head above, encrusted with decades of hard water deposits.

Hot water exploded from the showerhead, pelting Reggie's head, face and body, thousands of hot, tiny, wet needles. It felt wonderful. He opened up the paper wrapper on the tiny bar of soap. There was no washcloth in the bathroom, so he soaped up as best he could. He rinsed off quickly, and stood motionless under the showerhead, the gentle sting of the hot water slicing into his pores, running furious rivulets down his skin.

He breathed deeply, his rib cage expanding, his lungs filling with wet air. He felt heady, engulfed by that euphoria that comes from an influx of oxygen into the bloodstream. He exhaled, forcefully, through his mouth. He had to keep his head in the game. He could not allow himself to stop and smell the roses, so to speak. Even a temporary, seemingly innocuous distraction could prove fatal, if an attack came at that very instant when he was not aware of his surroundings.

Reggie reached down and turned the water off. Lingering water already in momentum inside the pipe, continued to drip from the showerhead. He stood in silence. He could not even hear his own breathing. He concentrated, listening for any sound on the other side of the curtain. On the other side of the bathroom door. Within the apartment beyond.

He did not hear anything. Somehow, tonight, that did not bring him any comfort. He knew the remnants of El Gecko's men, and the men El Gecko had worked for, would be out in force tonight, trying to track him down and kill him. They had to. It was a matter of honor with them.

It was also a matter of survival. They had to kill him, and kill him quickly, promptly, or other organizations would see them as being soft, weak. Vulnerable for a "hostile takeover", which usually meant a lot of blood and a lot of bodies as the outside group fought to wrestle the business and the revenue from El Gecko's bosses.

Reggie gently pushed the curtain aside, from right to left, gingerly trying to not generate a lot of noise as the metal rings scraped along the aluminum tubing above his head. He still heard nothing. Still sensed no threat.

Good.

He stepped out of the shower and onto the floor mat. He shook excess water off his hand, picked up his handgun to move it out of the way. His fingers curled around the worn cotton towel underneath it, lifted it up away from the upside down trashcan. He placed his handgun back atop the trashcan, and toweled off quickly, efficiently.

He folded the towel over once lengthwise, then hung it from the imitation chrome towel rack attached to the cinderblock wall. He noted as he turned away that the whole rack bowed a bit under the weight of just the one towel.

He picked up his handgun, made sure the safety was still on. Satisfied, he twisted the dull door handle and pushed the door open. Steam billowed out, pushed into the blackened room by the air movement created by the door movement. He padded across the forty-year-old shag carpeting – did they even make that stuff anymore? – to his bed. He tossed his handgun down. He grabbed his duffle off the floor, tossed it onto the rumple sheets in front of him.

He unzipped the bag, began pulling out fresh clothing. He stepped into new underwear first, then pulled up his dark green pants to buckle them around his waist. He faltered a moment, looking at two different shirts, trying to figure out which one he would wear.

The moment lingered. Reggie could not make up his mind. His eyes moved back and forth between his two choices.

"I'd go with the black mock turtle."

The voice from the far dark corner of the room, even though spoken softly, exploded through the silence. Reggie, startled, eyes wide, dove for his handgun, flicked the safety off, and aimed at the darkness.

"Freeze, motherfucker," he growled.

He sensed no movement in the room. Whoever it was, was using the darkness as cover. Like a goddamned ninja or something. Concentrating and squinting in the gloom, Reggie thought he could just make out the barest beginnings of a shadow. More amorphous than anything else.

He retrained his weapon slightly, pointing more directly at where he perceived the threat to be. "Okay, dickwad," he said. "Come out slowly with your hands where I can see them."

"Dickwad?" the voice responded. It sounded as if whoever was there was trying to keep from laughing. "That's amusing, Reginald."

Looking down the length of the barrel of his handgun, putting his sight right in the center of where the voice was coming from, Reggie's brain hit a fog bank. Something recognizable about the voice. Something half-remembered.

"Wait a minute." His voice was unsure, faltering.

"Yes?"

"We've met before."

"Very good." The person in the shadows seemed genuinely pleased to be remembered. Perhaps it was a rare occurrence for him.

"Step out of the shadows. Come into the light. Let me see your hands."

The figure moved slowly, serpentine. Like coils unrolling, revealing themselves slowly, luxuriously. Like blurred wisps of smoke on a moonless night, all fog and darkness began to coalesce.

Into a dark solid mass.

He moved laterally in measured steps, careful to not alarm the already frightened police officer holding a large caliber firearm, zeroed in with a laser like focus on everything he did.

The vampire stepped forward out of the shadows. His hands out to his sides, palms open, empty, and facing forward. Reggie truly saw him for the first time.

He wore dark pants, expensive, and shoots of good quality, a navy mock turtle of his own, and a long duster-like, black trench coat, with the top collar popped up, hiding a part of his lower jaw. Moisture from outside still beaded on the waterproof material. He wore wraparound sunglasses, black and opaque, completely hiding his eyes. His frame was thin, almost slight. To the casual observer, he might appear frail.

Gaunt, Reggie thought. The man is gaunt.

And pale, Reggie's mind confirmed. Very pale. This disturbed him more than anything else up to this point.

Translucent. Yeah, that's the word. It was like his skin was fucking translucent, or something. Reggie could just barely make out a thin, spiderweb-like latticework of dainty blue blood vessels tracing underneath the yellowish skin on his cheeks and chin.

Reggie continued to scrutinize this... very strange, completely unique person. Average height, maybe five six, five eight, tops. No taller, of that he was certain. Long face, angular features. Sloping nose, high cheekbones, pointed chin. Thin, colorless lips gave this guy's mouth a cruel look. Like his mouth was not really a part of his body, but just a gash in his lower face that occasionally opened up.

And then there was the dark hair. Lank. Limp. Like it wasn't even alive. What the hell was wrong with his hair?

Then Reggie really figured out what was wrong. He put it all together, the look, the hair, the skin. White, lifeless, sallow, with a bloodless, almost yellowish or grayish hue.

"That's far enough."

The vampire stopped.

"Any weapons on you?"

"Not in your definition of the term."

"What does that mean?"

"I carry no gun or knife. I have no need for them.."

"Sit down."

The vampire obeyed. He sat down on a decades old, decades out of style chair with a plain wooden back consisting of two upright spines and a single, curved piece of wood about six inches wide connected and glued between the two. The upholstered seat had lost its dubious cushioning long ago. The chair creaked under his weight as he sat.

The vampire crossed his legs easily, held his palms out, upwards. The corners of his mouth lifted into a patient smile, his teeth still hidden beneath his lips.

"Okay," Reggie started. "Let's start with the basics. Who are you?"

"Someone who has taken a special interest in your continued well being," the vampire answered. "Someone who does not want to see you murdered by the cartel." He slowly leaned forward in his chair. "Someone who can help you track down the traitor in your ranks who betrayed you."

Then he eased back in the chair again.

Reggie's handgun stayed pointing at the vampire's chest. The vampire noticed the muzzle never wavered, never trembled. He allowed Reggie to continue to believe he was in control of this situation.

"So tell me the truth," Reggie said. "You're with the cartel?"

"No."

"You a cop?"

"No."

"Then how the hell do you think you can help me?"

The vampire folded his hands in front of his stomach. "I bring *unique* abilities to the table."

"Like what you did at the ship? How'd you do that, by the way?"

The vampire now looked directly at the nervous policeman. "I can say the words, convey the thoughts. But it may be quite difficult for you to accept them." The vampire paused briefly to let that sink in. "You see, my dear young officer, my... abilities arise from the reality what I am."

Reggie frowned slightly, confused. "And what, exactly, is the reality of what you are?"

"You will not like it."

"I already don't like it."

"You will not believe it."

"I probably won't."

"I am a vampire."

Reggie stood there, stock-still. His stomach heaved a little; his mind asked himself if he had truly heard what he thought he had just heard. But outwardly, his facial expression did not change. "That's the stupidest thing I've ever heard," he responded at last.

"You wound me, young man," he spoke with an edge to his voice. "I would never lie to you. And you offend me at the suggestion."

"Well then, please forgive me, sir." The tone was thinly veiled sarcasm.

The vampire rankled, moved slowly in his chair. "If I am to help you, we cannot move forward like this."

"Meaning?"

"You must first be amenable to my help. You must understand, accept, and believe I am indeed, a vampire."

A grin struggled across Reggie's mouth. "Just to clarify, when you say vampire, you're talking about drinking blood, coffins, crosses, all that shit, right?"

"I drink blood to survive," the vampire answered. "I don't do coffins. Too claustrophobic. I lie in a bed, in a dark room under the protection of some ridiculously thick and heavy, and rather musty curtains. As far as crosses go, I find myself rather fond of them. More specifically, what they represent."

"And what do they represent?"

"God, goodness, compassion, kindness. Redemption," he added after a pause. "I believe in the existence of God, make no mistake about that. I just do not understand his intent. Maybe someday I will have a chance to ask Him about it."

"Dude, I think you're one of the most convincing con men I've ever seen."

The vampire cocked his head slightly. Reggie watched him reach up, grip the earpiece of his sunglasses within the tips of three long, slender fingers. Reggie frowned a bit again. He had not noticed the long slim fingers earlier, or the long, pointed, claw like fingernails.

The vampire slowly removed his sunglasses, revealing his huge, crystalline, black eyeballs. They looked like two polished obsidian orbs. Reggie actually took a half step back. In credit to his training and professionalism, he did not panic. He did not scream. The gun muzzle never moved off its target.

The vampire was impressed. He blinked his eyes, then smiled. He opened his mouth, bared his fangs. The frown furrows across Reggie's forehead deepened.

Still sitting as comfortably as he could sit in such an uncomfortable chair, the vampire unfolded his hands, but kept his legs crossed. He gave Reggie a moment to take it all in.

"We shall now conduct... an experiment," the vampire announced.

"W – what?"

"An experiment," the vampire replied. "We shall test a theory under controlled conditions and observe the outcome. Like the scientific experiments you enjoyed so much in college chemistry."

"How did you now I had a blast in chemistry in college?"

"I know a great many things about you, young man. And I must tell you, I have become a fan of you. Both as a cop, and as a human being. You are a good man, Reginald Downing. Your heart is in the right place. Your mother and grandmother did a wonderful job raising you. You make me proud."

Reggie heard the genuine pride in this person's voice. But he heard something else mixed in the tone, too. Was it... ? No, it couldn't be. Did he notice genuine affection?

Reggie zeroed back in on the moment. "What about your experiment?"

"Ah yes. The experiment."

"Just to satisfy my own morbid curiosity, what do you have in mind? I mean, how do you intend to prove to me that you're a vampire, like out of an old Christopher Lee movie?"

The vampire grinned. "Ah, yes. Christopher Lee. My favorite." Then the vampire looked at Reggie, dead serious, with those disconcerting black, lifeless eyes. "I want you to shoot me in the chest."

"Excuse me?"

"Rest assured, you shall not succeed," the vampire said with utmost confidence. "But I want you to try."

"Why?"

"It is crucial to the success of the experiment."

"But why? Why do you want me to shoot you?"

The vampire smiled, his fangs showing again. It creeped Reggie out.

"I shall anticipate the moment you begin to squeeze the trigger," the vampire said. "I will wrench the gun from your hand before you have a chance to squeeze off a round. Now, it may hurt your hand a bit," the vampire warned, "but rest assured, it is not my intent to injure you in any way."

Reggie turned this over in his mind. The vampire simply sat there, smiling, showing his fangs, his black eyes, though dancing, were as dead as a corpse, and as cold as the grave.

Reggie's finger began to tighten around the trigger.

Moving so fast he could only be seen as a blur, the vampire bolted from the chair, sped across the room, and wrenched the gun out of Reggie's hand before Reggie could react.

Reggie's eyes grew wide once more. His mouth dropped. Sweat popped out across his forehead and upper lip. His pulse shot up to over one hundred.

The vampire smiled warmly, trying to be disarming. He expertly spun the gun around his hand and extended his arm towards Reggie. He was offering the gun back to him, grip first, the muzzle pointed at his own chest.

Respect.

Reggie, mouth still open in shock, reached out tentatively, eyes darting back and forth between the grip of his gun and the vampire's face. The vampire stood still, an undead statue. Reggie's fingers curled around the gun's grip and squeezed tight to handle the weight. The vampire's own talons uncurled and retracted, allowing Reggie to control of his weapon.

The vampire stood there, hands at his sides. There was nothing left for him to say. The human would either wrap his mind around this new reality, a reality that included the existence of vampires, or he would not. He cocked his head slightly. His glasslike eyes regarded Reggie quizzically.

Reggie dropped his hand to his side, gun barrel pointing downward. He stared at the vampire before him, trying to comprehend how all this could be possible.

"You're not bullshittin' me, are you?"

The vampire merely shook his head. Then he sat back down, crossed his legs easily. He draped one arm over the back of the chair.

Then Reggie's brain began to fire again, recounting the events aboard the freighter. "That quickness. Those claws. The teeth. That explains the *Sulu Sea*."

"They were bad people," the vampire stated. "You know that. They all wanted to kill you."

"They still do." Reggie slipped his handgun into the worn brown holster attached to the side of his hip at the belt. "Why spare Rudy?"

"Rudy?"

"Hispanic fellow," Reggie described. "Five foot seven. Clean-shaven. Short hair."

"Ah yes." The vampire nodded. "Think of it as a professional courtesy."

"Professional courtesy?"

"He is a killer. Like me. A professional. He moved like a soldier."

"Rudy was a Marine. He did tours in the Middle East."

"He has obviously made some bad choices," the walking corpse replied. "I can identify with that."

"I've made mistakes in my time, too. So what?"

"He is in a bad business, but he is not a bad man," the vampire responded. "Given the proper push, he may opt for a different path." The vampire paused. "I attempted to supply him that."

Why do you talk like that?"

"Like what?"

"So.... properly, I suppose. You never use contractions."

"Really? I had not noticed."

"It's weird, man."

The vampire shrugged. "I have no desire to disconcert you. I simply... speak the way I speak."

"He's still guilty of a dozen Federal felonies," Reggie recited.

"Who?"

"Rudy Valdez."

The vampire nodded, then said, "That is your concern, not mine."

Reggie's forehead furrowed again. He shook his head.

"You are, no doubt, quite hungry." The vampire said it as a statement of fact. "You have not eaten in hours. In fact, you have not eaten properly since this whole thing began."

"How can you know that?"

"The 'how' is not important. Suffice to say, I know."

"You really creep me the fuck out," Reggie said, pointing a finger in the vampire's direction. "No offense."

"None taken."

Reggie stood there, looking at the sitting vampire. Vampire? Jesus. If vampires were real, then what the hell else was out there?

The vampire read the cop's mind, but did not answer the question. It was better if the young man simply did not know.

He stood up. "Let us dine an evening repast."

An evening repast? Seriously? "Wait a minute," Reggie said. "You want to go eat? What kind of vampire are you?"

"I shall not eat any food," the vampire grinned. "But you will. You have more questions. I shall answer them. I have decided to reveal all to you."

"What are you talking about?"

"Later," the vampire assured him. "Let me buy you a decent meal."

Journal entry February 3rd

I recently saw on the TV the news that two misguided souls who, in a fit of misguided religious fervor, decided to swear out a jihad, and stage an ill conceived, poorly planned and executed attack on American soil, in the heartland.

Simpletons.

They attacked a convention center in Texas. Yes, just the two of them. Just imagine. Two gunmen, with no backup, attacking a convention center ringed by off-duty cops and private security (read, MERCENARIES).

It did not end well for them.

I am reminded there are many soldiers, sailors, airmen and Marines, coming home from the endless wars overseas with highly honed, lethal skillsets. The type of skillsets that once learned can never be unlearned. And are never fully be put to rest.

Ever.

These skills lie just beneath the surface, beneath that thin veneer people call "civilized behavior". Lurking, waiting, seething, coiled like a spring, begging to be unleashed.

One.

More.

Time.

I keep reading about these terror groups who threaten to come to the U.S. en masse and kill every man, woman, and child that does not convert to their ways. And to prove their point, they behead journalists, slaughter charity aid workers and priests, rape and torture nuns, or set fire to prisoners who have been confined in a cage and doused in gasoline.

They are cowards of the worst kind.

If they do come here en masse to the United States, with so many combat-skilled and battle-hardened veterans walking the streets, these "holy warriors" are in for a rude awakening.

In 1941, in the days after Pearl Harbor, Japanese Admiral Isoroku Yamamoto, the brilliant naval warfare strategist and architect of the Pearl Harbor attack, was crestfallen when he learned that the U.S. aircraft carrier fleet had been at sea and not destroyed in the raid. Although the Emperor and the Japanese High Command deemed the attack a success, Yamamoto felt it a failure. He considered it to have sealed Japan's fate. He is quoted as having said, "All we have accomplished today is to awaken a sleeping Giant, and filled him with a terrible resolve".

We currently have private gun ownership in this country at roughly 50% of the population, owning roughly 200 million firearms We currently have 1.5 million active duty military. And we have over 22 million combat veterans, itching for a fight.

God help anyone who thinks they can come here to this country, and wage a war against us on our own soil.

They too, will awaken a sleeping Giant, and fill him with a terrible resolve.

They will find a gun barrel behind every blade of grass.

CHAPTER SIXTEEN

Rudy Valdez left his Banker's Hill apartment late in the afternoon. His footsteps echoed off the walls of the deserted hallway. He made his way down the creaking wooden staircase. The front door opened silently, he noticed. It usually creaked. He supposed someone had finally taken a can of oil to the aging hinges.

Thick dark blue and gray clouds smudged the sky's palette, resembling a gigantic finger painting assignment. Cooler already by several degrees, the air tingled. The fading sunlight deepened to burnt orange at the horizon. Swirling shadows elongated, black fingers creeping across the concrete as day quickly fled the night.

He pulled his coat collar up around his throat as he skipped down the steps to the sidewalk. It felt good, it felt comforting, to have a high caliber handgun strapped inside his left armpit again.

He did not really know how tonight would play out. Summoned by Rick Oakley, supposedly at Mr. Vargas behest to a meeting at one of Mr. Vargas's warehouses. Even though Rick had assured him all was well, even though Rudy wanted to believe it, he carried his gun anyway.

Always plan for the worst-case scenario.

Rick had never lied to Rudy. In his own brutal way, Rick was an honest man. Unusual, given their line of work. If Rick planned to kill you, you would know. And you would know because, he would simply kill you.

Rudy considered taking the bus into downtown and running standard counter surveillance patterns for a while. Law enforcement might have put a tail on him since being released. Rudy rather liked the bus and trolley system when moving around San Diego. He liked not dealing with the hassle of parking, which was becoming worse and worse in this city. But if things went sideways later, he would need to beat feet, shoot his way out and affect a fast getaway.

Rudy moved towards his car, eyes always darting. One was always vulnerable when paused getting into or out of a car. Try to focus on reflective surfaces, car windshields, glass windows. Look for anyone coming up behind you.

Parked in a small lot around the back of the apartment building, the metallic gray Mini Cooper waited. Rudy had bought it for cash off the showroom floor about a year ago. A lot of people Rudy's age drove smaller cars like this. His intent was to blend in, not stand out.

Plus, he got great gas mileage.

His handgun still held fifteen rounds to a clip, and he carried four extra clips. So Rudy had seventy-five rounds on his person, just in case. Rudy was aware California had passed a law limiting the number of rounds to a clip to ten rounds each. Good thing Rudy was a criminal. Otherwise he might have gotten worried.

What the hell good was that law going do? Did anyone really think this was going to stop men like Rudy? The law tipped the balance in the criminal's favor.

All in the name of making "the streets" safer.

Oh, the streets were safer, Rudy smirked as he unlocked his car door. Safer for guys like me to do what we do. Do those idiots in the Legislature truly believe we get our weapons and ammo from gun stores?

He inserted the key into the ignition, twisted it all the way to the right. The engine roared to life. Rudy shifted into reverse, backed out of his parking space, shifted again, and sped off. Spinning tires kicked up gravel as he disappeared into the street traffic outside his apartment.

It was dark now. Rudy turned on his driving lights. No rain today. The pavement was dry.

Having grown up in the Midwest, Rudy had learned how to drive in all kinds of weather – wind, heat, rain, snow, ice, you name it. But out here where it only rained about twenty days out of the year, local drivers turned into maniacs at the first raindrop on a windshield. They either drove thirty miles per hour under the speed limit, or they drove eighty-five on the freeways, passing on both the left and the right, whizzing by sane drivers who know to slow down, hydroplaning be damned.

Rudy glanced in his rearview, put his blinker on as he traveled south on Fourth, heading downtown. He turned right, now heading west. He stopped at a red light on Third. The light changed to green, and Rudy hit the gas, let the clutch out, and moved forward. Heading west, he saw the glittering lights of San Diego bay.

He could see the lights of Anthony's, a local seafood market and restaurant, sitting where it had sat for fifty years, built on stilts out over the water.

Just north of that was the Maritime Museum with its menu of period ships and boats. Tall ships, rigged masts, a couple of submarines from eras past, even a large steam-powered ferryboat that had ferried passengers from San Francisco to Oakland from 1898 to until the early sixties. Hell, they even had recently restored and out on display a Coastal Patrol boat that had seen combat action from the Mekong Delta to the DMZ during the Vietnam War.

But the real jewel in the Maritime' Museum's crown, was the iron-hulled tall ship, the *Star of India*. Moored at the pier closest to the road and less than one hundred feet from Anthony's, Rudy could see her red and black sides and her creamy white sails, fully deployed and lit for dramatic effect. No matter how many times he saw her, bobbing gently at her moorings, he was always impressed. She was a beautiful ship – a work of engineering art, really – and an important link between the present and California's maritime history.

Unfortunately, Rudy had other, darker things on his mind this night. He put on his blinker again, and turned left onto what the locals called PCH – the Pacific Coast Highway. Heading south once again, he glanced into his mirrors. He did not notice any cars following him. He inhaled deeply, breathed out a huge sigh of relief.

He could turn left onto Broadway, head through downtown. It would be a more direct route to his final destination. But things were starting to get jumping in the Gaslamp, and traffic could get snarled at a moment's notice. He did not want to be late. These were not people who took kindly to being kept waiting, and the excuse of "I got stuck in traffic", even if true, simply would not fly.

So Rudy kept driving, past the intersection of PCH and Broadway, heading south. He shifted into the left hand turn lane at Harbor Drive, and stopped, anticipating the protected green arrow. As he waited, his eyes drifted around him. Across the broad intersection was the entrance to Seaport Village. He could see the one hundred year old carousel spinning, carrying delighted kids and indulgent parents, going around and around.

Rudy had no children of his own. His occupation pretty much precluded a so-called "normal" lifestyle.

But Rudy had made his choices, he knew it, accepted it, and did not feel much regret. His life was what it was, and by and large, he was good with it. There were consequences to every choice made in life, his uncle used to tell him, so make your choices wisely, be man enough to face the consequences, and you'll be okay.

Rudy's father would not approve of the choices he had made. But they were his to make, and he had made them. He had lived with them, and their inevitable consequences. Like getting arrested and thrown in jail.

But even Rudy had to admit, things were getting old. He did not want to be in the drug smuggling business forever, and he had been frugal with his money.

He lived below his means, had close to mid-six figures in the bank, and as much more neatly tucked away in various instruments. He rented a safe deposit box filled with cash, physical gold and silver, both in ten-ounce bullion ingots. Also included in the deep box was a nylon duffle bag, neatly rolled up and tucked into one corner of the box, and a .45 caliber automatic handgun, fully loaded with an illegal clip that held fifteen rounds, and with three extra clips, also illegal, also fully loaded.

The red light went out, immediately replaced by a green arrow. Rudy put the car in gear and turned left as he accelerated through the intersection. Now on Harbor Drive, he drove east, the expensive hotels and the expansive Convention Center to his right, and expensive high-rise condos and the bustling beehive that was the Gaslamp to his left. His boss lived in one of those high rises, he mused. Very high up. Very posh. Great view from the balcony, as he remembered.

Rank had its privileges, even in the drug trade.

He motored past the Gaslamp and Petco Park, the baseball-only stadium built several years back for the Padres baseball team. Then the buildings blurring by got scarce. More undeveloped land. Train yards to the right. He continued on, leaving downtown and the East Village, crossing a bridge into Logan Barrio on the left, and Port of San Diego docks and warehouses to the right. Lots of heavy industry here now, some large defense contractors like NASSCO who built ships for the Navy, and smaller businesses that supplied them or subcontracted work from them.

He slowed the mini down as he came to a red light intersection. If he turned left, he would be a on a surface street that served as a feeder to an onramp for the Coronado Bay Bridge. But he turned right, into what appeared to be an industrial park, heading towards the docks. He made a few quick turns, winding his way through a maze of weathered, nondescript, colorless warehouses that all looked alike and all looked like they had seen better days.

He made one last, slow turn, and inched down the narrow drive, barely wide enough for two cars to safely pass if going in the opposite directions. As he moved down, the headlights throwing yellow pools of illumination out in front of him, he scanned the warehouses to the right with increasing concentration.

He was close now.

He knew where he was going. He stopped his car, parked it beside another larger, splashier car, a red late-model Mercedes. So Rick Oakley was going to be here, he mused. This should be interesting.

Rudy got out of his car. Usually, Rudy felt he had nothing to fear from Rick. And although Rick had been good natured and reassuring earlier, Rudy still felt ill at ease. He never felt he could ever really trust Rick, because he had seen Rick be nice to someone one minute, and jab an ice ick into their carotid artery the next as if it were nothing. Just part of the job, a function he sometimes performed. Nothing more.

How could he ever truly trust a guy like that?

Rudy felt better knowing he was packing heat himself. He hoped he was just being paranoid. But sometimes, when someone had been nicked, "upper management" decided it prudent to eliminate any potential security leak.

But Rudy had proved himself, hadn't he? He had put his life on the line in gunfights, knife fights, and close-quarter hand-to-hand combat for Mr. Vargas. Hell, Rick Oakley and he had fought side by side more than once.

That shit had to count for something, right?

Rudy locked his car, pushed a tiny button on the key ring to set the alarm. A loud squeak erupted from somewhere under the hood, and his headlights blinked twice in rapid succession. Then the car went dark and silent, resting, awaiting his return.

He turned his head and scanned the area as he deposited his keys into the right front pocket of his jeans. He saw no one else around. The warehouses were dark, silent, and squatting. Dark pane-window eyed gargoyles, bursting to take flight into the inky night sky. No noise, no light, no movement.

Creepy as shit.

If someone was out there watching him, a sniper, maybe, with a high-powered rifle and a laser scope, Rudy could not detect them.

Hell, he thought as he began slowly walking towards the door of the warehouse in front of him. If they're that good to set up on me, then they deserve the shot.

The bullet would come from behind, and aimed at the center of his upper back, over the spine, between the shoulder blades, center of mass. Most likely either a 30- or 50- caliber round, traveling at over three thousand feet per second. Even at over a quarter mile away, the bullet would take less than two seconds to travel from the end of the rifle's muzzle to impact. Even at a half mile, it would take less than four.

He would suffer no pain, just an astonishing impact, like getting slammed with a sledgehammer. The bullet would drill through his chest cavity, pulverizing bone upon entry and exit, rupturing the aorta, the vena cava, possibly one or more chambers of the heart, and collapsing at least one lung.

The transferred kinetic energy would throw him forward hard into the door now in front of him. He would slide down the door to the ground, leaving greasy red stains on the metal. He would die gasping, wondering what the hell had happened, why he was suddenly so fatigued, struggling so hard to breathe...

But none of that happened.

Rudy reached out and grabbed the hook–style door handle. His fingers curled around it, and he pushed down. The handle moved at his command, and he pulled the door open. He stepped inside, into the dark hallway. He stood there a moment, getting his bearings.

His eyes adjusted, ciliary muscles relaxing, pupils expanding, twin apertures on creation's most miraculous cameras. All was quiet. No sound, except for his own breathing, and the pounding pulse from his own beating heart. The hallway in front of him remained black as midnight. Beyond that, at the end of the hall, he detected a faint pool, a paleness of the gloom, seen through the glass top half of the door at the end of the hall.

He moved forward, methodically, one foot in front of the other. His shooting hand never wavered far from his handgun underneath his coat. He could almost imagine invisible cobwebs hanging down from the ceiling, dancing across his face as he passed underneath all but the lowest hanging threads, gossamer tendrils. He practically half-expected for a zombie or a vampire to jump out at him, its rotting face screaming and moaning, milky eyes bulging, arms outstretched, fingers clutching for the soft flesh on his own throat. Mouth open, lips pulled back, long fangs ready to sink into his neck...

Rudy shivered, shook his head, angry with himself. Too many damn horror movies, he told himself. Maybe I should start watching comedies – or love stories, he thought.

He managed to get to the far end of the hall without being eaten alive by rotting bloated zombies, or being drained of his life-giving blood by some Euro trash wannabe Dracula. The heavy metal industrial type door sported a large window taking up almost half the upper portion of the riveted frame. Even in the pale light, he could see the tiny chicken wire embedded between the two layers of glass, reinforcing the pane.

Through the glass, he could see the expansive floor of the main warehouse. He remembered both the delightful and horrible events that had taken place here. His paranoia returned. He wondered whether this next experience would be delightful or terrible

He hesitated a moment. His hand drifted upwards from beside his thigh, reaching for the door handle. He noted it too was a hooked lever. A simple pull up or push down would be enough to open the lock and push through the doorway. His hand hovered for a moment longer, tension knotting up in his neck, between his shoulders.

Face it like a man, he told himself. Everybody dies.

Don't be a pussy.

His fingers curled around the door handle, tightened around it in a firm grip. He pushed downward without much thought. He heard the tumblers in the doorframe click open. He turned his shoulder towards the door and pushed, putting his weight behind it to

move the heavy door. The door gave, pushing open without any
noticeable sound, and Rudy stepped through the frame and into the
huge, high-ceilinged room.

Rudy paused, allowing the door, on its own hydraulic piston,
to close behind him. To his left, nothing but gloom. Within the
gloom, he could make out row upon row of boxes and wooden
crates, arranged neatly to create wide lanes in between them, wide
enough for forklifts to maneuver. These boxes and crates, which
contained legitimate manufactured goods, were stacked atop each
other over twelve feet high. Mr. Vargas's import and export business
was a legitimate enterprise that laundered his gains from his more
shady endeavors.

"Ah, Rudy!" A voice, familiar, cracking the silence.

Rudy's head turned in that direction. Down at the end of a
wide lane, under a shaded industrial lamp that shone its yellow light
directly downward, a misshapen, bent, grey metal desk of
questionable age and origin squatted low to the ground. Behind this
desk, sitting in an equally antiquated Government – surplus swivel
chair covered in a matching grey fake leather material, was Mr.
Vargas himself, smiling, like he was welcoming a guest into his
home. He motioned with his hand for Rudy to join him.

Real friendly.

Rudy spun on his heel, began walking down the long lane
towards his boss. He now noticed Rick Oakley standing beside
Vargas, slightly behind him and to his right. A few other trusted
confidants stood in the shadows to Vargas's left. Everyone seemed
to be at ease, smiling. No tension.

Everyone's eyes were on him. His right hand never ventured
far from the handgun just beneath his jacket. Since everyone seemed
to be smiling at him as he approached, he smiled back. Smiling
would not cause him to hesitate –not even for a millisecond - if he
suddenly felt the need to kill them.

When he was about twenty feet away, he saw Mr. Vargas
slowly rise from his chair behind the desk. Oakley grabbed the back
of the chair, pulling it back and out of the boss's way. Vargas smiled
warmly, made his way around the desk and stood in front, directly in
front of Rudy as he approached. Vargas opened his arms wide.

"Rudy," he greeted.

Rudy was less than ten feet away. "Mr. Vargas."

Vargas enveloped Rudy in a huge, affectionate embrace. More than a bit surprised, Rudy finally patted Vargas on the back, perfunctorily returning the hug.

Vargas grabbed him by the shoulders. "I'm glad you're here," he said. "It wouldn't be right to get started without you. Not after everything you've given in service to me, and the organization. And certainly not after what you've been through the past couple of days."

Vargas motioned to a chair facing the desk. "Please. Have a seat."

Rudy glanced around. He knew all the men here were dangerous, trained and experienced killers. Yet none of them gave off a threatening vibe. So Rudy sat down.

Vargas waked back around the desk. Oakley grabbed the back of the boss's chair as Vargas positioned himself in front of the cushion. As he bent his legs to sit, Oakley moved the chair towards him, seating him, and helping move the chair forward until it was a comfortable distance from the desk itself.

"You said something about getting started, sir," Rudy stated. "What's going on?"

"We're handling some business tonight," Vargas replied. "Business that will affect the organization. And since you are an integral part of our organization, it affects you, too, in a very real way."

"I don't understand, sir."

Vargas smiled indulgently. "Look. I know you thought we were going to snuff you," he said. "Nothing could be further from the truth. I never had any doubt you'd keep your mouth shut to the cops. Sanctioning a hit on you never crossed my mind."

Rudy shifted a bit in his chair. He wanted to believe this was true.

Vargas bent to one side, reached down behind the desk. Rudy stiffened, his hand drifting across the front of his unzipped jacket, his eyes glued to Vargas's every move, every nuance. But when Vargas sat back up, he held a thick envelope, tannish brown in color, almost like a paper bag. He sat the package down on the desktop. Then he pushed it forward, towards Rudy.

The room was silent for a moment. Rudy did not move to take possession of the curious package.

"What is this?" Rudy asked.

"Four hundred fifty thousand dollars. U.S. currency. Cash, of course."

"What for?"

" Consider it your Golden Parachute. A reward for services above and beyond the call of duty," Vargas responded.

"Are you retiring me, sir?"

"I am giving you the choice. Continue serving, or you can opt out. You can retire now if you want. You've earned that option."

Rudy slowly reached out across the desk and took possession of the moneybag. "This is a very generous offer. Can I think about it?"

"Of course."

"Thank you."

Vargas looked around the area. "Now," he said, with an air of formality, "on to new business."

Suddenly, the air seemed filled with static electricity. The men in the area tensed a bit, anticipating their boss's next words.

"I have run this organization for a long time," Vargas began. "We have prospered. All of us." The men in the room nodded in agreement. "But as we all know, nothing lasts forever," he added. "I myself have had a good, long run. I have risen, and I have no desire to fall. So as of tonight, effective immediately, I shall retire – both from this organization, and the business it serves."

Absolute silence in the room. The air seemed heavy with confusion, doubts about the future.

"Every great organization grows until one day it becomes self-sustaining. It takes on a life of its own, and becomes bigger, more powerful than any one man," he instructed.

"Our organization is no different," he concluded. "The important thing is to appoint a new leader who has the knowledge, skills, and moxie to continue the company along its current path with a minimum of upheaval. Someone who will take the reins and continue down the path we have already set." He sat back in his chair.

"I have selected Rick Oakley to be my successor," he announced. "I am confident all of you will give him the same duty, honor, service, and loyalty you gave me."

Now Rudy understood it all.

Vargas stood up, motioned to the chair. "Mr. Oakley, the chair, with its inherent headaches and heartaches, is yours."

Oakley stepped forward without hesitation. He sat down in the chair, easing himself into it. He used his legs to force the chair closer to the desk as Vargas took a step back into the shadows.

"Thank you, Mr. Vargas, for your faith in me to take the helm of our organization." He looked over his shoulder at Vargas. "I can assure you of one thing, sir. You will not be disappointed."

Vargas nodded.

Oakley turned to look at Rudy, paused his gaze there for a beat, then glanced around at the rest of the assembled men. "Now. On to new business," he announced. "We still have a problem with this undercover cop, this Reginald Downing."

A murmur of agreement rippled among the men. Oakley noticed even Rudy nodded his head in agreement. He saw the anger and sense of betrayal in Rudy's eyes. That's Rudy, he thought. Loyal to the end.

"The cold, hard fact is, this organization is under threat of imminent danger." Oakley paused for the dramatic effect. "Make no mistake about it, gentlemen. We are in harm's way.

"As you know, I am ex-military. Quite a few of you are, as well. So let us speak as military men."

Oakley paused, giving them a few seconds of realize they were witnessing not only a change in leadership, but also in leadership style. Oakley planned to run the organization like a military unit -- small, elite, highly trained, highly skilled, highly disciplined. Highly motivated men, all operating as part of a larger team, a well-oiled machine. Oakley was expecting - no he was *demanding* - military efficiency.

No words spoken; no questions raised. None were needed. Everyone knew the score.

"I've pondered this. I believe in order to safeguard the organization, Reginald Downing must die."

Another murmur of approval rippled amongst the men. Oakley noticed them looking amongst themselves, nodding, responding in a positive manner.

"Gentlemen, let me be clear," Oakley continued. "I am not a fan of killing cops. Bad for business. If anyone has a better idea, now's the time to speak up."

Silence in the room.

"I'm serious. If anyone has an idea that resolves this without killing the cop, I'm all ears."

Continued silence.

"Very well. This is the hand we've been dealt, gentlemen. So let's handle our business. Otherwise, this business *will* handle us."

Oakley stood up, the meeting officially over. Several of the men began to move towards the door, talking amongst themselves. Oakley looked at Rudy, who sat still and silent in his chair.

"If I were you, Rudy I'd play it smart. Take the money and run. You've got other resources, cash stashes, investment portfolios."

Rudy said nothing.

"Get in your car, man. Drive off. Go somewhere nice and quiet, live off your investments."

Rudy glanced away, thinking things over. Then he looked back at Oakley. "I can't turn tail and run when my friends are in danger."

Oakley, nodded, truly impressed. "Okay then. Help me finish this. Then you're officially retired. And I'll double the money Vargas gave you."

Rudy stood up. "Agreed."

The two men shook hands, each with firm grips. Then Rudy turned and walked back the way he came, melting into the gloom.

"A natural warrior, that one," Vargas commented.

"That he is."

"You knew he'd stay?"

Oakley nodded.

"What if he had opted out?"

"He didn't". Oakley turned to Vargas. "You should be getting out of here. A whole shitstorm is about to come raining down."

Vargas knew Oakley was right. They shook hands, then hugged, patting each other on the back.

"*Vaya con dios, amigo,*" Oakley said.

Vargas smiled, nodded. Almost overcome with conflicting emotion, he turned and walked away, away from his friends, from his colleagues, from the business he had built. But he was also walking away from double-crosses and turncoats. Undercover policemen. Assassination attempts.

He was walking towards more money than he could ever spend, towards a modern, modest house on a white sandy beach, just feet away from clear, azure blue waters teeming with fish. Vargas had taken up skin diving and snorkeling on his visits down South, and the reef about one hundred yards out from the shore provided an abundance of marine life – fish, crustaceans, and more.

Oakley sat back down at his desk. Heavy weighs the crown that sits upon a troubled brow, he reminded himself. He pulled out his cell phone, dialed a number. It picked up on the second ring.

"Good evening, Mr. Police Man," he greeted. "Do you have the home address on that cop of yours?"

CHAPTER SEVENTEEN

The vampire maneuvered the Lexus through the street traffic with practiced ease. Even with the sunglasses back on, he saw everything with perfectly clarity and definition. His peripheral vision was unencumbered, having expanded when he had been reborn a child of the night. As a result of his altered predatory DNA, the vampire had a full one hundred eighty degree active field of vision.

Reggie, beside him, appeared to be at ease, casual. He glanced out the window at the passing city streets, the people walking by, living their lives. But he also noticed everything. The fine detail of the car's interior, the hand stitched leather. The smooth, unhurried motions of the vampire driving the car. The pale bony hands and long, slender fingers curved around the padded steering wheel.

"So," Reggie said, "do you have a name, or should I simply call you 'Vampire'?"

The vampire smiled. "I was given a name at birth, just like you," he answered. "I do not identify by it much. I use one for business purposes."

"You have a job?" The vampire nodded. "What do you do?"

"I am a stockbroker," the vampire replied.

Reggie stared at him, mouth agape, assuming this was a joke.

"I specialize in the Asian markets. I work at night from home."

"Man this is too much," Reggie said. "First I find out vampires exist, then I find out I have a vampire guardian angel, and he's a fucking stockbroker?"

"We all have bills to pay."

"What about client meetings?"

"My clients prefer anonymity, as do I."

"Convenient."

"It is the nature of many business dealings these days," the vampire opined. "We insulate ourselves away from others. Anonymity implies a level of safety."

"Safety from what?"

"From whatever people are afraid of. Young people these days seem afraid of real human interaction."

"Human interaction can be risky."

"No excuse," the vampire countered. "Human relationships have been risky since the beginning of time."

"Maybe things are worse now. More complicated."

"Poppycock," the vampire responded dismissively. "There lies nothing new under the sun, my dear boy. It seems to me that people now possess fewer skills and less patience when dealing with difficulties that inevitably crop up in all human interactions."

"Maybe people simply don't want to get hurt when a relationship goes bad."

"That is a cowardice, and you know it," the vampire spat. "Without being brave enough to take the risks, you may never get hurt. But you also deny yourself the reaping of big rewards."

"No guts, no glory, is that what you're saying?"

"Precisely."

They drove in silence for a bit. They crossed through a green light where Park intersected with University.

"Where are we going?"

"You prefer diners."

"How did you know that?"

The vampire pulled his shades down on his nose, glanced over the top of them at his passenger.

"Of course," Reggie said, answering his own question. "You're a vampire."

The vampire, smiled, pushed his glasses back up on his nose, covering his eyes.

The Lexus slowed. The vampire put on his blinker, got into the far right lane. Traffic ebbed and flowed at the next intersection, allowing the vampire to turn right onto El Cajon Boulevard. They headed east, moving down a hill, bottoming out quickly at Florida Avenue, then climbing up the other side. The vampire put his blinker on again, dutifully checked his driver's side rear view mirror, then seamlessly changed lanes to the left.

"You're quite the careful driver," Reggie observed.

"I have no desire to be interrogated by law enforcement."

"Tickets can get real expensive real fast, right?"

The vampire considered his next words carefully. "Law enforcement and I have not always seen eye to eye."

Reggie took in his breath, a prelude to asking another question. But the vampire switched lanes again, and came to a halt in a left turn lane. Reggie looked ahead, and saw an all-American diner diagonally to the left. The sign proudly proclaimed they had been in continuous business since 1949.

The vampire cranked left on the wheel and hit the gas. They lunged forward, flashing across three lanes of oncoming traffic, and landed safely on a side street. The Lexus slowed immediately, and turned right into the small parking lot behind the building.

They got out of the car. Reggie stretched his legs and arched his back, hands extended high over his head. The vampire locked the car with his keychain remote. They started walking towards the sidewalk.

"It's chilly tonight," Reggie said.

"I had not noticed."

"Do you even feel the cold?"

"Constantly. That is why I had not noticed."

Reggie glanced over at his new guardian angel, amazed by the irony of that term. Dark hair, limp like old seaweed, pale skin, almost transparent, dark clothing that seemed to make him even more a part of the shadows and a thin, lean frame.

A slight silhouette, someone who knew what it was to hunt, and also knew what it was to be the hunted. The dark sunglasses, hiding those alien black eyes, all accentuated by the long coat. Even in the semidarkness of the frigid evening that looked like it was going to become foggy before too much longer, enough light shone that Reggie could tell the coat had been treated with oils to make it rainproof. Water would bead up and roll off.

They walked around to the front entrance. The vampire held the door open for Reggie to walk through first. Even though Reggie knew who and what the vampire was capable of doing, he had no problem walking in first, effectively turning his back on this creature. Reggie knew the vampire genuinely meant him no harm. If he had any malicious intent, the vampire could have, and would have, simply slaughtered him in the hotel room.

Reggie stepped into the narrow foyer, and was greeted by a chest-high sign inviting guests to seat themselves. As he finished scanning the sign, he sensed the vampire step inside, the door closing behind him.

The diner was long and narrow, with a long counter on their left, accompanying barstools bolted to the floor. The counter made a hard left about fifty or sixty feet down, disappearing from their line if sight. On the right, next to the large windows that looked out on El Cajon Boulevard, a series of booths stretched towards the back for nearly fifty feet as well. More booths lined the far wall, mirroring the left turn the counter took. Even more booths and tables for four hid in an overflow area, but that area was closed at the moment. The decor was of modern manufacture, but the design in keeping with the ambience of a 1940's diner.

Reggie moved down the walkway between the bar and the booths. He selected a booth at the back, nearest the blocked off area. He sat down in the far seat, making sure he was facing the door through which they had just arrived. The vampire slid into the booth on the opposite side, his back towards the door.

A middle-aged Hispanic man, with a graying moustache and an expanding middle appeared almost immediately. He welcomed them to the diner, and placed plastic laminated menus in front of them both. He asked what they would like to drink. Reggie ordered an iced tea. The vampire ordered the same. The man smiled and nodded, then disappeared as quickly as he had come.

"I thought you could only drink blood and water," Reggie said softly.

"Tea is not much more than colored water."

The Hispanic busboy returned, placed their drinks in front of them. Each man thanked him. The busboy smiled graciously and nodded, then retreated once more.

"So what can you not drink?" Reggie asked.

The vampire stared out through the window a moment. "Anything other than water, and a bit of tea," he said finally. "No coffee, unless it's black, and I hate black coffee," he added. "No alcohol. No milk."

"And regular food?"

"I am allergic to it," the vampire answered. "I get physically ill. Nausea, vomiting. Abdominal cramping. A rather disgusting diarrhea."

"Damn," Reggie said. "That sucks."

The vampire grinned at the humor. "Indeed."

A young woman, tall, gaunt, pink hair the color of bubblegum, and body tattoos and facial piercings, stepped up to their table. Her nametag greeted the world as Suzie, and she stood beside their table, pen in one hand, notepad in the other.

"Good evening, gents," Suzie said. "What can I get you tonight?"

"Swiss and mushroom burger, medium, and onion rings," Reggie ordered.

She jotted down the particulars, and turned her head to the vampire. "And you, sir?"

The vampire's smile had vanished. His long face and narrow features appeared to be more severe behind his sunglasses. The telepathic waves coming off Suzie struck him, and he did not like what he sensed. Domestic violence, he knew. He could not tell if she was the perpetrator, or the victim.

"Just the iced tea for me, thanks."

"You sure? The food's good here."

"I am certain it is," he responded, modulating his tone carefully. He did not want to create a scene, but he wanted her away from him quickly. He could not guarantee controlling his urge to tear her head off her body.

"Last chance, honey."

And yours, he thought. "The tea is fine."

She spun on her heel and walked away. The vampire's eyes followed her from beneath his dark shades.

Reggie reached across the table, tapped the vampire's arm. "What's wrong?"

"Nothing," the vampire snapped. When Reggie continued to stare at him, the vampire said, "Something about her. Something most distasteful."

"Like what?"

"The stench of evil. It follows her around, like bad cologne." He leaned in closer to Reggie. "And this is not the time or the place to find out what it is."

Reggie sipped his iced tea, then remembered he had not sweetened it. He grabbed the tiny dish on the table that contained several measured packets of sugar and artificial sweetener. He pulled out four sugar packets. He opened them into the glass, where the sugar cascaded into the tea, where it continued downward towards the bottom of the glass. He picked up the long narrow-necked spoon and stirred.

"You know, we're still just tap dancing around the real issues here."

The vampire cocked his head, intrigued. "How so?"

"I don't believe for a minute you picked my name out of a hat. It's no accident we met. That was no random act of kindness the other night, any more than it's a random act you protecting me now."

The vampire shrugged, his coat moving upward around his neck and face. For a brief instant, Reggie thought he looked like a huge bat, like something out of an old black and white horror movie.

"So the question becomes, or rather, the question remains, why me? Why save me? Why am I so important? More pointedly, sir, why am I so important to you?"

"Bravo," the vampire beamed with pride. "That is the relevant question, is it not?" The vampire took another carefully measured sip of his tea.

"I understand why you stay in the shadows," Reggie said. "By saving me, you've stepped into the light. You wouldn't do that unless you had a damn good reason. I need you to tell me everything."

"Oh, believe me, my child, I fully intend to."

Reggie asked, "And why do you call me, 'my child', or 'my dear boy'? Any why do you do it out of affection, and not condescension? And why is it that it doesn't offend me when you do it?"

Suzie came prancing back towards them, Reggie's food piled on a plate in her right hand. Reggie sat back and let her place the platter in front of him.

"Thank you," he said.

She smiled. "You're welcome, hon," she said. She looked at the vampire. "How you doing with that tea?"

The vampire reached out quickly, grabbed her gently but firmly by the wrist. Reggie watched with alarm, but said nothing. Watching, he saw Suzie's face register alarm, then quickly go blank. Her features relaxed, her breathing slowed. Reggie knew something was going on, but he did not know what. But he knew not to interfere.

The vampire smiled reassuringly, let go of her wrist, and patted her hand.

"Everything is fine. Thank you, Suzie."

Her eyes blinked a few times, like she was coming out of a trance. Her brow furrowed slightly, confused. Then everything seemed to be all right. She turned around and walked away towards the kitchen. She did not look back at them.

"So what's the deal with her?" Reggie asked.

The vampire, who had been watching her walk away, turned his attention back to his companion. "She is a victim, not a perpetrator."

"That's a shame."

"Yes."

"Is there anything we can do?"

"Already done. I suggested to her to leave him." The vampire leaned forward, then whispered fiercely," Real men don't hit."

"You think she'll do it?"

"Unknown."

Reggie picked up the rolled napkin, which had his silverware inside, and unrolled it. He placed his cutlery on the table beside his plate, laced the napkin in his lap. He picked up his fork, and stabbed at the steaming food. The vampire watched him hoist the first bite into his mouth.

"You want to know why I saved you. The answer is simple."

Reggie looked at the vampire, waiting for the next shoe to drop.

"We are... related."

Keeping his face carefully neutral, Reggie asked, "How so?"

"By bloodline," the vampire answered. "You are my direct descendant."

Reggie, not believing, cocked his head to one side. "You do realize that... well, that....."

"What?"

"Well, that... that you're white, and I'm black."

"Skin color matters little when two people are truly in love." Loss and sadness resonated in the vampire's voice. The corners of his mouth turned downward. His chin dipped, his body sagged, decades of regret weighing him down.

The morose tone made Reggie sit still and pay attention. He hardly dared breathe.

"Reginald, my lad" the vampire said, taking off his sunglasses and looking directly at Reggie, "this will be difficult for you to believe."

"What?"

The vampire removed his opaque glasses. "I am your great, great grandfather."

Reggie searched the face of the creature sitting across from him. He recognized earnestness in the vampire's voice. He saw no hint of guile in those unblinking eyes.

Reggie cleared his throat, took another bite of food. He needed a moment to turn things over in his mind, to think. After chewing and swallowing, he sipped his iced tea. He was buying time, stalling. Then he looked directly at the vampire.

"First, put your shades back on. No one needs to see that." He waited as the creature across from him complied.

"Now. I think you'd better tell me the whole story. And I mean, everything. Leave nothing out."

"Everything," the vampire repeated wistfully. He looked at Reggie and nodded. "I promise."

Reggie smile encouragingly, then continued eating. His companion, the ancient creature sitting across from him, this vampire, began to tell his story.

The story of his brief life.

The story of his violent death.

And of his rebirth into Darkness.

CHAPTER EIGHTEEN

The first thing you should know me is my name. My real name. The one my parents gave me. My human name. It will become relevant as this conversation continues.

I was born of man and woman, just as you were. I was named and known as Edwin Thaddeus Marx. Does the name ring any bells? No? Did your mother or grandmother ever mention someone named Eddie? Eddie Marx? Did you ever meet your Great, Great Grandmother, Danae? No? Yes? Perhaps when you were quite little. We shall progress to that in the fullness of time.

I was born in Hoboken, New Jersey, October 14, 1889. The family name Marx is of Germanic origin. It goes back, in various spellings well over a thousand years, both in Germania and other parts of Eastern Europe. It shows up in several Germanic and Slavic languages, in one form or another.

My father, of course, was an immigrant. He was a butcher by trade. No big surprise. This was a time when young men often grew up working whatever the family business happened to be. My father, my father's father, and his father's father before him, had all been butchers, both in the old country and here in "the New Land". That is they called it.

The Land of Opportunity.

My parents' dreams of wealth and comfort were much sweeter than the reality they faced. As you and I know, reality rarely lives up to the hype.

My mother was Bonnie Johns. Johns is an Anglo-Saxon name. It is probably where "Thaddeus" came from. Her people had started out in England. They moved to Ireland in the Middle Ages when England was trying to repopulate that country. Land was cheap. In some cases it was free. So Commoners could move to Ireland, stake a claim, receive ownership of the land, and live there. Instant equity, instant prosperity. Then the Potato Famine changed all that.

But I digress.

Bonnie Johns became Bonnie Marx when she married my dad. Back then all women did that. Keeping a maiden name or becoming a hyphenate was never contemplated by women of the time. What can I tell you? It was a different time, a different society with different norms.

A different world.

I was an only child, which was unusual for that time. Birth control as we understand it now was practically nonexistent in those days, except for the rhythm method and the "sheath" – what you would call a condom. I seem to remember overhearing my mother and father talking about the terrible time she had in childbirth with me, and that the doctor had said other children were not possible. It is a vague memory, as I was very young. I am sure they thought they were having a private conversation. Such matters are usually considered "husband and wife stuff", intimate things kept private between a married couple.

But a six-year-old boy growing up alone and inventing imaginary friends to play with knows how to hide under a bed and keep still and silent. The plaster walls and wooden floors of our cramped apartment did the rest, allowing the slightest sound to reverberate and carry.

My dad worked hard for his money, and did not make a lot. Often, in hard times, when times were tough for everyone, he was actually paid in meat. We might have gotten behind on the rent a few times, but we never went hungry when he was alive.

Can you imagine something like that in this day and age?

My father never actually owned any of the butcher shops he worked in. When he came here, he had to start over at the bottom. An entry-level position, as it were. He was strictly the hired help, and back then, just as now, no one makes more money than the boss. No big deal, no resentment on my part. It was simply how things were.

My father died when I was eleven, in 1901. He took ill in the fall. It did not start out as much, just a cough. Then the fevers started, the cough became productive, and he got sick, weak, and pale. The cough got worse, more liquid in the noise. We knew he was in a bad way. His skin went to ashen gray. He had bluish tint at the lips and fingernails.

We finally called a doctor who took a look, told us it was pneumonia and there was nothing he could do. Dad was too far gone, the case too advanced. The doctor said he was sorry, and left.

Naturally, I understand now what was happening. Bluish skin is called cyanosis, and it is caused by hypoxia, the lack of oxygen. At the time though, I just knew he looked like a dead man.

His cough got worse, his sputum going from yellow to green, and finally to brown and red, tinged with blood. Every time he tried to wheeze in a breath, you could hear the fluids gurgling.

He died that winter. It was a blessing. His muscles had withered to nothing. He looked like a skeleton covered in flesh. I was there in the room when he passed. His final breath left his chest with a small sigh, his eyes partly closed as the ciliary muscles relaxed, he went limp, and that was it. His remains just lay there, silent and still, meat on a slab.

My father was only forty-one years old.

Mom and I were, of course, devastated. We faced a bleak, uncertain future. These were the days before life insurance was available to those of us of "modest means". Life insurance then was a luxury of the rich.

We were on our own.

Then we realized we were lucky in a way, luckier than most in similar situations. Mom had mad skills as a seamstress. Within a week, she started taking in work from people in the building where we lived. We had to make ends meet so we weren't tossed out. Her work was so consistently good that before we knew it, she was handling work from not only our building, but from all over the neighborhood.

Even with Mama's sewing, food was scarce. There was no welfare, no food stamps, no housing subsidies. The neighbors helped when they could. They would bring extras they had, leftover food, that kind of thing. Sometimes, hand-me-down clothes, shoes their children had outgrown. They knew our circumstances. They understood. And being the good decent compassionate folk they were, they wanted to help out.

We even had to take charity from the Church a time or two. That embarrassed Mama the most. She could rationalize the gifts from our neighbors as them just being "neighborly". She was being "polite" to accept "gifts". She told herself that if they offered and we accepted, it was okay. As if we did not truly rely on them to stay fed and clothed. But going to the Church, that was different. That was desperation. There was no way to sugar coat that.

Thank God for Mr. Brennerman. If I ever see heaven, I hope I see him. I would like to say thank you.

Brennerman owned the butcher shop where my worked. And when I say he was old, I mean *old*. This guy was seventy if he was a day. Tall, lean, a shock of gray hair that was almost white, and a thick handlebar moustache. Tough as a two-dollar steak. Worked every day of his life. He died cutting meat at his butcher table, the victim of a massive coronary. I kid you not.

Brennerman felt a certain responsibility for us. He made sure we had "meat for the lad", as he called it. He would come by in the evening, a couple of times a week, ostensibly to just "check on us, make sure we were doing okay", and he never failed to drop something off to help tide us over. Usually it was the cheap stuff. You know, deli meats, bologna, some ham, chicken, maybe pork. Sometimes he would come around and bring ham hocks or neck bones and Mom would make stew or season a pot of slow-cooked beans.

We did not eat meat at every meal. That was not the norm back then. You had meat at one meal, usually dinner. Breakfast was porridge, a hot cereal not too different from oatmeal or cream of wheat. Lunch was usually a sandwich, or a hunk of hard bread and some cheese, something like that. Hard bread was sort of like what you would call a baguette now, or a Shepherd's bread. Nowadays it is considered gourmet or artisan. When I was a kid, it was simply what we had.

Mom never remarried, even though she was quite a bit younger than Dad. She was quite the looker in her day, and she had her suitors. But she showed little interest in speeding into another marriage. She did what she could with the sewing income, but once Brennerman died, the sewing money was simply not enough.

I was not a particularly gifted student. English, History, that sort of stuff I could handle, because a lot of it you could do at your own pace with the book right beside you. But science ate my lunch, and math completely baffled me. Which is ironic, considering how I make my living now. My grades were passable; nothing to write home about.

By the time I was fourteen, school held little appeal for me. Teen years are rough even in the best of circumstances. I had no vision for my future. I was growing wild as a weed, and did not have the heavy hand of a father figure in my life.

Other than my mother, I did not feel particularly connected to other people. I was friendly enough to other boys and girls, and they were friendly enough back. But I was an acquaintance only. I was not their friend, nor were they friends of mine. And I was okay with that.

Now, my Mother was a good and decent woman. And I knew she loved me. But there was an emptiness in her after my father died that never got filled again. Not in this world, at least. It was always there behind her eyes, underneath the surface. Even when she smiled or laughed, there was a note of sadness in it. I recognized it for what it was. That sense of emptiness and bleakness of future eventually permeated the entire apartment, and every part of our lives.

To her credit, she always stressed the importance of school, of getting an education. But I personally thought it a waste of time. Part of that whole bleakness of future thing. It seeped in, a slow and insidious disease, trickling down into my soul, and coalescing there.

And festered.

Everywhere I went, everything I saw took on that same bleakness and hopelessness. The beauty of this world faded; vibrant colors dulled and muted until everything became desaturated.

I felt a duty, an obligation to my mother. I was tired of seeing my mother's hands red and inflamed from hours of work, her fingers bruised or bloodied. So I started cutting class to look for a job.

There was a small grocer a couple of blocks from our apartment. It was not much more than a fruit and produce stand, all cheap wooden tables, apple boxes, and half-bushel baskets underneath a canvas tarp on the sidewalk. They had a small store inside, just two or three aisles of sundries, dry goods, that kind of thing. And as it happened, it was on the way to school.

So I bolted at lunchtime one afternoon. I ran like hell. Legs churning, arms pumping, absolutely terrified a teacher, or truant officer might see me. Truancy was a serious thing back then. Infractions carried serious repercussions. I hid behind an old maple tree, catching my breath, hands on my knees, chest heaving, certain that I would be caught and punished.

Well, lo and behold, nothing happened. No footsteps thudding my way, no angry shouts. I had successfully ditched school. A whole new world with new and endless possibilities had opened up. I could do whatever I wanted to do. I wanted to go get a job.

I walked the rest of the way, not nervous at all. I guess I should have been, but I was not. The thought that the grocer would say "No" never really occurred to me. Even at that age, failure was simply not an option for me.

It was the afternoon when I got there. The guy who owned the place, Mr. Davidson, stood by an old steel produce scale weighing out zucchini squash for Ms. Di Novi. Once they were done, he asked me how he could help me. I told him I was looking for work. He asked me how old I was, if I was in school. I told him the truth. He asked me why I thought I needed a job.

I told him the truth.

Davidson knew my Mom, of course. He knew our situation. He told me he would let me work two hours a day after school, and four hours on Saturday, from eight until noon. He'd pay me cash money every Saturday, ten cents an hour. I was going to make a dollar forty a week.

Don't laugh. A buck forty was decent money for a kid back then. With the extra money, we'd be able to eat better, maybe save up and get some better clothes.

I asked if I could start right then. He smiled, and told me to start the next day, after school. That right now I should go home and tell my Mom. Grinning ear to ear, I turned to go home.

He stopped me dead in my tracks. He gave me a stern look, pointed his finger at me, and said if I ever skipped school again, he would fire me on the spot.

I nodded my head. I knew he meant it.

Then I took off running again, just as fast as I could. I ran the remaining two blocks so fast it seemed like time had compressed in on itself. By the time I got to the third floor landing, I should have been practically prostrate with exhaustion, but I somehow managed to stagger down the hallway and to our apartment.

My Mom was sitting to the right, about seven feet inside the door. It was just a big room with a living area defined by an ancient and uncomfortable settee and a couple of scarred wooden chairs that had seen better days. She always sat there in the late afternoon, taking advantage of the sunlight streaming in.

She was hemming a set of curtains for the front window of the deli around the corner when I come barging in, sweaty, clothes soaked, ready to keel over in a dead faint. I was so out of breath I could not speak.

Naturally, she was alarmed, thought I was scared or in trouble. She jumped up from her seat, dropping her curtains to the floor. She demanded to know what was going on, why I was in such a state, and why I was home so early from school.

When I finally had enough air in my lungs, I told her about getting hired by Mr. Davidson. At first she could not believe it. I think she was as stunned that he hired me as the fact I took it upon myself to ask.

So anyway, I went to work. Davidson was true to his word. He paid me a dollar forty every Saturday afternoon, in cash from his own pocket.

Mom had made it clear if I did not keep my grades up, she would make me quit. I knew she was not fooling around. So I did my homework at night on the big dinner table after Mom and I ate. She would clear away the dishes, and I would wipe down the table. Then I would get to work.

Weeks went by. Then months. Winter passed. Summer was coming. Davidson offered me two dollars a week if I could work for him all day every day in the summer. Of course, I said yes.

Mr. Davidson added to my responsibilities. I was designated the delivery boy. So I spent a lot of time lugging groceries and bags of fruits and vegetables around, pulling a small cart behind me. But I loved having a job, loved having money in my pocket. "Two nickels to rub together", my mom called it.

I gained upper body strength lifting all those bushel baskets of produce, bending and stooping, hauling that damn cart all over half of Hoboken.

One of the places I delivered to was a small "private club" on the corner of twelfth and Elm. Yes, one of "those places". You know. Old-world *Mafioso*. The real thing. They played cards outside, or stood around smoking, always not too far away from the entrance. After a few deliveries, they knew me by sight. Whenever I came along, they would all smile and wave. They would say, "Hi, Eddie!", or, "Hey Little Man!".

Now, no one called me Eddie. Not even my Mom. But I knew these guys, all dressed in dark suits, slicked back hair, and greasy smiles, would not take kindly to being corrected. Calling me Eddie was their way of including me. In their minds, they were being friendly.

Gino Vinetti ran all the rackets in that part of Hoboken. He loan sharked, booked numbers, ran girls, you name it. The cops knew of course, but they were on the payroll. They weren't going to do anything.

One sweltering August afternoon, Mr. Davidson stopped me, looking very serious. He handed me a small package, about three and a half inches by about seven inches, the size of money printed prior to 1929. It was maybe a half-inch thick.

I knew what was wrapped up in the layer of butcher paper. I got nervous. He told me to put it in the bottom of the basket so no one could see it, and to hand the money to Mr. Vinetti himself.

No one else.

So now I wasn't just a delivery boy. I was now a bagman. And just like that, my brief but disastrous criminal career had begun.

When I arrived at the club, the guys outside stepped closer to see what I had in the cart. They grabbed whatever they wanted from the paper bag I had put aside just for them. That way they did not steal from paying customers.

I informed them I had a special delivery for Mr. Vinetti. When they asked me what it was, I showed them.

One of the guys, Thomas, a real psychopath among criminals, reached out his hand, offered to deliver it for me. I took a half-step back. I was told to hand this over to Mr. Vinetti and no one else. Thomas told me to quit kidding around. I looked him dead in the eye and told him I was not kidding. I was not handing the envelope over to anyone but Mr. Vinetti, and if anyone tried to take it, I would punch him in the mouth.

Thomas face clouded with anger. Dark eyes turned mean. Real fast. He took a step forward. I took a step back. I clenched my fist and eyed the point of his chin.

Now I had been in a few fistfights at school. Back then, a bloody nose or a black eye was no big deal. It was a normal part of growing up. But I knew if I hit Thomas, he would beat me senseless. But there was no way he was getting that envelope from me without a fight.

Milo, an aging Sicilian with the physique of a fireplug, put his arm across Thomas' chest, told him to take it easy. I was just following orders, doing what I was told.

Thomas glanced at Milo, then back at me. After a second, Thomas relaxed, took a step back, and lit a cigarette. Just like that, my first run-in with Thomas was over.

It would not be my last.

Milo shouldered the door open. Lots of natural light streamed in from the windows. Ceiling fans overhead, placed about ten feet apart, spun lazily, stirring the air. Not that it did much good.

We moved further inside. A cook wearing a dingy T-shirt pushed his massive belly through a swinging kitchen door. Milo nodded, hoisted the basket up onto the counter. The cook grabbed the basket without a word, swung around and pushed back through the door into the kitchen beyond. The door swung closed and he disappeared from my view as Milo wiped sweat off his brow.

The heat was getting to Milo.

As for me, my heart was pounding inside my chest. I knew I had stepped into a completely different world. A world of hard men and harsh rules. Of illegal conduct, and fast money. Of cheap women and hot lead. A world of back room deals, back alley politics, influence peddling, illegal money, ill-gotten gains. A world where brutality was expected, respect was commanded, loyalty rewarded, and betrayal got you killed. A gangster's world.

And it excited me.

Milo looked over his shoulder at me, then nodded towards the rear of the place. I looked past him. The big booths in the back, for all the best customers. The most important clients. The private conversations.

Sunlight streamed through the west-facing window, all golden straw across the black and white tiled floor. I remember, seeing the particles of dust, the dirt and silt from outside, dancing on the air as it wafted in from the alley.

Gino Vinetti was the epitome of Old World Mobster. Older than Milo and much smarter, he sat alone in the best booth in the house. His coat hung on a wooden hook nearby. Even though he was inside, he still wore his hat, a fedora that matched his gray suit. Sitting in his shirtsleeves, the cuffs rolled up past his hairy wrists, he puffed on a cigar while he counted a pile of money.

Gino – and no one, and I mean NO ONE called him Gino back then; he was Mr. Vinetti, or Don Vinetti – looked up as we approached. Milo stood a little straighter, then spoke formally, and with much deference. I stood behind Milo, and a bit to the right. I wanted to see as well as hear what was happening. Milo introduced me, that I worked for Davidson the produce grocer, and I had been entrusted to make a delivery to Don Vinetti.

Gino nodded his acknowledgement, took the cigar out of his mouth, and tilted his head a bit to get a better look at me. I put my shoulders back and tried to stick my chest out, you know, stood up straight and all that. Just like my Mom had told me all my life. He said he knew me, had known my father. He added that he had not seen me around with the other kids for a while.

I glanced at Milo, whose face told me nothing. I cleared my throat and spoke up. I told him that I had been working after to school, and doing my homework at night after dinner, which did not leave much time for play. Now that summer was here, I was working full time for Mr. Davidson.

He asked me to step closer so he could get a look at me. I did what I was told. He held out his hand, palm facing upwards. I dutifully placed the package in his hand, taking care to do it right. His eyes followed the envelope from my hand to his. Then his eyes shifted back to me. I pulled my hand back, then let my arm fall to my side. He sat back, very much in control. He pocketed the money without counting it in front of me.

He told me that he knew my mother, had spoken to her a few times when they had passed each other on the street, that kind of thing, that he had known her since before my father died. He was sorry that Dad had "passed on" as he put it, and then he crossed himself, like it was rote or reflexive, done without thinking.

Don Vinetti looked directly at me and asked if I knew what was in the package. I simply replied, money. He asked if I knew how much money was in it. When I told him no, he asked me, why not, had I not peeked inside? When I shook my head no, he seemed to like that.

Finally, he nodded, and I knew the meeting was over. The tension in the room dissipated rapidly. He flipped a quarter at me across the table. Without me even thinking about it, my shoulder moved, my arm extended, my hand shot out, and I caught the coin in the air.

He smiled again and told me, nice reflexes. He told me that it was my tip, and to keep it. Now, a quarter was not much in the grand scheme of things, not even back then. But it did have spending power. I thanked him, and he told me to "not be a stranger".

I said yes sir, then turned around and made for the front door. Milo fell in behind me. But even with him there, blocking a direct path and line of sight between Gino and me, I could feel those eyes watching me, searing through me with laser-sharp intensity. Seeing how I would handle myself in his presence, at least until I could get out the door.

Would I continue to move along, like it was just another stop along my route, just another piece of business in a day filled with different pieces of business? Or would I lose my cool, trip, fall, otherwise betray my age, my awkwardness, my nervousness?

As I slowed down near the closed front door, Milo opened the door for me. I looked up at him, and told me with a knowing grin that he would "see me around".

If I had known then what I know now, I would not have walked out of that "Private Club" that day. I would have run as fast as I could. Like all the demons of Hell were after me.

One morning a few weeks after, Mr. Davidson told me to go directly to Mr. Vinetti's club. From now on, I would work for Gino. Mr. Davidson told me not to worry, he would drop by my apartment and square things with my Mom. I would be making more money working for Mr. Vinetti than he could afford to pay me. What I did not know at the time is that Davidson got paid money as consideration for losing an employee.

Gino and the boys started me on the ground floor -- running all their errands. I delivered laundry to the cleaners. I picked up their tribute money, brought it back. As it turned out, Mr. Davidson was just the tip of the iceberg.

When people in the neighborhood had a problem, needed money, had a disagreement; they didn't go to the banks. They didn't go to the cops. They either handled it themselves or they went to

Gino. Like they would have back in the old country. Gino loaned money, blessed weddings, meted out punishment, settled spats before they became disputes, and settled disputes before they became blood feuds.

But then were his other businesses: illegal booze, drugs, gambling, and prostitution. Whiskey and whores. Lots of money then. Just like now. Money made from the weakness of some, and the misery of others.

And Gino was the parasite that profited from it all.

Word got around that I worked for Gino. Boys that used to give me a hard time smiled and waved whenever they saw me, or gave me a wide berth and left me alone. When I would go around to pick up the merchants' tributes, many of them wanted me to make sure that I relayed "their best to Mister Vinetti". The pharmacist at our local drugstore would sometimes let me have a free seltzer water. The fellow that ran the mercantile would sometimes let me take a gumball or a piece of licorice.

Mom and I had meat every night at dinner, cold sodas for the hot days, and we could finally afford better clothes, better shoes. Mom was even able to take it easy with the sewing, ease up a little. She was getting older by then, and her hands were starting to give her problems. I wanted her to rest.

Mom did not like me working for Gino. Not one bit. She knew very well what Gino Vinetti was. She was not naïve to the ways of the world. She knew how things worked, that extreme violence could erupt at any time and for any reason, without warning. Because back then, just as much as now, violence was simply a way of life.

I was just a kid, making deliveries now, no big deal. I was kind of like a mascot. It was a good time for me. Well, I thought it was. But the die had already been cast. I would not remain a kid forever. Eventually they would bring me in on bigger, more dangerous jobs. Things that damaged and destroyed property. Things that scared people. Hurt people.

Killed people.

Eventually, they demanded I take on responsibility and do a man's job. And when that time came, I did.

Being connected to Gino had its perks. Nobody bothered me. Everyone was nice to my Mom. And if one of the local merchants tried to stiff me on the tributes or give me hard time because I was just a kid, I had Gino's guys in my corner. Believe me, anyone who tried pushing me around never did it twice.

In the beginning, they sheltered me from the real violence. I knew it was going on, of course, but I never saw it. The slapping around of the working girls if they got mouthy. The beatings dished out to deadbeats that owed them money. Or the murders of anyone who betrayed them.

I thought folks were showing me respect. In truth, they feared Gino, but I could not make that distinction. I just enjoyed the attention. In fact, I came to expect it. Even at seventeen, I had no problem "reminding" some shopkeeper of who I worked for if I felt I had been slighted.

Funny thing about human nature, that slippery slope we can all slide down. I'm talking about the insidious nature of sin. It starts out innocent. Innocuous. But once you get used to it, get accustomed to crossing the line, the line ceases to exist.

And so it was with me.

Before long, I was spending all my time with Gino and the guys. I was making more money, wearing suits and ties just like the rest of the guys. I stayed out late every night, much to my mother's chagrin. I did not carry a gun, but I had a straight razor in my pocket. Gino approved. He felt a young man like me needed a little something extra to protect himself.

My mother was constantly on me about them being a bad influence on me. She was right, but I did not want to hear it. I spent less and less time at home. By fall of that year, 1907, I was living in a small room in the back of Gino's club. Broke my mother's heart when I moved out.

Things were never the same between us.

The room itself was nothing special. It smelled of onions. Small, metal spring bed frame, thin, lumpy, uncomfortable mattress. A beat up and scarred wooden three-drawer dresser squatted against a wall. A lavatory mounted in a corner provided me a place to wash up and shave. Floorboards creaked even under my moderate weight. Like I said, just a room.

It was my first home as a man.

One day late in the fall of 1908, this storeowner, an old guy named Vincenzo Scarpaccio, refused to pay. He said he was tired of paying for "protection" he did not need. I reminded him who Gino Vinetti was. He said he did not care. He was not afraid.

I was flummoxed. In all the time I had been collecting, no one had ever simply refused. Oh, a few had grumbled, complained, and talked trash, but in the end, they paid. I understood. They had to talk tough so they could still have some respect for themselves as men. I would always say thank you, I was always polite, always respectful to them.

I reminded Mr. Scarpaccio of his arrangement with Mr. Vinetti. The old man cursed Gino, cursed me, then he spat vehemently on the floor between us. An ultimate insult at the time.

I took a breath, straightened by coat. I told him that Mr. Vinetti would be very disappointed, and I bid him good day. He replied that I was no longer welcome in his store, and that he was sure my mother was ashamed of me, and that she probably regretted having conceived me.

I usually reminded folks I was Gino's gentle side. The other men in his crew were the wrecking ball. They could deal with me, or with them. Their choice. But I decided right then and there, Scarpaccio no longer had a choice.

Later that night, few of Gino's boys paid him a visit. Old man Scarpaccio opened the door and immediately, three burly Italian guys in suits slammed him up against the wall and held him there. Terrified, he knew better than to scream. The third guy, Thomas, the one who never really liked me too much, opened up a razor blade. Waved it in front of Scarpaccio's nose. Told him he had heard about how he had "talked tough to the kid" earlier in the day, and did not want to pay. Then Thomas reminded him that one way or the other, everyone paid. Then he stepped to one side, turned his head towards the open door. Scarpaccio's gaze followed his.

I walked inside. Cool, mean, angry. In control. I looked at Scarpaccio, glanced at the men as I unhurriedly crossed the floor. I nodded to Thomas as I went by. His lip twisted upwards slightly at one corner of his mouth.

I kicked Scarpaccio in his old shriveled balls so hard I lifted him off the floor. Even the guys holding him winced. All the color left the old man's face. His knees buckled. He fell to the floor with a solid thump. He lay there on his side, curled into a fetal position.

I stepped back and kicked him in the face. The sole of my shoe split his lip open and knocked out two teeth. It knocked his head back and ricocheted it off the wall. Hell, even Thomas was shocked. He took a half step back. I lifted my foot up and stomped the side of Scarpaccio's head, bouncing it off the floor. By this time, he is crying and wailing like a lost child.

Thomas stepped forward, reached out to take my arm. I threw a glare at him that stopped him in his tracks. I kicked Scarpaccio's arms out of the way, and I straddled his torso, settled my weight. Then I punched him. Hard. Once, twice, three times, four. Blood spattered on my clothes, across my shirt, across my tie, across my face.

And I told him, calmly, matter-of-factly, to never disrespect me, or Gino Vinetti. He nodded. And I told him to never, ever talk about my mother ever again. He was forbidden from even mentioning her name. Not just in my presence, but in anyone's. And that if I ever heard that he had so much as mentioned her name to anyone, even in polite conversation, I was going to come back, to his house, with these men, and kick him in the face until I kicked him to death. I would leave him drowning in a pool of blood and snot in his own kitchen.

There was a deathly silence as I let this concept sink in. Thomas and the boys were awestruck. A cat screeched out back in the alley. Inside that room, you could have heard a pin drop.

My blood still up, I glanced up at them with hard eyes, challenging them. They had never seen me like this. None of them were about to challenge me that night.

Not even Thomas. At least not then.

Scarpaccio was still spitting blood and teeth out his mouth, trying hard not to choke to death right in front of us. I smiled, kneeled down, and asked him gently if he understood. I gave him permission to nod if that was all he could do.

He nodded.

I asked him if he doubted my sincerity.

He shook his head.

Satisfied, I stood up. I straightened my bloodied tie. I unbuttoned my spattered coat and smoothed my ruined shirt, tucking it in around the waist. I adjusted my rumpled coat, buttoned it back up – which was the style back then – and pulled my shirtsleeves down at the cuff underneath.

I looked at the men, asked them if they had a problem with what had gone on here? They all shook their heads.

No, kid. No problem.

I made to walk away, then I spun around with such speed no one saw it coming. I kicked Scarpaccio in the gut so Goddamned hard it moved his entire body across the floorboards.

Then I spat in his mangled face.

I told him I would be coming by the next day for his payment. And it had better be fucking ready. And it had better all fucking be there. Every fucking penny. *Capice?*

I turned and stalked out without waiting for a response, tolerating no interference, and without speaking another word to anyone.

CHAPTER NINETEEN

Things changed after that. Word got around what happened. Everyone in the neighborhood looked at me differently when I strolled down the sidewalk. Gino's boys no longer treated me like a kid. By making such a brutal example of Scarpaccio, I had just sent a message. Not only to the neighborhood, but to the rest of Gino's boys. *Do not mess with me.* And the message to Gino himself was, *I have potential. I have ambition. I know how to make things happen.*

Gino was impressed. Scarpaccio had the money ready prior to noon the next day. He could hardly look at me. And he Goddamn sure never gave me any more trouble.

Ever.

Mr. Vinetti counseled me that violence should only be used as a last resort, but that if violence had to be used, it had to brutal, bloody, and public. Violence had to be a reminder; it had to send a message, just as I had done. He said he would rethink my place within the hierarchy of the gang. And of course, that is precisely what it was - a gang. An ongoing criminal enterprise, as your police brethren call it.

And boy, was I ever about find out the hard way about that.

In addition to my weekly collections, Gino put me in charge of collecting from the local nightclubs. I was still living in that converted storeroom off the kitchen at Gino's headquarters, but I was moving up. Before he sent me out, he called me, Thomas, Aldo to a meeting. He declared me a man, and a full member of the crew. Aldo grinned approvingly. Thomas did not. Then Gino declared I was now in charge of collections from the bars and nightclubs he owned, ran, or extorted money from.

Thomas bristled. The nightclubs had been his gig. It was bad enough I was being promoted, but he was being demoted at the same time. He asked Gino why the job was being taken away from him.

Gino understood Thomas had a legitimate gripe. So he told Thomas the terrible truth. It was because even at just eighteen years old, I had shown more initiative, more daring, and more decision-making ability in dealing with Scarpaccio, than Thomas had shown in years. Thomas was a good man, but he was a born follower, not a leader. He was destined to always be a foot soldier, nothing more.

Thomas grimaced with anger at Gino, and hatred towards me. I thought just for an instant, he was going to pull his gun and start blasting away. I think he thought about it. But he understood the Life, and said nothing more. I knew a new battle line had been drawn. Thomas would never accept me in this new role, would never take orders from me no matter what Gino said.

This was a problem.

Maybe Thomas always saw me as a potential threat. Maybe he knew he could never control me, all the back to that first time I came by, and was ready to hit him rather than give the money to him.

Maybe he envied my youth. Thomas was in his mid-thirties and had nothing to show for it. No home, no wife, no children. Gino did not pay that well, and Thomas spent money as fast as he earned it. He had no savings, no nest egg, no retirement, nothing to call his own.

Then again, some people hate for no reason.

Gino declared the new arrangement effective immediately. My first collection would be that night. After we had left the table, Aldo pulled me aside and told me that he would keep Thomas in line. I had my doubts about that, but I was grateful for the help.

I went back to my room. I buffed out my shoes, washed my face. I picked up the straight razor lying on the sink, stared at myself in the mirror. I knew Thomas would turn on me the first chance he got. He would simply not be there when I needed him, or worse, he would take me out himself. So I took the folded razor, slid it into my coat pocket. Not much defense against Thomas's gun, but if I could get close enough… well, you can guess the rest.

There I was, certain of betrayal, preparing for war. I was hardly old enough to shave, and I already thought like a gangster. I dressed like a gangster. I acted like a gangster. I plotted like a gangster. I coveted power and money like a gangster.

The mistake was, I actually thought I *was* a gangster.

The first few weeks went smoothly enough. Thomas gritted his teeth and did what he was told. But I never trusted him to have my back. Some of the nightclub owners showed surprise at the shift in power, but never said anything about it. These were not poor, extorted shopkeepers. No, these men were corrupt themselves, gangsters of their own accord. Some were tied to the New York boys, some to Chicago. They understood paying a small tribute to the local Don was simply good business. It was showing respect.

Back then, there were rules. And I mean, *real* rules. Everyone followed them. No one killed each other over a measly two percent of gross. They just charged more for the drinks and the food. It is not like now where street hoodlums slaughter each other over ten bucks and a pair of sneakers, or shoot a ten year old because she's playing in the wrong playground.

One of the places we collected from was a run-down gin joint located in the part of town where black people congregated. Typical place for the time. Dimly lit, small tables, rickety chairs, wooden flooring, tiny stage in one corner, just enough room for a couple of musicians against the walls and one singer out front. Bumpy, the owner, tended bar so he could keep an eye on things. He wanted to make sure people had a good time, so they'd come back and keep the money flowing. He also wanted to make sure no one was starting trouble, and of course, he wanted his cut of any less than legal goings on. Lastly, tending bar, he could make sure his employees weren't cheating him.

We collected from Bumpy every week, near the end of the night on Saturdays. So we always got there when the place was winding down. We always entered quietly through a side entrance, walked directly to the bar. Bumpy would always ask us if we wanted anything, compliments of the house. We would always thank him and decline, and simply ask for our package. He would always have it with him, slide it to us across the bar. We would take it, pocket it, thank him, and walk out. Usually took about three minutes, start to finish. In, out.

But there was this singer there. Beautiful young girl, skin a caramel brown, high cheekbones, tumbling black hair, sultry voice. Usually performed in a dark blue sequined dress. Plunging neckline.

Smokey, is the only way to describe her.

Her name was Danae. Danae Jefferson. I see by your reaction you know the name. Now you are starting to piece it together.

Danae was about twenty then, rumored to be a direct descendant of the union between Thomas Jefferson and Sally Hemings. Danae was your great, great Grandmother, Reggie.

And I loved her. So very much.

Bumpy introduced us. The band was between sets. The men had gone out back. She leaned at the bar and drank sarsaparilla. Danae did not drink alcohol. She said it would affect her singing voice.

We talked a bit. I was nervous because she was so beautiful. But she was a sweet girl, well mannered, very polite. She knew I was tongue-tied in front of her. She thought it was cute. She was charming, and put me at ease. I told her I had enjoyed her singing, what I had heard of it. She told me I should come in on a night when I was not working, and take in a whole set

Well, I did just that. I ventured out one night, alone mind you, into Bumpy's club on a Wednesday. I enjoyed her set. All the neighborhood gangsters knew who I was. More importantly, they knew who backed me. They did not like me coming around, but they had to tolerate it.

I had been coming to Bumpy's for a while. They had gotten used to me by then. But eyes were still glued to me whenever Danae came over to my table in between sets.

It was all quite innocent at first, I assure you. Right from the start, we both seemed to see past the color of our skin. I was interested in what she had to say. She was quite intelligent, you see. She read newspapers every day, trying to educate herself in all kinds of subjects. See, she had never gotten past the eighth grade. It bothered her, made her feel less.

But there were angry murmurs throughout the club. You know what I mean. The talk was immediately that I was using her, getting a little taste of brown sugar, all that nonsense. A lot of that stuff went on back then, mind you. White men going out, leaving their wives at home, then coming over to the far side of town, sampling some foreign flesh. I can understand why folks thought I was doing the same thing.

But I swear to you, I always had nothing but the most honorable of intentions towards her. There was nothing illicit going on between us those first few encounters at the club. Well. Not at that point, at any rate.

Hey, do not look at me like that. I told you, I was in love with her. We finally started sneaking away from our respective groups of friends and acquaintances after about four months of small talk and flirtation.

We became romantically involved, which was a much bigger deal back then than it is today. Nowadays, an interracial couple is no big deal. Back then, it was not only considered immoral and wrong, it was actually against the law. You ran the risk of beatings, lashings, and lynching. People got killed or castrated over this kind of thing when I was a young man.

But we were young and in love. We did not worry about such things. We knew we were unique, and that our love was a love that had never been experienced by anyone else, ever, anywhere, in the history of the world. We would find a way to fly in the face of convention, and find a way to be together, forever, until the end of time. We told ourselves that as we stole precious moments and even more precious hours, in cheap rented rooms accessed through back alleyways, consummating our love.

You're looking at me like that again. I told you she was your great, great Grandmother. And I am your great, great Grandfather. We did not accomplish that feat via Immaculate Conception.

Of course, no matter what precautions we took, no matter how careful we were, the truth got out. It always does, does it not? Word got back to Gino Vinetti regarding Danae's and my torrid affair. Quite frankly, he did not care. As long as I was taking care of business for him, he would not interfere.

So things went on as they did for several months. There was a lot of resentment among Bumpy's crowd. Danae endured terrible ridicule and harassment. Sometimes she would be crying from the hurtful insults and taunts when I saw her. I offered, on more than one occasion, to "take care of the situation". But she knew what I was, knew what my definition of "taking care of business" meant. So she always told me no, she would deal with it. She always got a certain look to her face when she had made up her mind about something. I learned to recognize that look and to just shut up, because nothing I said would change her mind.

One year passed into another. Danae kept singing at the club. I kept collecting for Gino. Thomas was still a prick, and Aldo was getting old, tired. Gino just kept being Gino. More gray hair, more lines on his face.

I started getting a hint of trouble on the horizon. Thomas became quiet, withdrawn. He still followed orders, but his eyes were getting dangerous. After years being around dangerous men, I knew when things were about to explode.

I tried talking to Aldo about it. He told me if Thomas was going to make trouble, the best thing to do was stay out of the way. I argued that any trouble Thomas made would be directed at me. Aldo just shrugged, shook his head sadly, and told me he was retiring. Gino had already okayed it, and he could not protect me any longer.

I started carrying a loaded revolver that very day. Even though I was a gangster, I always had my guys backing me. Like I said before, most people just paid the money to keep in business and avoid trouble. Old man Scarpaccio notwithstanding, high-order violence was not my strong suit.

So Danae and I made a plan. If Thomas made trouble, it meant an all-out war against Gino. Aldo would be of no use. I found out later that Aldo had made a side deal with Thomas to stay out of it if Thomas would simply not kill him in return. I am sure that it sounded like a good deal to Aldo at the time.

Poor bastard.

Anyways. Back to the plan. I had found out that interracial marriage was legal in France. Had been since 1833. Both Danae and I had been saving our money for months, squirreling it away. For now we had a concrete goal. We were going to elope, book passage on a steamer ship to France, get married, and live happily ever after.

Unfortunately, happily ever after only happens in fairy tales.

One week later, Thomas walked into Gino's place with three men from a rival gang Thomas had struck an alliance with. They stood at the table where Gino was eating his eggplant parmesan.

Thomas pulled out his revolver, and put a round right through Gino's face. The old man tipped over backwards in his chair and spilled onto the floor. Thomas then put two more rounds into his chest.

Aldo was sitting at the bar eating some minestrone. Thomas put the gun on him as he walked towards the exit. Aldo sat where he was, his hands up. Thomas got close, told him to stay out of it since he was retired, and eat his soup. Aldo turned back and put another spoonful in his mouth. Then Thomas shot him in the back of the head, splashing Aldo's brains into his soup bowl.

All the noise finally brought the fat cook out from the kitchen. He froze in shock behind the bar. Thomas told him to back into the kitchen. The cook disappeared. Then Thomas and his new associates left the club.

And came looking for me.

As Gino and Aldo were being executed, I was in bed with Danae in a small room on the second floor of Bumpy's place. Bumpy had softened his stance regarding our relationship once he realized we really cared for each other.

Bumpy was a good sort. I always liked him.

An urgent knock came on the door. Bumpy himself stuck his head in before we could respond. His face was drawn, his forehead sweaty. He relayed the news.

I threw the sheets off me, grabbed my clothes. Danae did the same. I told her we had to leave town, head to France right then, that night. I told her to pack a bag, bare essentials only. I had to get back to the club, to my room off the kitchen. I had over four thousand dollars in cash hidden under the floorboards in the corner. And this was when four thousand dollars was a lot of money. I told her to go out front. I would use the fire escape. We would meet back in one hour. There was a freighter leaving for Europe on the morning tide. Three hours tops and we'd be aboard, making good our escape.

Happily ever after, right?

She was scared, of course. She could barely hold her hands still long enough to button her blouse. I smiled, reassured her everything was going to be fine. I had no intention of fighting Thomas. If Thomas wanted control, that was fine by me. I just wanted out.

She nodded, tried to smile back at me, but failed to be convincing. She put her shoes on while I tucked in my shirt. She smiled and waved as I threw my tie around my neck, allowing it to drape down both sides. I grabbed my coat and threw open the window. She closed the door behind her as I climbed out.

Out on the fire escape, with her safely on her way, I took a deep breath to calm myself. Gino was dead. Aldo was out of the picture. There was nothing standing between Thomas and me.

I have to admit, I was afraid.

Once my own pulse began to stabilize, I climbed down the swaying metal ladder and jumped the few feet down onto the dirty, uneven alleyway. It was raining that night, and the cobblestones were slippery. I stumbled, went to one knee.

I stood up and took about three steps, then heard someone call my name. I froze in place. I recognized the voice.

Thomas.

I turned slowly, keeping my hands very still. Thomas and a thug I had never seen before stepped forward out of the shadows. A third guy materialized out of the gloom at an angle behind me and moved slowly to the right.

Ambush. And they had me dead to rights in a crossfire.

Holding his gun on me, he cordially informed me of Gino's untimely death, and of Aldo's, then informed me that from now on, he would be in charge of things. He asked me what I thought about that.

I told him congratulations. It was all his. I had no intention of interfering. I just wanted out. I would leave Hoboken right then, that night, never to return. I promised I would be out of the country by sunrise.

He smiled a cruel smile, asked me if I really thought that would happen. He had me where he wanted me, and giving me a pass was not in the cards. I decided I would die fighting.

I moved diagonally to my left, while reaching into my coat pocket for my gun. Thomas fired, missed. I got my gun out, brought it up, fired.

Once.

Twice.

I missed both shots.

Then it felt like I got hit in the chest with a sledgehammer.

Stunned, I staggered backwards, fell down into the mud and drainage that trickled down the center of the alleyway. My gun clattered to the ground, out of reach, useless.

Thomas and his men walked up on me. I will never forget lying there, looking up at a black velvet sky, my chest on fire, my breath coming in ragged gasps as my lungs filled with blood. And then those three faces appeared, hovering over me, angels of death. Not what I wanted to see in my last moments on earth.

I croaked Danae's name.

Thomas assured me he would personally inform her of my unfortunate demise. And that afterwards, he was going to find out what it was about her I was so attracted to.

Enraged, I tried to sit up, but could not. One of the thugs asked if they should kill me with a second shot, but Thomas said no, no need to waste the bullet.

Let me suffer.

They turned and walked away. Leaving me where I lay, like a piece of human garbage.

So this was how my life would end.

All my decisions, all my choices, all my actions, had lead me to point, that alleyway, that night. And all my hopes and dreams, all my pursuits of better days, of a peaceful life in France with Danae, flitted away with each drop of blood that flowed out of me.

And I realized how stupid I had been, about all of it. A life of crime always ended one of two ways: either jailed for life, or like where I was right then, dying violently and alone.

Tears of rage ran down the sides of my face. I kept trying to get up, but it was like someone had nailed me to the ground. As my eyes rolled around in my head, I saw the gloom and shadows swirling both from the amber lights of the rooms and buildings nearby, but also from my own fading consciousness.

I sensed movement, vague and ambiguous. Then I realized someone was moving towards me. I assumed Thomas and his goons had come back to finish the job, or to just taunt me while I died.

But no.

It looked like a woman. Swirling, silent, ethereal. Beautiful. An angel, perhaps? But no. Of course, no. She was quite real, just no longer of mortal flesh.

My vampire mother.

Her skin was pale; the palest I had ever seen. White. And thin as gossamer. I could see tiny blue blood vessels spreading upwards across her cheeks. She looked freshly young and impossibly old at the same time. She walked steadily towards me, but she moved in a

way I had never seen a woman move. Not faster, not slower. Just...
different.

Unnatural, somehow. Like she was not walking at all, but
gliding.

I found out later that she had simply happened into the
alleyway just as I was jumping to the ground. She had hidden in the
shadows and had watched events play out. She did not interfere. Not
her business.

She showed no fear or angst as she knelt down beside me.
She seemed well acquainted with the sight of blood. My strength
was slipping away quickly. And yet, she did not make haste. She
looked me up and down like she was examining a specimen, with a
cool sense of detachment.

She took my dripping red hand, closed her eyes. She gasped
in surprise, breathed in, her breasts rising against the thin material of
her blouse. She said she knew I was a criminal, but that there was
good in me, too. She said I was dying, but what if I could get
revenge on the men who had shot me? How would I like to live
forever, and never have to worry about dying again?

Is that something I would want?

I could not speak at that point; I was too weak. I simply
closed my eyes and nodded once.

Her eyes sparkled in the night, glassy black, bottomless,
soulless orbs. Her mouth opened and I saw fangs. She descended and
sank her teeth into my neck. It happened so fast, I did not have time
to feel the pain. After she had drunk from me, she cooed me like a
mother with a frightened child. She soothed me and stroked my hair.
She assured me that death would be only temporary, that one must
die in order to be reborn.

And that is the last thing I heard as a mortal man.

The whole vampire motif of having to remain dead for three
days and rising on the third night as a vampire is bunch of hooey
made up by religious fanatics in Europe in the Middle Ages. It was
conjured up to be an unholy correlation with the scripture of Jesus
Christ rising from the dead on his third day. It was just another way
to push the narrative that vampires were of demonic origin and
inherently evil. Fear is the most efficient form of enslavement.

True, I have met some vampires who actually fit that bill. But most of us just want to be left alone. And for the record, I never went to hell. I do not remember ever meeting the Devil, and I have never, to the best of my knowledge, ever seen or been seen by a demon.

Just wanted to put that out there.

The reason why I intervened on your behalf should be obvious by now. You are a good man in a dangerous line of work. And you are my great, great Grandson. I could not sit idly by when I had to power to stop a terrible fate from befalling you. If you were a bad person, a drug dealer like you pretended, I would have let nature take its course.

You look outraged. You should not be. Would I have stood by and let you die if you had knowingly followed a dark path, even though you ware my direct descendant?

You bet I would. And I will tell you why.

Every man must take responsibility for his actions, his choices, his decisions, his life. You make good choices, you reap the rewards. To the victor go the spoils. But the flip side is if you make bad choices, you shoulder the burden; you take the blame.

But either way, everyone gets what he or she works for.

I woke up disoriented and quite naked. I was resting on a slab in the city morgue. This was the next evening. A new vampire does not get bitten and change all in one night. It takes closer to twenty-four hours. The change from human to vampire is a process, and like I said before, you have to die before you can be reborn.

I took the first of many nightly gasps of cool air flowing into deflated lungs, filling them with earthly atmosphere, and filling my chest with pain. I tried to move, but I was stiff, like I had been in bed a week. I finally swung my legs over the side of the coroner's table and pushed myself into a sitting position.

I looked around the room. Things seemed different somehow. Colors seemed to be more muted, but I saw clearly in the dark room. There was no light source. I looked over my shoulder, saw a closed door that lead out to the entry room. Light shown a yellow sliver under the door. Someone sat at a desk outside, scribbling reports and filling out forms. I knew he was there. I could smell his scent; could hear his scribbling as the pencil brushed across the paper. And internally, I felt a rhythmic beat.

Lub-dub. Lub-dub.

It was the beat of the Coroner Assistant's heart.

New and powerful instincts kicked in. I leapt off the table and landed on my feet, nimble as a cat. I scanned the room, my eyes adapting remarkably well to the darkness. My tongue flicked across my new fangs.

And then I saw her, the mysterious woman from the night before. Standing still and small, for she was a petite thing, in a far corner. She watched me, smiling with approval. She nodded encouragingly.

I asked her exactly what was happening? How could this be? What had she done to me?

She held a bundle under her arm, pressed tightly to her body. She told me I would need these and held out the bundle, which proved to be a change of clothes and an old pair of shoes.

I glanced down at myself. I was standing naked in front of a strangely beautiful woman. And yet I had no feeling about it one way or the other. No pride, no fear, no shame, no arousal. It just did not seem to matter. The bullet hole in my chest was healed, scarred over. I felt no pain. I did notice my skin had the same pallor as hers. She assured me this was normal.

As I dressed, she explained in that strange accent of hers that she had done what I had asked. She had made sure the gangster's bullets did not kill me. I had died, yes, but I now lived again. But this new existence came with a strange and terrible price.

I was *vampyre* now. Like her.

As vampires, we would sustain ourselves by drinking blood, human blood. We would never get sick . We would never grow old. We would never die. We would heal from injuries, regrow severed limbs.

We were stronger than humans, much stronger. And faster. Oh, so much faster. But though we could not die, we could be destroyed. Sunlight was Death to us, and we had to, um, "keep our heads", as it were, if we were to survive. Decapitation will kill me just as dead as sunlight.

I tucked in my shirt. She asked me if I was hungry. I said yes. She smiled and suggested we exit out the back. We stepped out into an alleyway. I stopped as my senses became bombarded with the sounds, smells, and tastes of the world outside.

I staggered back initially. It was overwhelming.

She knew what I was experiencing, and reassured me. She was reading my emotions, my mood changes. She waited a moment for me to take everything in. When I finally relaxed and stood straight again, we went forward towards the street.

We walked down the street, mingling with the humans. No one seemed to notice us, our pale skin, our hungry stares. She explained that the hunger was an instinctive thing. And she educated me on the basics of this new Life in the Shadows.

We did not need to feed every night, and we certainly did not have to drain our prey to the point of death. If the victim died, we had to sever the head from the body, otherwise that human turned into a vampire that we would be responsible for.

I asked her how that was possible: that our bite and death would make a new vampire? She replied that it simply was, and had always been so. She did not require a deeper more detailed explanation. She knew it to be fact, accepted it. She suggested I do the same.

We moved on, down dimly lit streets, scuttling through back alleyways, slinking close to the shadows, slithering into the seedier side of Hoboken. The neighborhood where I had grown up.

All the buildings looked familiar, and yet somehow different. I recognized the tenement building I had been raised in. The building my mother still lived in. I stopped and looked upward at the third story apartment where I knew my mother still abided. An orange glow emanated from the window, warming the night around it. I saw a shadowed figure, a woman, step to the window and pause as she looked outside, then pulled the curtains closed with a flick of her wrists that sent the cheap cotton material fluttering.

It was my Mom.

I had not seen her in a while. Quite a while, actually. She had aged beyond her years. She was a little heavier now, her hair gray. Ashen skin, worry lines across her face, her eyes rheumy from stress and heartbreak, her back mildly stooped from the weight of the world she carried. I saw, sensed and knew all of this in an instant. And I knew, with a heavy heart, that I had wronged her. I had added to the burdens of her life, that indeed, much of the burden she bore, she bore because of me. How I had disappointed her, wounded her, abandoned her.

She Who Was With Me read my mind. She admonished me against stopping in to see her. I told She Who Was With Me that I needed to see her, however briefly, to apologize to her, to explain – well, explain what? Came my mentor's terse response. She told me my appearance, my deathly pallor, sharp fangs that I kept running my tongue over, and my black glassy eyes would do nothing but terrify my mother. It would shock and horrify her. A bad situation made worse, so to speak.

The vampire beside me gravely warned me to not contact any of my mortal friends, contacts, family, or lovers. Even Danae. I told her I must see Danae. Danae was why I had chosen this path rather than Death. She stood firm, instructing me I must have the strength to make a complete break. My old life was over. A new one had begun.

The need to feed pulled at me again, became uppermost in my mind.

A word about the Hunger is in order here. Again, do not believe the baloney you see in the movies or on TV. Hunger does not turn us into salivating maniacal monsters any more than we can turn into bats. But it does become one's primary motivation.

As we glided along in that seedy part of town, we must have been an unusual sight. She a petite, slim, strangely exotic woman in a thick red velvet dress that plunged at the neckline and fell to her feet, and me, a pale, gangly man with a flat face, no hat, no necktie, and no coat – only pants, shoes, no belt or suspenders, and a plain white shirt with long sleeves that did not quite extend down to the wrists of my newly longer arms. And yet we moved along in this dangerous place, neither one of us felt threatened.

No one accosted us. People on the sidewalk looked away. A few altered course to avoid us. We were the predators, and the prey somehow knew it. And like all prey in the animal kingdom, they got out of the predators' way.

I asked my teacher, whom we should target? She asked me whom I would like to target? I thought a moment, and then told her I wanted to target a criminal. A bad person. Someone who deserved to be drained of blood, and possibly die a frightful death, if it came to that. She smiled, showing her fangs. She liked that idea.

We stopped at a corner, where we could watch people going into saloons and speakeasies, staggering out, random people walking down the street. She told me to pick one person out, and concentrate on them. I did as she asked, and realized what she was trying to teach me.

If I calmed myself to stillness, I could sense the auras of the humans around me. I could sense who was good, who was bad, who was in between. In time, I would hone this skill to where I can do it at will, turn it on and off like a switch. And I found out later that if I could touch a person, I could see into their souls, know everything about them, everything they've done. Every person they ever hurt, every sin they ever committed.

But that night, I was a newborn vampire, trying to understand my new senses, my new powers.

We decided on a prostitute who plied her trade nearby. This was a safe choice. Rough men with dark souls and violent tempers frequented the brothels here, and it was not uncommon for young ladies of the evening to be killed or go missing, never to be found. If she survived, no one would ever believe the truth. If she died, she was just another whore who went missing.

She stood on a corner a block away, wearing a threadbare blouse and long skirt of faded red. She was probably late twenties, but a rough life and barebones existence had made her look closer to forty. She reeked of desperation and sadness. I had found a hat outside a store as we had walked along. It fit fairly well, maybe a little tight, but I could wear it and not look ridiculous. So I pulled my hat down low to hide my face and approached. My teacher followed behind me at a distance.

The hooker, who was familiar to me and went by the name Trixie, saw me heading her way. She took a step further out onto the boarded sidewalk as I approached. With my head down, we exchanged pleasantries. She did not recognize my voice. With my hat low and my head pointed at the ground, my face was hidden. I feigned embarrassment.

She asked if the woman with me wanted to watch or participate? I told her she would most definitely participate. Trixie quoted her price, and I agreed. She turned to go inside through the front door, but I stopped her. I asked her if there was a back way, as my partner and I required discretion.

She smiled and nodded, thinking she understood our intent. She motioned with her hand for us to follow her around the corner.

We followed and stepped into the deeper gloom. As my mentor caught up with me, our hostess was assuring us of her utmost discretion, and further assured us of her tender talents, as she had entertained couples such as ourselves before.

The vampire beside me smiled, stifled a laugh, and replied, "I doubt that."

Something in my Vampire Mother's voice made the woman turn around. I raised my head and looked her square in the eye. She took in our pale faces, our black eyes, our hungry mouths.

We moved quickly. We grabbed her at the wrists and the mouth, pushing her against the rough-hewn wall of the building. Pure instinct took over. I could hear her heartbeat, smell her fear. Feel the humidity from the sweat on her skin. It excited me, intoxicated me. I could see the gentle pulse under the alabaster skin at the side of her neck. My mouth opened and I descended upon her. That blood was the sweetest I have ever tasted in over a hundred years.

No one ever forgets their first time.

I do not know my Vampire Mother's name. She never told me, and I never asked. She taught me only the most rudimentary of vampire survival skills, and then she was gone. I never saw her again after that first night.

My Vampire Mother was careful, unhurried, sublime. The word "dainty" comes to mind. She hardly spilled a drop on the ground. Not me, man. I was a slobbering fool. Not for the woman, of course, but for her life-giving blood. I was as sloppy as a Saint Bernard at a water trough.

It was like a drug that first time. It was as close as I ever came to being high. Oh, that warmth. That pulsating warmth. The slick wetness of it. Even the coppery taste.

I made a rookie mistake. I reveled in it jut a bit too much that first time. I drained the poor woman to the point of death. Suddenly, Trixie was limp in my arms, a lifeless doll. I could barely hear her heartbeat as I came out of my euphoric trance.

Vampire Mother scolded me on my lack of self-control. She told me I could not allow Trixie to become like us. I did not know how to be a vampire myself. How could I possibly teach anyone else? My choice was quite simple. I asked how, and she told me to snap her neck. Right away.

I obeyed quickly, snapping Trixie's neck with a quick twist to the right, her pliant spinal cord coming apart as the cervical vertebrae gave way, killing her instantly. It was easier than I had expected. A person's neck is actually quite thick with muscle, bone, tendons running everywhere. It takes an enormous amount of torque, the proper force at the proper time in the proper direction, to do it and do it right. But with my new vampire strength, it popped with little effort.

Trixie was nothing but a meat sack now, a limp bag of bones. Dead weight, she slid out of my hands. I left her where she fell, and my mentor and I calmly walked away, wiping our mouths. She then gave me the rundown on being a vampire.

Bottom line, crosses do not paralyze us with fear, nor do we curse God. At least, no more than mortals. We are not compelled to sleep in coffins. Those of us who do have either a morbid sense of humor, or a proclivity for the macabre. Stakes through the heart just piss us off. Silver bullets through the heart? Wrong legend. Same result. We just keep coming.

Shoot us in the head, now you are getting close. That will stop us temporarily. A shotgun blast to head? That will kill just about anything. I have never heard of one of my kind coming back from that.

And as I said earlier, sunlight is Death to us, pure and simple. We sunburn and blister in seconds. We swell, bleed, and char in less than a minute. We burn to the bone like a fire victim in less than two.

Think of it like albinism on steroids.

Do not ask me why or how. I do not know the why or how. I simply know it is.

My old life was gone. I had a new one in return. It was up to me to make it right.

But I was no longer human, and new rules constrained me. I could no longer engage in most "human" activities. My emotions remained largely the same, but the physicality had changed drastically. Daylight was nonstarter, obviously. Eating human food, too. I can drink water, and water-based liquids. Tea, and coffee a little bit. Black only. No sugar, no cream. Anything else makes me violently ill.

Sex was done, too. Over. Kaput. Forget about it.

I told She Who Made Me again about Danae. I explained our situation, our plans for our immediate future. What was I to do?

My vampire mother listened to my every word. She nodded at all the appropriate times, looked sympathetic to my plight. She told me the best thing I could do regarding Danae would be... nothing. Stay away entirely.

Of course, this was unacceptable to me. I loved Danae, and nothing, not even death, could stop us from being together. She reminded me that I was different now. I looked different, smelled different. Humans would never accept me. They would fear me. In the end, they would hate me. Danae would hate me. I was in what you might call a "no win" situation.

I told her she was wrong; she was wrong about Danae.

Vampire Mother told me to do as I desired, but be prepared for things to not work out. She advised me to make my appearance the following night. Dawn was coming. She would make sure I survived that first night, but after that, I was on my own. Her obligation would be at an end. But this first night, her job was to teach. My job was to learn.

I was impatient, of course. Most young men are. A sign of immaturity, I think. Over time, we learn the benefits of allowing events to unfold in the fullness of time.

Vampire Mother and I walked the streets. Trixie's blood peppered the front of my shirt. Even in the night air, it had dried rusty brown sprayed across the white material. My companion, of course, was neat and tidy. She told me she understood the bloodlust that had overcome me, but warned me to keep it under control.

Control was the secret of anonymity, she explained. And anonymity was the key to survival. That was probably the most important lesson I learned from my Vampire Mother.

It was the rule I broke in order to save your life.

Now, I am exposed. The truth of what I am is in danger of becoming public knowledge. Can you imagine what would happen in this day and age if people were to find out that vampires actually exist?

I simply cannot have that.

We need to keep you alive, and that means killing the men who are coming to kill you. Once it is done, I must fade back into the darkness, and you must go on with your life. That day-to-day struggle of life's peaks and valleys is for you and you alone.

But know this, my son: from now until the day you die, your movements will be known to me. If you ever need me again, need my special brand of assistance, believe me, I will know.

In that sense, I will always be there for you.

I swear it.

CHAPTER TWENTY

Detective Reginald Downing sat silent in his seat. Overwhelmed by the story he had just heard and shocked by the vampire's matter-of-fact candor, Reggie's mouth hung open, his eyes wide and unblinking.

The vampire had stopped talking, and now sipped from his glass of iced tea. Smooth, unhurried movements. If Reggie had not known better, he might have assumed the creature sitting across from him was alive, mortal. A bit pale and sickly looking, but mortal nonetheless.

But Reggie did know better, didn't he?

The story the vampire had related was fantastic, incredible. But Reggie understood, on a visceral level, that every word was true. Another realization hit home, like a baseball bat to the center of his forehead.

Vampires were real.

And this vampire, this creature who subsisted on human blood, the walking corpse that had been shot, left for dead, delivered from Death, and now sat before him, was indeed his great great Grandfather.

"I understand now why you helped me." Reggie's voice sounded hoarse. "And thanks again for that. But how did you know when and the where?"

"Elementary, my dear Watson." The vampire smiled and flicked his wrist. "I have been aware of you since the day you were born. I have kept tabs on you."

Reggie was not sure he liked the idea of a supernatural monster keeping tabs on him. The vampire sensed his tension.

"Nothing intrusive, I assure you."

"What then?"

The vampire leaned forward, elbows on the table for the first time. "Remember in middle school, you wanted to go on that eighth-grade overnight to Big Bear?"

"Mom said she didn't have the money."

"Times were hard for you and your Mom."

Reggie nodded. "She was working two jobs most of my childhood. I think she was looking for another part time job back then."

"And what happened?"

"She found a money order in the mailbox with..."

"The precise amount of money she needed to send you." The vampire finished. "Plus a hundred dollars for spending money."

"That trip meant the world to me," Reggie said, remembering. "Thank you."

"It was my pleasure."

"Mom never said where the money came from."

"She did not know."

"Think I remember her saying there was a letter in the envelope."

"Instructing her to use the money for its intended purpose."

"The letter was not signed."

"Of course not."

"What else did you help us with?"

The vampire tilted his head upwards and to the right, a subconscious action taken when accessing that area of the brain that retains long-term memory. "I attended your college graduation. The top bleachers in the back."

Reggie remembered graduation. It was eight o'clock, in June. "The sun was still out. How did you get inside without frying?"

"Long pants, long sleeves, gloves, SPF 60 sunblock on my face and neck, and a broad brimmed hat. I waited until dusk before leaving."

Reggie contemplated this, nodded. Then the slaughter aboard the *Sulu Sea* came rushing back. Had it been less than two days since? It already seemed like a lifetime ago.

The vampire smiled. If he had been a human being and not an unnatural creature, Reginald would have thought that his great great Grandfather was smiling warmly at him.

"So you know my father, then?"

The vampire's smile fled his face. "Yes."

"Where is he?"

"Passed on."

Reggie took the information in, nodded solemnly.

"Please know, I had no hand in it." What else could the vampire say after delivering such news?

"It's all right. I never really knew him."

"He was an addict. Your mother, God love her, had terrible taste in men."

"She's still alive, you know."

"And living a life of self-imposed celibacy," the vampire said. "Hence the past tense regarding her sexuality."

"Aw man," Reggie said, sitting back and waving his hands. "Don't talk like that."

The vampire was confused. "Why not? All humans are born sexual creatures. Of course your parents, your grandparents, and so on were sexual beings in their youth. Be glad they were. Otherwise, you would not be here."

Reggie pushed the disturbing mental images out of his mind. "What about my grandfather?"

"On your mother's side? Wilfred. My grandson. Married Dottie, your maternal grandmother in 1951. Got shipped off to war in 1952. Korea. Died for his country at the Chosin Reservoir, but not before making sure the bloodline continued."

"My mother."

"Exactly."

"Wait a minute. Grandma Dottie remarried. He's dead now. But they had another child. Haven't seen him since I was a kid"

"Clarence. He did a stint in the Army. Fought in Vietnam. Bounced around a bit after he got back like so many of them did back then. Lives in Sarasota, Florida. Owns a car dealership down there."

"Good to know."

"Not much for family ties," the vampire added. "He was a lonely kid before Vietnam. Confused. Never really fit in. Then what with his experiences during that war, and with all the drifting afterwards, well," he shrugged. "He never married."

They sat in silence for a bit. The waitress came by, asked if they needed anything else. They did not. She left the bill turned upside down on the table, walked away with a smile.

The vampire put his cold withered hand with the long fingers, claw nails, and mottled skin over the slip of paper. He drew it to him, picked it up. He regarded the math work on the ticket, adding the numbers in his head. He nodded to himself.

"Everything okay?" Reggie asked.

"Fine," the vampire answered. "Did you get enough to eat?"

Reggie grinned. His great, great Grandpa was making sure he was full. "Yes."

"Would you like some dessert? Some pie, perhaps?"

"No, thank you. I'm fine."

The vampire looked around the room, peered through the tinted glass outside. Reggie knew that the vampire saw everything.

"Is everything all right?"

The vampire looked at Reggie from across the table. "Yes. Fine." The vampire moved towards the edge of his seat. "We must not stay in one place too long."

"Roger that."

They each slid out of the booth, twisting their torsos, contracting their core muscles, extending their legs. They were so similar, Reggie thought. They both moved, both breathed. Both possessed cognitive abilities, both experienced emotions. But only one of them was alive. The other had been dead for over a century.

What surprised Reggie was that he was already accustomed to this new reality.

The vampire led the way through the narrow confines of the restaurant. Reggie followed three feet behind him. Back in "cop mode" now, his eyes moved all around, taking in his surroundings. Red vinyl-covered booths squatted on his left. The old-fashioned Americana greasy spoon counter stretched into the distance on the right. The individual stools boasted padded seats covered in matching red vinyl and small backs so a diner could stretch during a meal.

A young black man ate a tuna melt and onion rings at the counter, fourth seat from the cash register. Interwoven tribal tattoos adorned his arms. Dreadlocks tumbled down to the middle of his back. He paid no attention to Reggie or the vampire.

In a booth to the left, the second booth from the main entrance a Hispanic family ate dinner. The father, trim, in his thirties, sat with a plate of tacos, beans and rice in front of him. His wife, young and attractive, ignored her Denver omelet with cottage fries to help feed the infant with them. The baby, a girl judging by her pink clothing and pierced ears, appeared to be about six months old. Secured in her car seat and wedged in between the back of the booth and the table's edge, she held a Vienna sausage in each chubby little fist. She looked from one hand to another, trying to decide which one of eat first.

Reggie grinned as he passed by. The baby saw him, responded in kind, grinning from ear to ear.

Horn's office looked like something out of an old pulp novel. Scarred desk bolted to the floor, yellow pool from above illuminating the center of the cluttered desktop. The light mellowed outward from the bright center dimming to amber, then farther out a coalescence of musty brown. The squeaky Government-issue chair at a forty-five degree angle. Metal bookcases lurked in the murk. The cheap white coffee maker, indistinct in the shadows, sat unused. A small red light at the base announced electricity coursing through its twisted umbilicus.

Horn, tired and heavy, sat opposite the amber perimeter. The high-backed chair groaned with every move, every shift of his considerable weight. Horn thought it felt like he had a spring trying to coil its way up his ass.

The acid reflux burned in his throat. He grimaced at the taste of bile on his tongue. He turned quickly and spat something thick and green into the trashcan beside him.

Where the hell had he hidden those chewable antacids? Even as a Captain, he was not immune from office thieves. He had left personal stuff like chewable antacid tablets on or in his desk before. He would come in the next day or Monday after a weekend and find the bottle either missing, or the supply inside seriously depleted.

Horn had been down that road before in his Navy days. And Horn was a fast learner. So he now hid stuff quite well, often under lock and key. Problem was, sometimes even he could not find it when needed.

Like right now.

Where the hell did he put it...?

Oh yes.

Right side, top drawer.

He grabbed the drawer handle and yanked. He snatched the pill bottle out, muscled the top open. He shook the open mouth over his bear paw of a hand, popped several into his mouth. The fruity taste hit his tongue just as he began chewing. He forced the lid back on, tossed the bottle back into the drawer, pushed it closed with his knee.

Where the hell was Castle?

His stomach grumbled. He was hungry. The sun was long down outside. Darkness spilled in through the windows, punctuated by artificial beams from the gulag-style lamps affixed outside.

He had not eaten since about one that afternoon. And he had not eaten well. Something greasy. Unhealthy, and of low quality ingredients. Wrapped in a flour tortilla. Typical cop cuisine, best left forgotten. He had eaten simply to fuel his body. Too bad the fuel had been crap.

Horn absently wondered if his case of Cop's Crappy Diet contributed to his acid reflux. That and the general stress of the job, of course. Then add his latent angst about the divorce and his stalled life in general into the mix, and *voila!* Instant GERD.

Looking down at his desk, glasses perched on his nose, he concentrated on work. Crime scene photos from the *Sulu Sea* Massacre stared back up at him. He picked up the picture of T-Ball's twisted corpse. Exsanguination was the actual cause of death, according to the coroner. The gaping neck wound had been designated as the cause of the exsanguination. The broken bones had been an effect of being tossed aside with considerable force. The rending fractures to the cervical vertebrae from C-2 through C-4 had shredded the spinal cord embedded within the bones.

But who - or what - killed like this?

The crime scene technicians (Horn referred to them as the CSI geeks) had reported the wound appeared to be a bite, not something made by a knife or other bladed weapon. The skin and underlying blood vessels had not been sliced or incised, they had determined.

They had been torn.

Torn asunder, was how the CSI geeks had termed it. When pressed on the matter of what kind of animal might have done this, the CSI Head Geek and All Around Guru had told Horn over the phone – off the record, of course – that the forensics fit for a human bite. The bite radius, the imprints of the various teeth: molars, bicuspids, central incisors all matched.

But with one significant exception.

Whatever had done the biting also exhibited distinct, unmistakable bite marks of two upper jaw canine teeth measuring somewhere between a quarter and a half inch longer than the surrounding teeth. The canines in the lower jaw impressions were unremarkable.

These fangs, for lack of a better term, in conjunction with tremendous bite force of the jaws of whatever had done this. Far surpassing the bite force of a human, it had been sufficient to rend five layers of skin and subcutaneous fascia, puncture blood vessels, and then a wrenched outward motion thereby tearing tissue asunder. There was that term again.

Torn asunder.

It kept coming back to that term. This was the key to the case. He knew it, but could not fit the pieces together. Not yet. But he knew they fit. And he knew that when they did, he would not like the picture they revealed.

And it frightened him.

The doorknob clicked as it turned. The office door swung open with a thump. Horn jumped, startled. He dropped the photo he was holding.

"Sorry," Nick Castle said as he shouldered his way through the door holding two paper bags. They looked heavy and in danger of tearing at the bottom. The detective quickly moved and placed the bags gingerly on the closest edge of Horn's desk.

"Didn't mean to scare you."

Horn's heart rate was slowly returning to a normal sinus rhythm. "That's all right. What did you get?"

"Filipino."

Castle grabbed the top of the bags and made a swift downward motion from top to bottom. The paper bags ripped loudly, revealing wax paper food containers. Horn noticed that one could say Castle had torn the bags asunder.

Damn. Now he had that phrase on the brain.

"Pancit and lumpia. Pork adobo. Steamed rice." He pointed to each container in turn. "I got plenty of soy sauce, too. And sweet and sour sauce."

Horn smiled appreciatively. "Outstanding." He jammed some of the gruesome black and white photos into a dull brown file folder to protect them, then dropped the file onto the far left side of his desk.

Castle produced paper plates, napkins, and plastic forks from a thin plastic bag. They opened the containers and began filling their plates.

Castle hoisted a forkful of pancit. "So did you solve the case while I as gone?"

Horn grunted. "I know everything we need to solve this case is right here," he said, putting voice to his frustrations. "We've got all the pieces, but they just don't fit together in a way that makes any sense."

"Maybe we need to open up our minds a little bit on this one."

Horn stared at Castle askance. "'Open our minds'? Are you going all hippie dippy new age bullshit metaphysical on me?"

Nick nearly choked on his food laughing. "Not exactly," he said when we could breathe again. "But here's the thing. Like you said, it doesn't make sense. I agree."

Horn crunched on a lumpia roll, waiting for Castle to continue. He loved pork lumpia. He loved pancit. Maybe we would retire to the Philippines. He would probably weigh four hundred pounds, but he would die a happy man.

"So the pieces must fit together in as way that doesn't make sense. But that's not a problem."

"Why not?"

"Process of elimination. Eliminate what we know is false. Then, whatever is left, no matter how improbable, must be possible."

"I knew it," Horn sighed. "You are going hippie dippy new age bullshit metaphysical on me."

"It's stupid to keep banging our heads against a wall, Captain. We have to approach from a different angle."

"Which is?"

"Take drugs out of the equation. Take the weapons out of the equation. What's left?"

Horn was on the same page now. "He was there to save Reggie's life."

"A guardian angel," Nick nodded. "Let's assume we're correct. How does he get his intel?"

Horn shrugged. " Beats me. But, he knows about the ambush. He shows up, slaughters everybody, saves Downing." He paused. "That's assuming Downing isn't lying about all this."

"He's not lying, Cap. About any of it. The forensics back him up." Castle wiped his hands on a napkin. "Downing's an honest cop. You don't like him because he's sassy."

"Sassy?" Horn echoed. "I hadn't noticed."

"He's smart and pays attention to detail. He respects the rule of law; takes solid cases to the D.A. You know this. But you're looking to make him out to be a bad guy."

"Oh?"

"Yes sir."

Horn ate in silence a moment. Castle went for seconds on the pancit.

"Pretty brutal assessment of your superior officer," Horn said at last.

"Am I wrong?"

"No," Horn heard himself say. "Look. I'll admit I've driven the car into a ditch. Time for something new. You're driving the rig now."

Castle's chest swelled a bit. "Let's assume I'm right. Why would this guy care about a cop being murdered?"

"Friend? Family?"

"Why did Downing not know him? Why did he not recognize the voice? Cross out family or friends."

"Perhaps someone with military training. Spec Ops skills, that kind of thing?" Horn mused aloud. "Nah. The computers would have picked it up."

Castle sighed in exasperation. "The only play we have is to talk to Downing again."

Horn checked his watch. "When do you want to do that?"

"Before the cartel does."

"And before his JTF." Horn added. "I never liked Walt Coulter."

Castle knew there was more to that than Horn was saying, but he let it go for now. "But where would he go? We have to assume they know about his apartment."

"It's just a cookie-cutter McCondo we confiscated in a drug bust. San Diego PD's been using it ever since." He grinned again. "Not even Coulter knows that."

"You really don't like him."

"I don't like most people," Horn replied. "Most people are full of shit."

"You like me."

"You're not so full of shit," Horn conceded. "Besides. I've simply... grown accustomed to you over time."

Horn tossed his plate in the trash and pushed upwards with his powerful legs to stand. His chair squeaked as rusty casters rolled it away behind him. The movement was quick for a large man; so fluid it was almost graceful.

Castle reminded himself to never underestimate Horn. He looked big and slow and overdue for retirement, but in a "push come to shove" situation, this guy would go toe to toe with anyone, and probably hold his own. He watched as Horn opened a drawer, pulled out a Colt Python.

Castle was impressed. A four-inch anodized barrel with ventilated rib on top, custom sights, plus a custom black rubber combat pistol grip with molded finger grooves. He blew air through his pursed lips in appreciation.

A massive weapon, it looked intimidating even in Horn's oversized fist.

The Python was of classic handgun design: an old-fashioned double-action revolver, with a spinning cylinder that held six .357 magnum rounds.

It was a hell of a reliable weapon. Revolvers tended to not jam in the heat of battle. On the other hand, with double action and no automation, one had to cock the hammer back each time, or squeeze the trigger hard enough to cock the hammer back so it could drop onto the firing pin.

"Where the hell did you get that hand cannon?"

"Since I graduated the Academy. Bought it as a graduation present. Carried it as my service weapon for the first few years." He shoved it in the waistband at the back of his trousers, careful that his belt loop did not get hung up on the hammer.

"You think we'll need that tonight?"

"You never know."

Suddenly, Castle's 9 mm Berretta, with four clips carrying a mere sixty rounds seemed rather inadequate. Castle stood, adjusted the pistol on his hip. Horn was already turning away, grabbing his coat off the old coat rack near the door.

Castle was careful to close the office door behind them as they left.

Rick Oakley stood off to the side, watching his men prepare for war. He pretended to not be nervous. He also pretended it did not bother him that he was no longer a glorified foot soldier himself.

Of course, that was false. But he was now head of a large, transnational, multimillion-dollar drug smuggling empire. He could not get his own hands bloody. It sent the wrong signal, the wrong message.

His job now was similar to any C-level executive at any "respectable" company in the world. He delegated the dirty work to the underlings. He had keep his eye on the big picture. He had to have vision for where he wanted the organization to go in the future.

But as any C-level executive can attest, any tenure can be... tenuous. If business runs on supply and demand, an executive's survival runs by the law of the jungle. The strong, the cunning, the ruthless, the merciless thrive. Any sign of perceived weakness can be like blood in shark-infested waters.

He had been in charge less than twenty-four hours, even though he had been in this business for almost twenty years. It felt like his first day on the job, and a bit... awkward.

As far as he could tell, no one else shared his unease. Everyone went about their business. The new foot soldiers were no longer regular gunmen. Every foot soldier now wore body armor, and each man carried mobile tech and coms.

Oakley listened to the metallic cacophony of crisp sounds: rounds pushed into clips, the springs recoiling against the resistance, the snapping in of the clip into the magazine of the oiled weapons, and the following snap as the weapons were locked and loaded, ready for firing. Then the comforting clicks of safeties being flipped expertly into place.

Rudy Valdez stepped up to him. "The men are ready, sir."

Oakley nodded. Rudy looked perfectly at ease in the new gear. Combat boots, dark cargo pants with the legs bloused just above the boot tops. Black mock turtleneck underneath matte black body armor with regimented plates that reminded Oakley of a scorpion's back. An earpiece wirelessly connected to a two-way radio in a Velcro pocket near Rudy's hip.

"Let's go over the strategy again," Oakley said.

"Find and kill Reginald Downing."

"Tactics?"

"We employ a two-pronged attack," Rudy recited. "He will mostly likely go to one of two places. His apartment – his *real* apartment," Rudy added for emphasis, "or his grandmother's house."

Oakley nodded.

"We deploy two teams of six men," Rudy continued. "We set up surveillance at each location. When he shows himself, secure any escape route. We trap him, corner him, and kill him."

"No collateral damage. I expect Grandma remains unharmed."

"Understood, sir."

Oakley glanced past Rudy, saw the other men. Some he knew, some were new. He trusted none of them the way he trusted the man in front of him. He wondered if he could possibly talk Rudy into staying on.

"Make sure they understand."

"Understood, sir."

"All right. Make it happen."

Rudy turned around and walked slowly towards the other eleven men. Most of them were mercenaries, hailing from a military background. Rudy had handpicked them based on this criterion. Oakley had explained to Rudy a few hours prior how he wanted to create a well-oiled operation. That meant employing operators with military proficiency.

Rudy had selected his operators for the night, gave a few the night off, and fired two more whose sloppy habits made them liabilities.

These men understood chain of command. They would obey orders without question, or Rudy would shoot them. Violent death was part of doing business, part of the life. They understood this as well.

"Okay, guys. Mount up. Terminate with extreme prejudice. Check your targets. No collateral damage."

None of the men spoke. They simply nodded their heads.

Rudy nodded back. They all turned and walked out of the warehouse, filing silently, one after the other, through the narrow, industrial metal door. When the last one went through and disappeared, the door closed shut behind them.

Outside, the kill squads moved towards two large Land Rovers. Black and shiny, with options that made them look reminiscent of military vehicles, the machines waited. Six crammed themselves into one, and six more folded and fitted themselves into the other. Doors closed. Men adjusted themselves inside, trying to get comfortable for the ride ahead. Discomfort frayed even the most professional person's nerves, made them distracted, irritable. Such distractions often lead to delayed responses and sloppy performance.

Sitting in the driver's seat of the lead vehicle, Rudy made sure his weapon was within easy reach to bring to bear at the side window, but kept the muzzle hidden from the casual observer with an outside view. He turned the key, started the engine.

"Radio check. Melvin. You copy?"

"Read you Lima Charlie," came the immediate response from Melvin, who sat in the front passenger seat of the other vehicle. Besides Rudy, Melvin a disciplined, no-nonsense black man, had been with the organization the longest, and had the strongest military background.

Melvin had done eight years active duty Army. He had been part of a Stryker force, and had completed combat tours in both Iraq and Afghanistan. But Melvin had found out the hard way when he got back that two tours in war zones with a body laced with scars, a chest full of medals and the often empty, perfunctory "thank you for your service" from civilians who had no fucking idea what his service had entailed, simply did not pay the rent. And legit jobs were scarce in a "recovered economy" that had never truly recovered.

"We'll set up at Downing's apartment," Rudy said.

"Roger that," Melvin replied. "To Grandmother's house we'll go."

Rudy grinned. "It's important for a man to have a sense of humor."

Headlights snapped on. The two vehicles edged forward, Melvin's falling in behind Rudy's. They crept through the maze of narrow lanes that snaked between closed and quiet warehouses and storage spaces. Some had been leased or were owned by both legitimate businesses and by more covert enterprises. At this time of night on the weekend, they sat dark and still.

They eventually wound their way out of the maze and came to a stop at the main gate. Open to the street, no guard. No witness. A major thoroughfare lay ahead of them, two-way traffic coming and going in each direction. Rudy looked right, looked left. He put his blinker on, turned left. He accelerated gently, stayed within the speed limit.

Behind him, the other vehicle did likewise. Melvin came to a full and complete stop. He put his blinker on, looked both ways. Only then did he turn right, accelerate gently up to just within the speed limit.

The last thing anyone tonight needed was to be pulled over by a local *gendarme* for a minor traffic violation. They would have to kill a cop just for doing his job, and in public no less! It was something none of them wanted to explain to the new boss.

CHAPTER TWENTY-ONE

The vampire maneuvered his Lexus through the early morning streets with fluid grace. It was well past midnight, actually past one. Not much traffic out on the road now. He realized time might become a factor soon.

"So was Danae a hottie?"

The vampire, distracted, did not comprehend what had been asked. "What?"

"Was Danae hot?" Reggie asked again.

"She was very beautiful, and I loved her," the vampire replied from behind his opaque glasses. "And yes, she could certainly be... sultry when she wanted to be."

Reggie grinned. "So great great Grandma was a hottie?"

"Yes," the vampire admitted. He smiled wistfully at an intimate memory "I suppose, in the current vernacular, she was indeed a hottie." He pronounced that last word haltingly.

"So what happened when you saw her again?"

The wistful smile disappeared. The vampire glanced his way, then faced the road in front of them. His expression was flat.

"I can't believe you loved her that much and never snuck back to see her."

"Vampire Mother told me not to."

"But she was only your Vampire Mother for one night," Reggie countered. "After that, you were free to make your own decisions, right?"

The vampire shrugged. He remembered the wide eyes, the open mouth, the look of absolute horror on Danae's lovely face. He remembered her recoiling from him, from his cold touch. Her involuntary gasp at the sight of his eyes.

His fangs.

Her screaming at him. Calling him "demon". Calling him "monster". Her jabbing forefinger pointing to the second story window through which he came come, ordering him to leave, now, to leave *her*, and never come back.

Ever.

"Things did not turn out as I had hoped," the vampire said.

She had screamed that the man she had loved was dead, and the unnatural, unholy thing standing in front of her was NOT Eddie Marx.

"So. She threw your ass out, then?"

He remembered the rainy night in the filthy alley where he had died. Dying would have been preferable to what he felt that night, skulking away into the darkness. For without Danae, was life worth living?

The vampire drove for bit in silence. "I was dead." His voice was forlorn, in danger of breaking. "She felt it would affect our relationship."

"She had a point."

The vampire did not answer. He sunk down a bit in the seat. The movement pushed his collar up over his chin. The corners of his mouth turned down.

Reggie finally got an inkling the depth of the vampire's pain wondered if a vampire could cry. "Hey. It was a long time ago, man."

"Not for me."

"What about Thomas?"

"Thomas?"

"The guy that shot you?"

"Ah. Him." Reggie saw the vampire he had come to know returned. "Oh, I killed him," he replied casually. "Slowly. It took hours. But I made certain he suffered an eternity." The corners of his mouth turned upwards into a dreamy, contented smile.

"Sounds messy."

"It was."

Reggie shuddered. "Sounds like he got what he deserved." He looked at his great, great Grandfather. "But then again, so did you."

"Excuse me?"

"You made your choices.

"When you put it that way, you make it sound bad."

"Your choices got you killed. You hurt the people you loved."

They stopped at a red light. "Where are you going with this?"

"I just want you to know I've heard your story. I believe you. Every word. But you got what you got because of the choices you made."

"As do we all," the vampire said.

The light turned green. The Lexus moved forward. "Destination?"

"East Village," Reggie answered. "Just south of Market."

Rudy Valdez sat in the Land Rover, parked on a narrow side street perpendicular to his target. Down the block, the front entrance to Reginald Downing's apartment. It had been recently refurbished, only a facelift, an unimaginative paintjob to the front facade. The faded side was still its same old self. The building itself must have been in good condition, though. Reggie's apartment sat n the second floor over a convenience store. The store was closed, dark, and quiet.

This area of San Diego had been until recently slums, residential hotels, vacant lots, old buildings dark and evil, with windows broken out and resembling jagged teeth. The bums, drug dealers, crack whores, and other assorted "undesirables" had been rounded up, arrested; pushed out of the area so college students, art students, and young professionals could move in to the refurbished, brightly urbane buildings in their shiny new neighborhood.

Rudy glanced at his watch. Almost zero two hundred. No movement on the street. His operatives had alighted when they arrived and melted into the shadows. They assumed flanking positions. They had set up interconnecting fields of fire at all angles, effectively surrounding the building from about one hundred feet away. Two had climbed onto nearby rooftops to recon from sniper positions. Nothing larger than a cat would be able to move without someone detecting it.

"Stay alert", Rudy whispered into his mic. "This guy might show any time."

"He may not show at all," came a response.

"Identify yourself."

"Razor." Razor was the street name for the sniper on the roof above, set up with a line of sight into the window of Downing's apartment living room.

"You're right," Rudy allowed. "He might go to Grandma's house instead."

'Or he's already in the wind."

"Maybe," Rudy said. "Or, he may show up in the next two minutes."

Three blocks away, the vampire parked in an empty parking spot along the street. Trees and buildings obscured their view of the apartment. Reggie noticed a change in the vampire's mood. He was quiet now, mouth drawn into a thin line, his jaw set. And Reggie knew that if his own personal Vampire Protector had dropped into combat mode, he should do the same.

"So what's the play?"

"They lie in wait for you."

This simple truth, spoken by this century-old creature, fell like a steel curtain across Reggie's consciousness. Death was out there, waiting for him.

The vampire inhaled, steeling himself. "My son, if sinners entice thee, consent thou not. If they say, Come with us, let us lie in wait for blood, let us lurk for the innocent without cause. Let us swallow them alive as the grave, as those that go down to the pit."

The vampire opened his door and slid out. Reggie did the same. The vampire motioned for Reggie to follow close behind him. The vampire immediately went to the sidewalk, hugging the shadows he knew so well.

As they crept forward, the vampire spoke again. It was not more than a husky whisper, but Reggie heard every word clearly. And he would remember them for the days of his life.

"My son, cast not thy lot in with them. Refrain thy foot from their path. For their feet run to evil and they make haste to shed blood."

The vampire paused. Reggie saw him sniff the air, then stick his tongue out. Somehow his tongue extended farther out than he had ever seen anyone else's. The tip of the vampire's tongue was not blunt and rounded, but rather ended in a muscular tip. Watching, Reggie was reminded of a TV special he had once seen about snakes, about how they flicked their tongues to taste the smells of its environment.

Finally, the tongue rolled back up into the vampire's mouth. He turned to Reggie.

"For surely," he continued, "they lie in wait for their own blood, they lurk for their own lives. So are the ways of every one that is greedy for gain; which takes away the life of the owners thereof."

"What is that?"

"The Bible," the vampire replied. "The book of Proverbs. Chapter one, verses ten through nineteen. I thought it fitting."

He turned away from Reggie and moved on. Reggie followed, falling in close behind him. They moved in silence along the deserted streets. Everyone was already home, either asleep, or close to it. Good, the vampire thought. All the easier to separate the scents of the men ahead and pinpoint their locations.

All the easier for him to slaughter them.

As they moved closer, multiple scents assailed hit him: gun oil, graphite. Sweat, starched clothes. Antiperspirant. Even fresh polish on their boots. Locations were becoming clear to him.

"Men ahead," the vampire whispered. "Your apartment is surrounded."

Reggie reached behind himself, pulled his handgun out. He flicked the safety off.

"I live the next block up. Across the street. Above the convenience store."

The vampire nodded, came to a stop. He melted deeper into the shadows, right up next to the building, shaded by trees planted recently at great expense by the city of San Diego.

Ahead of them, the intersection of Market and Sixteenth lay waiting. Buildings on all four corners made for easy cover. The convenience store sat at a ninety-degree angle from them. Immediately beside the store's entrance, a narrow doorway and stairway lead upstairs to an apartment facing onto Market. The traffic control lights were on timer, and cast little usable light and shadow. One halogen streetlight illuminated the scene at strange angles, spears of stark light and black shadow, dark as ink.

"They are here."

"Where?"

"Down this street to the left, around this corner. Another a half block to the rear to cut off any escape route out back."

"There is no back way out."

"They do not know that," the vampire replied. "There is a sniper on the roof cross the street. And one or two others." The vampire pointed to the roof. "See that glint?"

Reggie peered upwards to the roof across the street. Unmistakable. It was a rifle barrel.

On the rooftop, Razor kept a steady eye through the scope, but also kept the other eye open to retain peripheral vision. He detected movement.

"Wait a second," he spoke softly into his mic.

"What?" Rudy asked over the com line.

Razor ignored him for a moment, peering away from the scope at the intersection of Market and Sixteenth. He though he had detected movement. Nothing now, though. Maybe a trick of the light?

On the street below, the vampire gently nudged Reggie farther back into the recesses of the darkness until his back was against the building.

"Razor, acknowledge." Rudy ordered through the com line.

Razor heard it. He swung his gun around to the far side of the intersection. "Thought I saw movement." He peered down through his scope.

"Where?"

"Northeast corner. Confirming now. Nothing through the lens. Switching to IFR."

The vampire turned and threw his body around Reggie's giving him a bear hug.

Razor switched on his infrared switch. The sightings through the scope changed. Anything generating heat would light up orange, red, yellow, or white, depending on its temperature. It would be obvious from the muddy blues and greens of the cooler objects in the target area.

Razor scanned the area. "Nothing," he reported. "False alarm."

He swung the rifle back around, turned off the IFR. He set up once again aiming at Reggie's apartment.

The vampire stepped back from Reggie, patted him on the shoulder. He turned and pointed again, this time at an alleyway about halfway up the next block. Reggie peered, following the vampire's thin long finger.

"I can't see anything."

"I see it," the vampire whispered.

"What?"

"A Land Rover. I can see the hub cap emblem on the front tire."

"A car parked in an alley? You're concerned over that?"

"Who parks a seventy thousand dollar vehicle in an alley in San Diego?"

"Someone getting stoned? Getting laid?"

The vampire turned his head. "And you believe that?"

Reggie admitted to himself he did not.

"You need to take care of the two around the corner and in back. Can you do that?"

"Yes."

"I mean, kill them."

"I know."

"Leave the rest to me."

Reggie shuddered.

"You will be exposed once you are on the street, so wait about fifteen seconds before you move. I must take the sniper on the roof."

"Fifteen seconds?"

"I only need ten."

Reggie nodded.

"Do not die," the vampire said.

"I won't."

"Do not miss."

"Believe me, I won't."

The vampire picked up on the simple confidence of his descendant, a consummate professional in his own right at what he did for a living. The vampire smiled with affection, and nodded. He turned towards the street, towards his enemies.

Then he was simply... gone.

Across the street, past the intersection, on the roof of the three-story building, Razor gazed through the scope. He sensed, rather than saw, a flutter move from left to right across the eyepiece.

Nothing more. A shimmer, really. He felt a slight rush of wind, above him, to his right. He glanced upwards.

Something hit him with so much force it knocked the wind out of him. He skidded across the rooftop, away from his rifle.

Eyes blurry from the impact and disoriented by his ass over teakettle tumble, Razor did not understand he was seeing. A thin man, not particularly tall, incredibly pale. Long black hair, wearing sunglasses in the middle of the night. The man silently held the sniper's rifle in his hands.

Long fingers. Sharp nails.

Claws?

Razor assumed his life was over. He expected this strange man to point the rifle at him. Using his bare hands, he bent the barrel to an impossible angle and broke - no *shattered!* - the plastic stock with a great wrenching motion. He made it seem easy. Like child's play. Pieces clattered onto the rooftop.

Instinct kicked in. Razor clambered to his feet and reached for his pistol. But the strange man was already moving towards him as he brought the pistol out of its hiding place. His long coat billowed in the wind as he moved.

Like a big black bat flapping its wings.

Razor heard a soft hiss, saw claws out. And did Razor actually see fucking *fangs* in this guy's mouth? Razor brought the weapon to bear, pointing at his assailant, extending the arm.

Those sharp claws –talons, really – neatly sliced through the bone and sinew at the wrist, severing Razor's hand with surgical precision before he could squeeze the trigger. The useless appendage flopped to the ground in a spray of liquid crimson. The gun clattered harmlessly, still cupped in Razor's severed hand, finger still on the trigger.

Razor stared uncomprehendingly at his forearm as warm red blood pumped out, spilling across his boots. No pain, he thought. No jagged rending of flesh. Just a neat thin slice. Those claws must have been sharp.

Sharp as a razor.

Razor smiled at the irony.

Holding his spurting stump in his one remaining hand, Razor sank to his knees without realizing it. His whole world, his entire universe seemed to be comprised of only this terrible wound he continued to stare at, but never seemed too worried about.

He looked up; saw the demon monster in the shape of a man standing over him. A man wearing dark, expensive clothes glared down at him from behind those sunglasses. He saw, or rather, he sensed another rapid movement.

And then he sensed nothing at all ever again.

The vampire had slashed Razor again, this time across the throat, nicking the right carotid artery, perforating the esophagus, cutting through the larynx, and coming out the other side, nicking the left carotid for good measure. He moved out of the way as bright liquid scarlet sprayed six feet. Razor pitched forward onto the deck, blood pooling rapidly even as the heart seized and stopped beating forever.

The vampire stepped back farther to keep from getting Razor's blood on his shoes. Not only did he not want to leave footprints, but his shoes cost over four hundred dollars, and well, he *really* liked his shoes.

He disliked working in such a sloppy manner, but he was pissed and wanted to make a statement to whoever had sent this man, the one he had just turned into a human Pez dispenser.

You did not threaten the vampire's family and live.

Over his shoulder, he heard the running footsteps and rising heartbeat of his great great grandson. He turned and moved quickly to the edge of the roof. He wondered if Reggie had a silencer. When he heard a rapid, clipped *pop! pop!,* he guessed he knew the answer. He did not hear returning fire.

Good.

Then the vampire saw movement on the roof across the street, atop his descendant's apartment. A man's head popped into view. And like the man he had just killed, he had a firearm and a headset.

Not good.

A static squawk erupted behind him. "That's gunfire. Did anyone make contact?"

The vampire was already moving towards the slain assassin's body. "Report."

The vampire pulled the headset off the dead man's head. He held the mic close to his mouth. "Leave Downing alone, now and forever, and I will let you live."

Stunned silence on the other end.

In the distance, another *pop! pop!*

"All units respond. I say again, all units respond."

"They can't."

Silence. Then, "Who is this?"

The vampire recognized the voice. "I gave you a chance at the docks to change your ways and lead an honorable life," the vampire said. "Pity you did not take it."

Silence again, then, in earnest, "Who *is* this?"

"I am Death," the vampire replied, quoting Oppenheimer. "The destroyer of worlds. And I have come for you."

The vampire dropped the headset to the ground. He turned and focused his attention on the assassin across the street. Working up his anger, his seething hatred of men such as these, he stepped back two paces, then pushed off to get a running start. He accelerated quickly and pushed off with his left foot just as he reached the leading edge of the roof.

The vampire leapt in an upward motion, flying out into space. He felt no fear as his body reached the zenith of his arc. He felt suspended for a moment, fully forty feet above the pavement, in the middle of a jump from one building to the next, spanning four lanes of street, two sidewalks, fully sixty feet from point A to point B. Then his momentum coupled with gravity, now past the apex of the arc, and he began to descend as his body decelerated.

Gravity, air friction, curvilinear motion, he thought. Gee, physics can be fun.

He targeted his enemy as the rooftop rushed up underneath him. He landed hard on both feet, knees bent to take the shock and distribute it throughout his body. He tucked and rolled like a landing paratrooper.

The man on the roof, had a large head, square jaw, and was clean-shaven like he had been taught in boot camp. Rippling musculature, close-cropped blonde hair and ruddy skin, he spun round in surprise upon the vampire's thudding impact. He wielded a modified M4, with a shortened stock, night vision scope, and a silencer attached to the barrel. He registered someone suddenly in close proximity. He opened fire in semiautomatic mode, one round fired each time he pressed the trigger.

The vampire neatly ducked and moved, bobbed and weaved, easily avoiding the bullets. He likened them to metal mosquitos. They buzzed nearby, a nuisance looking to bite. But he slapped them away.

The big man paused, confused. He was a crack shot. Frustrated at missing, he watched as the figure in the gloom rolled away from the bullets and rose again to a standing position. The big man could not see his face as he stood in the shadows, but this idiot was just standing there, an immobile target. He raised his rifle to his shoulder.

Big mistake.

The vampire rushed forward, grinning. He heard the click as the big man switched to full auto. It mattered not. Before the big man could squeeze the trigger again, he was already dead.

The mercenary felt a terrible raking sensation across his torso, a deep rending, then a spreading warm wetness near his hips. Had he just peed himself? He looked down at his front.

Four large rents in the fabric of his shirt, below his body armor, just above his pubis. The spreading wetness was not just urine. Yes, his bladder had been punctured, but blood poured down his pants legs, spilling across the rooftop, pooling between his feet.

He heard Rudy yelling into his earpiece for all units to respond, to report, to say something. Anything. None of this made sense. And it made no sense to him when the creature – for surely this was no *man* - ripped the M4 out of his hands.

The vampire grabbed the big man's face and wrenched his head to one side. The vampire then opened his mouth, bared his fangs and descended downward. Blood, thick and coppery, bubbled into his mouth.

Thirsty and needing sustenance, the vampire drank his fill. His physical strength expanded. The dead man must have been a health nut, for his blood was chock full of vitamins. When he had drunk his fill, the vampire hoisted the limp meat-sack up, heaved it over his head, and flung the corpse off the roof. It plummeted to the ground below.

Reggie moved past the first man he had just killed. He stopped just long enough to pick up the fallen man's rifle, which was also equipped with a sound suppressor. He pressed the stock into his shoulder and aimed ahead as he moved. Safety off. Finger on the trigger.

He saw the other mercenary, an older black man, first. He did not hesitate. He fired once, blowing the top of the man's head away. His target dropped dead like a sack of potatoes.

Reggie advanced on his target's last position. He did not let his guard down until he confirmed the kill. Confirm the kill? Hell, the bastard's head looked like a bloody fucking canoe.

Across the street, down the block, Rudy grew truly alarmed. He keyed his mic as he got out of the Land Rover.

"Melvin, Rudy. Come in."

"Send it," came the tinny, crackling response.

"Men down, men down. They're here. We need backup." Rudy locked and loaded.

"Say again?" Melvin's voice sounded incredulous.

"Get here now. Come in hot." He flipped his safety off.

"Roger that."

Rudy pushed his back into the rough brick of the building at the entrance to the alley. He held his weapon close, barrel upwards, but suddenly it brought him no comfort. Somehow, someone had managed to silence five trained men.

Just like someone had managed to slaughter seven people at the *Sulu Sea* the other night. He had not been spared because he had outwitted, or outfought, that unseen opponent. He had been granted a reprieve, by that guy up on the roof with Razor.

A sharp sliver of ice-cold fear, unannounced and unwelcome, stabbed down his spine. It settled in the pit of his stomach. His dinner threatened to explode out of him.

For some reason, he thought of T-Ball's mangled remains. It had looked like a pile of slop; unrecognizable as the remains of a sentient (or in T-Ball's case, partially sentient) being that had actually lived.

Something was terribly wrong here. For the first time in a long time, Rudy did not think was going to make it.

Something fluttered up above, just at the top of his peripheral vision. A bird, perhaps. At night? He looked up. He saw a black blob, hurtling off the rooftop across the street, from atop Downing's apartment. The fluttering he had sensed were not wings, but were arms and legs pumping as someone – some thing! – leapt off the roof and hurtled towards him. As it flew closer, it materialized: long black coat flapping behind him, gray skin with a yellowish tint, severe cheekbones, long face, pointed chin, cruel mouth.

Rudy's mind came to stop. This could not be happening.

The thing landed with a thud on the concrete just a couple of feet away from Rudy. Shocked into stillness, Rudy watched as the thing in front of him, crouched down from absorbing the impact of the fifty-foot jump from the rooftop and across the four lanes of the street, rose up and stood before him. The demon brought a hand up in one smooth motion and ripped the heavy sunglasses off his face, revealing the cold, unblinking glassy black orbs he usually kept hidden.

Rudy moved. He tried to bring his weapon to bear. Too late.

The creature snarled, revealing sharp predatory fangs. He grabbed the barrel and wrenched the weapon out of Rudy's hands before Rudy could squeeze the trigger.

The last thing Rudy saw before the lights went out was a mildly misshapen hand with long slender fingers ending in sharp nails extending towards his face and throat.

Journal entry, 02 March

I had not spoken to anyone about Danae in almost a century.

Experiences both bitter and sweet shape us, mold us into who we become. Our own memories, unique perceptions, and lessons learned season us for life's inevitable ups and downs. Over time, memory fades, and the more jagged edges dull, become less cutting. Bring a particular trauma back up, and it all floods back. An ugly wound, long thought healed, reopens with all the pain, and rawness of the first time.

Danae lived out the natural cycle of her life, and has long since passed away. But she still lives on young and fresh, strong and beautiful in my most cherished memories.

But there was my ill-fated attempt to reestablish contact with her. I waited a few weeks because I first had to take care of a thorn in my side named Thomas. Once I knew the police were writing his murder off as just another gangland killing, it was safe to move about.

I entered Bumpy's through the back door a little after one in the morning. My new vampire hearing had detected her voice while I was still halfway down the same alley where I had died. Wearing a long coat, black broad brimmed hat, and having the collar turned up, most of my vampire features were obscured, and were further hidden by the low light, cigarette smoke, and the general inebriation of the patrons.

Danae had one more set and would finish up around a quarter of two. Then she would slip behind the bar, and take the narrow back stairs up to her room where she would change before bed. I was waiting for her when she entered the room, closing the door behind her.

I sat on a bare wooden chair, leaning forward, looking at the flooring. When she first walked in, all she could see was someone in dark clothes, long coat flowing over the chair seat, broad brimmed black hat hiding a face.

She demanded to know who I was, and what I was doing in her room. In my own swirling emotions, I found I could not speak. She mistook my silence to mean something it did not. She reached into folds of her skirt and pulled out a knife with a gleaming four-inch blade to protect herself.

I spoke one word: "Danae".

Of course, she recognized my voice. She started to run across the room. But an outstretched arm and the word, "Don't!" stopped her in her tracks. She immediately became wary, then fearful as I explained to her what had happened, that I had been shot, that I had died, and that I had been given a second chance. I had been reborn, but forever changed.

She told me she loved me. Whatever trouble I was in, we would face it together. We could still go to France, leave right now tonight. She could be ready in ten minutes.

I took off my hat, lifted my head, and stood up.

And in that one instant, that one pivotal moment in my existence, all my worst fears in both life and in death came true.

Her face froze. Her breathing stopped, caught in her throat. I heard her heart skip a beat, sort of a cardiac shudder. Then it began pounding hard and fast like a jackhammer. I saw her face change to anger.

I could hear the blood rushing through her veins. It excited me, but not in a good way. I immediately realized how difficult a life with her would be, only having nighttime hours together, putting myself in a constant state of check, denying my new nature, knowing I would hear the blood in her veins, smell it, and covet it.

I attempted to calm her down. I explained to her what had happened in the alley that night, the choice I had made, and what I was now.

Much to my surprise, she believed me, believed my story. In fact, Danae knew and understood exactly, precisely what I was. African folklore that had been handed down to her from her grandparents, who had been born slaves on a plantation in Mississippi, had included ghost stories containing all manner of supernatural beings, including vampires.

And that was when I detected a second heartbeat. Smaller, faster, coming from her lower belly. And while I was certainly no doctor, even I knew what that meant. I was shocked and elated.

I was going to be a father.

But Danae made it clear I was not welcome here, that she never wanted to see me again. She further made it clear she would raise our child on her own. I was no longer the man she had loved. That man had died in the alleyway that night. The creature standing before her would never be welcome in her home, her life, or the lives of her children.

Crumbling inside, I told her that I understood; that because I loved her, I would respect her wishes by keeping my distance. But she was family, my family, and so was our child. I would watch from afar, but not interfere unless I felt compelled to do so by extreme circumstances. Life and death, that sort of thing.

She said she would not want my help, even under those circumstances.

I planted my feet. Squared my shoulders. Looked her in the eye and informed her she would have my vigilance and my protection whether she wanted it or not. And I would watch over our descendants through the years.

I swore my undying love to her. Then I adjusted my hat, buttoned my coat up to the throat, then slipped out the window and onto the fire escape.

True to my word, I never went back to that room with the tiny window looking down onto that alley where I died. I wanted to go back every night for years. Sometimes, respecting the wishes of others is the hardest thing you can ever do. And sometimes the only way to show someone you love them is remain absent from their lives.

I only broke my word once.

It was the early seventies. She had moved out west to be with family as she got older. Coincidentally, I was already out here. I had felt the psychic link immediately, and for years fought the urge to go see her. But the night came when I had to.

She was quite elderly by then, well into her eighties, almost ninety. Time had ravaged her body. She was hospitalized, her body failing. But her eyes still saw clearly; her mind still sharp as ever.

Two or three hours prior to dawn, I crept through an unlocked door on the ground floor of the hospital and up a back stairwell that opened onto the hallway.

I moved like a wraith along the silent hallway, clinging to the wall, using the shadows. Up ahead sat the nurses' station, in its requisite pool of light. The nurse sat in a rather uncomfortable-looking chair, writing in a patient's chart. I stretched forth my arm, fingers extended, palm towards her. In my head, I concentrated and said one soft word, "Sleep".

The nurse exhaled, a quiet sigh. Her eyes closed and she slumped forward in her chair, her head coming to rest on the chart she had been dutifully updating. The nurse would awaken in about one hour, disoriented but otherwise unharmed.

Blocking out all distraction, I followed Danae's weakening heartbeat. I crept into her room. She lay on her back, asleep, bed tilted into a semi-sitting position. Her eyes were closed, her head turned towards me. A single light shone above her, a weak amber glow so as to not disturb her slumber.

Even from several feet away, I could smell the decay, the stench of the cancer that had spread throughout her body, literally rotting her from the inside out.

My anguish knew no bounds.

*Even though the woman in front of me was wrinkled of skin, grey of hair, and fragile of body, her features remained familiar. All I saw was the same woman I had fallen love with so long ago.
Her eyes opened. She knew someone was in the room, thought was the nurse. I whispered her name from the darkness. Recognition registered in her eyes, and I stepped forward.*

I smiled, pulled a small chair forward, and sat down. She asked me, How I had found her; why I had come? I told her I knew she was sick, that I had come to see her once more. I could not bear the thought of us never having a chance to say goodbye.

She whispered she had thought of me often, wondered if I had survived. She said she had appreciated the fact I had kept my word, and had stayed away. And from her heart, she apologized for how she had acted that night in the speakeasy. She said she knew she wounded me terribly.

I took her hand in mine. Weak fingers curled around my cool palm. Death was imminent. I told her she had nothing to apologize for. I understood her horror at what I had become. In retrospect, I felt she had chosen wisely. She took comfort in that. She had been burdened with doubt all those years.

I asked her if perhaps she would like to forgo death. I could give her a choice most people did not get. She could die; cancer would take her soon. But if I bit her, she would wake up new again, a vampire like me. She would be forever young, like she had been, so many years ago.

She declined. She had lived a full life. She preferred to pass on rather than become something unnatural. Then she added, "No offense".

I told her I had been called much worse over the years. And "unnatural" was indeed as accurate a description as any. I asked if she was certain. She was.

I nodded my head, tilted down to kiss her hand. She reached out to me. I stood from the chair and bent across the bed, hugging her, embracing my woman, my love, my lost potential, my reason for living. She squeezed back, and it was like the decades fell away. I was a young man again, alive, with a beating heart and warm skin, feeling all the love I had for this woman who made me want to be a good man, a better man. Get out of my life of crime, go straight, get a job, and be a real man – a good and faithful husband, a loving and devoted father.

All those things I never had, never experienced. All those things I lost because I chose to become a gangster, a cruel criminal, a bad and brutal man.

Her strength faded quickly. I eased her back onto the sheets. I did not realize I had picked her up off the bed in my arms. Her body seemed so frail, arms and legs like twigs. Looking up, she pointed to my face. I touched my cheek, looked at my finger.

Tears.

Up until then, I did not know a vampire could cry.

She told me I needed to go. She knew she did not have much time left, and she knew dawn approached. I kissed her lips one last time, told her how much I loved her.

"I love you too, Eddie. I always have".

My heart swelling and breaking at the same time, I backed into the shadows. I left the way I had come: as a wraith, a shadow, something sensed, never fully seen.

Danae passed away just before dawn.

So from that night until now, I have been, and shall always remain alone.

CHAPTER TWENTY-TWO

Rick Oakley sat at his desk awaiting an update on the operation. Tense, he tried to calm himself, tell himself "no news was good news". He stared at his cell phone as it lay in front of him, silently willing it to ring. And yet it refused to bring word of success.

He had spent many years on the front lines. First as a combat Operator in the Army, followed by time as a "soldier of fortune", which was simply a mercenary going by another name. Then, as a soldier/enforcer/executioner for Vargas.

Events had transpired so quickly in the last few days. The bloodbath aboard the *Sulu Sea* still rattled him. His contact within law enforcement told him that they theorized the perp was a lone, master assassin not involved in the trade.

Without knowing this outsider's motives, it was impossible to predict his movements. What did he want? What was his end game?

Oakley suspected Vargas had cashed out and bailed because he had seen the writing on the wall. He saw danger looming; knew what was coming. Oakley hated him for it, but he also admired him at the same time. If he had been in the same position, he would have done the same thing. Smart move. Not brave, mind you, but smart.

Oakley had instructed his personal bodyguards to move the desk from the middle of the warehouse floor into the smaller office off to the side. With a solid wooden door that could close and two walls made of wood from the ground to about three feet up, and double panes of heavy glass from there up to the ceiling, it seemed a more appropriate place for "The Boss".

The office was easily defensible. Facing the glass, no one could sneak up on him. The wall behind him consisted of two layers of heavy metal, part of the outside of the building. He made a mental note to have the current panes replaced with bulletproof glass as soon as possible.

Ever the soldier, his eyes systematically darted around the room. He looked for weaknesses in the construction, found nothing glaring. Rigging the office for audio and video surveillance would be simple. He also saw several places in the room to hide a weapon: a handgun here, a combat knife there. He identified where he could hide a loaded shotgun (preferably with a pistol grip) and it not be visible from outside.

Tim, a youngish man with long hair and a cruel face appeared outside the office door. Clothed in dark fabrics, covered in a leather jacket, Oakley could tell the man worked out. Oakley motioned for him to enter.

"Boss, you need to hear this," he said as he walked quickly into the office. He moved fast enough for his flowing hair to fan out away from his head, bouncing on his broad shoulders.

Oakley stood from his chair behind his desk. He took the set and keyed the mic. He heard Rudy calling for responses from his crew, and getting none. He heard the tension in Rudy's voice, then heard him calling out to Melvin's crew for reinforcement.

He keyed the mic again. "Rudy, this is Oakley, come in."

Silence on the other end.

"Rudy, this is Oakley. Come in."

Silence at the other end.

"Mount up," Oakley commanded. He handed the handset and earpiece back to Tim.

"Yes sir." Tim spun around on his heel, almost a perfect one-eighty, a military "about face" maneuver, and walked out. He clipped the handset and repositioned the earpiece as he went. No drama. No flurry. No wasted movement.

Oakley grabbed his cell phone off his desk. He slipped it into his right front pants pocket. Just like he had done thousands of times over the years. Habit made one more efficient, more proficient. Habit reduced the chance of mistakes. This was something Oakley had learned long ago. He patted the back of his pants. His wallet was still there. He patted under his left arm with his right hand. His handgun was there, fully loaded, securely holstered.

He stepped to one side, pushed his chair back up under the desk. Another habit. Stay neat. Stay tidy.

He exited the office, locking the door behind him. Tim and the other bodyguard, Ronald, geared up. They each pushed their heads through the tops of their body armor, then fastened everything in place using the attached Velcro straps. Each man slid their handsets into pockets on the front, adjusted their earpieces. They picked their weapons up, snapped in fresh clips, locked and loaded.

Then they each grabbed several extra clips of ammo. Loaded for bear, they were.

"Ronald, right?" Oakley asked.

Ronald, as black as Rick was white, nodded. "Yes sir."

"Background?"

"Active duty Army, sir. Did six years. Tours of duty in Iraq and Afghanistan."

"Any problems pulling the trigger?"

"None I'm aware of, sir."

Oakley grinned, nodded. He looked to Tim. "And you?"

"Third Marine Division. Did four and out. Two tours in Iraq."

"Marines?" Oakley grinned. "With that head of hair?"

Tim grinned. "I've been out a while, sir."

Oakley nodded. "The Op tonight may be going sideways. Bad shit's happening at Rudy's pos, and Melvin's team is en route to reinforce. We'll backfill Melvin's pos."

"We're going to go sit on Granny?" Ronald asked.

"By the time tonight's done, we may have to shoot Granny right through her silver-haired head."

Reggie stalked through his tight, orderly apartment. He wielded a fully loaded 357-magnum handgun in his right hand. He had drawn the drapes over the window facing the front of the street.

At the vampire's urging, he had left the lights off except for a small lamp near the door. A small light also shown above the stove in the kitchenette. The door and the first few feet inside bathed in light, while the hallway dimmed to darkness. Anyone standing in the region at the entrance to the living room would be backlit, a perfect target, while they would only see blackness in front of them.

Reggie admitted the vampire knew how to set an ambush. And he certainly knew how to use the night to his advantage. Like camouflage, or something.

Great, great Grandpa was one hell of an ambush predator.

Reggie crept from his unused bedroom into the living room. He padded past his easy chair, his favorite place in the apartment. It was set directly in front of and about six feet away from his high definition TV. He did not have cable, but he had Internet service, and enjoyed watching movies and TV shows on a streaming media service.

But there would be no binge watching tonight.

Rudy Valdez, unconscious but alive, duct tape applied to his mouth, wrists, and ankles, currently occupied the chair. His face was marred where the vampire had grabbed him, his sharp claws digging into the skin. Reggie could make out the pattern of the vampire's hand by the position of the wounds and the bruising.

"Men coming." A disembodied voice coming in softly from a far corner of the room.

"You sure?"

"Two of them."

"Just two?"

"On the other side of the door."

Reggie began to say something more, but a discreet knock at his front door stopped him. He looked into the darkness of the room where he knew the vampire stood, a still silent shadow slightly blacker, darker, denser than the gloom around him. Then he looked down the hallway.

Another knock sounded. This one was louder, longer. Less discreet, more insistent. The next knock would probably be closer to indignant pounding. The kind of thing that drew attention and woke up neighbors.

Reggie sidestepped to a covered position. "Wait a second," he called out as casually as he could. When gunfire did not immediately erupt, he pointed the gun at the door and crept down the hallway, staying to one side.

Steeling himself as he went, he cocked his weapon, ready to fire in an instant if he felt threatened. He stopped inches from the door and listened. No sound came from outside that he could hear. He carefully placed the muzzle of the gun right over the wood of the door. Hot, heavy rounds would punch straight through wood and pulverize flesh and bone on the other side.

He held is breath, peered intently through the peephole in the doorway. With the distortion of a fisheye lens, he recognized the parties outside. He relaxed, flicked the safety back on.

He opened the door. Castle and Horn waited. Reggie stepped aside, opening the door wider. The two detectives slid inside, and the door shut softly. The deadbolt shifted into the jamb.

"Reggie, you all right?" Castle asked.

"Barely."

"Where you been?" Horn demanded. "I saw that Range Rover down the street. Doesn't look like it belongs here."

"It doesn't." Reggie motioned them into the depths of the apartment. "It belongs to a kill squad sent here to kill me," he said as they walked down the hallway and into the main room.

"And where is that kill squad now?"

"Dead."

They all stopped in front of Reggie's easy chair. Rudy was now awake.

"How the hell did you capture him?" Horn asked.

Before he could answer, Castle asked," Who killed the team?"

"I killed a couple of them," Reggie stated. "The rest, well... I had help."

"Help, huh?" Horn echoed. "Like you had help aboard the Sulu Sea?

There was a pause in the conversation. Rudy's eyes glanced from one policeman to another.

"How did you capture this guy?" Castle asked.

"Actually, I didn't," Reggie said.

"Who did?"

"I did."

Everything in the room simply... stopped. A whisper, from out of the black recesses of the room. The whisper froze Castle and Horn in their respective spots, the softness of the voice somehow chilling them with a deep, unreasoning, irrational fear.

The barest hint of a grin passed across Reggie's lips. "Like I said. I had help."

Horn and Castle stared into the mercurial dark. Slowly, silently, the shadows swirled, coalesced, took shape and mass. The vampire, still in shadow, glided forward. Full coat flowing almost to his ankles, his hands in his pockets, his collar turned up. The duster was unbuttoned, and his immaculate clothing, the dark cashmere mock turtle and gray pinstriped custom tailored pants, hand-stitched and dyed black leather belt peeked through.

He stopped in front of them. His head tilted down a bit, his wraparound sunglasses were still secure to the upper half of his face.

Through the specs, he looked down at Rudy, realizing that he was hungry again. Rudy, aware of his presence, stared up at him, eyes wide with apprehension.

"Let's get something out of the way right now," Horn growled. "Are you the same guy who killed all those assholes aboard the *Sulu Sea*?"

"Yes," the vampire answered, unafraid, and without hesitation.

Horn, shocked into silence, looked at Castle. Castle stared back at him. They looked to Reggie who only shrugged.

"Sir," Castle started, "did you intend to kill everyone?"

"Only those in my way."

"You were there for Detective Downing?"

"Yes."

Maybe the stranger's pallor came from the gloom he stood in. "But not kill him?"

"To protect him."

"Yes," Horn interrupted. "And by the way, thank you for all you've done to keep him alive."

The vampire nodded, brought his hands out of his coat pockets and shrugged. "Not at all, good sir."

Horn tilted his head. Who the hell talks like that these days? "Downing, who the hell is this cat?"

"He's my – his name is... Eddie Marx."

"Are you wanted for any crime in the United States?"

"None that I am aware of."

"So what are you?" Castle asked. "Some kind of hired killer?"

"A hired killer?"

"Yeah. Like some ninja assassin, or something."

The vampire was so surprised he convulsed with a short laugh. Mouth open wide, his fangs were on full display. Horn and Castle's mouths fell open.

The vampire recovered quickly. He had been found out.
Oh well.

He stepped closer, into what little light was in the room. The pallor to his face and hands did not warm to a human skin tone. It remained dull gray, waxy, dead.

He held up his hands, exposing his extended fingers and claw like fingernails. "What was your last question, young squire?"

"Wh - What are you?" Castle stuttered, barely able to get it out.

"I am... a vampire."

"*Vampiro!*" Castle spoke, stepping away and crossing himself. "*Madre de Dios!*"

The vampire started to tell Castle it was okay, but there was no point. Reason could not penetrate this kind of fear. So he sighed in frustration, said nothing.

"This is bullshit," Horn stated.

Irritated, the vampire turned his head without moving his body. It was like his head was simply on a thin stick, not attached to muscle, bone and sinew. He focused on Horn. Saw the waves of fear wafting off him. The man did not understand the reality of the situation. The vampire was trying very hard to not demonstrate that reality.

"Downing, what the fuck kinda bullshit is this?" Horn demanded. "This guy's full of shit. And so are you!"

"What did you say?" The vampire's words were almost silent, but most insistent. Simple words, filled with icy menace.

The room went silent again. All movement stopped. Suddenly, the air was heavy as lead.

"What?" Horn was genuinely confused. He thought he had made himself quite clear.

The vampire now swiveled his body to the same direction as his head. Downing knew this could not be good. He also knew not to interfere.

"I asked you a question, sir. What did you just say?"

Horn suddenly found himself considering his options. Finally, stupidly, "I said, that you're full of shit, and so is he."

The dull skin at the corner of his right nostril pulled up. A snarl crossed the vampire's lips. His fangs showed. He ripped off his sunglasses; let them drop unheeded atop Rudy Valdez's chest.

The vampire lurched so quickly across the room Horn never even had a chance to draw his gun. The vampire grabbed him by the throat with one hand and by the belt loop of his pants by the other and lifted him forcefully off the ground. He slammed Horn's massive body into the ceiling so hard dust shook from the wood.

Castle gasped and began crossing himself once again. Reggie simply stood back and watched. Rudy figured the little guy had to be on drugs.

No matter how much he would try in the years ahead, Horn would never forget what he saw as his vision cleared. Below him, holding him up above his head as if he were almost weightless, the vampire glared up at him. Pale dead skin, black, unblinking eyes that blazed with anger and a hint of red; an ugly mouth filled with teeth, armed with fangs. This small guy, about five foot six, maybe seven, probably a buck forty five dripping wet, stood under him, hoisting him up, balancing him easily.

This person – no, this creature, this walking corpse, this *unholy fucking thing* below him, holding him in the air without the slightest trace to physical strain, was a vampire.

Vampires were real.

Oh my God. Vampires were fucking real. Horn had to concentrate to keep from shitting his pants.

"From the smell I am sensing, you, sir, are the one full of shit," the vampire said. "Would you like me to carry you to the bathroom?"

"Mr. Marx." Castle had found his voice. "Put him down, sir. Please."

The vampire did not take his eyes or his angry face off the enormous black man he held above him. "Detective Castle, is it?"

"Well," the Latino stuttered, "it's actually Detective Sergeant."

"Detective Sergeant," the vampire said back, "I get the feeling you are a good and decent man. And since you have done nothing to impugn my great great grandson's reputation," he paused snarled, baring his fangs for Horn's benefit, "I am inclined to consider granting your request."

"Thank you. Uh, sir. Uh, Mr. Marx."

"Look at me, sir." Horn looked at the vampire in his black, bottomless eyes. "Do I look like the kind of person you want to provoke?"

Horn tried to answer, and found that he could not. The vampire's grip around his throat made vocal communication impossible. Grimacing in pain and diminishing oxygen, he shook his head.

Reggie cleared his throat. "Grandpa?"

The vampire glanced over his shoulder at his great great grandson, then back up at Horn. "You do not deserve my mercy. But you have good and faithful friends. On that count, you are indeed a fortunate man."

The vampire lowered Horn until he was standing back on the floorboards of the apartment. He let go of the man's throat and waist.

"I care not what you think or say to me. Do not ever speak to my great great grandson in such a foul manner again." He leaned in close to Horn, bared his fangs. "Ever."

Castle had his phone in front of him. "You said your name is Eddie Marx?"

"Yes."

"Wow," Castle said in awe. "I found you." He held up his phone screen towards he rest of them. "Says you were a gangster back in New Jersey. You died young."

"I am familiar with the circumstances of my death, young squire."

"It also says your body went missing from the morgue," Castle added. "They never found it."

"I am also aware of the circumstances of my rebirth."

"So, with you being, um," Horn rasped as he massaged his bruised throat and neck, "what you say you are, that's how you took out all those guys at the *Sulu Sea*."

"The speed and strength you experienced here is nothing," the vampire said without boasting. "I possess a capacity for violence and brutality the likes of which you have not seen," he added. "That includes the *Sulu Sea*."

"Jesus," Horn muttered, remembering the *Sulu Sea*.

"Must be hard," Castle said, "keeping a secret like that."

The vampire turned his head towards Castle. He smiled benevolently. "I am not the only man in this room with a secret."

Castle tensed. "What do you mean?"

"You know what I mean." He took a step forward. "You should tell them."

Castle broke out into a nervous sweat. The vampire smelled the sweat mixed with deodorant under his arms.

Reggie and Horn stood still. Now what?

"These men are your friends," the vampire said. They will understand."

"What are you talking about?" Horn asked.

"Oh, it's nothing bad," the vampire reassured everyone.

"If you can read my thoughts, you know I why can't."

"Your fears are understandable," the vampire cooed gently, "but they are groundless. Times have changed."

"Castle, what the hell is this?" Horn demanded.

"Gotta admit, I'm curious now," Reggie chimed in.

Horn and Reggie stared at him. Castle's tension and unease continued to build, rising to a fever pitch.

"I already know."

"Know what?" Horn demanded, exasperated.

"And I still know you to be a good and decent man," the vampire continued, ignoring Horn's interruption. "I also know you to be a clever cop who pays attention and thinks outside the box." The vampire shrugged. "See? It has not changed my opinion of you."

"Nick, just spit it out, man," Reggie said. "Trust me, he won't let up until you do."

"I'm gay," Castle blurted out, a bit too loudly for the room. "I'm gay, all right? You happy now?" he asked the vampire, then looked at his colleagues. "I'm gay, guys. I always have been." The admission seemed to drain all the energy out of him. He looked as though he might swoon from exhaustion.

Horn and Reggie, silent, looked at him. Then they looked at each other. The vampire stood aside, silent and aloof. Rudy Valdez lay bound and gaged in his chair, the duct tape adhesive irritating his skin.

"That's it?" Reggie said. "That's your big secret? Dude, I had you figured out ages ago."

"Huh?"

"So you're gay. Big deal," Horn shrugged. "Fang Face over there is right. You're still a good cop. You're still a good man. And I'll still go through a door with you, anytime, anywhere."

"Anybody in the Department gives you shit about being gay," Reggie said, "you let me know. I'll kick their fucking ass."

"I'll stop trying to fix you up with my niece," Horn promised.

The vampire walked over to Castle, put a comforting hand on his shoulder. "Feel better now?"

"Yeah, I do, " Castle answered.

The vampire stepped back, turned to the room. "For if we must be damned, then let us be damned for who and what we truly are. Agreed, gentlemen?" Both Horn and Rudy nodded in assent.

"Excellent," the vampire grinned. And speaking of that..." He walked over to Rudy.

"I allowed you to live following the *Sulu Sea* because I sensed you were a brave, but misguided young man. I had hoped to give you pause, make you reconsider your life of crime."

Rudy stared up at the vampire, who simply picked up his sunglasses, put them back on. "Sadly, that was not the case." The vampire moved his arm quickly, hand and fingers extended. No one had time to react. But rather than slice the man's face or cut his throat, the fingernail of one slender digit ripped the duct tape from Rudy's mouth with the delicacy of a surgeon's scalpel.

Rudy gasped, terrified. "I'm sorry, sir," he said quickly. "I did not understand."

"More is the pity."

"No. Please. Jesus Christ, I'll never do it again."

"Too late for that, numb nuts!" Horn hissed.

Rudy looked pleadingly up at his dark angel. "You gotta help me."

"No, young squire," the vampire shook his head, "I do not."

"I'll never break the law again," he pleaded. "I'm done. I promise!"

"I believe you," the vampire returned truthfully. "But I shall not interfere with man's justice. You must accept the consequences of your bad deeds." Rudy's face froze in disbelief. "Perhaps you will appreciate whatever freedom awaits you when you get out of prison. You will be aged and gray by then, but at least you can have what I never had."

"What's that?" Rudy asked.

"A rest of your life." The vampire stepped back, partially blending in with the gloom.

"I get it now," Reggie said. "Why you hate criminals so much."

The vampire's body did not move. His head turned, as if on a swivel, to look at his descendant.

"You see in them that which you despise in yourself."

"I see a life that could have been," the vampire said with an infinite sadness. Every man in the room noticed. "What I could have had with your great great grandmother," his voice, a wisp of vapor, cracked a bit. He paused to gather himself. "If only I had been a more honorable man."

"Wait a minute," Horn interjected. "A white man and a black woman in the early nineteen hundreds? That was illegal back then. And condemned by both races. You would have gotten your asses kicked."

"When you are truly in love, the color of a person's skin matters not."

"Pretty progressive for a guy born a hundred and thirty years ago."

"There is only one race, Captain. The *human* race."

Horn considered the vampire's wisdom, gained over a life of over one hundred and thirty years of bitter experience, pain, and death. Maybe he needed to quit giving his son shit because he was dating a white girl.

"Let's get back to business, shall we, gentlemen?" Castle said, stepping forward.

"Right," Horn agreed. "Okay, Rudy. Here's the deal. You're going to jail no matter what. But how much time you do might be another matter."

"You mean, I help you, testify and shit, for a reduced sentence?"

Horn nodded.

Rudy computed his options. "Hell, man, what do you want to know?"

Horn smirked. "Honor among thieves."

Rudy looked wounded.

"Captain," the vampire said, the voice of wisdom, "self-preservation is the most ancient of all human instincts. There is nothing to be gained from mockery."

"Point taken." Horn turned his attention back to Rudy. "What's going on?"

Rudy nodded towards Reggie. "It's all about him."

"We already know that."

"No. You really don't."

"Enlighten us."

Rudy spilled the beans. He told them everything. About Vargas retiring, Oakley assuming command, his determination to run the crew like a military unit.

"A crew run by ex-military types and mercenaries, and run to a high level of efficiency?" Castle summarized. "That's bad."

"That ain't all." Rudy told them about the two teams sent out this very evening.

Reggie's tension rose immediately. The vampire felt it several feet away.

"Where did the other team go?"

"Your grandmother's house."

Reggie bolted forward, eyes afire with rage. His face flashed murderous intent. Arms out in front of him, hands open, he lunged at Rudy.

"YOU MOTHERFUCKER!"

Horn stepped in front of Reggie, a human brick wall. He grabbed the young detective by the shoulders. Reggie's forward movement came to an abrupt halt.

Reggie grabbed his firearm in the small of his back. He brought it out and around Horn, knowing a round was chambered, and flicked the safety off in move smooth motion. What kept him from killing Rudy Valdez that night was Detective Nick Castle, a once closeted and now outed homosexual, a veteran policeman, and brave Latino, stepped into the space between Reggie and Rudy, eliminating any clear line of fire.

Reggie knew he was outmaneuvered. "Goddammit!" he shouted in frustration as he stepped back.

"You better pray to God nothing happens to her," Horn said over his left shoulder, speaking to Rudy.

Rudy nodded, then shifted his eyes to Castle. "*Gracias, hermano.*"

Castle looked down his nose at Valdez, a withering sneer of utter contempt upon his curled lips. "*No estoy su hermano, puta.* I didn't do it for you."

Rudy shifted in his chair. "When Mr. Vampire here started taking out my team, I called for backup. The other team barely got on location at Grandma's house. And they were under orders to conduct surveillance only. They never would have breached the perimeter unless under direct orders."

"You keep talking in the past tense," Castle observed.

"Where are they now?" Reggie asked.

"On their way here to save me, of course," Rudy responded. "Hell, I'm surprised they're not here yet."

CHAPTER TWENTY-THREE

Time ticked towards the dawn. At zero three twenty, a Land Rover, exactly the same in style as the one that sat empty in the alley, slid up to the red light at the intersection. Melvin, sitting in the front passenger seat, quickly scanned the streets, the intersection, the convenience store building. The store was dark except for one light above the door, probably left on to illuminate the sidewalk for the CCTV camera attached to the wall.

Melvin turned his head to his left shoulder, so the men in the back seat could hear. "Reconnoiter."

Doors opened, bodies alighted, doors closed without slamming. The men knew their jobs. They scattered, taking different tacks and angles.

Inside the vehicle, Melvin pointed through the light, which had just turned green. The driver followed the finger, seeing the head of Rudy's command vehicle at the entrance to the alley. The Land Rover rolled through the empty intersection.

"This doesn't make sense," the driver said. He ran a nervous hand through his wiry red hair.

"No, it does not," Melvin confirmed. He looked hard at the alley as they inched along. His mind recorded all he saw, ready for instant recall later if need be.

"Recon. Report."

"Recon One. Man down."

"Recon Two. Man down. Disemboweled."

"Say again, Recon Two?"

"I said, *disemboweled*, sir.

Melvin and the driver looked at each other, their tension rising. That was not standard procedure for any police department.

"Recon Three. Man down," came the next verbal communiqué. "Slaughtered, sir. Like an animal attack, or something."

"Recon Two. Two more. Head shot."

What the hell was going on here? "Recon One, Two, and Three. Surround the building. Hold positions." He motioned to the driver. "Let me out." He opened the door and stepped out as soon as the vehicle got close to the sidewalk. He walked away, weapon ready, muzzle pointed down as the vehicle moved off discreetly, no screeching tires or revving engine.

Melvin crossed the street, checked the silent vehicle at the alley entrance. Keys dangled in the ignition. Driver's side window rolled down. No blood. No broken glass. No dented metal. No torn pavement. No pitting from ricocheted bullets. No spent shell casings.

No obvious signs of struggle inside the vehicle, or immediately outside on the ground. It was like the entire team had been set upon by... ghosts, or something.

This shit was getting unnerving.

And what the hell happened to the sniper?

Melvin looked across the street, and saw a dull light on in the upstairs apartment. He detected no movement. That did not necessarily mean anything. Now where would a sniper set up?

Melvin's head turned from the window and arced back to his side of the street, and stopped at a rooftop nearby. That had to be the place. He glanced back into the dark recesses of the alleyway. About ten meters behind the Range Rover, a metal ladder crawled up the side of the brick building, providing access to the roof.

"All units, I say again, hold position," Melvin ordered again. Tensions were running high. He could hear it in his men's voices. "Snoop," he said, referring to his redheaded driver, so called because he loved listening to Snoop Dog, "I'm going topside."

"Roger that," Snoop responded.

Melvin stood at the foot of the metal ladder, rusted rungs every twelve inches leading up. The bolts securing the ladder to the building looked loose.

Just peachy.

He stepped onto the bottom rung, grabbed the rails with his hands, then shook vigorously, testing the strength of the ladder tie downs. Nothing pulled away from the building. No bricks loosened, no rivets or bolts fell from above. Melvin scampered upwards, moving quickly. He reached the top in seconds and hopped over the ledge onto the roof.

The mercenary immediately dropped into a low crouch. He brought his weapon up to shooting position scanning for signs of movement. Looking down the sights, past the barrel, nothing seemed out of place. No movement, no incoming fire. Keeping his level of mental alertness high, he stood up, reaching his full height.

Melvin advanced. Keeping his weapon in firing position, stock pressed firmly into his shoulder, both eyes open looking down the sights and past the barrel that was perfectly parallel to the ground, safety off, trigger finger alongside the trigger guard but not on the trigger itself, he stayed alert, paying attention to his periphery as well as his primary line of sight. Danger could come from any direction; Iraq and Afghanistan had taught him that. He crept quietly, moving in a measured, practiced shuffle, always placing his back foot precisely where his front foot had previously been. His legs never crossed over. Such a move bound up one's legs and could put one off-balance at a most inopportune moment.

Pressing his back against a patina, corroded air conditioning unit, Melvin paused, listened. He heard traffic on the distant freeway. He heard a siren to the east, far away. Other than that, nothing. He pushed off the air conditioner and continued his shuffle forward, whipping to his left at the portion of the rooftop he could not before see now came into view.

And what a view that came into focus.

Continuing forward, Melvin scanned in all directions, even straight up. He noticed the shattered rifle. Plastic pieces scattered haphazardly, the barrel bent upwards almost ninety degrees. Next thing he saw looked like something out of a Halloween store, a detailed replica of a human hand holding an automatic pistol.

Melvin paused, gulped. The pistol was real. So was the hand. So was the thick gooey blood that had leaked out at the wrist.

Melvin glanced farther ahead and saw Razor's crumpled body, sort of turned away from him. He glanced around, wary of a trap. But he was alone on the roof, so he moved quickly forward, and dropped to a squat beside was had once been a fellow professional. He checked carefully on and around the body, looking for wires or anything else that would make him think Razor's body had been rigged to blow.

He found none. Just a nauseating amount of blood. Razor's entire body was surrounded by it.

Melvin exhaled, steeling himself what came next. He rested the stock of his weapon on his crouched thigh, barrel pointing skyward. He reached out with his left hand, grabbed the blood-soaked clothing at Razor's shoulder. Then he pulled, turning Razor towards him.

Melvin muttered, "Jesus!" as he reflexively recoiled backwards, falling onto his butt. Razor's half-decapitated head lolled around like the head of a sadistic jack in the box.

He keyed his mic. "Recon One, Two, and Three. Report." Each man reported all clear. "Snoop, I'm on my way back down."

"Roger," Snoop responded.

"All units converge on the stairway up to the cop's apartment. Let's get this shit over with."

Reggie's apartment remained dark. Everyone with the exception of Rudy stood, listening.

"It's quiet," Horn whispered, his eyes gazing helplessly about the darkness. "Too quiet.

Reggie suppressed a laugh and shook his head as he crossed his arms. "I can't believe you actually said that."

"What?" Horn did not understand the reference. Reggie did not answer, just kept shaking his head.

"You see?" Horn barked at the vampire. "This attitude right here. This is why I ride his ass so much."

"Your own insecurities make you a fool." The vampire's words floated like feathers across the air, yet managed to cut through Horn like a switchblade.

"What do I have to be insecure about?"

"Your wife left you because you put the job before her."

"I had to –"

"You hardly see your children," the vampire continued. "This job is all you have. But it does not have the luster you hoped. You have paid a price above rubies, and yet you have nothing of any true value to show.

"But your biggest fear is, what comes next? What life will you lead in retirement? Die an angry, embittered old man, alone and forgotten by everyone who meant anything to you?"

The vampire's words had been softly spoken in a staccato, matter-of-fact delivery. He had hissed no venom during his exposition. He had not passed judgment; he had simply given voice to facts. And Horn, bear of a man he was, suddenly appeared very small.

The vampire turned his head again, then allowed his body to follow. He glided closer to the window. He took off his sunglasses, allowed his eyes to take everything in. Movement across the intersection. More down the street, rolling towards them.

His hearing kicked in. The faint thudding of footfalls, combat boots with thick rubber soles, contacting the concrete sidewalks below. He started picking up breathing patterns. Then heartbeats.

Several of them. From multiple directions.

Then his sense of smell informed him. Even his sense of taste. The smell and taste of sweat on the early morning air. Their sense of grim purpose. Their urgency. Even their tension and creeping fear had a distinctive smell.

The vampire put his shades back on. Time was becoming a serious factor in his personal equation. But the job was not yet done. The men coming after them were not fools. They had lost comrades at his hands, and they knew they were advancing towards him when every instinct they had was screaming at them to retreat.

"Saddle up, boys," the vampire said.

"What?" Reggie asked.

"I heard it in a Randolph Scott movie once."

"Who's Randolph Scott?"

Shocked, the vampire wanted to explain, but thought better of it. "Prepare for battle."

Every cop in the room checked his weapon. Rudy Valdez looked around. He realized he was in direct line of sight to the barred front door. That meant he would be the first thing his colleagues would see as they stormed through the door, adrenaline pumping, weapons aiming, trigger fingers squeezing...

"Guys?" Valdez spoke. "Can someone please move me out of the direct line of fire?"

The vampire grabbed him and deftly lifted him out of the chair with one arm. "Where would you like me to put him?"

Reggie motioned. "Just over there in the corner."

The vampire dropped Rudy to the floor, unmindful of the pain the short drop caused. He was listening to the men downstairs as they breached the iron security door.

"They're in the stairwell," the vampire said. "Two by two. Steady. Very disciplined."

Horn stood beside the archway leading to the short hallway and the metal door. Firearm ready, he held a cellphone to his ear. He called for backup as Castle dropped to one knee in the shadows opposite the archway.

"They're right outside," the vampire whispered.

"You could take them all out," Horn suggested.

"And rob you of the pleasure of doing what deep down you want to do?" the vampire shook his head. "I think not, sir."

Reggie had moved quietly away to his bedroom. He entered back just as quietly. He held a second gun in his hand. The vampire approved. His great great grandson had made his decision: if he was going to die, he was going to die fighting, protecting his friends, protecting society from the scum of the Earth.

The vampire's chest swelled with pride.

"We ain't taking prisoners tonight," Horn instructed. "Got it?"

"I'm good with that," Castle growled, his blood up.

Reggie moved like a cat, both pistols aimed at the hallway. "Let's kill these fuckers," he said. "We gotta get to Encanto, check on my Grandma."

A bright flame, burning quickly, accompanied by a foul odorous smoke and a hateful hiss, engulfed the metal door at the end of the hall.

"Breach!" Horn barked.

The door blew inward with enough force to swing open and slam against the wall. The door twisted and bent off its top hinge. The bottom hinge twisted as well, but held. The heavy door swung slightly at an absurd angle.

An acrid aroma assailed the vampire's nostrils. C4 mixed with Semtex. Damn! The vampire's face twisted in disgust. It fed his determination. He crouched, ready to spring, ready to fight, ready to kill, prepared to die to protect his family.

An unexpected quiet ensued. The smoke from the explosives wafted, suspended in the air. A tiny red beam pierced the veil, bouncing along the particles floating in the air. They shone metallic as the intense light burned through. Another beam appeared, performing its own dance. Then another, and yet another.

Laser sightings, attached to automatic rifles, held by dangerous men, intent on trouble. Expert killers looking for a target.

The vampire glanced down at Rudy. He put his extended index finger to his black lips, indicating for Rudy to remain silent. Rudy understood, fervently nodding his head.

The quiet lingered. Then, like ghostly wraiths coalescing, the mercenaries appeared one by one as they materialized out of the cloud. Not a word spoken, no hand signals given. They inched forward down the hall, vengeful spirits, silent as the grave.

Into the Kill Box.

Castle fired first, his weapon deafening after the tense silence, and struck his target in the throat, just under the chin. The upward trajectory of the bullet sent it through his brain and out the top of his head. Part of the mercenary's skull flopped open. He was dead before he hit the ground.

Automatic gunfire erupted, laser sightings bouncing around, bullets biting into the walls ahead. Horn waited, crouched low to avoid injury, then committed to the attack. The big man spun into the Kill Box and fired his Python. He aimed just a tic above the dancing laser sightings, and two more fell. Then he spun back out of the way, bullets sending plaster near his head spraying, falling like chalky dust.

Castle reloaded, and took aim just as Reggie stepped up. He opened fire with both pistols. Castle fired as well. In the mist, they could see bullets impacting, and men's' bodies twisting backwards crashing to the floor.

Another quiet ensued. Then the sound of coughing, of ragged breathing. It sounded wet.

Reggie, Castle, and Horn all advanced down the hallway. Blood and brains splattered the walls like a gruesome Jackson Pollock mural. Blood rivulets, crimson amoebic pseudopods, inched their paths across the wooden flooring.

The only man left alive, a black man, shivered and convulsed on the floor. A pink frothy blood trail trickling from his mouth and down his chin. He clutched tightly at a wound at the side of his rib cage, a vulnerable area not protected by his body armor.

Horn kicked the man's gun away. "What's your name, son?"

The black man set his jaw, narrowed his eyes. He was not going to say a word.

"His name is Melvin."

Horn, Reggie, and Castle turned and looked at the vampire. He strolled casually up the hallway. He seemed completely at ease, as if walking among multiple dead bodies in an apartment smeared with bullet holes, blood, and gray matter was something he did every day.

"All right, Melvin," Horn continued, "you were at Reggie's grandmother's house when you got called off. Who backfilled your position?"

Melvin coughed, wincing in pain. Then he spat pinkly in Horn's face.

The vampire's head twitched. His ears perked. "Sirens."

"I don't hear anything," Castle said.

"You will," the vampire assured him. Then to Horn, "Time is of the essence, Captain."

Horn pulled out a handkerchief, wiped the bloody phlegm off his face. He assessed Melvin's condition, and mentally projected Melvin's chances of survival. He stuffed the handkerchief back in his pocket.

"You've got a collapsed lung," he pointed out. "You're going into shock. You're developing a tension pneumothorax. As your lung collapses, it shifts inward, pushing your trachea and your heart out of place. It's a life-threatening emergency as your heart cannot beat in its proper rhythm, and the one good lung you have left can't inflate the way it's supposed to."

Horn stood up, crossed one hand over the other. "You know what the difference is between you and me?" Melvin was in too much pain to answer. "Ten minutes from now, I'll still be alive." Horn smiled, then simply turned and walked out.

"I cannot be detained by the police," the vampire spoke up. "We must check on my granddaughter."

"I'll hang back, " Castle volunteered. "Go guys. Head out. I'll handle the uniforms and the press."

The vampire drove efficiently through the deserted streets. Reggie sat in the passenger seat beside him. Horn took up most of the back seat. Reggie was tense, but under control. His heart beat loudly in the vampire's ears, his blood surged through his arteries, gurgling like water in a pipe.

Glancing up through the rear view mirror, the vampire regarded Horn. The big man stared through the window at the dark landscape blurring by, silent and grim. He was feeling old emotions, the vampire realized. The firefight had brought up bad memories. The vampire did not probe further. The big man deserved his privacy.

"Where are we going?" the vampire asked.

"Encanto," Reggie replied.

"Precisely where?"

Reggie gave him the street address. The vampire nodded.

"Twelve minutes," the vampire said. Then he added, "You were betrayed by one of your own."

"Who?"

The vampire eased the car through a turn. "His identity will be known soon."

Horn peeled his eyes away from the window and stared at the back of the vampire's head. "How can you be so sure?"

"Human nature," the vampire answered. "Reginald is alive. The cartel's plan has unraveled. The drug lord and his top henchmen must come out of the shadows to handle this themselves. That will include the turncoat."

"I think you've seen too many movies."

The vampire grinned. "Perhaps."

"Turn left up ahead," Reggie said.

The Encanto neighborhood is located in Southeastern San Diego close to its border with National City, populated with a high percentage of African Americans and other minorities. The old buildings, cracked sidewalks and crumbling curbs made silent testament to the neighborhood's decay and the residents' meager incomes. City politicians always promised money for improvement projects, but the programs never materialized. More than once, monies meant for infrastructure maintenance, upgrades, and repair somehow got diverted to other, "higher priority" projects. The projects almost always happened to be in more affluent areas of town: La Jolla, Point Loma, the Gaslamp.

Meanwhile, Encanto and its residents of modest means and working class backgrounds, were simply forgotten. The neighborhood withered. Drugs, gangs, street crime rose, but the residents endured.

The Lexus crept down a narrow street, lined on both sides by houses sagging with age and hopelessness. At this time of morning, most of the houses were dark. Some had a single dim bulb shining, but it was more of a nightlight in case someone woke up and, half asleep, needed to stumble to the bathroom.

"Which one?" the vampire asked.

Reggie pointed. "Last house on the left."

The vampire parked the car further down the block on the opposite side of the street. He shut the engine off. Somewhere in the night, a dog barked. They all got out.

Reggie glanced at his Grandmother's house as he counted his remaining ammo. "There's a light on."

"Does she usually have one on at night?" Horn asked.

"Sometimes."

"This is different." The vampire's words were barely more than a whisper. But intense.

Instantly fearful, Horn and Reggie froze and looked at the vampire. His face was awash with murderous intent. His nostrils flared. The right side of his upper lip curled into a snarl, revealing his right fang again.

"What's wrong?" Horn asked. "Is she in there?"

The angry vampire did not answer. He stood there, trembling. Both Horn and Reggie were glad neither of them were the objects of his rage.

"Come on, Grandpa Eddie," Reggie prodded. "Is Grandma Lottie in there?"

"Yes." His voice was still a whisper.

"Is she all right?"

"For the moment."

"Are they in there with her?"

The vampire swallowed, then, "Yes."

"Her life is in danger."

"Yes." His whisper had become a growl.

Horn and Reggie flicked the safeties off their firearms. Horn nodded to his fellow officer, a man he had grown to respect, then moved left. Reggie went right. They fanned out in a classic flanking movement on the house, executing the move with military precision.

The vampire stalked forward, right up the middle, heading directly towards the front door. His Baby Girl, his Lot-Lot was inside.

And he was absolutely going to kill anyone, *ANYONE*, who tried to harm her.

CHAPTER TWENTY-FOUR

Reggie's apartment buzzed with activity. White tarps covered the bodies. CSI techs photographed blood and brain splatters. Others walked carefully through the hallway and into the apartment itself, fluidly videotaping their progress with high-def camcorders.

Castle stood on the small stoop at the top of the stairs, outside the apartment itself. Yellow police tape crisscrossed the entrance. A young uniformed officer climbed the stairs towards him. She was young, probably a rookie, he thought. She pushed wavy red hair from her face.

"Detective Castle?" she asked, a bit out of breath.

"Yes," he answered. He had never felt so calm as he did at that moment.

"Officer Wahl," she introduced herself. "The Watch Commander is downstairs. He wants to debrief you."

"Of course," Castle smiled. He started lightly down the stairs. He got a few feet down, then turned. Wahl was at the yellow tape, craning her neck to see inside.

"Officer Wahl?"

The young officer jumped at the sound of her name. She stepped back.

"Have you ever responded to a crime scene like this? Multiple bodies, savage damage done on a scale like this?"

"No sir."

"Steele yourself, then go on inside," he said. "Tell them Detective Sergeant Castle said it was okay. Have one of the techs lift a tarp. Take it all in: the look, the sounds, the smell. It won't be pretty, but it's important that you see this."

She stood there, not understanding. But that was all right, he thought.

"Go on," he waved. "You'll thank me someday."

Castle turned and descended the stairway. The last step was not wood, but concrete, part of the foundation of the building. He stepped on it and out through the doorway. The early morning air had never smelled so sweet.

The Watch Commander, a lifer dog with frayed gray hair and a leathered face that reminded Castle of an old catcher's mitt approached. Castle waited. He shook Castle's hand. "Looks like you took out some real bad-asses up there."

"Yes we did."

"So who was up there with you?"

"Captain Horn and Detective Reginald Downing."

The Watch Commander eyed him hard. "So there was no one else?"

Castle shook his head. He hoped he appeared emphatic. "No sir."

"And you're sure of that?"

"Yes sir."

"You sure you don't want to change that?"

"Why would I, sir?"

"Well, because I've got an eyewitness, that Rudy Valdez character, who says there was a fourth person up there with you."

"He is mistaken."

"He says there was a guy named Eddie Marx. Scary guy."

"He must be confused."

"He is, is he?" the Watch Commander was not buying it, but Castle did not falter. After a pause, the Commander asked, "And where are Downing and Horn now?"

"Following up another lead, sir."

"How convenient."

"It's an urgent matter of public safety, sir."

The Watch Commander digested this. "So it was just you, Horn, and Downing, and no one else. That right?"

"Not another living soul, sir."

Standing outside Lottie's house, the vampire felt an unfamiliar twinge of regret. The dilapidated house in front of him had seen much better days, many years ago. He wondered briefly if in keeping his promise to Danae to not interfere in the lives of their descendants, he had left them to lives worse off than they deserved. He could have helped more. Danae was still alive then, but still. He certainly could have contributed anonymous money. After all, he had over twenty-seven million in various accounts spread halfway across the globe.

A promise is a promise, he told himself. A promise kept is a promise kept. But his promise had been to Danae, and she had passed. And now, he found himself wanting to become more involved.

He glanced to his left and to his right, saw Reggie gliding towards the front and heard, rather than saw, Horn huffing and puffing around towards the back. He glanced upwards, saw the second floor window.

Open.

Drapes fluttering.

Reggie crept up towards the front porch and small front deck cautiously, firearm in front of him. He blended in with the shadows of the trees, the light poles. He silently climbed onto the railing. His footfalls on the wooden decking made almost no sound. He paused, glanced through the window. Grandma Lottie's curtains were so old they were gossamer thin. Quite easy to see through and access the situation within.

He did not like what he saw.

He turned to whisper to his ancestor, but the vampire was already walking. Two steps and he, without any obvious effort, leapt straight up, over the covered porch, and disappeared from view.

He keyed the walkie-talkie function on his phone, whispered, "In position?"

"In position," came Horn's ragged whisper.

Reggie's palm made contact with the doorknob, his fingers curled around its circumference. He applied the lightest touch, gingerly turning. The knob gave easily. When pushed, the door gave without resistance. Looking both at the top of the jamb and along the bottom, he noticed no wires, no smell of Semtex or cordite to indicate the door was rigged with an explosive device.

He let go of the doorknob, let the door swing slowly inward. No big sounds, no crashing of glass. Just a slight ruffle from outside, the tinny squeak of an unlubricated door hinge. Steeling himself for what was coming next, he stepped across the threshold of his Grandmother's house. It was the first time in his life he had ever contemplated the possibility that he might not walk out of that house alive. He pushed himself through the small foyer and into the living room.

Everyone was there.

His Grandma Lottie, elderly, a bit overweight and going gray in her late sixties, sat in a threadbare easy chair, her dingy bathrobe wrapped around her, cinched tight at her waist. Sandals on her feet, fear and worry on her face.

Directly behind her, Rick Oakley stood, his left hand lightly touching her shoulder, his right hand holding his large caliber hand cannon pointed absently at the base of her skull. His face, cruel in repose, betrayed nothing of what he might or might not be feeling at this very moment.

It took every fiber of discipline in his being to keep from shooting Oakley in the head right then and there. He barely noticed the two other sides of beef standing on either side of Oakley. One white, one black, both muscular, both professionals, about three feet off.

Well there you have it, Reggie thought. Diversity in hiring at its finest.

He glanced at them simply to memorize their positions within the room, which he now thought of as another Kill Box. Other than that, he did not care about them. They did not matter.

They would most certainly never leave this house alive.

"Evening, Oakley."

"Evening, Officer."

"Grandma. You okay?"

"I asked them to leave," she replied. "They refused."

"I got nothing against your Grandmother," Oakley said. "I got no reason to kill her."

"Then let her go. Your beef is with me."

"Can't. Not yet. I need her as leverage to make sure you play nice."

Reggie glanced behind them, beyond them. A large arched passageway lead directly from the living room into the dining room, and on to the kitchen. The very same kitchen where Horn would now most assuredly be hiding, waiting to emerge at just the right moment.

Now would be a good time.

"What makes you think I'll do what you want?" Reggie asked, trying to stall.

"Because if you don't, I'll be forced to kill Grandma – no offense ma'am."

Grandma Lottie bristled.

"And you think killing her will make me more compliant?"

"Something has to," Oakley answered. "You don't want to die alone, do you?"

Reggie grinned. "What makes you think I'm alone?" He craned his neck and called out: "Captain. Horn!"

A groan escaped from the darkness beyond. Oakley and his team turned their heads, unconcerned. The sound of feet shuffling, then Horn, bloodied, defeated, unarmed and with his hands atop his head, materialized out of the shadows, being followed closely by someone else.

Reggie took his eye away from his gun sights. His face fell in shock. Then he stared down the barrel through the front sights once more.

Horn shuffled further into the room, into the light. Behind him, using Horn's girth as a human shield, walked Special Agent Walt Coulter. His eyes were on Reggie; Horn's own firearm was in his hand, pointed at the back of Horn's head.

"Sorry, Reggie," Walt said.

"How much they paying you?"

"Enough to take early retirement. My paperwork went through yesterday."

Reggie glared at him with open contempt. "So it's just about money?"

"Of course," Coulter said, careful to stay behind Horn. "Nothing's been the same since 2007. The stock market came back, but not the economy. Not really. I've got to think about the rest of my life."

"As opposed to the lives of your men?"

Coulter did not answer.

"As you can see, we seem to be holding all the cards," Oakley said.

As if on cue, a shuffling bump, like someone running their knee into a nightstand, came from above, on the second floor.

"You think so?" Reggie asked.

Oakley leaned close to Lottie. "Miss Lottie, you told me no one else lived here with you."

"No one else does."

"Then what just happened upstairs?"

"I don't know."

He motioned for Tim the Bodyguard to investigate.

Tim moved quickly but unhurriedly around the perimeter of the room and stopped at the bottom of the narrow, angled stairway. He pointed his weapon upwards towards the top of the stairs, listened. He lightly put one foot on the staircase, then another. In perfect shooting position, he slowly ascended the stairs until he disappeared from their view.

In the few seconds of silence that followed, everyone simply stared at each other. Then the night was torn asunder: a brief staccato of automatic weapons fire, a man's high-pitched scream cut short, then a sound resembling the loud tearing of wet cloth. And then...

Silence.

A thin rivulet of blood appeared, pouring over the edge of the top stair they could see. It dripped down the stained wallpaper, diffusing into the tired fabric. The rivulet became thicker, redder, began spilling over and onto the floor with an audible sound.

Everyone with the exception of Reggie seemed to be in shock.

Slow, steady footsteps sounded across the boards upstairs. Ronald raised his weapon to fire. Oakley motioned for him to stand down. Ronald obeyed.

Footsteps at the top of the stairs.

"Grandma, I'm getting you out of here."

Footsteps sounding again, this time descending the stairs.

"Don't worry about me, Reginald," she said bravely. "I'm not afraid to meet my maker."

The vampire, bloodless skin, lank hair, black sunglasses, dark cashmere sweater and pinstriped slacks, London Fog overcoat, glided down the stairway and into the room. He reached up with both hands, popped the collar on his coat.

"Don't be so quick to die just yet, Lot-Lot."

Reggie watched Grandma Lottie as the vampire slowly came into full view. He saw surprise on her face, heard her gasp. But she was not afraid of him. It was something else, something.... then it hit him.

She recognized him.

"Gentlemen," he greeted as he extended his arms out away from his body, "I am not carrying a firearm."

Oakley said, "Light him up."

Ronald brought his weapon up and fired a short, contained burst. The weapon belched fire, bullets impacting the vampire full in the chest. He staggered back and fell heavily to the floor.

"Hey. GQ Dude," Oakley taunted what he thought was a dead human, "you're supposed to bring a gun to a gunfight." He began to chuckle.

Ronald joined in.

Even Coulter smiled.

They stopped abruptly when the corpse sprung up from the floor and onto his feet in one quick movement. He pointed at Ronald, livid.

"This was a four hundred dollar sweater! You ruined it!"

Ronald, looking like a ten year old who just got caught with his hand in the cookie jar, stuttered. "I'm... I'm sorry."

"Cashmere wool. Imported from Scotland."

"I'm sorry!"

"Hey," Oakley said, "I know you. I saw you at that club downtown. Fetish."

The vampire reigned in his indignation, nodded. "Indeed."

"So what are you doing here?"

The vampire tilted his head slightly. "Giving you a choice."

"And what choice is that, exactly?"

"Let Miss Lottie go free. Unharmed in any way. Do it now. Surrender yourselves without further violence or resistance to these policemen, and face prosecution for your crimes."

Oakley pretended to consider this. "And if we choose to politely decline, sir?"

The vampire's mouth was a cruel, thin line. "None of you make it out of this room alive."

Oakley glanced to Ronald, then to Coulter, then back to the vampire. "Like I said before, we're still holding all the cards here."

The vampire took off his sunglasses and grinned. The criminals all took a collective gasp. He lifted his sweater upwards, exposing his grayish torso. The bullet wounds were already almost healed, jagged black holes against colorless skin.

"Just in case anyone thought I was wearing body armor." He pointed at Oakley. "You put a gun to the head of my Lot-Lot? No way you live."

"What the hell are you?" Oakley asked. His voice was a harsh whisper.

The vampire lifted his head towards Heaven. "And lo, I saw a pale horse, and the rider of that horse was Death. And all Hell followed with him." The vampire lowered his head, and glared at Oakley with a palpable malevolence, black eyes somehow blazing with a hint of red, fangs long and sharp. "I am Death, Mr. Oakley. I am the Destroyer of Worlds. And I am here for you."

The room exploded into action. The vampire leapt through the air, blazing eyes glassy, mouth open, fangs bared. Oakley moved the handgun off Lottie, aimed at the vampire, fired.

Reggie spun to his left as the vampire leapt, dropping to the ground and taking aim at the bewildered Ronald. He shot three times: two in the side of the chest, one in the head as Ronald twisted backwards from the impacts.

Horn, still holding his hands up, moved fast, caught Coulter off guard. He drove his right elbow down onto Coulter's collarbone. It gave with a satisfying crunch. Coulter winced and grunted, dropped his pistol. It clattered to the floor as Horn spun to his right and drove his left fist directly into Coulter's nose, breaking it.

Coulter dropped like a load of bricks.

Oakley fired again, missing the vampire a second time. How can that be, he wondered as the vampire crashed into him. They fell to the floor in a tangle of arms and legs.

Reggie lunged for Lottie. "Grandma!"

Grandma Lottie pushed herself up and out of the chair. He grabbed her, put a protective arm around her, lead her towards the front door. As they got towards the foyer, they paused and looked back.

The living room, partially lit, was a kill zone. Ronald lay dead, brains and blood pooling around him. Whatever was left of Tim still spilled blood over the staircase and down the wall. Coulter was out cold, bleeding profusely. Horn had turned him over on his side so he would not choke on his own blood.

Reggie understood. This was not out of kindness or compassion. Horn wanted that Goddamn dirty cop motherfucker to live so he could be tried, convicted, and sent to prison. Everyone knew what happened to cops in prison.

It would be a fate worse than death.

Oakley, for his part, was fighting a losing battle and he knew it. As he wrestled with this unholy thing atop him, he knew his opponent was stronger, and that his strength would fade quickly. But he was going to go down fighting.

Die like a man.

Suddenly, the vampire released his grip and leapt to his feet. Oakley, in shock, watched as the vampire danced, like boxer, and motioned for him to join him.

The bastard's taunting me.

Oakley clambered awkwardly to his feet. He assumed a classic defensive stance, legs shoulder-width apart, hands in a modified boxing position, taught long ago in a boot camp that seemed so far in the past. Right at that moment, he could not remember the name of his drill instructor.

The vampire grinned again. He was enjoying this. "Quickly or slowly?"

"Huh?"

"Do you wish to die quickly or slowly?" the vampire asked. "Choose now, or I will choose for you."

"I don't want to die at all."

"No one does," the vampire said. "Yet, we all must."

Oakley moved forward quickly, closing the gap on his opponent. He unleashed a flurry of flawlessly executed punches and kicks. His opponent somehow blocked, ducked, dipped, bobbed and weaved, avoiding an onslaught that would have – should have! – killed him in a matter of seconds. And to make it worse, the toothy bastard was chuckling under his breath, laughing as he did so.

He executed one last sidekick. His opponent blocked the kick easily, and in one fluid motion, grabbed his leg and twisted hard to the left. Oakley lost his balance and fell to the floor.

The vampire checked his watch. "Gentlemen, time has become a factor."

"Handle your business, Grandpa."

"Lot-Lot, you do not want to see what happens next."

Reggie guided her out the front door.

By now, Oakley was on his feet again. "What the fuck are you?"

The vampire grinned again, all teeth and fangs. His eyes looked like those of a Great White Shark.

Pure predator.

"I am simply... your worst *fucking* nightmare."

Oakley attacked again. But this time, instead of having his fun, the vampire stepped forward through the kicks and punches and grabbed Oakley by the throat. He lifted him up off the ground with one hand, easily, as if he were weightless. Oakley tried a futile counterattack, as his feet dangled several inches off the floor.

The vampire slammed Oakley into the wall so hard the sheet rock gave way. "Do you believe in God, Mr. Oakley?"

"What?"

"God. Satan. Heaven. Hell."

"Nope. Never have."

"Pity," the vampire said. "I do." A hint of remorse in his voice.

"Why?"

"How else do you explain me?"

Oakley, snarling with primal rage, clawed at the vampire's face. His fingernails tore thin slivers of skin. The vampire winced, pounded Oakley into the wall until the sheet rock lay on the floor in pieces. White silt floated down through the air. Oakley kicked at his opponent, kicked him in the belly. Hard.

The vampire dropped Oakley as he staggered back two paces. The force of the impact had surprised him. Of course, the vampire did not worry about internal bleeding.

Oakley attacked again, swinging a hard right. The vampire caught the swing at Oakley's wrist and elbow, twisted and turned, which drove Oakley to one knee to keep from having his shoulder dislocated. The vampire shifted, turned again, put his foot into Oakley's ribcage, and pulled.

HARD!

Oakley screamed, first in shock, then in pain and terror. The vampire pulled harder, screaming and laughing in sadistic pleasure, taunting his victim. A terrible wet sound began.

Horn turned his head when the shoulder popped out of socket. "Jesus."

Reggie reentered just in time to see it. The vampire ripped Oakley's right arm out of its socket at the shoulder, rending flesh and sinew, pulling the appendage away from the jagged stump.

Arterial blood sprayed everything: the walls, the ceiling, the vampire himself. Anything within five feet got soaked bright red.

Instinctively putting his left hand to his right shoulder, Oakley clamped down hard, trying to stem the bleeding. He somehow forced himself to his feet. Why was the room spinning?

The vampire was in no humor for mercy. Holding Oakley's amputated arm by the wrist, He began swinging it in a savage arc, bringing it crashing down upon Oakley's head. He beat Oakley over the head with his own severed arm three times before Oakley began to wobble. The vampire reached out with his free hand, grabbed Oakley by the shirt, held him up. Then he beat Oakley over the head with his own arm again.

Over and over.

Again and again.

Blood spurting in all directions.

Finally, the vampire allowed Oakley to fall in a semiconscious lump at his feet. He tossed the useless arm aside.

Knowing he was dying, Oakley rasped, "Fuck you and your Lot-Lot. Fuck your whole goddamn family."

The vampire dropped to his knees, straddling Oakley. He slapped Oakley on the forehead, laying him our flat. He used his claws to rip open Oakley's sweater. He then joined his hands in front of himself, where Oakley could see, pushed the backs of his hands together, fingers interlocked.

Ten razor-sharp claws, all pointed at Oakley's chest.

The vampire drove down with all his might, even putting his weight behind it to build momentum. His nails sliced through Oakley's skin easily, drove deeper down to bone, then past that. Fingers curled through soft tissue, braced against bones inside.

Oakley was glassy-eyed with shock.

The vampire grinned thinly.

The vampire then threw his body backwards with a shout, wrenching upwards and outwards, ripping flesh, rending subcutaneous structures, breaking bones.

Oakley's chest burst open, popping ribs off at the sternum, opening up the entire chest cavity. More blood erupted, fountaining out. Without missing a beat, the vampire jammed his left hand into Oakley's chest between the lungs. He smiled down at Oakley, having found what he was looking for. The vampire twisted and wrenched his hand backwards simultaneously.

The last thing Oakley saw in this world was the vampire, triumphant, holding his prize aloft: Oakley's heart. Still beating. The vampire opened wide and bit down into it, sucking out what he could as more blood dribbled out from the torn arteries.

Fade to black.

The vampire held the heart above his upturned face, mouth open, and squeezed the muscular organ. Blood ran thick, a congealing syrup, stringing downward into his mouth. He swallowed, tossed the heart aside, forgotten. He looked up, and saw Horn staring at him, a combination of shock, horror, and morbid fascination on his face.

The vampire shrugged. "What?"

"Is that some kind of a vampire thing?"

"Yes."

"Remind me to never piss you off again."

The vampire looked down at his clothes. Dripping red everywhere. They were ruined. No matter. They could be replaced.

Reggie moved deeper into the room. "Time marches on, Grandpa."

"The police are coming," the vampire said.

"I don't hear anything," Horn answered.

The vampire grinned. "You will."

Reggie moved over to Coulter. He looked up at Horn. "May I have the pleasure?"

"Of course, kid."

Reggie put the handcuffs on Coulter. He was still unconscious.

The vampire moved towards the door. "I really must be leaving."

"But what about all this?" Horn asked, motioning to the carnage all around.

"You will think of something."

Outside, the vampire instinctively checked the sky to the east. The pale blue of the coming dawn shown, blending to a deeper blue overhead, and black in the west. He saw Lottie standing in the small yard. He went over to her.

Her eyes grew wide at his appearance.

"Please excuse my appearance, Lot-Lot," he said. "Things got messy.

"You saved my life."

He took her hands in his. "I am so sorry for all this. I am sorry you became involved."

"Those men made their own choices."

The vampire nodded.

"But Uncle Eddie, and I guess you're not my real Uncle, are you, where have you been since I was nine years old? How come you look the same now as you did then?"

"I am not your Uncle. I am your Grandfather."

"You mean -!"

"Your Grandmother Danae and I loved each other very much. We were young. We thought the world would change to accommodate us. It did not."

"And your appearance?"

He glanced at the east once more. "Dawn is approaching. I really must be going. May I come by and visit one night soon? I would love to give you answers to your questions."

"I'd like that."

The vampire reached out and stroked her cheek. "I love you, Lot-Lot."

"I love you, too... Grandpa."

He smiled at her, his face conveying the purest love.

And then, he was gone. Disappeared in a blur, a wraith, a spectral tendril, as if he had never been there, indeed as if he had never really existed at all.

Journal entry, Wednesday, April 15

It has been a while since I wrote a journal entry. The reason for my negligence is a happy one. I have been spending more time with my family. Lot-Lot and I have had several happy discussions late into the evening regarding my past, my plans to elope with Danae.

How those plans were derailed.

She understands why I made the choice I did, to become what I am. And she understands the nature of my promise to Danae regarding non-interference. But she also feels the burden of that promise can be lifted now without dishonor since Danae has been passed on for forty years now.

So in keeping with my newfound familial ties (and to make up for lost time), I bought my Lot-Lot a house. I figured it was the least I could do, seeing as I had a heavy hand in ruining the one she lived in before. Naturally, she had been resistant to so lavish a thing, until I disclosed to her my true net worth, accumulated over the span of my existence.

She felt better about it after that.

When one has a net worth like mine, buying a vintage three-bedroom craftsman two blocks down from where you live seems a small thing. So we found one she liked, I forked over the cash, made sure her name was on the deed, and let the realtor hand her the keys. I visit often, several times a month, and we have a lovely time.

I never truly understood until recently how being with family fills one's heart and feeds one's soul.

Reginald is doing fine. He got a medal and a big promotion at work. He is a Lieutenant now. He actually insisted that the ceremony be held during evening hours so I could attend. Such a wonderful man my great-great grandson is! Now if he could only meet a nice girl...

*In the weeks following the destruction of the drug smuggling empire
Reginald had infiltrated, much else has transpired. Captain Horn,
who was awarded a medal during the same ceremony as Reginald,
put in his papers and has now retired from the force. He still lives
quietly and alone in that tiny apartment. But at my continued urging,
he has reached out to his children. They are supposed to meet for
coffee next week. I hope all goes well for them.*

*Coulter was formally indicted, arraigned, and held without bond.
Because he was a cop, they put him into the Protective Custody Unit.
He was found with his throat slit like a hog the very next morning.
So much for Protective Custody. As far as I am concerned, it could
not have happened to a more deserving fellow. I hope the blade was
dull. I hope he suffered greatly.*

*As for me, life goes on. I wake up. I work. I make money. I eat. I
occasionally go out and hunt. It's much the same, night after night,
like my life is on a permanent loop.*

*But I get to visit my Lot-Lot. And I get to see my Reginald. I have
gained a peace and a sense of kinship that I have never felt since I
was a young boy living in that terrible tenement in Hoboken.*

*I must complete this entry with dispatch. I am having the guys over
for horror movie night. Reginald is coming over, so is Horn. Nick
Castle too. We do this quite a bit. We sit and watch movies most of
the night. They eat pizza, popcorn, and drink beer, all that stuff. We
all have a great time. They especially love it when I laugh
uproariously at the vampire movies.*

Hollywood never gets it right.

CPSIA information can be obtained
at www.ICGtesting.com
Printed in the USA
FFOW01n0925290518
46941777-49200FF